TEEN
FRANKENSTEIN

HIGH SCHOOL HORROR

TEEN
FRANKENSTEIN

CHANDLER BAKER

FEIWEL AND FRIENDS
NEW YORK

A FEIWEL AND FRIENDS BOOK
An Imprint of Macmillan

Our books may be purchased in bulk for promotional, educational, or
business use. Please contact your local bookseller or the Macmillan Corporate
and Premium Sales Department at (800) 221-7945 ext. 5442 or by e-mail at
MacmillanSpecialMarkets@macmillan.com.

Library of Congress Cataloging-in-Publication Data
Names: Baker, Chandler.
Title: High school horror : teen Frankenstein / by Chandler Baker.
Description: First edition. | New York : Feiwel & Friends, 2016. | Summary:
"When science prodigy Tori Frankenstein accidentally kills a teen boy in a
midnight car accident, there's only one thing for her to do—use her
science project to bring him back to life"—Provided by publisher.
Identifiers: LCCN 2015021555| ISBN 9781250058744 (hardback) | ISBN
9781250068873 (trade paperback) | ISBN 9781250080288 (e-book)
Subjects: | CYAC: Scientists—Fiction. | Dead—Fiction. | Horror stories. |
BISAC: JUVENILE FICTION / Horror & Ghost Stories. | JUVENILE FICTION /
Fantasy & Magic. | JUVENILE FICTION / Love & Romance. | JUVENILE FICTION /
Action & Adventure / General.
Classification: LCC PZ7.1.B35 Hig 2016 | DDC [Fic]—dc23
LC record available at http://lccn.loc.gov/2015021555

Book design by Eileen Savage

Feiwel and Friends logo designed by Filomena Tuosto

First Edition: 2016

10 9 8 7 6 5 4 3 2 1

fiercereads.com

For my parents, Coni and Mike,
for nurturing my love of books

ONE

The Seventh Rat:

We've retired Mr. Bubbles Six. The new specimen is a field rat acquired from outside the main house. I'm pleased with the find. He's two ounces heavier than Bubbles Six, who recently lost his fur in a small fire. I consider the extra mass to be advantageous. Bubbles Seven has slightly coarser and more tawny fur, but he comes to us already missing a toe. Will run the first tests tonight and report back findings.

— — —

Yesterday I didn't win a Nobel Prize. I didn't win one last year or the year before that, either. Each of these stacked up behind me in a neat little pile of non-Nobel-Prize-winning days. And I hated every one of them.

Marie Curie didn't have a Nobel Prize when she was seventeen, either. But then again, Marie Curie lived in Paris, which might as well be located in a different solar system from Hollow Pines, a dead-end Texas town that sucked you in up to your ankles and held you there fast and tight as quicksand.

Seven feet belowground, in a tornado cellar dug beneath the soil of the world's biggest cultural black hole, Owen Bloch and I toiled to fix our problem of scientific obscurity by extracting a dead rat from a jar of formaldehyde. Dressed in a dingy white lab coat that fell to my knees, I pinched the tail through a pair of latex gloves while Owen slid a metal tray under the rodent and sealed the lid on the rotten-egg smell that wafted from the jar. Drops of formaldehyde, the color and consistency of pus, dripped from the nose of Mr. Bubbles, the posthumous star of our experiment. Mr. Bubbles came from a long line of Mr. Bubbleses before him. The tip of his tail draped like an earthworm over my right wrist as I lowered him to rest, bellydown, on sterile metal.

A roll of thunder rattled the shelves already sagging under the weight of cleaned-out pickle jars and sent their contents sloshing against the glass walls, where they caused the floating animals inside—lizards, fish, and, in one case, a roadkill armadillo—to sway suspended in the murky liquid, as though to music. On the counter below, liquid bubbled in a series of Erlenmeyer flasks attached by rubber stoppers and glass tubing. Steam gathered in the bottle necks. A sticky red substance coated a microscope slide clipped on top of the scope's stage.

A flash of lightning illuminated the cracks in the cellar door. The exposed lightbulbs hanging overhead flickered dark and then bright. Owen scratched the scalp beneath his shock of sandy-blond hair. "Not to be a cosmic buzz kill, but a wise man may consider, you know, *not* throwing down serious kilowatts in the middle of a lightning storm while standing on a damp floor." He stared down at his sneakers, laces untied and dragging on the dirt-covered concrete. He was wearing a red T-shirt with the words *Homo sapiens inside* printed on the chest.

"Don't be ridiculous. We're too close," I muttered. The chemical stench burned my nostrils as I bent closer to Mr. Bubbles to take inventory of our last experiment's leftover effects. We'd only just begun using this rat tonight, but already he had a singed ear, which I marked down in my black-and-white-speckled composition book before gently lifting the curve of his snout to reveal the enamels of two teeth sticking out from the gums. I noted this, too, along with a spot on his right shoulder blade where the brown fur had begun to blanch as though it'd been bleached. I circled the location on the Mr. Bubbles diagram.

Owen slumped down onto a stool and lifted his glasses to rub at his eyes. "Here's the thing: It's midnight. On a night before which we have to get up for government-mandated compulsory education."

I was in the middle of rolling over the dead rat to examine his belly but stopped to glare at him. "Was that Edison that said, 'Try, try, and stop trying again after midnight'?"

His head drooped, and he peered up at me, forehead wrinkling and mouth crooked into half a smile. If Owen were an animal, he'd be a lemur, one of those long, slender animals, with concave chests and beady eyes. "You're a little frightening." He held his finger and thumb an inch apart. "You know that? Just a little."

I lifted my eyebrows. I found it hard to carry a dead anything without giving off an at least slightly off-putting impression to the general human populace. Owen was different, though. I plopped the rat down on his back with a thud and got to work examining the claws. Owen slid off the stool, made his way over to a cluttered pile of discarded machinery parts, and began tinkering with an old clock. This was his thing. Owen liked to tinker. He kept a stash of old radios, model airplanes, desktop computers, and random car parts just so he could take them apart and put them back together in a new way. I was sure there was some psychoanalysis in this hobby ripe for the picking, but I never questioned his love for tiny machinery parts and the desire to know what made them tick. Instead, when I found a discarded DVD player on the side of the road, I just loaded it up and gave it to Owen as a gift. He was, as a friend, very easy to shop for.

"You should reset the rattrap." My breath caused one of the whiskers on Mr. Bubbles's nose to quiver. "We'll need another one soon."

I listened to the cranking of a ratchet screwdriver.

"But we just got this one," Owen protested. "What about the test-animal application?"

I rested my chin on my knuckles and brushed a strand of hair out of my eyes. "That'll take too long. Stop being such a baby."

Only the first Mr. Bubbles had been secured through "proper channels." As far as our biology teacher knew, we were still using the same one. Owen said sometimes he heard rats shrieking in his sleep.

I glanced up at the other jarred specimens, their eyes magnified in the curved glass cases, each one carefully preserved for laboratory study. I inherited the storm cellar from my father, where he'd kept his lab equipment in a shelter that was supposed to protect him from the very thing he was chasing. Once he was gone, Mom wouldn't step foot inside. Memories, to her, must look like ghosts.

The cellar was a cluttered, misshapen hideout carved into the red dirt with a hatch door in the ceiling that let people in and kept tornadoes out. A worktable occupied the center of the room, still draped with Dad's old maps and Doppler coordinates. In the corner, next to the chalkboard, sat an old, claw-foot bathtub. Shelves lined the surrounding walls crowded with weather vanes, old fan parts, wheels off a rusted tricycle, and dim jars of syrupy liquid. My father had collected other assorted items for his laboratory, too: a gurney, dusty Victorian-era textbooks—many first editions—a collection of surgical utensils, a generator, a transistor radio, clouded beakers, a model skeleton, a gopher skull, and a preserved pig heart. Much like a living, breathing thing, the cellar laboratory reflected a kind of organized chaos in which I knew where everything was and yet somehow always managed to uncover new treasures.

I stifled a yawn and drew myself back to the work, dragging my finger over the curling pages of my notebook. Inside, I'd scribbled a short list of variables: kilowatts, conductors, incision points. Each separate attempt had been crossed out. I was missing something. Something tantalizingly close and just out of reach, like a word tingling the tip of the tongue. The answer was there, buried in the pages of my

notes, in the texts I read, in the diagrams I designed; it was all there—
it had to be—and yet it may as well have been hieroglyphics.

The scent of burning skin still hovered in the room, mixing with
the fresh chemical cocktail that was leftover from when a dead lizard
had fried to the point of extra crispy earlier this evening. The reptiles
never worked. Their scales hardened and their wiry bodies blackened
around the edges, turning stiff and brittle under the shock. Still, I
swore this time—I *swore*—that the lizard's foot had moved just
before he turned into an unappetizing, reptilian potato chip.

I drummed my fingers on the metal tray, trying to mentally unlock
the answer from Mr. Bubbles as if it were hidden not in my careful
methodology but there underneath his matted fur.

"It has to be more volts," I said at last.

The clink of metal parts stopped. *"More?"* And then it resumed from
Owen's side of the room. The twisting of a screw and the sound of a
tool being dropped onto a pile. "Maybe it's the incisions," he said.
"Maybe if we attached the wires to the external layer of the epider-
mis, then—"

"No, it's not the placement." I'd studied the anatomy time and time
again. I'd spent late nights trying every other point of entry for the
wires, and no configuration came close to working except for this one.
"At fifty watts I got his tail to move."

"At fifty watts Mr. Bubbles started smelling like chicken-fried steak
and Einstein tried to eat him," Owen pointed out. Einstein was my
bulldog.

"More," I said. "It's got to be more." This time I didn't wait for Owen
to question me. I gathered a jar of brine water, our makeshift diathermy device, a bouquet of multicolored wires, and our scalpel. I
cut back and forth across the room, weaving around odds and ends.
Owen set down the clock and screwdriver and quietly joined me as
I cleared a spot at the worktable.

Without further argument he bent over the kilowatt meter, calibrating it to measure out the correct level of energy—sixty watts. His tongue stuck out the side of his mouth in concentration. He positioned his back to face me as I made deep, fresh cuts in the hide of the dead rat, a part which always made Owen squeamish. A cord trailed from the generator to the kilowatt meter to which the wires were attached. One set of frayed wire ends dangled inside the jar, magnified by the brine water. I inserted another set of copper wires into the incisions.

Another rumble of thunder rolled through the cellar, this one longer and more menacing, like the growl of a feral animal. I pulled a cord above the worktable, and a lamp flicked on, spotlighting Mr. Bubbles. Owen looked up from the kilowatt meter, his tongue still squeezed between his teeth. He pushed his glasses up the bridge of his nose and tilted his chin as though to say, *if you must.*

I took a deep breath, savoring this moment, the one of possibility just before fates were made or broken, when everything felt balanced on a pinpoint. I took a deep breath, put my finger underneath the switch, and flipped it.

The dials on the rudimentary kilowatt meter sprung to life. Four small circles aligned on the face of the meter, each with matching needles that spun to different points like hands on a clock meting out energy. As with a spark traveling the wick of a dynamite stick, I saw the moment the volt hit the vat of brine water from the small twist of wire and the tiny ripple that grated the surface before the other wire began to tremble almost imperceptibly.

The smell of burning fur began to radiate. The rat's good ear curled downward and then, so fast I almost couldn't believe it happened, his tail swished from one side to the other. My eyes widened. The electricity built up and up. Mr. Bubbles shook violently. Nearby, Owen pulled his shirt over his nose. Then the tail that had just twitched began to blacken from the tip up toward the base until half of the pink appendage was charbroiled. His claws shriveled. His fur began to smoke. Coiled tendrils twisted, dark and shadowy, into the light.

"It's going to work. It's going to work," I chanted, almost in prayer.

Smoke was now choking the room. The body of Mr. Bubbles was shriveling.

"All right, that's enough, Tor." Owen pinched his nose.

I flattened my palm over his arm. "No, wait, hold on." I inched my nose closer. The heat dried my eyes. "Come on. Come on," I urged.

It was Owen who broke. He hit the switch just as another crack of lightning blasted through the cracks in the hatch. The charge died at once and the needles fell back to zero position. Slowly, I stepped up to the edge of the worktable. I stooped down to peer at the shriveled rodent and, with my gloved finger, nudged him in his little rat ribs.

For a second, I had a harebrained hope that he might stir after all. And then . . . his whiskers fell out.

TWO

hy·poth·e·sis: a supposition or proposed explanation made on the basis of limited evidence as a starting point for further investigation; a proposition made as a basis for reasoning without any supposition of its truth

Postulation: A refining of galvanic reanimation will result in the stimulation of vital forces to the point of resuscitation.

List of variables: kilowatts, point of entry, mass, density, conductor, methodology

Progress: none to report

— — —

It's an absolute scientific fact that thunder is the sonic shock created by a sudden increase in both pressure and temperature at the exact moment the lightning expands its surrounding air too fast. Not that anybody in Hollow Pines cared much about facts, aside from Owen and me. I flipped the switch on the windshield wipers and they beat faster, groaning across the slick glass. Defeated, I'd dropped Owen off at home around half past one, just as the storm, which had been rattling and kicking at the hatch door, decided to unleash its torrential downpour. Rain pelted the forest green hood of my Mercury Grand Marquis, lovingly known as Bert. But it was the wind that kept pushing poor Bert off to the left, across the road's yellow dashed line. Nature's way of throwing a tantrum, I supposed.

In response, I gripped the oversized steering wheel so tightly the blood drained from my knuckles as I pulled myself to the edge of my seat and peered over the dash into the blustering night. Lightning split the darkness horizontally, forking into electric veins that pulsed through the gray-black sky, hanging heavy and thick as a corpse's skin over the farmlands.

"Just a little bit farther," I pleaded with Bert. He had a bad track record of getting me stuck in situations that nobody would want to be stuck in. It was Bert that'd made me late for the PSATs. My mind chewed over the events of the night, the stack of mounting failures that rubbed at my nerves, the unshakable feeling that the answer was obvious only I was somehow too thick or nearsighted to see it.

Thunder rattled the cup holders, and I put my palm over the top of an empty can of Dr Pepper till it stopped. I gnawed on my lip, rifling through my brain the same way an ordinary kid might the pages of a textbook, before making another go of concentrating on the highway instead of the rat.

The sky hovered tangibly above like a ticking time bomb. My headlights scouted the road ahead by inches not feet, and the rain fell in white sheets I could hardly see through. It was only when I was practically even with it that I could read our city sign: WELCOME TO HOLLOW PINES, TEXAS!, with an exclamation mark, like Hollow Pines was some place to get excited about.

I peeled a hand off the steering wheel to fiddle with the radio; the speakers were drowning in static. I slammed the heel of my hand onto the dash, but the faint buzz of static persisted. I cursed at the station before fumbling for a scratched CD I kept in the side-door compartment. A halting, stop-and-go version of the White Stripes' first album crackled through as the city-limits sign melted into the rain. The dark silhouette of cornstalks blurred in the faint glare of my windows, and from here the two-lane country road started to curve around town. I forced Bert to stay centered.

Just then, my phone buzzed in the center console. A text from Owen flashed on the screen:

Eureka!

Lightning flickered overhead. Eureka?

Oh my god.

Eureka!

This was it. The breakthrough. The universal code of scientists everywhere. Eur-freaking-eka.

I shoved the phone into the pocket of my zipped hoodie and glanced up. For an instant, time was suspended like two objects dropping through a tub of high-density glycerin. There was the car. There was me. And then . . .

There was him.

He appeared in the middle of the road like a highwayman's ghost. Rain tumbled down around him, and the golden glow of the headlights lit up his white face as he screamed.

My foot fumbled for the brakes. My elbows straightened. I pushed back into the headrest. Wheels skidded and the moment filled with cottony silence. Then Bert's nose plowed into him with a sickening thud.

THREE

Scientific Method, Step 2—Applied Research:

Professor Giovanni Aldini first performed the process of galvanism in 1803. The process of galvanism involved three troughs that combined forty plates of zinc and copper and were applied through the arcs of two metallic wires descending from the ear to the jaw. The first experiment took place on the severed head of George Forster, who was hung for an hour at Newgate Prison at subfreezing temperatures for the drowning of his wife and child in the Paddington Canal. Aldini secured the body and succeeded in causing the jaw to quiver and the left eye to open.

— — —

The body hit the hood. The windshield splintered into a star. I ducked as the clunk of shoulders and boots pounded the sunroof on their way to the trunk.

My foot finally slammed on the brake, and Bert's tail whipped sideways. I slid to a stop, facing the opposite direction from where I began. I turned the CD off and could hear my heart hammering. My hands shook.

"One Mississippi . . . two Mississippi . . ." My breath wavered. I cut the engine but left the headlights on.

There, in the middle of the road, lay a heap. It wasn't moving.

I squeezed my eyes shut. This was not happening. I was supposed to go to Harvard or Penn—not penitentiary. But all I could see was his face lit up by the glow of headlights. Over and over, I saw his features morph into surprise.

Swallowing hard, I unlatched the door. Rain poured over me as if from a showerhead. Sodden strips of auburn hair, dangling almost to my shoulders, cleaved to my throat and chin like leeches.

It was the sort of moment that didn't seem real. The part in a dream where you suddenly become self-aware and start looking around for clues that your surroundings are projections. But the asphalt was hard beneath my sneakers. The rain turned my thin black sweatshirt into dead weight that stuck to my ribs and clung to the waist of my jeans. I gulped a sticky wad of saliva, and the roar of the storm grew louder.

One foot in front of the other, I trudged on wobbly legs closer to the heap. The nearer I got, the more human the heap became.

My insides lurched.

"Hello?" I yelled through the sheets of rain. I glanced back at Bert looming in the distance. I'd seen horror movies begin this way. "Hello? Are you all right?" I used my cupped hands as a megaphone. There wasn't so much as a flinch.

I should leave. Right now. Get in my car and go. To Mexico, maybe. The thought lingered, but only for that instant.

"Sir?" I called, louder this time.

Rain continued to splash onto the blacktop. I swiped strands of hair off my forehead and ran the rest of the distance, at which point I immediately wanted to revisit that whole Mexico thing.

His teeth chattered.

At first, he didn't look at me and that was bad, but then he did and that was worse. He had eyes the color of maple syrup. Wide and alert as a cornered animal. His jet-black hair was plastered to his forehead, and he lay flat on his back, one arm stretched out with his palm open like he was waiting to be crucified.

Not knowing what else to do, I kneeled on the road and took his hand in mine, our skin slick with water. Drops poured down my nose and into my mouth.

"I'm so sorry," I sobbed. Or at least I thought I sobbed. I couldn't tell on account of the monsoon beating down against us. "I couldn't see you. Or I mean, I didn't see you," I corrected myself. I hated to lie, but not nearly as much as the thought of telling the truth.

His eyes seemed to register me for the first time. He had high cheek-bones and tan skin, the good looks of a high school Homecoming king. He was about my age, too. There was a gash over his left eye-brow, but the rain fell too quickly for him to bleed much. I bit my lip and glanced away from his face, my own eyeballs stinging.

Farther down, dark crimson bled through his white V-neck T-shirt, spreading into fuzzy edges on the fabric. My stomach flopped over like a beached catfish.

His Adam's apple spiked. He looked up at the sky and then back at me.

Gently, I peeled the edge of his shirt up over his ribs. A long, curved gash ran down his side from just below the right side of his breast-bone to the top of his hip. Pink, tattered skin flayed open, creating a crevice where blood pooled and oozed while he panted for breath.

"It's not that bad," I told him, knowing full well it was exactly that bad. "See, I'm—" I patted myself until my fingers closed around the hard rectangle of my phone still stuffed inside the pocket of my jacket. I pulled it out. "I'm calling 9-1-1 right now. They'll be here any minute." He nodded a silent agreement and I felt a ballooning in my throat.

I pushed the top button. The screen stayed dark. Frantic, I pushed it again, hands shaking more than ever now. It'd been working two minutes ago when I got Owen's text. This time I held down the but-ton. I tried counting to five. Counting to five felt like an eternity. Noth-ing happened except the boy moaned.

I shook my phone as hard as I could and held it up to my ear as though I might hear the ocean if I listened hard enough. But it was no use. The screen was soaked.

I felt the corners of my mouth curl downward and my face break apart with the horror. My phone was waterlogged. No help was coming. Not quickly, anyway. I took the phone and threw it against the concrete. It split open on the pavement. I wanted to scream, but the sound was trapped inside.

"It's okay. Don't worry." I pushed my hand into the gummy swamp of his side to stanch the flow, but blood oozed through my fingers, and more pools of red leaked onto the concrete than I had hands for. The asphalt had ripped into his legs, leaving tears in his jeans that revealed bloody scrapes of road rash. I sucked in a lungful of air. "Okay. You wait here." Like he was going anywhere. "I'm going to get help. I'll be back before you know it, I swear."

His hand squeezed tight around mine, clamping down on my bones. I stared hard at him, refusing to cry out in pain. "All right, I'll stay," I said at last, and his grip loosened. "I'm sorry. That was stupid. I'll stay."

Shiny red bubbles started to form at the corners of his mouth. Trying to look unfazed, I tucked my toes underneath the back of my jeans and rocked. One of my hands held his, and the other pressed into the chewed-up edges of his wound. Without thinking, I began humming the tune of one of my mother's old hymns. I had to hum with such force to be heard over the raucous weather that my lips tickled and I felt my nose get twitchy. But still, I hummed on.

I was in the middle of the chorus when his head jerked off the pavement. His eyes went round and rabid. I froze. His chest heaved.

He gasped in one desperate inhale and said, "Meg," before his head fell back to the ground.

FOUR

Observations: A pattern has emerged regarding the use of the brine water in the experiment. Aldini used troughs with zinc and copper, but I've found the solution of saline to be a better conductor. Brine water was first used as a conductor in the early nineteenth century. When the brine water is used, the core body temperature of the subject heats up more before burning than during experiments without. At first, I marked this as a correlative relationship, but enough evidence has been gathered that I'm prepared to count the use of the conductor as a cause for better results.

- - -

I unlaced my fingers from the boy with the bluing lips and bent my ear down to meet them. Not even a tickle of air escaped his open mouth. I pressed my fingers into his glands, pushing through sinewy flesh in search of a pulse, but the veins remained flat and still. Placing my hands, palms down, on his chest, I leaned in with the full force of my weight and pumped. I pushed into his ribs until my muscles burned and breath rushed through me like fire, and when I couldn't pump anymore, I tilted his head back and pressed my lips into his. He tasted like blood and rain as I blew as much life into him as I could muster. It wasn't enough.

With each thrust, his body plopped against the pavement. At last,

I collapsed onto his chest, crying big, fat tears until they collected in the back of my mouth and threatened to drown me.

I didn't know how long I stayed like that, lying with my cheek flattened against a bloody T-shirt, but by the time I peeled myself away, I was numb. And not in the metaphorical way, either. My nail beds tingled. I couldn't feel my face. There was the feeling that my head had literally separated from my shoulders and was starting to float off.

My palms bit into the blacktop as I levered myself to my feet. I walked in a trance back to Bert. I should have asked his name. Why hadn't I asked his name?

I slammed the door. The cabin filled with silence even though outside the rain kept beating down. Water trickled through the cracked windshield onto the dash, reminding me of what had happened, just in case I tried to forget.

A blank pair of hazel eyes stared back at me in the rearview mirror. Smudged liner smeared down pale, pink skin, creating an ink-blot test on my face. I played with the volume dial on the radio, but the engine was cut, so nothing happened.

I clutched my forearms, wrapping them around my stomach and hugging. "I . . . k-killed him."

There, I said it.

My forehead fell to the steering wheel. I was at a point beyond tears. On the road to total ruin, there was anguish, hopelessness, misery, despair, and then there was me. My temples throbbed. A dreamlike quality still shrouded the recent chain of events, and it was that surrealness that kept me from crumpling in on myself like a paper bag. But before long my legs were restless and I couldn't sit still with my thoughts. I reached for the door handle once more and stepped out onto the shoulder of the road. The rain's initial fury had ebbed from a torrential downpour to a soggy mist. The asphalt took on the translucent sheen of wet oil reflecting a cloud-obscured moon.

I paced the length of the car, back and forth, shaking my head.

I couldn't just *leave* him there while I went for help. I glanced over at the body-shaped heap down the road. Someone might think they'd come across a hit-and-run.

My phone. My stupid phone. Already I was imagining my picture plastered on a public service announcement that warned against texting and driving. My heart slipped lower.

What did Owen mean by *Eureka* when he texted, anyway?

Eureka. I shook my head. That text had seemed so promising for a single moment.

More pacing. My shoes struck out at the pavement.

This was why we needed a breakthrough in the first place. If—

I stopped dead in my tracks. Owen had a breakthrough.

That was it. My heart beat faster. If we discovered how to make Mr. Bubbles come back to life, then I could save the boy. I could do better than any hospital or doctor. I could do what medicine couldn't.

What if what was wrong with our project wasn't the process but Mr. Bubbles himself? More mass. More watts. The blood in my veins buzzed as if charged with electric volts. I tried to shove the thought into a corner of my mind like a pile of dirty clothes pushed into the back of the closet. But the more I paced, the more the idea kept tumbling out and spreading.

The thing was, once I did this thing, there'd be no turning back. One door opens and every window in a thirty-mile radius slams shut. Except through the open door, the boy might live. He might *be* the breakthrough. It only takes one person brave enough to find out. That person could be me.

I felt my gait take on the grim weight of an executioner's march, even though the execution had already taken place. As I drew closer, the boy's glassy eyes became unavoidable. Hard and unseeing as marbles, he stared up at the night sky like he might be studying the constellations. What *had* he been doing walking across a country road in the middle of the night during a thunderstorm? And who was Meg?

A pang of guilt twisted through my side. Dogs started barking in the distance. I looked over. Every light was on in the closest farmhouse. The highway butted up against a fence connecting the cornfields, but the fields were huge. Surely nobody could hear the crash from here, let alone see it. I quickened my pace and the dogs barked even louder. A correlating relationship, not causal, I had to remind myself. If two events occur together, that didn't mean they had a cause-and-effect relationship. The dogs weren't barking because of me. They couldn't be. Could they?

I took a deep breath, then crouched and slid my wrists underneath his armpits. The heft of his torso pulled me down. My back strained against the mass of what felt like a six-foot-two linebacker.

I arched, hoisting him higher on my skinny frame. My thighs quivered as I shuffled backward, taking tiny steps in the direction of Bert. I really should have pulled the stupid car closer. I wrapped the body in a bear hug. My fingers barely touched across his chest and I caught a whiff of tropical-scented shampoo.

After a few feet, my biceps were screaming for mercy. I let his upper half collapse onto the road. Stretching, I wiped a hand across my forehead and felt a smear of wetness the texture of leftover jam. I jerked my hand away. My fingers were covered in a fresh coat of blood.

"Oh god." I coughed, hocking over my shoulder.

I squeezed my eyes shut and lugged the boy back upright. His jeans skidded across the blacktop.

"Almost . . . there . . ." I huffed as if he were somehow invested in the journey. With a final heave, I leaned my unwilling passenger up against Bert's back tire. His chin slumped onto his chest and a chill ran through me.

I popped the trunk. I started with his upper body, digging my shoulder into the boy's belt buckle, and winched him over my shoulder so I could use the full force of my body to propel him up into Bert's spacious trunk. There was a clunk as his skull hit the trunk's fiber-glass lid.

His legs hung out the rear end like a dead deer. I swung one limb over the side, where it landed on the black carpeting with a dull *ker-thunk*, then the other. Crystallized in time, this was the sort of life moment that'd be better left on the side of the road like discarded lug-gage, and, in truth, I never thought I'd be the girl to cart around emo-tional baggage. It was almost comical how wrong I'd been. Because I was clearly more the type of girl who took her mistakes, bundled them up in the back of her car, and drove.

FIVE

The Final Dissection of Mr. Bubbles Six:

I began by carefully removing the skin to expose the muscles below, using scissors and forceps. I began the incision at the top of the neck and continued toward the tail. The muscular structure, including the biceps brachii, the triceps brachii, and the latissimus dorsi were all still intact despite the effects of the higher electrostimulation, a fact which is promising. The lymph glands, however, appeared darker than on Bubbles Four or Five. Will preserve them along with the heart, lungs, and liver for the laboratory.

— — —

I cut quietly across the lawn to Owen's window on the rear side of a large brick house. Owen had one of those houses you could just tell had a real family inside. Trimmed shrubs, a pebbled walkway leading up to a cheery red door, and a wooden bench swing that hung from one of the trees. I stalked through the grass. We didn't hang out at Owen's house much. Mainly because we didn't like his housekeeper chasing us out of rooms or his mom constantly checking if we wanted cookies. Plus, his house didn't have a place where it was okay to store flammable liquids.

I looked both ways, then tapped the glass. "Owen," I hissed. His light was off and my breath fogged up the glass as I smushed my nose to the windowpanes. "Owen! Owen Bloch, open this window right now!"

When I couldn't see movement in the shadows, I dug the tips of my fingers underneath the sill and tried to pry it open myself. I was making zero progress when the window slid open and Owen popped his head through. His hair stuck out at sharper angles than usual and he wasn't wearing his glasses. He squinted out into the night. "*Tor*, is that you?"

I was instantly annoyed. Owen had a breakthrough and now he was *sleeping*? "I'm sorry," I said. "Do many other girls stop by your window in the middle of the night?"

He fumbled around inside and after a moment located his glasses. Spectacles in place, he squeezed his eyes shut, shook his head, and yawned. "I'm going to guess there is a ninety-nine-point-five percent chance that whatever it is you're about to tell me could have waited until morning."

Misty rain still drizzled from the sky, and the dull rumble of thunder sounded in the distance as if the clouds were hungry. I crossed my arms, impervious to the droplets that were turning my skin cold and slick. "Further proof that you're not very good at statistics."

He scrunched his forehead, and it was as if his retinas snapped into focus and he was seeing me for the first time. "Is that *blood*?"

I swiped my hand across my brow where the blood was beginning to coagulate. "Don't worry, it's not mine."

Owen disappeared from the window. I heard rummaging around, bedsprings squealing, sheets rustling, car keys jangling. "And that's supposed to make me feel better?"

His foot shot out the window, followed by a leg and then the rest of him.

"Well, it's definitely not supposed to make you feel worse." It was only when we were halfway back to the car that I realized we'd left his window wide open. I didn't mention this to Owen, who was trying to keep up while at the same time hopping on one foot and attempting to wrestle on his second sneaker. The presence of another person made me feel more calm and in control. I took quick strides around the front of the car and dropped into the driver's seat. Time was of the essence.

Owen stood slack-jawed outside the passenger-side window. "Um, Tor . . ." He was seeing my car for the first time. Jagged cracks branched out from a crystalline puncture wound in my windshield, and my hood looked like the site of a meteorite crash. "Are you sure you're all right?"

"*I* am fine. Now can you please get in?" My mind spun with echoes of imagined sirens. As I closed the door and moved the sole of my foot to the gas pedal, I knew that the truth would color Owen's view of me. Maybe forever. He'd look back and remember that I'd been calm—*too* calm. But this had always been a problem for me. I'd never acted like people wanted me to. I didn't cry or get weepy when I was exhausted. I didn't wonder why I hadn't been invited to so-and-so's birthday party. I didn't doodle boys' names in my notebooks. Instead, I pulled the tails off lizards and observed them until they grew back, or pinned dead beetles to corkboards so I could label them with their proper scientific names. That was *my* thing.

Still, I knew the whole morbid tale would sound so much better when I told it to Owen if only I'd been trembling and sobbing from the moment I showed up. I thought about this as he made a show of clicking his seat belt into place and checking the tension in the strap across his chest. I swallowed hard. I was too focused on the end goal now to revert back to quivering girl in distress. He'd probably love a quivering girl in distress. All guys did. Even Owen, I bet.

A few houses down, I had to make a three-point turn to go back in the opposite direction. A single thud sounded from the trunk. Owen twisted to stare into the backseat. "What the hell was that?"

I flipped the windshield wipers on, but the blades got stuck on the fractured glass. I didn't reply.

Owen flattened his shoulder blades to the seat again. He raked his fingers through his hair and flicked on the cabin light. I felt his attention square on me. I set my jaw and drove faster down the glistening pavement. The neatly hedged community gave way to a long stretch of road where telephone poles stood like sentinels and thirsty grass unfurled over long stretches of flat land. The heat of the small cabin lamp warmed my forehead.

"Have you seen yourself?" Owen asked. I glanced sideways at him. His eyes pinched at the corners, betraying a look of genuine concern. "Because you look like you've just survived a bombing or something. Tor, I think you should pull over. I think you may be going into shock." He reached his fingertip out, and I flinched when he dabbed at the streaks of blood caked at the edge of my hairline. "Did you hit a deer?" He sank back into his seat. "God, you could have died."

Shock. That was a good one. Perhaps I could be going into shock. I tried that on for size, remembering the feeling of numbness that came over me when I'd . . . when he'd . . . *God*, maybe Owen was right.

"I didn't hit a deer," I said. I snuck a glance in the rearview mirror. A knotted nest of hair formed a clump about an inch above my left ear. Then there was the blood. More blood than I'd remembered. It was much worse than the stains left from when I'd swiped my hand over my brow. I must have gotten more on me when I'd put my face to the boy's chest. Now, his blood smeared over my cheekbone like blush.

I reached up and clicked the light off, bathing the cabin in darkness. We were getting closer to home. The houses got smaller and squatter, though farther apart, and instead of trimmed bushes there were crooked mailboxes and sneakers dangling from the telephone wires.

"Owen," I said, tightening my grip around the steering wheel. "Something bad happened." I stated this in the same way a counselor might gently break bad news to a child. "There . . . was an accident. *I'm* okay, but . . ."

This took a moment for Owen to register. His cheeks drooped. His mouth fell open. He turned in his seat again and looked at the backseat as if he had X-ray vision. Then he shook his head. "You . . ."

"I hit someone." The words came out totally wrong.

"But, Tor." He leaned away as though I were suddenly contaminated. "You can't just—I mean, you called the police, right?" Were there flashing red and blue lights? Were there sirens? Was I in handcuffs? No? Okay, so I didn't call the police.

"I tried."

"Tried?" His voice cracked. I kept driving. "There are only three numbers, Tor: 9-1-1. How does one *try*? Jesus . . ." He dragged the word along with his breath. The space between us went silent, like a bad phone connection. The question lingered in the air half formed. Finally, Owen plucked it and the words materialized. "Did . . . this someone survive?"

Survive. The phrasing was so hopeful. He could have asked if the someone died, but he chose to say *survive*, as though he could will it to be true. "No," I said flatly. "He didn't."

I thought I knew how Owen would react, but when I looked over at him again, it was pure, unadulterated horror that consumed the entirety of his face. The kind of knee-jerk reaction reserved for witnessing a mother strike her child or a man slice off his finger in a meat grinder. Owen cleared his throat and at the same time sewed up the wounded expression on his face so he wore a mask of calm.

Owen sighed deeply or as deeply as he could if he were to try to sigh while being asphyxiated, because that was how he actually sounded. "I'm sorry, Tor." There was more. I could tell. "We can figure this out. I'll go to the police station with you. We'll explain."

I looked up at him, dry-eyed. "No. We can't." It was too late for that.

Bert was already rocking from side to side as the wheels careened into the mud holes that pockmarked the dirt road leading up to my family's ramshackle, old ranch house. I cut the headlights and eased Bert through the rotting fence posts on either side of the drive.

I pulled up on the right side of the house, the side closest to the storm cellar hatch.

"And what do you want me to do? Tor, we don't have a choice. Don't you see that?" He was still trying. He was still at the first stage of grief—denial.

I pushed the car into park and turned in my seat. "There's no sense crying over spilled milk, is there?" In case he hadn't noticed, the decision was made nearly an hour ago.

Slowly, Owen released the clumps of sandy-blond hair and lowered his hands to his sides. "It wasn't milk, Tor."

There was nothing to say to that, so I got out of the car and went around to the back, where I clicked the button on my keys twice.

The trunk opened like the lid of a casket. The boy's face appeared, looking more corpselike this time. His lips were dry and cracked. The skin underneath his eyes had turned a deep purple. It was way too late.

"Owen," I said, staring down. "What did you mean when you texted, 'Eureka'?"

SIX

Applied Research: In the initial experiments of Dr. James Lovelock, a hot metal spoon was used to restart the circulation in the bodies of frozen hamsters. The key was to warm the heart first. If the entire body was warmed through a bath or other total-immersion method, the blood in the animal's limbs would resume circulation too quickly, thus stopping the heart entirely.

— — —

A night breeze blew the rain's leftover mist across my cheeks. From its perch on the roof, the old weather vane screeched on its hinges, causing my skin to crawl off the bone. Owen was halfway out of the car when he froze. "No." He held up one finger. "No, no, no, *nononono-nono*." Then he pushed all ten fingers into his hair and yanked at the roots. "No," he said one more time before pressing his forehead to the side of the car. There was a pause long enough to hear crickets chirping. "Tor, I was talking about that Bruce Willis movie." It was as though someone were strangling Owen from the inside. His voice was hoarse and he stammered. "I . . . I figured out a way to prove you wrong." My heart tumbled down my rib cage. We'd been debating the plausibility of time travel in that stupid pulp movie for hours last weekend. Owen looked up to the sky and rubbed his hand over his face. "The entire premise of the movie could be fixed if the audience just adheres to Stephen Hawking's chronology protection conjecture . . ." The end of his sentence then trailed off into nothingness. "*God.*"

The metallic scent of blood clung to the air, and my stomach gnawed on itself like a giant wad of chewing gum. "You *what*? Eureka, Owen! Do you even know what that word means? I thought you'd cured Mr. Bubbles. I thought you'd—"

He spun on me, the darks of his eyes pin sharp with anger as he took accusatory steps toward me. "I'm sorry for not *realizing* that texting *Eureka* would give you tacit permission to convert your car into a hearse!" His finger was now inches from my nose when he realized what he just said and looked back at the open trunk.

He made a gagging sound, and his chest curved inward. He covered his nose and mouth with his hand and muffled another heave.

Owen walked in a short loop and refused to look back. "Only you, Tor, only you would do something like this."

I leaned around the open hood of the trunk and peered up at the house. "Keep your voice down," I hissed, and listened for the stirring sounds of my mother. I thought back and was comforted by the memory of the open bottle of gas station wine, half empty, and that had only been at nine o'clock. I rested my palms on the lip of the trunk. "This doesn't change anything," I said. And it didn't, because even if I had known that Owen's breakthrough was not actually *the* breakthrough, I might have done the same thing. It was the spark of recognition caused by his text that set the wheels in motion, the detection of possibility. "Now, are you going to help me or not?"

"No. No way. I want no part of this." But his gaze seemed to land instinctively back on the stony face lying at the bottom of my trunk. "Christ, he's dead," Owen whispered, and I wasn't sure why he'd said that.

The boy's eyes were wide open, and they stared straight back at us. It shaved my nerves down like a cheese grater.

Owen pushed his thumbs into his eye sockets and squeezed his eyes closed like he was trying to gouge the image from his mind. "Think about what you're doing, Tor. There are . . . ethics to consider. Even if . . . even on the off chance that it . . ."

"That hasn't seemed to bother you before," I snapped.

Slowly, Owen raised his head and looked at me. "But this is a human we're talking about. You have to see the difference. You're playing God here."

"I'm not playing anything. I'm being a scientist." Owen's face twisted like he'd just bit into a lemon. I relaxed my shoulders and turned from the boy in the trunk-coffin. I moved closer to Owen until I could feel the heat from his chest. I grazed his hand with mine and peered up at him. "We have the chance to save him, Owen. To fix this." Owen started to open his mouth but I gripped his hand and held it. "You can't reverse the past." And Owen understood that I knew this better than anyone.

He looked away and pinched the bridge of his nose, the fight visibly draining out of him.

There was a long pause and then—"Okay." It came as a breath.

"Okay," I replied.

Without another word, we returned to the car. I ducked and slid my hands underneath the boy's shoulders. My back strained as I heaved him up, and his head flopped backward. His jaw fell open, exposing the roof of his mouth and a pink tongue contracting toward his throat. I grunted.

Owen muttered something unintelligible but reached for the boy's ankles. We dragged the body out, and his waist plopped onto the ground. Owen and I both shook out our arms and wrists. Silently, we grabbed either end of him. His body formed a swinging arc as it dangled. The stained shirt he was wearing slid up from where I was holding him by the armpits to reveal the bottom of the violent gash. Owen looked away.

We waddled with the cadaver between us to the hatch door and began our descent into the cellar. I picked my way backward down the steep flight of stairs, gingerly feeling for the next step. My grip on the boy was slipping. The belt on his jeans skimmed the edges. Owen had his tongue pinched between his teeth. His glasses were held on by only the tip of his nose.

The boy was heavy. Gravity seemed to be working double to pull him into the earth where he now belonged. With the end in sight, I hiked my knee under his back so I could reposition my grip, but when I did, I lost my grasp entirely. His torso crashed onto the stairs, and his legs were ripped from Owen. It was all I could do to jump clear as the body went tumbling down the remaining steps.

My eyes met Owen's. He massaged the spots above his eyebrows.

"That wasn't supposed to happen."

"None of this was supposed to happen."

"Right, well, at least we've got him down here." I clomped down after the body and stared at the placid face for a long second before diving into action. The key, I figured, was to act professionally. I'd go about the same preparations I would for any other lab and avoid addressing the reality of working on a human subject until the last second.

In a plastic tub I tossed alkaline, salt, vials, thread, a scalpel, and thin conductor wires—all the ingredients to land me on a TSA watch list for the next twenty years at least.

The variable, I thought now. That was the critical point. The trick was the level of voltage. Surely, Mr. Bubbles couldn't spring back from the dead because . . . because why? Because there wasn't enough power to reactivate the brain patterns. I found a dropper and added it to my collection.

The boy was different, though. There was so much more of him. My brain jumped to the image of his heaving chest. The strong line of his jaw as he clenched his teeth in pain. I shook the thought away. He was substantial. Yes, the brain was bigger, but with a larger proportion of mass located in the rest of the body. . . .

I jumped at the sound of a howl coming from aboveground. Owen and I shared another look.

Einstein.

I silently pleaded that she would get tired and settle down. But the howl continued like the wail of a werewolf during a full moon, and I knew there'd be no such luck.

"Wait here," I said, craning my neck to stare up at the cavernous ceiling. I shoved the bin of supplies into Owen's chest.

He straightened. "Hold on a minute. You can't leave me alone with . . . with that." He pointed at the dead body still sprawled at the foot of the stairs.

I stepped over a leg and climbed up the first few stairs. I could hear Einstein's bellows become more high-pitched and whinier. "Don't be ridiculous," I said. "It's not as if he's going to jump up and bite you."

A glance back at Owen confirmed that this was exactly the sort of thing he'd been worried about. "It's creepy is all," he whispered, as if the dead boy might hear him and be offended.

I reached the top of the stairs and pushed open the hatch. "I'll only be a second." A wave of fresh air hit me. Above, the stars were beginning to shine through the haze of clouds.

I moved like a cat burglar around the side of the house where inside I could hear Einstein clawing at the back door. My dog was a face full of wrinkles with a brown ring around her eye and a knack for thwarting the pursuit of higher knowledge, despite her promising namesake. She had only two talents: smelling and wreaking havoc.

The growl revved up. It was only a matter of moments before my mother would come looking for me to quiet her down. I tippy-toed over to the back door. Einstein's paw was splitting through the blinds, and I could see her shiny black nose peeking through.

I opened the door, and Einstein let out a squeal.

"Tor?" There was a voice in the darkness. I stiffened. "Is that you?"

"Yes, Mom?" came my tentative reply.

"It's late, *idnit*?" she asked. Her speech was throaty, and it came from the living room. There was rustling, and then she appeared in the doorframe of the kitchen still dressed in jeans and a moth-eaten sweater that hung off one frail shoulder. Her stringy hair was slept on, and she had that sluggish, hollowed-out look in her eyes that came from hours of television and too many glasses of wine.

"Sorry, Mom. I've been working." I held on to Einstein's collar while she wiggled her army tank of a back end and licked what was most likely blood off my jeans. Mom hadn't been the same since my father died. Sometimes it seemed like she'd died right along with him and left the shell of her body here to tend to me. It was like living with a ghost.

She smacked her lips and ran a finger over the cracked bottom one. "You know, young lady . . . God . . . punished Adam and Eve," she said slowly, as though she were sounding out the words. ". . . For eating an apple . . . from the tree of knowledge . . ." She wagged a floppy finger at me before dropping it limply to her side. "He could, Tor, you know he could." She was babbling her usual confused prattling of words when we crossed paths late at night, or sometimes not so late, sometimes already by dinner. Mom's church shows had been her refuge since my dad died. Sometimes she even joined ladies' Bible study on Sundays.

"Go to bed, Mom. It's late." At no point did she register my own state of disrepair, probably because I fit right in with the rest of the house we shared like two messy college roommates. A half-eaten piece of dried toast lay next to the sink, where dishes were piled up to the faucet. In the living room I could see a shirt flung over the back of a recliner.

"You go to bed." Her brow lowered over her eyes, and she looked like she was trying very hard to concentrate on this one specific thing she remembered, in her more lucid moments, that she was supposed to be doing—parenting.

"I'm going to bed," I lied. But Mom didn't budge, and I was beginning to conjure up some awfully creative curse words for my meddling canine. "Fine," I said. "We're going." I dragged Einstein past her to my bedroom, where I left the door open a sliver. My heart sank when I saw her sink back down onto the couch.

I lowered to the floor and waited to hear sirens. Sirens I knew must be coming. But all was eerily quiet except for Einstein's soft snorts. Every second I spent in my bedroom was agony.

After what felt like an eternity, my mother's snores filled the house. "Come on." I patted my leg, and Einstein waddled after me. We left Mom sleeping openmouthed on the couch with one arm dangling on the floor.

I had to carry Einstein like a sack of potatoes down the cellar stairs to the boy's body. It was exactly where I'd left it, which seemed to be fairly normal corpse activity. The only difference was that Einstein crouched to her belly and began growling in his general direction.

I patted her head. "Cut that out," I told her.

Owen emerged from the shadowed corner. "I don't know, she might have the right idea if you ask me."

"I'll make sure not to ask then." Retrieving the tub of supplies, I set to work, kneeling beside the boy. Transferring our methods from mouse to human anatomy wasn't an even swap. We'd need more of everything. I bit my lip, mind churning. "He should go *in* the brine solution," I nearly whispered. I twisted to look at Owen. "More of the conductor. He needs to be submerged." The brine—a solution of 26 percent sodium chloride and water—had been proven to act as a conductor. Each time we used the brine water the rat had moved a bit more than without. We had gotten the idea from Professor Giovanni Aldini, who began dabbing the inside of convicts' ears with salt water before trying to reanimate them.

"Are you—"

"I'm sure." I wasn't sure, but, in moments like this, it didn't help to be wishy-washy. "Help me move him," I said.

More obediently than I'd expected, Owen crossed the room, this time taking the upper load of the boy's body. I grabbed the ankles, and together we transported the corpse to the empty claw-foot tub. We gave ourselves to the count of three before hoisting him into the porcelain basin. His solid back made a hollow echo as he flopped to the bottom. Streaks of rust crawled up the sides of the bathtub and cascaded toward the drain, which I plugged with a rubber stopper.

I yanked off his shoes then leaned in to unfasten his belt.

"What are you *doing*?" Owen grabbed my arm.

"You don't honestly think we can shock someone in jeans, do you? Don't be such a prude."

Owen's face reddened to the shade of uncooked hamburger meat. I thought I heard him say something about common decency, but once I'd unbuckled the belt and the waist of the tattered jeans, he took one pant leg and we each pulled. I had been unaware that there were degrees of dead, but with his jeans removed, the boy somehow looked a lot deader. I pulled his shirt over his ears. The gash down his side smiled up at us, crimson and menacing.

Unclothed down to his boxers, I inventoried the full extent of the damage. Cuts of various sizes marred his legs, presumably from where he'd been sliced by shattering glass. A deep purple bruise colored the side of one thigh. I worked my fingers into a pair of rubber gloves and rummaged for a pair of tweezers before beginning to extract two inch-long shards that were lodged in his chest. Owen turned his back as I let each clink into an empty jar.

I reached for the stack of textbooks positioned nearby. Scraps of paper hung out of dog-eared pages. I selected one with a yellowing spine, my dad's old copy of *Gray's Anatomy*, and flipped open to a two-page spread detailing the nervous system to use as my road map.

I locked my teeth together and tried to steady my hand. The scalpel was cool and stiff between my fingers as I rolled the boy farther onto his side. Positioning the point at the base of his neck, I cut through the skin and muscles until there was a clear view of his spine. With more force, the scalpel dug into bone, and I found what I was looking for—the spinal marrow. I inserted one of the wires I'd gathered so that it touched the marrow with enough lead to trail out several feet once I laid him back down.

The next incisions were smaller. One on each temple with only trace amounts of blood. By the time I hacked through to his sciatic nerve, I barely saw him as a person at all.

Seconds slipped into minutes, and before I knew it, I'd skated through over an hour. My gaze flicked from one end of the body to another, searching for holes, searching for possible mistakes. Mistakes I couldn't afford.

I rubbed my eyes and then turned the nozzle on the faucet. Water poured over him, mixing with the blood to create a sickly red. Like thinned-out watercolor paints. I raked through every possible nook of my intellect. What had I missed? What could go wrong?

On some level I was there. My mind told my hands what to do and then they did it—basic chemistry, synapses snapping rapid-fire. I dumped the brine water into the basin with a splash. I felt as if there were a layer of Plexiglas separating me from the experiment and I was standing on the other side of it watching.

I nestled the wires into place, each now burrowed into one of the incisions. The next piece of the puzzle was the diathermy device. My crown jewel. The part that had taken me the longest to figure out. Even if the brain patterns were reignited by the jolt of electricity, the blood in the heart still needed to start pumping again, a problem first discovered—but not solved—by Dr. James Lovelock. I opened one of Dad's tool drawers and pulled out the ancient aircraft radio that I'd made Owen purchase on eBay. Owen was the machinery geek, and he'd retooled the radio until it was in working order and could act as a frequency transmitter to emit microwaves. Before, I'd tried to use heated metal, mainly spoons, to reheat the hearts of several Mr. Bubbleses. The problem was that if they ever woke up, they'd be met with third-degree burns. The radio frequency transmitter was a more humane alternative. I placed the clunky aircraft radio over the boy's heart and let Owen lean the boy's torso forward so I could duct-tape the device to his chest.

Meanwhile, my own heart was very much alive, pumping and halfway up my throat. Einstein army-crawled a few inches closer.

Staring at my handiwork with open eyes, it was the first time I could see the complete picture of what I'd done.

And it was a terrible thing.

Because there was a boy. And he was dead.

But instead of looking still and peaceful as he should have, I had sliced and sutured, cut open and inserted, and what was left was a monstrosity lying prostrate in a filthy tub. My limbs turned to wet cement.

Head down, Owen wheeled the kilowatt meter over. "How much?" he asked, his mouth pressed into a white slash.

I glanced over the notes I'd written, the bits of chicken scratch that were barely legible. "Five hundred and fifty," I said. Five hundred and fifty. The number seemed to ring in the air. Five hundred and fifty. Higher volts than any breathing human body could withstand. He shook his head, but leaned down, placing his elbows on the cart. Adjusting his glasses, he forced the dials to spin.

A cable snaked its way from the gauge, and I held the end in my hand, imagining the buzz of electricity coursing inside my grip, waiting to be unleashed. On the other side, the trail of yellow, green, and red wires leading from the boy's body floated in the brine water below.

I switched on the radio transmitter, then held my arm out over the water. I looked back at Owen.

"Famous last words?" he said, eyes burning with intensity.

"After this, maybe there will be no last words." I took a deep breath and released the fingers clutching the electric cable into the brine water.

Sparks created firefly bursts all around us. The cords churned up brine like a water moccasin. I crouched for cover as the storm cellar filled with the smell of smoke and burning hair. The body shook, trembling violently in the water like it was strapped to an electric chair. I turned my head but couldn't look away. The boy's face morphed into horrific grimaces. His tongue lolled out the side of his mouth. An eyebrow shot up to an unnatural height, and his pupils rolled back into his eye sockets until all I could see was white.

My throat caught fire. I felt bile rising up, dangerously close to reaching the roof of my mouth, and I wanted to scream and cheer and throw up all at once.

An earthquake swept through the mass of lifeless flesh, blurring lines and distorting the shape that once looked human.

Einstein scurried in between my feet. Then Owen was at my side. His hand reached out for me at the same moment a shower of sparks exploded from the kilowatt meter, and a shock jolted through the soles of my feet and raced its way up my body before my vision snapped off like the click of a camera shutter.

And there was nothing.

SEVEN

Observation: Initial inspection of the first human subject revealed the following injuries: hematoma above the sixth rib (2-inch diameter), laceration along right side of torso (estimated depth of ¼ inch), surface scrapes above right patella, right and left femurs, and left ankle (all minor), small laceration over left ocular socket (½ inch).

— — —

My eyelids fluttered open. Dust and dirt stuck to the lashes. The first thing I noticed was that the ground was in close proximity to my face. A groan came from somewhere nearby, followed by a whiny, "Cut it out."

I turned painfully onto my side. Einstein's tail was aimed at my face, and she was slobbering all over Owen. I pushed myself upright. Another wave of hurt shot through my body, like my skeleton was made up of one giant funny bone and I'd smacked it with a baseball bat. The tip of Einstein's white tail was smoking.

Beside me, Owen pulled himself to a sitting position with the slow deliberateness of a zombie from the grave. The full volume of his hair stuck straight up. His eyes were round saucers of surprise in his skull.

"Well, that was a shock," he said drily.

I patted the top of my own head, and my palm bumped against hair several inches above where it should be in relation to my scalp. I blinked and glanced around. The high voltage must have reacted with the damp floor, traveling to the spot where we stood and slamming Owen and me with an electrical punch to the figurative gut. Speaking of which, my stomach was killing me. The dirt and concrete must have saved us from the worst effects or else we'd be human French fries right about now. My heart flip-flopped unevenly in my chest. "What the . . . ?"

Wires cascaded from the edge of the tub. Empty. The transistor radio lay broken into clunky pieces on the floor nearby. I pushed the heels of my hands into my eye sockets. The veins in my head pounded.

Water puddled at the base of the bathtub. Smaller splashes formed a trail at even intervals, and that was when it hit me, coming back in a great, crashing tidal wave of realization. There had been a corpse there earlier. Corpses did not generally move on their own. Unless, of course, they weren't corpses any longer.

I jumped to my feet. Einstein skittered back. "Owen," I hissed, tapping his shoulder. As I did so, I turned and froze, my heart now missing a full beat. *Buh-boom. Skip.* Einstein grumbled then let out a hoarse bark.

"You know that feeling of when a semitruck is driving through your brain?" Owen asked, dragging himself to his feet. "Yeah, that." He rubbed at his temples, eyes squeezed shut.

From across the room, a boy stared directly at us. I tugged at Owen's sleeve. He registered the added presence in the room, and his mouth fell open.

My skin tingled. "*Eureka*," I said in a slow exhale.

It was not any boy. It was *the* boy, and now that he was standing in front of me, I could picture him again with his startled expression the second before my headlights crashed into him. He was wearing only his pair of dripping boxers and was slick-chested and wet like he'd just been born.

He cocked his head, examining us. Now upright, he was even taller than I'd thought. More substantial, too.

Owen put his hand up, palm facing outward. "We come in peace," he overenunciated.

I pushed his hand back to his side. "This isn't Roswell, you idiot."

I took a cautious step forward, heart pounding ferociously. The deep laceration that sliced down his rib cage looked dried out now, with cracked, shriveling edges. Wiry thread crisscrossed over the dark red gash where the edges of his flesh were sutured together. The other cuts and scrapes had also scabbed and turned colors. The whole of his torso was coated in angry red branches, like veins, spoking out from where the diathermy device had sat on his chest. I recognized these as the signs of high-level, direct electrocution, and my scalp tingled.

I wrung my hands together. "Okay, I'm just going to say it: You're not going to, like, kill us, are you? We don't have a zombie situation on our hands?"

He pursed his lips and sucked in his cheeks; his eyes were wide.

Einstein resumed her deep, throaty growl. "Right. Sorry," I said when he didn't respond. "That was . . . insensitive."

I looked over my shoulder at Owen, who shrugged and waved me forward.

There was a stillness about the boy in the way he stood that made me worried he'd endured some degree of rigor mortis.

"Let's start over," I said. "Hi." I waved.

His face was no more expressive than a marble slab. "Who are you?" His voice was low and flat.

"I—I—" I stammered, taking one step back without meaning to. "I . . . I'm Victoria." I tried to steady the trembling in my fingers. "But, uh, people call me Tor." Einstein waddled closer to me and took up residence behind my legs. Not much of a guard dog. "And that's Owen." I gestured over my shoulder.

"Hey." Owen's voice was hoarse.

Dark hair was matted down over the boy's forehead, and there was an almost imperceptible gray tint to his otherwise olive skin.

"*Victoria*." He enunciated my name slowly, like he was trying it out for the first time and couldn't quite decide if it sounded right. "Owen." He dipped his head, nodding toward Owen. "And who am I?" Slowly, he raised his hand and placed it flat on his chest.

This, I hadn't expected. "Who are you?" I asked. "You mean you don't know?"

He shook his head, deliberately, gradually, revealing the two razor-thin incisions at each temple.

This time I took several steps forward, walking over to the busted radio and tub of brine. I had to tilt my chin up to make eye contact. "What *do* you remember exactly?"

"Nothing."

I circled him, examining the crusts of dried blood. "A blank slate?" I stopped in front of him. "Where're you from?"

"I don't know." He knitted his eyebrows together. "Did you bring me here? I'm sorry. I don't remember you. Victoria." The way he said it was apologetic. Like one of those overly contrite British fellows from a Jane Austen novel, but without the accent.

Owen and I had never thought to consider how re-instigating the brain patterns might affect thought, especially memory. Naturally, we'd expected there to be complications. We'd just expected those complications to be those of a rat, or in other words, relatively uncomplicated.

Explaining the situation to a walking, talking corpse? Considerably more difficult. I took a deep breath. "Okay, then, there's something I need to tell you." I felt my mouth twisting to the side the way it did when I wanted to tell a lie. "Yesterday there was an accident." I stopped. "I feel like you should be sitting down for this. Do you want to be sitting down? The reason people are usually asked to sit down before receiving bad news is that it lessens the distance to fall, you know, if you faint or something." Like now was the time to play Human

Encyclopedia. He didn't move. Just stood there, arms pinned to his sides. "*Okay.*" I hesitated over how to proceed. Owen, of course, was being no help. I could tell him how he died. Or I could remind him he was walking the streets at close to 2:00 AM. I wasn't sure how much information was too much and how much not enough.

The point was he was here now. Breathing. He had a heartbeat even if he had no memory. I decided the best approach was clinical. Give him the facts that mattered. I would ease him into the full picture later. When it made sense.

"All right then." I clapped my hands together. "I . . . came across you last night," I said, choosing my words carefully. "And, well, there's no easy way to say this, but you died."

A strained gargle rose up in the boy's throat. For an instant, a look of panic flashed over his face like he was dying all over again. "Died?"

Owen moved to my side, adjusting his glasses to get a better look at the man-creature occupying space in our laboratory. "Great bedside manner, doc."

"I was going for the Band-Aid approach," I said out of the side of my mouth. "Rip it off and the worst is over."

"Do these look like Band-Aid problems to you?" Owen retorted in a stage whisper.

"Shut *up.*" I jabbed him with my elbow, and he jabbed me right back. I pressed my lips together and tried to seem in control. "I brought you here," I said. "Because I thought I could help." My words were coming rapid-fire now. "See, I've been working with Owen on reanimation. And"—I could hardly suppress a smile—"and, as you can see, it worked."

The boy blinked, once, twice, three times, and then he lurched forward. I shrank into myself. I had a vision of him mangling me to death like a grizzly bear, but then, when I was about to scream for help, he wrapped me inside a stiff hug.

His skin had the coppery tint of blood, and he smelled salty and a little sick with my nose pressed into his chest. "Thank you," he said. "Victoria. Thank you."

My lungs tightened at the word *thank*. I was the reason he was dead. A confession prickled on the tip of my tongue.

Just then, though, there was a pounding at the hatch door. "Tor! Are you in there?" Mom beat her fist against the entrance, and Einstein's howl joined the chorus.

I squeezed the boy's shoulders hard and wondered briefly if he was cold without any clothes on. "Don't say a word, 'kay? Owen," I said. "You two hide."

"Hide? *Where?*" He glanced around the knickknack-filled room. But I was already bounding up the stairs.

At the top, I slapped my cheeks and tried to rearrange my face into something that looked less guilty.

"Victoria Frankenstein, are you in there? It's seven forty-five in the morning. You're gonna be late for school."

Seven forty-five, I mouthed. I had a physics quiz first period. "One second, Mom," I said, shrinking back farther from the door. There was a crash of metal from down below. My shoulders jerked up to my ears.

"We're okay!" said Owen's muffled voice.

"Be. Quiet." My molars ground into one another.

"I hear you in there." Mom shook the latches on the door. She wasn't a morning person.

"Mom, I said I'm coming!" I licked the palm of my hand and used it to flatten the mop of hair sticking out from the top of my head, then added more saliva to try to smudge off eyeliner using my thumb.

"I'm counting to three, Tor. One . . ." I heaved the inner latch up and over, unlocking the hatch. "Two . . ."

With both hands I shoved open the door and climbed out. "I'm here," I said breathlessly, kicking it closed behind me. The sun assaulted my eyes. I felt like a vampire and immediately threw both arms over my head to block the light.

"What happened to your car?" Mom said without introduction.

"I—" I was still squinting against the brightness of morning. The rusted metal groaned on my father's weather vane, and Mom spared an irritated glare for the rooster outline that spun atop the post of cardinal directions on our roof.

In the events of last night I'd completely forgotten about my car. I cast around for a lie, a good lie, a convincing one. "I . . . hit a deer, Mom." There, that was believable. There were deer everywhere in Hollow Pines. "I'm sorry," I said, and I knew I probably should have felt worse about that fib than I did.

Mom appeared as though she'd been put together from a collection of chicken bones this morning, and I wondered if the light was too bright for her, too. Her teeth were still stained grape juice purple from her favorite brand of Merlot. I'd tried a sip once. It'd tasted like sweet vinegar and made my breath smell like rubbing alcohol.

"I swear, for how smart you are . . ." She didn't finish her sentence. Instead, she pinched her nose so that I didn't know if she was about to sneeze or yell at me. All I knew was that on mornings after she drank, she was in a rotten mood. Lucky me. "Who's going to pay for this, Tor? The tooth fairy?" At that, I felt a surge of righteous indignation. When it came to how parents were supposed to act, I wasn't the resident expert, but still, wasn't my mother supposed to thank God I was okay or something? Since my father died, she was always thanking God for everything else. "Can Bert still drive?" she asked instead.

And I thought about the two of us and how different we'd become from each other. Looking back, I found it nearly impossible to remember whether we'd started this way before my dad's death or whether it was his passing that had turned us both into creatures with our own thirsty addictions—hers to forget, mine to know more.

Seconds felt sticky and slow as I waited for them to tick by, and

I succumbed to the familiar, twitchy-fingered jitteriness of impatience I got when my mom took too long to understand something or forgot to set the oven timer. "It's only the windshield and maybe the fender," I said.

Goose bumps erupted on my arms as the weather vane let out another creaky howl.

"This is going to cost us your dad's Social Security check, you know that?" Her words rubbed at my nerves. Every time she mentioned my father, it was as if she put a special tone around it just to show that she thought it was his fault for dying. She glanced up at the roof again. "And haven't I talked to you about fixing that thing?" My arms prickled again.

I hated that. Mom didn't get anything. She didn't get why Dad chased storms and she didn't get science and she didn't get me. But that was all going to change now that my first big discovery was already here, just beneath our feet.

Eureka.

EIGHT

Conclusion: First human subject—reanimation a success! Submersion in conductor; higher voltage capacity; placement of incised wires on cranium and trunk stimulated all vital organs; possible injury to the hippocampus or reset resulting from localized charge to that area of the brain causing loss of memory; signs of electrocution present on torso.

— — —

I watched my mom's beat-up station wagon trundle out of the drive, leaving muddy tracks in the bogged-down dirt, when I noticed something. Or at least I thought I had noticed something. The soles of my shoes squelched onto the unpaved road as I moved closer to study the thing that I believed I'd seen—tire marks. Three sets of fresh tire marks to be exact.

The stench of rain tilled up notes of cow manure. Brown sludge oozed up the sides of my sneakers as I stepped closer, dodging the puddles left over from the night's storm. First, there was a set of tracks leading straight from the fence opening to where my car was now parked. I could see the small curve that my car took before stopping, and as I traced the path with my eyes, I remembered sitting behind the steering wheel with Owen beside me. Our argument. The enormity of what followed.

I bent down and studied the pattern, touching my finger to the imprints that were left over like fossils in the damp earth. Next,

I sidestepped over to where Mom's car had been parked, a stone's throw to the right of my driver's side door. Four craters were left where her wheels had sunk into the mud during the rains. I'd watched her leave and could now retrace the path. The tire marks bowed out from my own before converging again at the fence. I could recognize her tires by the three lines, crossed through by horizontal markings that looked like sketches of barbed wire.

My skin tingled as I slowly turned to the final set of tread marks. I brushed the dirt from my knees and scanned the yard. There were only these three sets of tire marks on the road. This was significant because the rain had started last night, leaving behind a fresh canvas, and now there were three where there should have been only two. Each set must have been left behind after the rain had died down. I swallowed.

The final set of tire marks veered sharply to the left, disappearing into a patch of grass. My heart pounded. I let my knee sink into the dirt. The third set of tire marks matched neither Mom's station wagon nor my Bert. The grooves in the dirt were thick and chunky, like rows of molars had taken bites out of the road. The pattern reminded me of my dad's old truck, the one my mom had sold, and a cold sliver of fear passed through me. Because there was only one explanation: Somebody must have been here.

I lingered over the strange trail even as the sun was baking the remnants into a hard mold. I tried to shake the crawling sensation out from under my scalp and, instead, headed straight for the house and into my mom's bedroom.

It smelled like cigarette smoke and the pages of old magazines. The room stayed dim, even when the sun was pointed straight at the rest of the house. The carpet was squishy beneath my feet. I tugged at the closet doors, and they opened like accordion pleats to a shallow two-rack wardrobe. My mom's clothes hung dull and lifeless near the center, an array of muted colors, sloppy cardigans, and ill-fitting pants.

I pushed those to the side to clear a path to the far right-hand corner, where, hanging untouched, were my dad's clothes. Once, when Mom didn't know I'd come in, I caught her smelling the sleeves of one of his shirts, just sitting there with her nose pressed into the fabric. I yanked down on the collar of a button-down, and it slid from the hanger. My father liked plaid, and by the time I left, I was cradling three shirts in that pattern along with a couple pairs of jeans.

I carried my stash to the cellar, no intention at all of going to school. I pried open the hatch door and descended the stairs at last. "It's me," I called, my voice muffled by the pile of clothes. I stopped at the bottom and dropped the garments on a clear square of countertop. From where he was squatting behind the lab table, Owen pulled a tarp he'd draped over himself and stood.

"What took you so long?" He swatted the blue plastic down toward his feet.

I hesitated, weighing whether to tell him about the unexplained tire marks that I'd found in the front lawn, until I made a conscious decision that Owen, who was already more prone to worry and paranoia than I was, didn't need to know unless and until there was actually something *to* know.

Right now, there wasn't. So I pivoted and spotted the boy, standing directly behind the model skeleton against the far wall. This time I raised an eyebrow at Owen.

"What?" he said, kicking the now crumpled tarp beneath the table. "You told us to hide."

The boy's form was in full view between each of the bones. "You can come out now. . . ." The boy had no name with which to finish the sentence. He didn't move. I came closer. "It's all right. My mother's gone." The boy stayed very still but was peering at me over the model skull. "No one's going to find you here," I said. "It's just Owen and me." I stretched my hand out toward him.

Cautiously, he put his palm in mine and allowed me to lead him away from the worst hiding spot ever. "I don't like it when you leave, Victoria."

The corner of my mouth twitched with the beginning of a smile. "I'm sorry," I said. "I'll try not to from now on."

His stillness seemed to suck the movement right out of his surroundings, like the air had turned stale along with him.

"First thing's first," I said. "Let's get you dressed." I reached over and tossed him a pair of jeans, boxers, and a shirt from my dad's closet. He immediately began sliding off his boxers. "Wait!" My hand flew over my eyes and I spun around, pinching Owen to follow suit. "Okay, proceed." I listened to the rustling of fabric and soft grunts for several moments. "Are you clothed?" I asked.

"Yes, Victoria."

Owen and I turned. The clothes may have been a bit out of style, but at least if he was going to be a walking dead man, he wasn't a naked one.

The boy looked to me expectantly, holding his arms out from his sides.

Owen checked his watch. "School's started."

I grimaced. Owen and I didn't skip school. In fact, we were never even late. For the past two years we'd won awards for perfect attendance. It wasn't so much that we thought we were learning anything as it was that people didn't get into Harvard without a pristine transcript.

"Then we better figure out a plan for tomorrow, Captain Obvious."

I crossed the room and pushed the metal gurney next to the boy. The black pad on top of the stretcher was cracked, revealing the yellowing foam inside. I patted the surface. "Can we ask you a few more questions?"

He hoisted himself onto the gurney. His bare feet dangled off the side. Einstein came over to lick his toes. I tried to scoot her away but she was very persistent about certain things and toe-licking was one of them.

I took hold of one of his wrists and pressed my fingers into the tendons at the base. A steady pulse coursed against my fingertips. "The voltage must have triggered some sort of restart in the brain patterns."

"But if there's no long-term memory, why has he retained his motor skills? How's he speaking to us?"

"Syringe and vial," I said, and waited while Owen retrieved them from a sliding tray of surgical tools. I took the syringe from him and pushed back one of the boy's sleeves. "Could be retrograde amnesia. The memories most likely to be lost are the most recent. Working backward it can go decades depending on the severity of the brain trauma, and it doesn't affect motor skills." I applied pressure above the boy's elbow. "This might sting." I glanced up at him. He was following every movement I made with his eyes. I plunged the needle into the blue vein at the crux of his elbow. As I pulled back the stopper, the vial filled with deep red blood.

"He didn't even flinch," Owen observed.

I slid the needle out of his arm. "Did you feel that?" I asked.

The boy stared down at the spot on his arm. "No."

I poked his shoulder. "How about that?"

He shook his head.

At this revelation, I reached for the back of his hand and pinched it hard, like a kindergartner with a vendetta. No reaction.

"How . . ." I trailed off. "But there can't be just nothing . . . can there?"

Owen rubbed his chin thoughtfully. "I don't know. I mean, twelve hours ago I might not have thought any of this was possible. We're kind of dealing with the definition of uncharted territory here. How do you feel right now?" he asked. The boy's brow lowered and his chin dimpled. "For instance, are you sad?"

The boy touched the back of his hand where I'd pinched it. "I don't know. I'm not sure." His jaw changed shape, teeth grinding beneath the surface, but otherwise his features remained impassive. *Empty*.

"That could just as easily be the lack of memory, though," I figured. "Without memories, what's there to be sad about, you know?"

"Amazing," Owen whispered, and we both stood for a moment, he and I, basking in the secrets of the universe that the two of us had unlocked. "He's truly a blank slate. Like a newborn baby in a teenager's body."

"For some reason I don't think we're going to be able to hire a babysitter for this one."

"So then what?" Owen asked. "We can't exactly hide him here forever."

"We don't. Hide him, I mean." I held the vial and deposited the contents of the syringe into it, then capped it with a rubber plug. With a marker I labeled it *Day 1*. "You're about our age, right?" The boy looked from side to side as if he wasn't sure I was talking to him. "Right, stupid question. What I mean is, he comes to school with us."

I stepped back and studied the two guys in the room. Compared with Owen, the strange boy was about four sizes bigger. His chest swelled where Owen's caved inward, but the boy, I thought, could pass for one of the athletes. Maybe.

I rubbed my temples. I was suffering from severe caffeine and sleep deprivation. If this ended up being a horrible plan, I could blame it on both.

Owen sighed. "He needs a name if we're going to make this work. I repeat, *if*." As though we had another choice. "You want a name, don't you, buddy?"

The boy cracked his neck. The popping of bones sent shivers down my back. "What kind of name?" he asked.

"I don't know. Whatever kind of name you like," I said, depositing the blood sample onto a test-tube rack.

"You can't use Owen," Owen butted in. "That's taken."

"Like anyone would want it." I rolled my eyes. "Open your mouth wide." He obeyed and I swabbed his mouth with a Q-tip, which I deposited into another vial for later testing.

The boy smacked his lips when I had finished, and I could practically see the cogs turning. Finally, once I'd shifted my weight several times over, he spoke. "Victoria, could you please choose?"

A pocket of air bubbled inside my chest. I couldn't swallow, and just when I thought I'd refuse the honor, it came to me like a vision. It was inspired. It was biblical. It was hard proof that I hadn't quite slept through *all* my Sunday school classes and that, occasionally, I listened to my mom.

"I've got it," I said, breaking into a broad smile. "Your name, I think, is Adam."

NINE

Preliminary test results taken within first 24 hours for processing: red blood cells uniform in size representative of 40% of total blood consistency; white blood cell count normal; blood serum—colorless, clear, without parasites or other bacteria; saliva pH—6.5

Conclusion: Safe for general population; will proceed with next stage of the experiment

— — —

Adam had now been alive—or dead, depending on how you looked at things—for over twenty-four hours. The previous day had passed with preparations and another near-sleepless night as I fretted over the details of my plan to take a corpse to Hollow Pines High School.

"One last time, Adam. What are you going to say to Mrs. Van Lullen when you see her?" My eyes flitted up to Adam's reflection in the rearview mirror. He was perched at the edge of Bert's backseat with his knees tucked up to his chest so that he could lean forward to hear Owen and me. I felt as if Owen and I were driving our child to his first day of school.

Owen twisted in the passenger seat to watch the recital.

"I am Adam Smith. I come from Elgin, Illinois. I am sixteen years old. I am a junior. Victoria is my family friend. I am staying with her while my parents wrap up our move to the Lone Star State. Please,

I would like to enroll in Hollow Pines High School." He finished his speech with a beaming smile.

Owen pushed his thumbs into his eye sockets. "That's it. We're screwed."

"We're not screwed." I took my eyes from the road long enough to glare at Owen. The rain had left behind muddy craters in the asphalt. The patchy tumbleweed grass that lined the side of it shimmered and looked slightly less cotton-mouthed than it had a couple days earlier.

We'd taken pains to make sure Adam's assumed persona would stand out as little as possible. We'd chosen "Smith" because it was the most common last name in the United States, and a hometown of Elgin, Illinois, because nobody in their right mind would make up the fact that they were from some Podunk, middle-of-nowhere town like Elgin.

Or Hollow Pines for that matter.

"Adam, it sounds a little rehearsed. Do you think you could do it again only try *not* to sound like you're reading from a cue card. Here, like this: 'Hi, I'm Victoria, but since that name sucks I prefer Tor. I'm from Hollow Pines. Turned seventeen in July.'" I raised and lowered my inflection to illustrate. "See the difference?"

Owen's jaw dropped. "Oh my god. Look at him. He's like a baby freaking bird when you talk."

I blushed. Adam had clearly developed an instant attachment to me. When I moved, he shadowed. When I spoke, you could literally see his chest puff up in anticipation. I had to continue to remind myself it wasn't adorable, it was dead.

Adam cleared his throat. "I'm Adam Smith. *I'm* from Elgin, Illinois." He stopped. "How was that, Victoria?"

Owen slapped his forehead. "You've created an imbecile."

"I have not." I gave Owen an extra slap on the head. The car careened across the dividing line, and I hurried to correct my course.

"Be nice. He's relearning, that's all." In the mirror, I could see Adam's lips working through his lines. "Adam, that was much better. Excellent."

"I'm sorry," Owen muttered, and stared out the window. "I'm nice. I'm just trying to calculate the maximum sentence for aiding and abetting." He twisted the nob on the stereo and flipped through stations until he found talk radio.

"Really. You think Mrs. Van Lullen is going to take one look at him and guess that"—I lowered my voice and turned up the radio—"that he's a walking, talking corpse. Be rational, Owen. For god's sake, we had a breakthrough."

"I am being rational, Tor. News flash: Our science fair project wasn't some well-guarded secret for which you needed national security clearance. We worked on it in the *biology* lab. At our school. You know, the one we're trying to enroll Mr. Stitchy McStitcherson in."

"Keep your voice down." I wrapped my hands tighter around the steering wheel. My stomach was already working itself over with worry well enough. "Do you have the paperwork ready?"

He pulled out a folder. In it, the forms we'd e-mailed to request from the school yesterday were printed. The imaginary Ms. Smith had a new e-mail address and Owen's cell phone number. "It's all here. I e-mailed it to the school last night, but we have it just in case."

"And your voice mail?"

He punched a number on his phone. It played a muffled recording of my voice, donning my best midwestern accent. "You've reached Marjorie Smith. Due to recent family events, I am tending to personal matters. I will return your call as soon as I'm able." *Beep.*

He nodded. "What's it called when a plan's a step below bulletproof?"

"Shot to hell," I said.

He grimaced. "Right, that."

As we got closer to the school, my legs began sticking to the fake leather seats, and it felt like ripping off tape every time I pressed the brakes. My armpits were Slip 'N Slides, and I knew my cotton socks were doing their fair share of sopping up my nerves.

My head was ringing louder than a bell tower as we neared the school. Buildings started popping out of the cotton fields. We passed the sprawling expanse of the Beverly-Tate plant, where the lion's share of this country's feminine pads and toilet paper was proudly produced.

We then took a right and my heart began hammering harder. The stadium loomed in the distance. "Adam?" I said as we pulled into the parking lot, the brick and mortar of Hollow Pines High sprouting out of the ground in front of us. "Just act normal."

We unclicked our seat belts. Car doors slammed. I ducked my head into the backseat. "Are you coming?"

"I am coming. Wait for me." Adam didn't notice when the top of his head rammed against the roof of the car. Each large foot clomped into the gravel and, once standing, he dwarfed me.

"This," Owen gestured, "is Hollow Pines High." Adam grunted and backed up against Bert. Owen thumped him on the back. "I agree, buddy. It's frightening. But you get used to it. Shall we give you the tour?"

The school was crawling with its morning bustle. Hollow Pines High School was a biosphere in which all species were forced to mix. A pickup truck sped past us, kicking up gravel and dust. We paused to cough and swat it away. Adam stuck close to my side.

"Those kids," said Owen, looking over to where the pickup was squeezing itself in among a line of other gas-guzzlers, "are called the Wranglers."

"As in the jeans," I explained.

"You thought that Wrangler jeans went out of style in the 1980s and you'd be right," Owen continued. "But the Wranglers believe it's their God-given duty to wear starched denim twenty-four-seven-three-sixty-five. Check out the ironed-in creases on those babies." We shuffled past three guys sitting in the bed of a pickup, sharing dip from a tin can of Skoal tobacco. They passed around a Styrofoam cup and took turns spitting into it. I shuddered and looked away. "Rumor has it, they even sleep in them."

Adam's face cracked open with what I believed was supposed to be a smile. He raised his hand in the air and waved furiously. "Hello, Wranglers," he shouted.

The kids in the truck glanced up and shook their heads before stuffing in another wad of chewing tobacco.

I grabbed Adam's arm and forced it to his side, shuffling him off past the line of trucks. My face flushed with heat. I made a quick wave and muttered an apology to the confused wannabe cowboys.

"Aren't those your friends, Victoria?" He pointed back to the Wranglers.

"Definitely not. Come on. We're headed that way." I gestured toward the mouth of the main building, where a stream of students was already pouring in. Owen and I had the worst parking spots. It was a hike.

"On your left, you'll see that we're entering the Bible Belt." A collection of kids wearing matching shirts busied themselves unloading posters from the trunk of a car. "They're harmless mostly, but if you so much as hint that you're having a less-than-perfect day, they *will* pray for you. You've been warned." I laughed when Adam sidestepped farther from them. "Over there, those are the Billys." Owen directed our attention to five husky guys tossing around a ball. "Redneck football players. They have a shocking amount of dudes named Bill. That's Billy. Then there's Billy Ray, and William. Those fine fellows"— we paused to watch Billy Ray crush a can between his palms, then use it to peg William in the backside—"those are God's gift to Hollow Pines."

"As you can see, God's fondness for Hollow Pines is questionable," I said.

Maybe it was seeing guys that looked like him or maybe it was the whooshing excitement of the football, but Adam began gravitating toward the Billys like they were the actual center of the class solar system. "Uh-uh." I snagged Adam by the elbow. "No way. We steer clear of them." I had thought Owen and my speech made that clear. "They're popular. And mean. That, my friend, is a bad combination."

We picked our way through the rest of the factions—Tea-Sippers, Kickers, and the Angels Camp Posse—and onto the school's crumbly lawn.

At the top of the walkway, a card table, manned by a bevy of Oilerettes, blocked the entrance. "Calendars! Only ten dollars! Show your Oiler spirit!" Paisley Wheelwright waved a glossy wall calendar overhead.

"That's the drill team, the Oilerettes," Owen mumbled to Adam. "Tor affectionately calls them the 'Whore Core.'"

"Can we please keep that between us?" I shot Owen a dirty look. But seriously, the school's cheerleaders were selling calendars of themselves. The campus of Hollow Pines High was basically where feminism came to die.

Nearby, I heard a gruff yell. "Ready, set, hike!" Out of the corner of my eye, I saw Billy Ray cock his arm back like a trigger and fire off a football.

"Incoming," Owen called out.

William ran toward us, his chin hiked over his shoulder. I watched his bright red hair and freckled face sprinting over, not looking where he was going. His eye was on the spinning ball and so was mine. Adam and I jumped apart and William threaded the space between us, narrowly missing a death stomp to my toes.

As the ball hurtled toward me, I did that awful thing girls do when they screw up their arms and elbows. I hated sports. Even more than that, I hated team sports. And even more than that, I couldn't handle balls flying toward my face. A chorus of squealing girls split the morning bustle just as William dove. He crashed onto the Oilerette table, squishing the smiling faces of the pom-pom-toting future Dallas Cowboys Cheerleaders of America and buckling the table's legs so that it pitched onto its side. As for the ball, it landed with a bouncy *ker-thunk* directly in front of Adam's feet.

"Did that even make sense in your head?" Paisley Wheelwright, pint-sized blond and summa cum laude in high kicks and spray tans, shrieked at William, who was crinkling glossy calendar spreads with his rear end as he tried to wriggle free from the wreckage.

"What?" He roughed his hair. "It's not my fault."

Feet away, Billy Ray clapped and held his hands out. "Toss me the ball, man."

Adam stared at the football, still rocking on the concrete walkway like a dying cockroach. Time seemed to freeze over. Slowly, Adam reached down and wrapped his hand over the leather laces.

William stopped his shimmy. Adam looked down at the ball then up at Billy Ray. I clenched my teeth.

Billy Ray rubbed the top of his shaved head and looked around as if to say *Are you seeing this?* "It's not a snake. It ain't gonna bite you." His accent made for a slow drawl.

Adam's expression was serene. His elbow arced back so fast that his hand was a blur of motion as he released the ball. It sped like an arrow straight into Billy Ray's gut. He grunted and doubled over, a whoosh of air rushing out of him.

Nearby, William was pushing himself off the broken table. He stopped to stare at Adam, then at Billy Ray, and then at Adam again, squinting one eye shut to look at him cockeyed like maybe he'd been seeing him from the wrong angle before. As he trundled past, he kept staring back at Adam and shaking his head. "You ain't gotta kill him, you know," he said before reaching his friend and clapping him good-naturedly on the back.

"See what we mean?" Owen asked, returning to join us.

Adam spun to me. "I killed him?" He pointed at Billy Ray, who was still rubbing his belly. "Can you bring him back, too, Victoria?"

"Shhhhhh." I glanced around, looking for anyone who might have overheard him. I pushed his arms down to his side. "It's called a figure of speech. You didn't literally kill anyone. But, just to be safe, let's not use the K-word in public. We don't need to draw any more attention to ourselves than . . . well, than you just did."

Adam appeared chastened while a group of girls stood whispering behind their hands and casting looks in Adam's general direction.

"Way to fly under the radar." Owen looped his thumbs under his backpack straps.

"It was one thing," I shot back.

"Hey, kid." I stiffened at the voice of my nightmares. The she-devil with horns that must have been hidden somewhere under all that highlighted hair. "Kid with the arm. Come over here."

Adam lifted his chin. "Me?"

Paisley nodded.

"You don't have to go to them," I said, but he was already walking over.

Paisley leaned against the side of the overturned table. "I don't remember seeing you around before, and Hollow Pines isn't exactly a big place. Who are you, anyway?"

"Hello. I'm Adam Smith. I come from Elgin, Illinois. I'm sixteen years old. I'm a junior. Victoria is my family friend. I am staying with her while my parents wrap up our move to the Lone Star State." Adam reached down and retrieved one of the scattered calendars from the ground and held it out for Paisley to take. "I can help." He picked up another calendar and tried to straighten the table.

"I'm—"

"You're the Whore Core." Adam smiled. "I remember."

I choked on my own spit. "Adam," I hissed, but kept my distance.

Paisley's eyes snapped to attention. Her left eyebrow arched slowly.

Her glance flicked to me. "Is that what they're calling all the girls who didn't make the spinster squad?"

I scowled.

Adam's brow dropped. "I don't know. I'm new here," he said with a tone of complete seriousness.

Paisley dropped into a seat behind the cash box. "I see that. Here." She shuffled around for an undamaged calendar. "For you, free." She flourished a silver marker from her pocket and signed her name across the front. Autographed it. Like she was famous. "Welcome to Hollow Pines, Adam Smith." She handed him the calendar, which he held clutched to his chest as he wandered back to me. "Hope to see you around more often." I turned away in case she did something truly gag-worthy like wink and I was forced to upchuck my breakfast.

"Look, Victoria," he said, showing me the calendar like a cat dropping off a dead bird to its master. "I got you this."

Owen snorted. I closed my eyes and counted to three. Then I took the calendar from Adam. On it, Paisley Wheelwright, Cassidy Hyde, and the rest of the Oilerette elite posed in bikinis and high heels with Crest Whitestrip smiles plastered on and glittery pom-poms clutched in hand. "Thank you, Adam," I said. "That's, um, that's very sweet."

He beamed. I swung my backpack around and stuffed the calendar inside as we ushered Adam into the administration office.

"Are you seriously going to keep that?" Owen asked close to my ear.

"What am I supposed to do, dump it in the trash in front of his face?"

The glass door swung shut behind us. "It's autographed. If I were you, I'd burn it."

The administration office had orange carpeting. I imagined it was meant to tie in with the school colors. It didn't. It was the color of Cheez Whiz.

"Shut up," I said, noticing that Mrs. Van Lullen was peering over her glasses at us. "We're on."

I squared my shoulders and strode up to the desk, wishing that I'd chosen something more presentable than a loose-fitting baseball tee. "Hi, Mrs. Van Lullen. I wanted to introduce you to a new student. This is Adam Smith. I believe his mother e-mailed you yesterday for the paperwork?"

Mrs. Van Lullen painted her lips into the shape of a heart and favored overstretched cardigans that never failed to clash miserably with the spray-on cheese decor.

"Nice of you two to join us today, Ms. Frankenstein," she greeted me in return. "May I see your guardian or doctor's notes for yesterday's absence?"

I winced. It figured that an otherwise perfect attendance record would be the thing to come back and bite us. "Um . . ." I made a show of patting down my pockets.

She waited until I finished acting. "I see," she said, jotting something down in a notepad with quick, staccato handwriting. "Adam, you said?" She didn't look up. Not right away.

I felt Owen prod Adam forward. He stood so still I might have sworn he was a mannequin. I nodded at him and he twitched to life as though remembering his lines. "I am Adam Smith. I come from Elgin, Illinois. I am sixteen years old. I am a junior. Victoria is my family friend. I am staying with her while my parents wrap up our move to the Lone Star State. Please, I would like to enroll in Hollow Pines High School."

Mental head-thunk. Owen sucked in his breath. Mrs. Van Lullen leveled her chin and stared at us. She was allergic to shenanigans, as she called them, unless said shenanigans came from the right sources, and those were, namely, the Billys and the Oilerettes. We were neither of those, and the wild knocking of my heart threatened to give us all away.

"Elgin," she said, only she drew the word out so long she could have said it twice. She crossed her arms over an egg yolk cardigan and pursed her lips. "You're awfully big, Adam. Did you play football where you're from?"

He looked back to Mrs. Van Lullen, holding her eye contact with the directness of a sociopath, and said, "I don't think so."

She frowned and slid the folder from the desk to examine. "You don't think so? It's hardly a trick question."

I glanced nervously between Adam and Mrs. Van Lullen and burst into spontaneous fake laughter. I slapped my knee. "Oh, Adam." I hiked my thumb in his direction. I was a terrible actress. Owen physically distanced himself from me like I was having a psychotic break, though perhaps that wasn't so far off. "This one . . ." I stuck with my nervous chuckle. "He's always such a kidder. You'll see." My laughter died under the hard stare of the administrator. "Er, no, he's never played football." I tugged at the hem of my T-shirt. "Adam here is a pacifist." He smiled in return.

"I don't like kids trying to be fresh with me," she said.

I cleared my throat. "He's not being fresh," I added. "On the contrary, he's downright stale, I think."

She slid her glasses down her nose and held out a printed sheet of paper. "It's too bad. We're always looking for good ballplayers around here." She flipped to the next page. "I tried your mother's line yesterday." She had returned to all business. "She didn't answer."

I swallowed. "I've known the Smiths for a long time, Mrs. Van Lullen. They're good people."

"That may be, but we need parental consent to enroll in the public school system."

"And you have it." I reached over the desk and pointed to the signature at the bottom of the page.

She gave a small huff and picked up the phone. "I'm going to try her again." She referenced the paperwork to dial the number for the fictitious Ms. Smith.

As soon as she finished dialing, a buzzing sound came from

Owen's pocket. We froze. Mrs. Van Lullen cradled the receiver against her ear. The phone kept buzzing at intervals.

"What is that sound?" she whispered, then shook her head and turned away.

My eyes bugged at Owen. *Silence it*, I mouthed. He fumbled in his pocket.

Finally, she clicked off the phone. "Went to voice mail again."

"Mrs. Van Lullen, with all due respect," I began. "It's Adam's constitutional right to be educated, and he's exercising that right, right here, right now. Are you really going to do something so . . . so *un-American* as to deny him his individual liberties?"

The second it left my mouth I felt the liquid in my stomach turn to battery acid. Her glare hardened. If there was one thing the folks in my town would-not-could-not stand for, it was questioning their patriotism.

"I'm just saying—" I started up again.

She held up her hand and I quieted. "Well, stop saying it." She set the open folder down on top of her desk. "Adam," she said, "you seem like a nice young gentleman, and if you're in a hurry to get into school, then *for now*," she stressed, "I'm not going to be the one to stand in your way. It's a noble thing you're trying to do here, furthering your education. I'll keep trying your mother, and I'm sure I'll get ahold of her." She squashed a rubber stamp into an inky sponge pad and pressed it on the front of Adam's file. "We could use more boys like you. Promise me you'll go see Coach Carlson? I trust you'll meet some excellent friends here soon."

When it was clear that Mrs. Van Lullen didn't place me in that category, I sneered my lower lip just a hair. She disregarded me and flipped the folder shut. With a smile meant only for Adam and definitely not for me, she handed Adam several pamphlets. "Enjoy Hollow Pines High," she said. "Go, Oilers!"

TEN

Stage 1 of the experiment concluded in a successful resuscitation of a dead human specimen. Circulation and organ functionality have resumed. Proper vital signs are present and being monitored. Plans for Stage 2 include integrating the resuscitated specimen into society to increase quality of life. Notably, this stage would not have been possible with one of the rat specimens, which makes this an exciting stage of development.

--- --- ---

They stuck you with the junior basics," I said, examining the schedule that Mrs. Van Lullen had printed for Adam. "What kind of transcript did you send?" I asked Owen.

Owen shrugged. "I didn't know. I went with the most average one I could find from Elgin."

"Sorry, I hope that's okay." I handed the schedule back to Adam, who held it daintily. The usual morning cacophony overtook the hallway. Muffled music played from headphones. Locks clinked open. The smell of Magic Marker wafted off poster board.

A foot outside the administration office, Adam stood frozen. Ice Age frozen.

"Let me see. It can't be that bad." Owen snatched the sheet of paper. "Here we go, US History, English 2, economics, Algebra 2, chemistry, PE, Global Studies."

Adam's eyes flitted around, taking in the hundreds of students who swarmed around us. His chest shrank inward and I cringed as he plugged his ears. He rocked back on his heels and then forward, back and then forward.

Owen was still busy outlining his day. "Okay, so you're on your own for history, but we all have English 2 together, lunch, and, hey, we all have PE together, right?"

I nodded but kept watching Adam. His eyes didn't stop moving from one side to the other, and from here, it looked as though he was trembling. I tapped Owen on the shoulder. "Um, nine o'clock," I said.

Owen looked up and dropped the hand holding the schedule to his side. "You've got to be kidding me. This guy is scared of . . . of what? Of high school now? He's gargantuan."

"He's *overwhelmed*."

"By what? By people? You're a person. I'm a person. He seemed cool five minutes ago. He was a regular charmer. A James Dean–type. Stoic. He was going to charm the pants off the ladies with all three sentences that he knows."

My shoulders dropped. I stepped in front of Adam and picked up his hand to hold between both of mine.

"Oh no, not you, too," Owen groaned. "If I knew all I had to do to get the ladies' sympathies was rewind evolution a few thousand years, then I would have limited my vocabulary to that of a fifth grader a long time ago."

I snapped my eyes at Owen and he shrank back. When Adam noticed me standing there, he stopped shivering. I had a flash of the boy in the middle of the road, scared and soaked through, our fingers braided together. I felt a surge of responsibility for him. I'd heard of soldiers coming back from war with a disease of the mind called PTSD, or post-traumatic stress disorder, which was caused by witnessing a violent event. And I'd known that in a town not too far away that's what was blamed when a young veteran shot twenty-one people including himself.

"It's very loud, Victoria." He stared down at his shoes.

I waited for him to look at me. "Adam," I said. "It's okay. I'm right here. We're going to be fine, you hear me? Fine." I squeezed his hand even though we'd already established that he couldn't feel it. It just seemed like the human thing to do. "Everything is going to go perfectly smoothly. I promise." I scanned the room. Yes, Adam had a bit of a sallow, haunted effect going on, but underneath it he was actually quite attractive. In an obvious, traditional way, too, with long lashes and nice teeth. In the halls of Hollow Pines High, good looks alone were powerful currency.

He let me hold his hand. "Victoria." He said my name with such devotion and with no purpose other than he seemed to like the sound of it. A piece of my heart chipped off and clattered down until it caught somewhere between my rib cage and belly button.

"Adam," I said back. The first bell rang. Students piled in on top of one another, but I stared into Adam's eyes for another moment longer. "Adam," I repeated, and I felt his hand relax under my palm.

When the moment broke, Owen and I led the way to a long row of orange lockers. I searched the numbers emblazoned at the top for his until I found it.

"Here it is," I said, pounding my fist on number 42. "Your locker. If you ever need either me or Owen and you can't get ahold of us, meet us here, okay? We'll come find you."

Adam surveyed the hall. I retrieved the combination lock Mrs. Van Lullen had given him and read the combo off a slip of paper. "60-28-63. Can you remember that?" Considering I was dealing with a boy with no memory, my hopes weren't high. "You can keep this sheet for a while," I said.

Adam peered at the dial. "60-28-63," he repeated.

Owen and I shared a look.

"60-28-63," Adam said again.

"Okay," Owen said. "Well, at least we know his neurons aren't *totally* fried."

I noted the marked improvement, then opened Adam's new locker and started putting some of his paperwork inside. "We can decorate your locker if you want," I said. "You know, if it'll make you feel more at home."

"Hi there." I twitched at the sound of another familiar voice. "Adam, right?" She extended a hand. "I'm Cassidy Hyde. I was at the table over there." She pointed over her shoulder. "My friend Paisley gave you that calendar." Cassidy laughed at this and shook her head, continuing to ignore Owen and me as if we were a pair of misplaced furniture. "Anyway, I'm number 41. Looks like we're neighbors."

"I don't live here," Adam said.

Her forehead wrinkled and she cocked her head, then laughed. "Funny." She turned her own combination lock. "And athletic. Rare combination."

I didn't bother to hide my scowl. I wanted to unhook her manicured nails from Adam and toss her across the room. Because even though Adam's brain had been busted, his eyes seemed to be working just fine.

So did Owen's for that matter. Cassidy Hyde watched her carbs. She did cardio outside of gym class. She carried a compact mirror and had a signature scent and signed her name in bubbly letters. Her aspirations consisted of being elected to Homecoming court and becoming Miss Texas. Not that I cared, but it seemed ridiculous for her to get so much attention for correctly applying eyeliner while I was slaving for a Nobel Prize. That was the thing about high school. They gave away prizes for who could be the least interesting.

The funny thing, though, was that Cassidy actually used to be kind of fat. When her family moved to Hollow Pines in seventh grade, she had these chunky moon pie cheeks and sausage fingers. Kids used to call her Princess Butterball when she wasn't listening. I didn't know if Paisley took a Xanax that day or if she just wanted someone to look better than, but Cassidy eventually worked her way into the in crowd and shed a few pounds until she fit right in with the popular kids. Secretly, I thought this pissed off Paisley. Not that she could say so now. When it came to the popular kids, I fancied myself a sort of behavioral zoologist that looked for patterns and natural hierarchy. Like just last year, the senior boys voted Cassidy hottest ass in the sophomore class. Personally, I'd rather be shot than receive an honor for the two bulbs of fat located on my backside, but I guess for girls like Cassidy that kind of thing was a big deal.

"Can I see your schedule?" She held out her hand.

Adam tentatively handed it to her. "I have English and PE with Victoria."

She peered up at me through her eyelashes. "How nice."

I cleared my throat as Cassidy was circling the classes she shared with Adam. "Adam, we really need to show you to your class," I said.

"Oh, I can take him." So now I existed. "We're in history together."

I offered a tight smile. A vision of Adam co-opted by Paisley, Cassidy, and their circle of bobble heads flashed before my eyes. *My* Adam. I created him. "It's okay. I promised his mother."

Cassidy shrugged, glossed lips pushing out into a pout. "Whatever."

"Come on, Adam." I patted my leg.

"He's not a dog." Owen leaned in and said this into my ear. I blushed and dropped my hand, but not before Cassidy rolled her eyes.

It only took a single second, but it felt like slow motion. Adam, with his jerky, unnatural movements, turned to follow me. His forehead slammed into the edge of the open locker door. *Thwack!* Followed by a clang of reverberating metal.

All three of us took in one collective gasp. The only one who appeared unfazed was Adam. He took a step back and then redirected his path so that the locker door was no longer blocking it.

"Oh my god, are you all right?" Cassidy cupped both hands to her mouth. Adam blinked. "You're bleeding!"

A thin trickle of blood ran from a small gash on his forehead, and Adam had exhibited absolutely zero reflex.

"Dammit." I rushed over to him.

"A blockhead and a klutz," Owen said flatly. "I guess that means we *don't* have a superhero on our hands?"

I stood on my tippy-toes and peered up at the cut, not able to stop myself from feeling like this was all Cassidy's fault. The cut was shallow, but head wounds had a way of bleeding more than they ought to. I felt my cheeks burn with annoyance. Two minutes ago Adam had outwardly been a perfect specimen. I poked at the skin around the gash.

"Pity, too." Owen clucked his tongue. "Because I was already coming up with names and everything."

My glare cut to Owen. "Would you like to know my names for you right now or would you like to *help*?"

"You should take him to the nurse's office." Cassidy buzzed around me.

"He needs space," I snapped.

Adam touched the injury. His fingers came away with a spot of bright red blood. "I'm sorry, Victoria." Then to Cassidy he said, "She had just gotten me cleaned up." His pale complexion and hollowed cheeks made him look doubly remorseful.

Cassidy did a double take.

"Inside joke." I pinched the gouge closed and applied pressure. "You wouldn't get it."

She gave me a *you're crazy* look before shaking it away. "He didn't even flinch," she said. "Christ, he's tough. He should try out for the team." Her breath was minty next to me. I wished people would stop saying that.

Just as we'd hypothesized, Adam didn't feel a thing. He was as impermeable to pain as a tank. This wasn't normal. Or good. Pain was an important evolutionary development that made normal human beings withdraw from damaging situations. Without pain, there was basically nothing standing between Adam and sticking his hand down a garbage disposal.

"I mean . . ." Adam wrinkled his forehead. "Ouch." His voice carried the same monotone, but he looked to me and Cassidy for approval. "Sorry."

I frowned. "It's not your fault." I released the skin and it started bleeding fresh.

"That might leave a scar, you know. But—" Cassidy leaned over to examine the sides of his face, where there were the remnants of Adam's incisions and other cuts and scrapes that already appeared older than they actually were. "Looks like you've already got a bit of a collection started. My mom can recommend a plastic surgeon. She got a face-lift last year."

The second bell rang. "Don't you have somewhere you need to be?"

"Sort of." She glanced at her watch and bit her lip. "I'll tell Mrs. Landers that he'll be late. See you around, Adam." She waved her fingers, spun on the spot, and headed back down the hallway, which was already being drained of students quicker than a flushed toilet.

"You should go, too," I told Owen. "There's no use in both of us getting in trouble. Make up something for me." The final bell was ringing. We were both already late. I grabbed Adam by the wrist and began towing him toward the girls' bathroom.

"Tor," Owen called after me. "Come on, Tor. You know I'm a terrible liar. People will see right through me. I have a very honest face."

But I just told Owen to stop being such a pansy and, after checking in both directions, pushed my head into the bathroom.

"Hello?" I asked. "Anyone in here?" When no one answered, I glanced both ways and pulled Adam inside. I stashed him in the large handicapped stall at the end and balanced on top of the toilet, between the feminine hygiene waste bin and the unraveling roll of toilet paper, so I could stand eye level with his cut. I leaned closer. It was a shallow wound, but enough to leave a goose egg. "You seriously couldn't feel that?" My voice dropped to a whisper.

"No." He stared up at the ceiling like he might catch a glimpse of the gash. "Is it broken?"

"Broken?" I smiled. "No, it's not broken. Just a cut. Although . . ." I leaned in. "Most people would have thought that hurt. If it had happened to Owen, he probably would have cried."

I hopped off the toilet and dug around my backpack until I found a bandage and a spool of surgical tape I'd used on Mr. Bubbles.

"You don't like Cassidy." He wasn't asking a question.

I remounted the toilet seat I was using as a stepping stool and paused. "I—who said that?" One of my shoes slipped on the seat, and I grabbed Adam's shoulder to right myself, knees wobbling for balance. "We're not in the same group," I explained, blowing a strand of hair from between my eyes.

"What group are you in?"

"Me? I don't know. I prefer to think of myself as an individualist." When Adam looked confused, I continued. "Fine, I guess you could say I'm a nerd, a geek, first stop on the train to Dork City. That's what you get for not wanting to peak by the twelfth grade."

"And what group am I in?"

I smiled. "You, my friend, are Dork City's newest resident. You're one of—" But a knock at the bathroom door interrupted us. I froze, remembering where I was and who I was with. Girls' bathroom with a definite nongirl. Not an ideal scenario.

I held my breath. The hinges creaked open and a man's rusty voice ventured a hello.

"Hell—" Adam responded loudly before I jammed my hand across his mouth, muffling the rest of the word.

Shuffling. "Who's in there?" From outside the stalls there came the sound of wheels rattling across the grout and then the *thwack* of a wet mop. The sopping yarn of the mop head dragged closer with each of his footsteps. "Who's there? This is a ladies' room."

I peered down at the dusty workman's boots of Old Man McCardle, the school's janitor, now pointed directly underneath our stall. He rattled the door. "Open up." He pounded his fist. "Who's in there?"

Seeing no way out, I piped up. "It's me," I tried.

The door stopped rattling. "I heard a boy's voice. There's someone else in there with you. Don't play me for stupid, young lady. I'll call the principal if you don't open this door right now."

My thoughts switched quickly to Adam's tenuous acceptance into Hollow Pines High, and my mind formed a snapshot of the walkie-talkie strapped to Old Man McCardle's uniform. I stifled a curse word and hopped off the toilet seat. Holding my breath, I slid the lock free. I was met with a view of the janitor's dingy brown uniform. Kids liked to say that Old Man McCardle was crazy because he yelled Bible verses at students who drew male genitalia on the lockers and didn't bother to make sure their empty bottles wound up in the trash cans, but really, it was just the fact that he was a janitor and smelled vaguely of gasoline and pickled eggs. My eyes traveled up to his cragged face. He blinked and took a step back when our eyes met.

"It's fine, really," I said, opening the door wider. "My friend here just bumped his head, and I was helping to clean him up. I'm sorry. It was just the easiest place to do it and, if we're being honest, aren't fixed gender identifications becoming a little passé anyhow?" McCardle looked from me to Adam, back to me again, then to Adam. His gaze lingered. I rolled my eyes. "Look, I promise, if I want to engage in any funny business, I will keep it to normal teenage locales. Back of cars. Movie theaters. Under the bleachers. That sort of thing."

Then, like a windup toy, Adam started his monologue. "Hello. I'm Adam Smith from Elgin, Illinois. I am sixteen years old."

McCardle's gummy lips worked without forming any words. He

backed up several paces, and before I could say another word, he had turned with only one last swift glance over his shoulder and was gone.

I grabbed my bag from the floor. "I would say that was weird, but, well, he's weird. We should go, though," I said. "He could be heading for reinforcements." I rummaged around the front pocket of my bag until I found a Band-Aid. When I pulled it out, I saw that the pattern on the bandage was of tiny green Yodas, which I recognized from a pack that Owen had received from his mom as a stocking stuffer last Christmas. "This will have to do." I motioned for him to bend down and then flattened the sticky parts to his forehead. I stood back to admire. Adam Smith was now tall, dead, and held together by a Star Wars–themed Band-Aid. And it was only 8:00 AM.

ELEVEN

A congenital insensitivity to pain may be caused by increased production of endorphins in the brain, a problem in the voltage-gated
sodium channel SCN9A, or lack of certain neuropathies. Children
with insensitivity to pain experience various problems, such as
biting off the tip of their tongue, untreated fractures, and
damage to the eyes. While the subject's pain insensitivity is
likely not congenital, I've marked the causes for further study.

— — —

Y ou're late, Ms. Frankenstein." Dr. Lamb's hand hovered over the
whiteboard, gripping a green dry erase marker. Turning, she
peered over her glasses at me.

Twenty heads swiveled in my direction. I found Owen seated on
the far side of the classroom in a middle row. Our eyes met, and
he shrugged, mouthed an apology, and scratched the back of his
neck with his pencil before staring down at the notebook in front
of him.

I dropped into an empty seat in the front row. "Am I really, though?"
I asked. Dr. Lamb was too New Age for seating arrangements, and the
back of the classroom always filled up first like the students were literally allergic to the possibility of learning. "I mean, according to
Albert Einstein, isn't all time relative, anyway?"

Dr. Lamb quirked an eyebrow. With her hair pulled tightly into a
bun, her needle-thin frame gave my physics teacher an uncanny

resemblance to a pin. "Time," she said, returning her attention to the whiteboard, "can be relative another day. Today we're looking at the Heisenberg Uncertainty Principle." She underlined each of the three capitalized words where she'd scribbled them in green marker.

"Who can tell me what that means?" Dr. Lamb glanced around the room, stashing the marker in the pocket of her white lab coat. As usual, she was met with crickets. I rested my chin in one palm and raised my other hand.

"Ms. Frankenstein?" Dr. Lamb crossed her arms and waited.

"According to Heisenberg's theory," I began, "there's a limit to the amount of precision that can be achieved when measuring the state of a system. The more precisely you measure the motion of a particle, the less precise your measurement of its position, for instance."

An exaggerated groan came from the back of the classroom.

"Very good." She pivoted back to the board and began drawing an axis for a graph.

I squirmed in my seat, my thoughts turning right back to Adam. Maybe Heisenberg's theory was true on a larger-scale system, too. Maybe, while I'd been able to measure the input—the electricity, the conductor, the positioning—to a high degree of precision, I'd let my finger slip on the output and that was where the uncertainty had slipped into the equation. I had no way now to measure what Adam had lost except to say that he seemed to have lost close to everything.

I glanced at the clock. Only ten minutes had passed. Dr. Lamb had sunk into the meat of her lecture, and instead of taking notes, I was worrying about Adam. Suddenly fifty unsupervised minutes felt like an eternity. I chanced a glance at Owen, but he was scribbling in his notebook, tongue pinched between his teeth.

A dead body was enrolled in my high school. There were approximately ten thousand things that could go wrong. I tried to concentrate on Dr. Lamb but could only grasp the movement of her lips without being able to assign any meaning to the words that were forming there, so, instead, I pulled out my black-and-white composition book and began scribbling notes from the last day and a half.

I was detailing my second line of observation when there was a jab at my back and my hand slipped, causing me to leave a long pen mark across the top of the page. I spun around in my chair. Behind me, Knox Hoyle was pretending to listen intently to Dr. Lamb's lecture. I grimaced. Knox had beady, foxlike eyes and a thin face partially obscured by a fringe of shaggy hair smashed underneath the brim of a ragged old ball cap. He was the punter on the football team and Paisley's on-again, off-again boyfriend. Together, they were the closest thing we had to a William and Kate. The secret to Knox's popularity wasn't that he was a good football player—he wasn't, he was terrible—but that he was the guy who knew how to get anything. Fake IDs, alcohol, hall passes. He was the favor guy, and everyone at school knew him because of it.

I turned back around, but no sooner had I done that than Knox's tennis shoe jabbed me in the spine again. My back stiffened. The rational part of me felt sorry for Knox that he had nothing better to do with his mind than formulate ways to mess with me, a girl who registered as a *point-nothing* on the social Richter scale. The more primal part wished I could dislodge his shoe and shove it in his mouth.

He had no idea who he was pestering. I had created life during the last few days alone, and he probably hadn't even finished last week's math homework. Come to think of it, I could be one of the most famous scientists in centuries already. Right up there with Darwin, Edison, and Faraday. I glared at the page in front of me and squeezed my hand into a fist. *Stage Two*, I reminded myself. We were only entering Stage Two. I had to bide my time, which meant for now, there was the eleventh grade.

When Knox rammed me in the back once more, I whipped around so hard I nearly pulled a muscle. "What is your problem, Hoyle?"

His eyebrows shot up in a look of faux-surprise. "*What?*"

"What?" I shot back. "Really?" *That weasel.*

"Ms. Frankenstein!" Dr. Lamb's face became pointy with annoyance. "Outbursts belong *out*side." She nodded toward the door. "No one here is above the rules, and that's twice that you've interrupted class today."

"But—"

She pointed the open end of her marker. *"Now."*

I ground my teeth together and clamped down on the monologue brewing inside me about how cosmically screwed up the high school universe was for *me* to be the one getting kicked out of class.

"Fine," I said, sliding my notebook underneath my arm and leaving behind a snickering Knox. It would be better for all humanity if we didn't have to breathe the same air, anyway.

I let the door close behind me too hard. The corridor was empty and hushed. The noise of the air conditioner through the vents thrummed behind the walls. I stood planted outside of Dr. Lamb's classroom for a moment while my chest rose and fell in rapid succession. Now that I had time to spare, it was a matter of determining how best to kill it. Right, well, I certainly had some experience in killing things, it seemed, so perhaps I should go check on that.

I adjusted my strap and took fast steps down the hall toward the history department. I'd taken US History with Mrs. Landers last year, and I recognized the door with the small, slender window carved into it and the blue cutout of North America. I slowed my pace as I approached and watched as my shadow crossed the seam of the wall and doorway. Adam was inside. A peek wouldn't hurt. One peek just to make sure he's all right.

I chewed on my lip and leaned over my toes to get a view through the narrow window. Mrs. Landers was writing something on the whiteboard. I scanned the students. At first, I didn't see Adam, and my heart skipped. The students were pulling out notebooks and pencils. Then, in the fourth row near the center, I spotted his hunched-over figure. He was curled over his book bag, one of Owen's old ones from last year. I held my breath as I watched him pull out a notebook and set it on his desk just like the other kids in the classroom. His eyebrows scrunched together. A sigh of relief morphed into a muffled gasp when he bent back over, pinched the bottom ends of his book bag, and turned it upside down to shake out the contents.

Several heads turned, including Mrs. Landers's. I ducked so as not to be caught spying. *Adam*, I mouthed to myself. *What are you doing?* I ventured back to the glass and craned to see. The students had settled. Adam's belongings were still strewn across the floor around him, but he'd found a pencil, which he now held poised over his open notebook. One eyebrow crawled higher on his forehead than the other, and it looked as though he'd stuffed his tongue into the pocket of his cheek so that it protruded in concentration. He returned his gaze from the whiteboard to the page when—*pop!*—the pencil snapped in two. The eraser end tumbled to his desk. I smacked my forehead and groaned audibly. Adam's eyes snapped to attention.

Victoria? I couldn't hear from the other side of the glass, but from the dozen heads that turned in my direction, I was sure he'd said it out loud. "Victoria!" This time he waved. Mrs. Landers, who, to be honest, had never really liked me, stared directly at me, her pillowy cheeks reddening. "Victoria!" Adam's smile took over his face, and he exclaimed loudly enough for me to hear. I felt my eyes widen. He stood up and the desk got caught at his thighs. "Hi, Victoria! That's Victoria! Come inside!" He beckoned me in with the hand still clutching his broken pencil.

I flattened my back behind me and slid to the ground, sinking my forehead into my hands. *Bad idea. Such a bad idea.* I didn't know how long I waited, but the commotion on the other side of the door seemed to die down and, in any event, Mrs. Landers must have been in a more lenient mood with the new kid than Dr. Lamb had been with me.

At this rate, Adam would cause as much disruption in the school day as a small tornado. He was big, enthusiastic, and, unlike any real high schooler I'd ever known, completely unselfconscious. Whoever he was, he was all Adam and he was all my problem.

The bell for the end of first period jarred me from my thoughts. A swarm of students funneled out into the hallway, and, from my vantage point on the ground, I could sense how Adam felt this morning. The crush of bodies, the explosion of voices, the slamming locker doors that rang out like gunshots, it was all a bit shattering.

I felt the weight of eyes on me and peered up. "Victoria." Adam cocked his head. "Why are you on the ground?"

I sighed and stretched my hand out to him, which he took. "I'm . . . hiding."

Adam looked around, nearly knocking over a ninth grader with his book bag. "From what?"

I dusted off the grime from my palms. "From reality." I shrugged. "Come on. We're only one-seventh of the way through."

I spent the rest of the morning escorting Adam from class to class. With each hour, I added more rules for Adam to live by. *Keep your shoes on your feet. Don't stick your head in the water fountain. Watch out for open locker doors, janitorial buckets, and people that are shorter than you.*

By lunchtime, I was exhausted. The cafeteria doors felt heavy as I tugged one open. We passed a tenth grader with frizzy red hair that stuck out six inches from his scalp.

"Adam, no!" I snatched his wrist as he was tugging at one of the tight curls, leaning in close to examine the unconventional hairstyle. I gave an apologetic wave to the boy and dragged Adam closer to the growing lunch line.

The corners of Adam's mouth drooped, and he nestled his offending hand close to his chest. "But he has hair like yours, Victoria." He ventured a sheepish grin. "It's pretty."

"Adam, I don't have hair like that." I self-consciously fingered my ends. "Mine's darker. Auburn. I don't know." I tried to cover the horror I felt at being compared to a boy whose head resembled a clown wig. "Anyway, that's not the point. You can't go around touching other people's hair, okay? It's not polite."

His chin lowered. "I'm sorry, Victoria."

I exhaled. "It's okay. Let's just find Owen and get some food. I'm starving."

I led Adam through the maze of lunch tables, where we found Owen and tried sneaking inconspicuously in front of him in line, but as had been the case all day, there was no sneaking Adam anywhere. He towered over everyone, and we were taunted until we were all forced to the back of the line.

"And the perks just keep on coming," Owen said.

"So there's a small learning curve." I moved up in the line and handed Adam a tray. Yesterday I'd been nervous to feed Adam. I could think of no way to test whether his body was fit to consume food without him actually consuming the food. I hypothesized that once his vital organs had been restarted, all systems, including the digestive, should operate as normal. I held my breath as he consumed one bite of a Whataburger Owen had picked up, then two, and before I knew it, he'd eaten both my burger and his along with the entire large fries. To my relief, he didn't short-circuit.

As we moved closer to the front of the line, I heard a thundering rumble from deep in Adam's belly. Owen's shoulders shook with laughter. I slid my tray onto the metal shelves. "Okay, Adam," I began. "You just tell the lady what you want, and she'll put it on a plate and hand it over to you."

He nodded while another rumble sounded from the pit of his stomach. I ordered the only thing on the menu that didn't look like prison food, a slice of pizza and a side of tater tots. I watched out of the corner of my eye while Adam pointed through the glass. I slid farther down the row and picked up two Cokes.

"Adam, I got you a—" But when he joined me at the cashier, my eyes nearly bugged out of my head. He grinned. His plate was a mountain of food. Mashed potatoes piled on spaghetti with gravy running into a puddle on the side of his plate. Pizza with tater tots half covered in a mushy spinach dish. I fought my gag reflex and forked over an extra five dollars to cover Adam's cafeteria feast.

"Are you sure that's what you want?" I squinted at his plate as we staked out a table near a row of trash cans.

"I don't know," Adam said.

Owen plopped a tray with pizza and tater tots down on the other side of Adam. "So I see we're still calibrating his taste palate." Adam's forehead wrinkled. He stared up quizzically at Owen. "Interesting tastes, my man." Owen patted him on the back. "March to the beat of your own drum. More power to you."

At this Adam grinned and eyed his plate greedily. He sank down into a chair and gripped the sides of his tray.

"Shoot, we forgot utensils for you," I said. "One sec."

But before I could return to the end of the lunch line, Adam had pawed a heap of mashed potatoes and spaghetti into his mouth and was slurping down a noodle. Brown gravy dribbled down his fingers. I hesitated, then lowered myself back into my seat. "Or . . . not."

He was already going in for another. This time he scooped up some of the spinach mixture and licked it happily from his hand. I pulled out my seat, shaking my head slowly as I watched Adam devour fistfuls of his food. Fatigue and hunger dragged at me as I rested my elbows on the table.

"Shouldn't we teach him about *silverware*?" Owen asked, curling the left side of his lip up and scooting a couple inches farther from Adam.

I blew bangs out of my face and stuffed the end of my pizza in my mouth.

Don't eat with your hands, I should have added to our list. But, instead, I just sighed, picked up a tater tot, and said, "Tomorrow . . ."

TWELVE

The closest comparison to the subject's experience of the world is that of a toddler. While he has retained motor skills and clearly some muscle memory, he is learning about how his surroundings work each moment. So far it seems the maturity of his brain and its size are resulting in a faster learning curve than a toddler despite following the same processes.

- - -

By the time I crawled into bed on the night of Adam's first day, fatigue had reached into the cavities of my bones and clogged them up like lead fillings. An hour ago, I'd carried a plate of brisket down to the cellar and put Adam to bed on his makeshift pallet, or at least I turned off the light, seeing as how you can't exactly tuck in a hulking teenage boy, regardless of whether he's alive or not.

I smiled faintly to myself as I switched on the bedside lamp. When we got home, Adam had tugged at the hatch door, clamoring to get in. As soon as he did, I could see the muscles in his jaw loosen and his hands unclench.

He was home. This was his lair. Maybe he'd be more like a superhero than Owen had thought.

Yawning, I jiggered open the nightstand drawer and pulled out one of my black-and-white-speckled composition books. Even as sleep dragged on me, I forced myself, in scrawling letters, to write down everything I could remember about the past two days.

I scribbled a reminder at the top and underlined it with blue pen. *Rule Number One: Catalog Everything.*

I didn't know when I fell asleep, only that once I did, it was restless, with dreams of splintering glass, and that sometime later I woke to pitch-darkness and the sound of rain pattering against the roof. Eyes unfocused, I felt around my bedspread until my hand found the lumpy outline of Einstein. She groaned and nestled deeper into the space beneath the small of my back.

A flash of lightning burst through the blinds. I let out a hoarse scream. A glimpse of a face hovered inches above mine, lit up and then disappeared into the night. I could just make out the fuzzy edges of a figure bent over the bed. I scrambled upright, tugging the sheets around my waist. A pair of eyes shone at me in the darkness, the rest of the outline stock-still.

I pressed my back to the cool wall behind my bed and twisted my fists around the cotton bedding. Einstein let out a soft woof but didn't stir.

"Victoria?" Adam's voice was deep and baritone.

I felt my tendons tighten into guitar strings at the base of my neck. I tried to swallow and wound up nearly choking. "Adam? God, Adam, you scared me." My eyes were beginning to adjust to the dim light.

"Did I wake you?" He touched my knee gently over the blanket.

I pulled the neck straight on a threadbare shirt I'd stolen from Owen. "It's the middle of the night," I whispered. "So yeah."

"Sorry." The pressure from his hand lifted and his silhouette retreated a few inches farther. The tracing of his body blurred.

"What are you doing here?" I was suddenly conscious of all the embarrassing items scattered around my room. A dirty bra hanging from the back of a chair. Yesterday's clothes still lying in a pile. A stuffed unicorn. The open notebook in which I'd been cataloging Adam's progress. I reached for that first, shut the book, and shoved it into my nightstand drawer.

"Victoria." The way he stood stiffly at the side of my bed was unnerving. "I'm scared."

I rubbed my eyelids, thick with sleep. "Of what?"

He pointed outside. I crawled to the end of my bed and peeled back the curtain, but there was nothing out there. Fat rain droplets plummeted past the window, splashing onto the lawn below.

I glanced back at him. "Of the rain?"

"I don't like it." I caught the tremor in his voice.

"I—" I started to tell him that was silly but stopped short. Instead, I crawled back to the head of my mattress, but this time scooted over. Adam hesitated and then sat down on the empty spot. There, he tucked his hands into his armpits and rocked slowly back and forth.

"When will it stop?" he asked.

I slid closer and put my hand on his back. The ridges of his spine pressed into my palm. I marveled at the way his rib cage expanded and shrank beneath it. So alive. "I don't know. Soon probably." My vision adjusted to the light. I peered intensely at his profile. The slight bump at the bridge of his nose like it might have been broken once made him seem all the more real.

He was real, I reminded myself. He was real because I made him that way.

I shouldn't have left him alone in the laboratory tonight. It was the accident. He must be having an adverse reaction to the thunderstorm because of the storm on the night he died. A fist squeezed around my heart. Which meant his memories were there, somewhere, waiting.

I decided to test the waters gently. "Is there a reason you don't like the rain?" I suspected that if he knew the reason, he wouldn't be coming to me for support, but if he'd uncovered the truth, I might as well know now. I studied the pronounced seam of his brow. So many answers locked away in that single head.

He shrugged, a very human gesture. He must have picked it up from Owen. Then he shook his head. His back curved into a C and his chin jutted over his waist. He turned his head. His dark eyes reflected tiny glints of light. "Can I stay here with you?"

I glanced at the door. The thunder drowned out the sound of Mom's wine-fueled snores. I pressed my lips together. "Okay. Fine." I let out a long breath. "But you have to be quiet. And leave before it gets light out, deal?"

"Deal."

I flipped off the covers and let him shimmy in next to me, where he pulled the sheets up to his chin. This time, Einstein lifted her head. The tags around her neck jangled, and her throat emitted a rough, uneven growl. She pawed her way closer to me, stuffed a cold nose beneath my arm, and whined.

Adam folded his hands one over the other across his chest. I wormed my way back horizontal, wedged in between him and the dog. The space between the sheets instantly grew warmer. Einstein's breaths quickly evened out into soft puffs on my skin. It was hardly like having a dead body in my bed at all. Adam smelled clean—like rainwater. The indentation made in the mattress by his form rolled me into him. I turned on my side and tugged the comforter underneath my armpit and tried to close my eyes and breathe normally.

I'd never slept in a bed with a boy, but it wasn't as if I was a total prude, either. Last year at the State Youth Science Summit, I'd made out with Daniel Berkovich, a senior from Southlake with an astrophysics project that didn't place. I let him feel under my bra and take down my e-mail address, even though I never returned either of his messages, mainly because I didn't see a point.

Adam was different, though. Adam was mine.

"Are you asleep?" I asked, low enough so that if he was I wouldn't wake him.

"No."

I twisted my chin over my shoulder. "What are you doing?"

There was a pause. "Thinking."

"About . . . ?"

"I don't like the rain."

I couldn't help it, I laughed, then tried to cover it up with the pillow. "Yes, I think we've established that."

"But I do like pizza," he continued, which was the least disgusting item he'd devoured off his lunch tray today.

I nudged Einstein away and turned over to face him. Our heads were on the pillows, my hands tucked beneath my cheek.

"I don't want to be blank, Victoria."

"You're not blank," I said. "You like pizza and . . . have full functionality of your motor skills. It's actually a huge stride forward in the human condition." Sometimes when I said things like that, I had a little voice in my head that sounded suspiciously like Owen and it warned me that not everything was an experiment. I hated that voice.

"I like the color orange, too, because it's the color of your hair. I like your hair."

I grabbed a handful and held it out from my head. "Again! My hair's not orange! It's—I don't know—amber or something."

"Then my favorite color is amber." He had the air of a schoolboy who'd just answered a very difficult question correctly.

I relaxed into the mattress and we lulled into silence. The invisible weight of sleep began to tug me under like an ocean tide. "You're not the only one who doesn't like storms," I said. "Sometimes, anyway." I wasn't even sure whether I'd said this out loud.

Half dreaming, I pictured my father wearing his yellow galoshes and yellow rain slicker while I watched from inside his pickup truck. He stared up at the sky holding an anemometer kit over his head. The gold cups spun like spokes on a wheel, measuring the wind. *Soon, Victoria, soon*, he'd said. But soon never came.

My eyelashes fluttered. I tried to focus on his face, but my eyelids fell shut. "Don't be afraid," I said. "Okay? Just don't. Because the truth is . . . well . . . we . . . shouldn't fear what . . ." And here sleep tried to tow me under to where my father waited in his yellow galoshes. "What we don't understand, Adam. That's what my dad used to say." I sighed.

I couldn't keep track of how many moments passed as my thoughts drifted into that tiny crawl space between dozing and waking. Only that it was enough for the sensation of falling to set in. I found my father again, gazing up at the clouds, watching lightning crack open the heavens like he was watching fireworks.

"Why doesn't he say it anymore?" Adam asked. The sound of his voice pulled me back.

"Because he doesn't say anything," I whispered. "Because he's dead."

"Then you should bring him back." Adam mimicked the quiet tenor of my voice.

I bunched the pillow tighter underneath my head. "It's too late for that," I said, and, unbidden, dredged up the image of my father once more, only this time his boots lay flat on the ground with the rest of him. The lightning generators that he'd invented loomed up into the angry sky above him. He'd been trying to harness atmospheric energy to disintegrate the atom and therefore, in turn, discover a super-energy source. Only he never managed it. A bolt of electricity had struck him in the heart, leaving red tree-branch scars across his chest and neck. He was dead and his experiment died along with him. After that night, I walked away from that forest and never returned.

There was a rustle of bedding, then so lightly I could barely be sure it was happening, Adam reached up and pet my hair in a stiff, unnatural motion. I let his hand rest there. "Thank you, Adam," I said. "That's very kind."

"Victoria," he said in that awestruck way that he had.

"Adam."

And with the last word falling partially formed from my lips, I allowed the part of me still clinging to reality to let go while the body of the boy I'd killed lay beside me.

THIRTEEN

Observation of subject's injuries show that all lesions and lacerations have formed scabs. Hematoma coloring has shifted to green, blue, and yellow hues at the outer edges. All signs point to healthy natural healing processes.

— — —

I woke up all at once, fingers splayed into stars on top of the mattress, head raised off the pillow, and breath coming in whistling heaves. My first thought was to feel around my left wrist and to panic for just a second when I found that the twine bracelet with the lightning charm my father had given me was missing. It took me several more seconds to realize that it had been missing for years and that it had been almost that long since I'd had the clawing empty feeling each time I noticed its absence.

I dropped my head back into the fluffy down. Thin light trickled through the shades. The space next to me was empty, and any trace of Adam had disappeared along with him. I sat up, rested my elbows on my knees, and cradled my forehead. Sweat prickled my skin like beads of condensation on a glass of water.

I pushed my fingers into my hair. My scalp was damp. Einstein lifted her chin and stared up at me through a face full of wrinkles. After a quick shower that left my skin pink, I wriggled into a pair of jeans and paired it with a T-shirt from my laundry pile. I found Mom in the kitchen cooking eggs. Mom's eggs only came one way—flat and dry. She smashed the spatula into one of the cooked yolks, and air whistled out of it. The shriveling whites crackled on the frying pan. When it was the consistency of rubber, she slid it onto a plate and handed it to me. I wasn't hungry.

"There's something you're not telling me, Tor," she said in a sing-song voice, baiting me, probing, like I should have known that these eggs came with an agenda. Mom wiped her forehead with the back-side of her wrist, then cracked another egg into the pan.

My first thought was of Adam. The thing I wasn't telling her was so big that it broke the scales of things that one would not tell their mother. I swallowed hard, clutching the ceramic plate to my chest. "What do you mean?" My voice sounded like it'd barely managed to escape the back of my throat.

She jostled the frying pan by the handle and looked up at me. Her eyes were cool and blue, clear as a mountain lake, clearer than they'd been in weeks. I'd come to depend on the layer of fog that kept her from asking too many questions about my life. "You know I don't like you keeping secrets from me," she said. "I know you think you're smarter than me, too, smarter than everybody maybe, but I'm still your mom."

Are you? I wanted to snap back.

But sticky saliva coated the roof of my mouth. My palms grew wet and I slid them into my lap. Einstein sat looking up at me, expecting a bite of my eggs. I ignored her, knitting my eyebrows together. "I don't know what you're talking about, Mom." Deny, deny, deny. Always deny.

Abandoning the eggs, she turned and placed her fist on the waist-band of her light-wash jeans. "Then how do you explain this?" She reached for something on the counter. My breath hitched as she re-trieved a dustpan and shoved the contents forward for me to exam-ine. "You're so careless with your belongings. First your car and now this? I could wring your neck. You know that? Who do you think's going to pay for a new phone? And this is after the car?"

I squinted at the pieces of shattered black glass in the dustpan. At first it was relief coursing through me as I realized that Mom didn't know about Adam, didn't even know I'd killed somebody. But no sooner had the glorious swell of relief washed over me than it was replaced with a sickening pit that opened up in the center of my stomach. The shattered glass in Mom's dustpan was the remnants of my broken cell phone, and the last time I'd seen that cell phone had been in pieces on the road. Blood thumped against my eardrums.

"How . . . how did you get that?" I stammered, touching my finger to one of the jagged edges to feel that it was real.

"How did I get it? Tor, you ain't *that* bright. It was right on the porch, apparently where you dropped it or ran over it or whatever you did to ruin a perfectly good piece of equipment. Doubt we'll even be able to sell this thing back to one of the infomercials now." She dropped the dustpan on the kitchen table and returned to the stove, where she removed the browning egg from the heat.

"On the porch?" I repeated more to myself than to her. The blood that had been pounding my eardrums now drained from my face.

"You and your father," she muttered. "Never did have any common sense when it came to things. Acting like money grows on bushes."

I felt as if a weight were clamping down on my chest and cutting off the oxygen supply. The world was in Technicolor. Just then the weather vane emitted a rusty shriek from above us so loud that it seemed to come up the pipes and echo through the kitchen. Mom slapped her spatula on the counter, rattling her half-empty cup of coffee. "I thought I told you to do something about that weather vane, Tor!" But I was hardly listening. My chair squealed across the floor, and I staggered upright, leaving my untouched egg on the table. "Where do you think you're going? Tor, I'm talking to you."

"I'm sorry, Mom. I'll . . . try to be more careful or something." I pushed past another kitchen chair that was in my way and brushed by my mother, who was shouting my full name like a voodoo curse.

"You've got to work on your priorities, Victoria. You hear me?"

The screen door sounded like a mousetrap snapping shut behind me. The air outside was swampy with puddled rain and early-morning sun. The day's first mosquitoes darted in and out of potted shrubs, and the weather vane creaked in short, spastic increments with the breeze. There was nothing left of my phone on the porch. I scanned the empty road that ran perpendicular to our driveway. In the dirt outside, I could only just make out the faded traces of that third set of tire marks. I felt feverish. Sick.

Somebody knew. If not about Adam, they knew what I'd done. They knew it and they hadn't called the police. Worry slid its way up my veins and through my heart. A thin trickle of sweat dribbled from my temple. They were toying with me. They wanted me to know that they knew. But why? Panic raked my insides. I scanned the horizon, but the yards around our home were empty.

I knew only that I had to destroy as much of the evidence as I could. As long as I could conceal the truth about Adam, it would only be my word against theirs. There was my car, but that could have easily been a deer, just like I'd said, and there was a body, but if that body wasn't dead anymore, then was it really a body?

I imagined my mom watching me from the window. I straightened my back and, trying to act normal, followed the familiar path to the cellar door and descended into the ground.

"Adam?" It was pitch-black. I felt my way down wooden steps that creaked beneath my weight. "Adam?" I counted the stairs. *Four. Five. Six* . . . On the seventh stair, I found the cord hanging from the ceiling and pulled. A single lightbulb switched on. Several feet in front lit up, but beyond the light's edges was darkness too thick to see through.

"Victoria." I couldn't tell from which direction Adam's voice came. Goose bumps shot up my arm. For the first time, I realized that I didn't have any idea what my creation might be capable of. In the cool darkness of the underground, the laboratory suddenly felt like his domain more so than mine.

At the bottom of the stairs, I found the switch, and the overhead lamps flickered, then settled into an electric buzz.

"Good morning."

I yelped and my hand flew to my chest. Adam was standing inches away, rail straight and still. I held out my finger while I waited to catch my breath for the second time this morning. "Good lord," I panted. "You scared me half to death." Then I quickly added, "Not that there's anything wrong with being a little bit dead, of course. The scaring thing, though, that seems to be one of your talents."

"I got you these." A stiff arm held out a flimsy bouquet of five white and yellow daisies. Their pitiful roots dangled from the bottom of his fist. He puffed his chest out and grinned.

I instinctively brought them to my nose. They smelled like fertilizer and lawn mower clippings. "Where did you get these?" I said slowly.

"In the field." He pointed up. "How did you sleep, Victoria? You looked very peaceful."

I set the flowers down gently on a counter. I ignored how creepy his last statement had sounded. "Did you see anyone? Did anyone see you?" I thought of the phone on the porch and the tire marks and—"Adam, you have to listen to me," I hissed, staring up at the ceiling to regain my composure. "You can't go wandering around up there without me. Someone might see you."

His chest deflated. "You don't like them."

My glance flitted to the wilted cluster. As a girl, I was pretty sure the female handbook required me to go gaga over handpicked flowers, but my idea of romance was more a Bunsen burner, an open flame, and highly combustible chemicals than candlelight and walks on the beach. "I do." I leveled my chin at him. "They're nice, but even still, you can't go wandering around."

"Why not?"

"Because you're different, and if people see you where you're not supposed to be, they might start asking questions. My *mom* might start
asking questions." *No one can see you*, I wanted to say. *No one can
know what you are.* But the words were choked by the still blooming
knowledge of the shattered cell phone and the foreign tire tracks and
the sinking realization that somebody knew my secret. Somebody
might even know about Adam.

The strands of worry hadn't left my blood, and I felt them itching
in my limbs for me to fix this. I crossed the room and dragged a metal
trash can to the center.

Meanwhile, a groove deepened between Adam's eyebrows. "I don't
want to be different. I want to be like you."

I ducked below the counter and crawled, the knees of my jeans dragging along the dirty floor. Behind a set of tool drawers, I stretched
my arm out and felt around until my fingers closed around crinkly
plastic. I pulled out the hidden garbage bag and dusted off my jeans.
"I'm different, too, just in another way. Trust me. You don't want to
be like everyone else. You're a breakthrough. A piece of history. But
for now, you're also a secret." Adam's face went blank again. "Don't
you want us to have our own little secret, Adam?" I asked. "Just the
two of us."

He seemed to consider this. "You and me?" I nodded. "Yes, yes I do."

"Good. But secrets have to be kept." I pushed my arm shoulder-deep
into the trash bag and pulled out a single article. "Otherwise they're
not secrets anymore. You understand?" The shirt was crusted and stiff
with dried blood. Patches of white fabric showed through. I bit my
lip and chanced a glance at Adam. His expression was still impassive, but his deep-set brown eyes were trained on the blood-soaked
clothing.

I tossed the shirt into the garbage can and pulled out the pair of
jeans, split where the road had torn into them. These were less gory

than the shirt, but the waistband had been soaked to the point that the denim was dyed an even red. Farther down, droplets had sprayed the legs like flecks of paint.

"What are you doing?" he asked when I dropped the jeans in after the shirt.

"Making sure no one takes you away from me." I rummaged around for the matches I used to light the burners and came back with a half-empty box. "We have to do all of this, keep all the secrets so that you can stay with me. That's what you want, right? That's what we both want." I struck the match head on the rough siding, and it burst into blue then yellow flame. I looked at Adam through the thin curl of smoke snaking off the lick of fire.

I let the match fall into the bottom of the trash can, then lit two more and did the same. It took several moments for the smell of smoke to reach me. Orange and yellow flickered against the gray metal. The fire flared, puffing up a thick column of smoke like a black belch.

Across from me, the flames danced in Adam's pupils. Smoke stung my eyes. I grabbed the nearest long, pointy thing I could find and prodded the fire with the wrong side of a broom. The once green handle came away charred. The cellar laboratory was thick with haze. Behind the fog, the floating specimens on the shelves looked like props in a haunted house, and the model skeleton, a set piece. I dropped one of Adam's bloody shoes into the pile and watched as the flames ate into the leather, and before I closed the lid, I added its mate.

A familiar rap came from above. *Tap-ta-tap. Tap-ta-tap.* The hatch door creaked, and sunlight flooded the stairwell. "Is someone barbecuing or did you recently pick up a nicotine habit?" Owen's shoes appeared before the rest of him did. The hatch door clanged shut.

"Owen." Adam pointed.

Owen's eyebrows shot up. "That's right, buddy. In the flesh. Not polite to point, though. We'll work on that."

Adam lowered his arm slowly to his side.

Owen sniffed the air. His eyes narrowed. He studied the trash can at the center of the room, then opened the lid. His chin snapped back and he waved away a cloud of smoke. Carefully, he peered over the edge and quickly replaced the lid. "Fantastic. Destruction of evidence. A shiny, new line for the rap sheet. Right after criminal conspiracy but before desecration of human remains. Now where do you think that goes on my college application?"

"If you want out, all you have to do is say the word," I said, crossing my arms.

"Really?" His tone was flat. "So I can just wave my hand and this all goes away?"

I responded with a signature eye roll. "Good morning to you, too."

He huffed. "Sorry, I'm fresh out of those. And anyway, that's not why I'm here." He glanced between Adam and me. "I'm here because I was listening to the radio this morning." Owen's penchant for tinkering left him with an alarming number of radios of all sorts and variations, which he kept in his room and his car and a few he'd left for the laboratory. There were foxhole, utility, weather, and battery-less radios, all makes and models that he'd fixed up into working order.

"Okay . . ." I gave a halfhearted shrug as if to say *So what?* "And that became newsworthy when?"

"It became newsworthy when I heard . . ." He cleared his throat and leaned in closer to my ear. "When I heard a broadcast that a boy's been reported missing."

FOURTEEN

Stage 2 of the experiment continues. The subject is blending into life at Hollow Pines High, which means we not only managed to resurrect a body from the dead, but have also made him a functioning member of society, passable enough that no one has questioned his postmortem state. Certain improvements could be made. The most pressing concerns remain memory and emotional functioning as well as pain receptivity.

— — —

The word *missing* rattled around in the space between my ears all morning.

Missing.

Missing.

Missing.

It played on repeat as I trudged through my early classes and I could concentrate on nothing other than those two syllables as I walked down the hallway to PE, there but not really there. Students streamed past me, a blur of movement. I kept my head down and weaved my way through the crowd.

It wasn't necessarily Adam, I had to remind myself. Boys went missing all the time. But it was hard to make myself believe it. If someone had reported Adam missing, or the boy that Adam used to be, then that meant somebody was looking for him, that somebody wanted to find him. It also meant that there was somebody who wanted to take Adam away from me. He had parents. He had—

There was a tap on my shoulder.

I jumped and yelped, "Meg!"

Owen popped up alongside me, and I squeezed my eyes shut, mentally chiding myself. So, yeah, there were a few things I had neglected to share with Owen.

"*Meg?*" Owen echoed my thoughts aloud. His shirt read *World's Most Complicated Equation*, followed by an illustrated version of *2+2=4.* "Um, no, just me. You okay? You look a little . . ." He widened his eyes behind his glasses and waggled his fingers next to his face. "You know, like you just saw Michael Jackson or something."

We passed the trophy case in the school's east wing, filled with ribbons and pennants and two state football championship trophies from a decade before. "Michael Jackson's dead," I replied.

"My point exactly. Now, who's Meg?"

"What?" My eyes cut to him and then back at my beat-up high-tops. "Oh, nobody. It's just"—I glanced over my shoulder—"the whole missing thing." A shiver ran through me when I said it.

He adjusted his glasses. "Yes, I got that. You may as well have a billboard attached to your forehead that says as much. You're acting weird. Maybe you should try acting a little, I don't know, less guilty. That or try to find the people that are looking for Adam."

"Are you kidding me?" I snapped. Two passing freshmen gave me a wide berth as they disappeared in the opposite direction. "Do we look like we're running a lost and found, Owen?" I felt my face go hot. I squeezed my hands into fists, and my knuckles turned a stark white. I wanted nothing to do with the missing boy, nothing to do with anyone who might have a stake in Adam.

And that was the whole problem with the idea of Meg. Right now,

I was Adam's world, but there was another girl out there and she must be important to be a dying boy's last word.

Owen pinched his shoulders to his ears. "I'm just saying that they must be worried about him, that's all."

"Well, stop saying," I said. "It's not as if we can return him in the same condition as we found him."

Owen held on to his words but gave me a long look that I knew was supposed to jump-start my conscience. He was always overestimating my conscience. "Come on," he said. "Don't you want to know anything about him? Don't you want to know if it's really him?" I plugged my ears and kept walking. Owen fell behind. "His name's Trent Jackson Westover!" I could hear his muffled call. "He's a sophomore from Lamar High School!"

I whipped around. Hair flew into my eyes and I peeled it away. "Will you stop it?" I marched over to him, grabbed him by the elbow, and, spotting the library's pale wooden doors, dragged him through them and away from the busy hallway. "What are you thinking?" I snapped. Glancing around, I shoved him between two stacks of books in the nonfiction section where nobody ever went. "I can't believe you'd say his name in public like that. Are you insane?"

"Are you?" Owen said, rubbing his elbow. On either side of us, hardbacks dressed in shiny plastic covers squeezed one another for space on crowded shelves. The smell of crisp paper and pencil shavings drifted from the pages.

My heart was pounding. I turned my back to him and paced the aisle. "What are we going to do?" I dragged my palm down the length of my face. Somebody knew about the car crash. Now somebody was looking for Adam.

"You could start by looking at a picture. Here." He held out the screen of his phone. I didn't want to look. What I wanted to do was avoid the missing boy, avoid the phone, avoid the tire marks. Despite this, I snatched the phone from his hands and held it close. "Is that him?" I asked. My breath fogged the phone's screen. "It's . . . tough to tell."

I squinted and angled the picture. The boy in the picture was smiling a wide, natural smile. His dark hair was longer than Adam's and covered the tops of his ears. It could be Adam's brother, but was it Adam? I really couldn't tell. I moved the screen closer to my nose and tried searching for the gold specks in Adam's eyes, but the photograph was too grainy to see.

"Well?"

I pushed the phone back in Owen's hand. "I don't know." I shook my head. "It doesn't matter. Whoever this Trent kid is, we have Adam and this doesn't change anything. Got it?" The bell rang, causing us both to jump. "Keep your head down and it will all be fine." Then I added under my breath. "I certainly don't think it could get any worse."

He held my gaze, and when several moments had passed, he sighed. "So I suppose now isn't the time to tell you that we're playing dodgeball today in PE."

Owen smirked like he'd just scored a point and headed for the doors, disappearing toward the boys' locker room.

HISTORY TELLS US that while others were slaving to invent cures for measles and polio and whatnot, some numskull was hanging out in his garage, scratching at his balls and coming up with the game of dodgeball. And so it went that every geek every day thereafter would suffer the curse of having balls chucked at his face, which, as far as I was concerned, was pretty much the modern-day equivalent of Zeus sentencing Prometheus to have his liver pecked by eagles on the regular.

Dodgeball. A Nobel Peace Prize ought to be given to the first person who can eradicate that festering boil on the heel of society.

Ten minutes later, this was me: black gym shorts cut perfectly to show off my little boy legs. Gray T-shirt to showcase my pit sweat.

Mismatched socks. Skin the color of jellyfish that worked double as a protective casing for my large intestines as well as a flashing neon sign to my classmates that read *Caution: This girl sucks at sports.*

I stood on the basketball gym's baseline shoulder to shoulder with Owen and Adam. It was a small consolation that Owen maybe looked worse in his uniform than me. Every bit of him was pointy. It looked as though someone had wrapped skin around a skeleton, and his shorts were entirely too short not to be reserved solely for European beachwear.

"Jenkins," yelled William. The process of picking teams should be outlawed. In fact, it probably was everywhere but Hollow Pines. I shifted my weight.

Blake Jenkins jogged over to where William was waiting with the rest of the chosen ones.

"Wheelwright." The other team captain, Knox, picked Paisley, his girlfriend. Surprise, surprise.

The sole benefit of my conversation with Owen was that it had taken the edge off my nerves. Bickering with Owen did that for me. I'd consider picking another fight later just to achieve normalcy. Standing next to Adam made me feel better, too. I hated letting him out of my sight, but if the experiment were to have any success at all, I realized, the science might require it.

Still, today, the day of missing boys and returning phones, I'd settle for keeping him nearby.

"Fernandez." William's team gained another player. I snuck a look over at Adam, where he waited, face serene.

He filled out the gray gym shirt that hid his red branchlike scars underneath. Thin scabs flaked from his shins.

Something pinched the back of my arm. "Ouch!" I yelped too loudly. The remaining losers in the line stared.

"Earth to Frankenstein," Owen muttered in a singsong tone. "You and your boy must both be in la-la land. They're trying to call him."

"New kid. *Hello?*" Knox clapped. "New kid. Over here. Christ, is he deaf or just mentally challenged?"

I elbowed Adam, and when that didn't work—"Adam, he means you. You're on Knox's team. He has a name, Hoyle," I snapped.

I leaned over to see how many people were still left unpicked—seven. I could have been imagining this, but I swore Owen tried to stand an extra inch taller just to get picked before I did. I tugged down on his arm and he wriggled away from me.

I rubbed the stinging spot on my skin where Owen had pinched me. Still feeling moody, I pinched him back. He let out a high-pitched shriek that sounded dangerously close to that of a little girl. I gave him a self-satisfied grin. "Well, if that doesn't get you picked, I don't know what will."

He glowered. In ninth grade, Coach Carlson had made Owen climb the hanging rope. He'd made it up five feet before his arms gave out and he slid back down. He had rope burn between his legs for weeks.

William chose the boy next to me and now there were only three of us left without teams.

I'd have smacked the smug look off Paisley's face if I didn't know for a fact that she could do push-ups. She whispered something in Knox's ear, and the next thing I knew the kid beside me was exhaling a held breath and then breaking rank with us.

"And we're last," Owen said.

I tapped my foot. "Seriously? That kid that just got picked has severe peanut allergies and carries an inhaler."

"Bloch," William called.

Owen squeezed my arm. "May the Force be with you."

What made it worse was that I knew the only reason Owen had gotten picked before me was that he was a boy. He even had to wear those dorky straps around his head to hold on his glasses.

A leftover reject, I slinked over to join Knox's brigade and tried to look useful. After all, Coach Carlson handed out actual grades in gym class.

Paisley toyed with a strand of hair and chewed gum in PE. It was a choking hazard. I hoped it worked. "Great. You're on our team." She pointed out the obvious.

"Trust me," I said. "The feeling's mutual."

Knox clapped his hands. "Spread out team. Give 'em hell."

The crazy thing was that Coach Carlson let us have dodgeball days as a break from running around the track in circles like hamsters, and other activities that furthered our physical education. Getting pegged in the boobs was supposed to be some kind of treat.

I went and stood in the corner next to Adam. "Do you know how to play the game?" I asked. He shook his head. "Just chuck the balls at the other team. Hit them, they're out. You get hit, you're out. Catch it, they're out again. Got it?"

"Hit them?" Adam turned and lightly punched the scrawny kid with the inhaler. "Like that?"

"Ow," the boy wheezed, rubbing at the spot where Adam hit.

I pulled him away. "No, with the balls." I pointed at the colored balls lined up at half-court. "You *throw* them." I mimicked the motion of throwing, though honestly I wasn't even sure if my technique was passable for a third grader.

Paisley wiped her hands on her shorts, focused and itching to run.

Coach Carlson balanced the whistle between his lips. "On your mark, get set." The whistle blew. "Play ball!"

Everyone but Adam and me charged to the centerline to make a grab for the dodgeballs. A second after, a ball whizzed past my face and I skittered to the side, narrowly escaping an immediate need for a nose job.

Adam picked up a ball. He turned back to me. "Don't worry, Victoria, I'll get him."

He cocked his arm back and hurled it at Daniel Ferrera. The ball zoomed through the air, nailing Daniel in the gut. He groaned and doubled over.

I slapped my hand over my smile. "Nice throw."

Adam shrugged and bent down for another. He pegged Caleb Bell so hard in the leg that Caleb had to limp over to the side of the court. And for that, I gave Adam a high five.

I jumped back when a ball nearly skirted my shirtsleeve. Adam instantly retaliated with a rocket to the shoulder of Spencer Hawkins.

At this point, a few other people on our team started to notice Adam's skills. "Toss him a ball," ordered Knox. Knox was shuffling from side to side like we were in the freaking dodgeball Olympics.

Another of Adam's missiles made contact. A loud *thwack*. Plastic on wet skin. He ducked, dodged, and shuffled. Teammates fell around him. I stuck close behind, using him like a shield. I glanced over. Knox was dripping sweat. Paisley was out. Adam, though, wasn't even short of breath. He was like one of those automatic tennis-ball machines.

He fired another shot. Bingo. Then another. A human strike force.

Knox hollered his appreciation. It was as if Adam were charged up on batteries. Or, I paused, watching him in awe from the free-throw line, an electrical charge. I felt my jaw drop. That was it.

In that instant, out of the corner of my eye, I saw a purple dodgeball floating toward me. I turned, but it was too late. The ball pegged me in the shoulder. Owen was just finishing his follow-through, a joyful gloat already parading over his face. He bounced up and down with one fist in the air.

"I got you!" he crowed. "I so got you!"

This was his mistake. Adam zeroed in on him like a fighter jet. Ready, aim, fire. Before Owen could calculate rate of speed plus velocity, the ball was already nailing him on the side of the head. I scrunched my shoulders as Owen's head snapped sideways. He stumbled and then his palms squeaked onto the gym floor.

Coach Carlson's whistle trilled. "Time! Time!" He waved his hands in the air. "Bloch! Get off the floor. It's a dodgeball not a meteor."

I ran over to Owen, who was scraping himself off the ground. He grabbed my hand and I hoisted him up. He cupped his ear and moved his jaw back and forth. "My ears are ringing, Tor. He destroyed my hearing. Ah! Ah! Ah! You hear that?" He pointed at his ear. "I'm completely tone-deaf now."

Adam appeared by my side. "I saved you, Victoria," he said happily.

Owen shrank back. "Don't be such a drama queen," I told him. He glared at me. "*What?*" I shrugged. "You have to admit, you're a little soft."

"Oh, I'm sorry I don't have the modern-day Prometheus to hide behind."

"You threw the ball too hard at Victoria," Adam said, turning cross.

"I threw the ball too hard?" Owen pressed his hand to his chest. "*I* threw the ball too hard?"

Adam got that deep furrow in his brow, almost like a caveman. "Yes."

I put my hand on Adam's shoulder. "Adam, next time let's agree to give poor Owen a free pass. He's one of the good guys."

"Good guys don't hit my—"

"Adam."

He dropped his chin to his chest. "Okay." He scuffed his shoe against the gym floor, leaving a black skid. "This game is confusing."

Our class was starting to funnel back into the locker room. Adam reached out his hand, which Owen reluctantly accepted.

"Let's go." I thumped Owen on the back.

"Smith!" It took me a moment to register that Coach Carlson meant Adam. The three of us spun around. Coach jogged up to us, whistle bouncing off the white polo that was working double as a bra.

Adam smiled when he approached. "Hi, I'm Adam Smith. I'm from Elgin, Illinois."

A slight tilt of Coach Carlson's head. "You ever think about playing football, son?"

"I threw one yesterday," Adam replied flatly.

Coach Carlson gave me an *is this kid for real* look. That was becoming a popular one when it came to Adam.

I cleared my throat. "He hasn't."

Coach Carlson eyed Adam from the shoes up. "Never?" He shook his head as if he thought we might be fibbing. In Hollow Pines, even toddlers had thought about playing football. "You like running around out here? Throwing balls. Catching things?"

Adam scratched his head, then there was that same spark in his eyes. He liked orange; he liked pizza. "Yes, I liked it a lot."

"You show promise. Come out to practice after school. I can't guarantee you anything about spots on the team, but I can promise there'll be a lot more where that came from." Coach gave a small salute and pivoted on his heel.

I trotted after him. "But Coach Carlson, don't you think that he should get settled in first?" I called after him. "Focus on his academics?"

Coach Carlson's butt cheeks sucked in the fabric of his mesh shorts and trapped it in the little triangle between his crotch, legs, and rear end. "That's enough, Frankenstein," he said without stopping. "Maybe you could learn something from your friend there. You know they don't give out trophies for who can study the most by the end of high school."

I threw my hands up just as he was disappearing through the open door to his glass-encased office.

"Actually, they do," I yelled. "It's called valedictorian."

He raised his eyebrows and tugged the blind cord, sealing himself off.

I stamped my foot, spun, and marched back to where Owen and Adam were waiting. "For the record," I said. "I think this is a very bad idea."

FIFTEEN

Half-life is usually used to reference nuclear physics and nuclear chemistry, but anything can have a half-life. It's the amount of time required for a quantity to fall to half its value from the first time it was measured. I shouldn't be surprised. Like I said, anything can have one. That includes a charged atom.

— — —

I didn't ask about football practice the whole ride home. Maybe that made me a jerk. Maybe that was what normal people did. The same kind of people who asked how people's days were or what was wrong when somebody was crying in the bathroom. Not me.

It was a relief to return home. My nerves felt like frayed wires, sparking with the memory of my broken phone, the tire tracks, and the missing boy. By now, I had a tiredness in my bones over the whole ordeal that made me eager to retreat into my own personal headquarters. Plus, hopefully we'd gotten this whole football thing out of our system. Since Adam didn't mention it, either, I felt validated in my usual rightness as I unbuckled my seat belt and climbed out of Bert.

Mom worked as a secretary at a small law firm during the day, but she moonlighted as a waitress at the Waffle House, and tonight she had the five-to-ten shift, so I didn't have to be on the lookout as we traipsed to the hatch. Adam's steps were heavy on the ground. Without a word, he stepped into the cellar in front of me.

He had taken four steps when he staggered, knocking hard against the railing. "Adam?" I said, alarmed.

He grunted and then pushed himself up. He got to the last few steps. His knee buckled and he staggered. Barely catching himself from crashing to the floor, he careened sideways.

I skipped down after him. "Are you . . . drunk?" It would be just like the Billys to haze the new guy. Would Adam know any better? He hadn't smelled like alcohol.

Adam groaned. I reached out a hand and spun him by the shoulder to face me. Upon seeing him, my heart leaped clear into my throat. This was not drunk. I almost wished it were. This was a thing far, far worse.

"Adam, you look . . ." I knew it wasn't the best bedside manner, but I couldn't help it. ". . . awful," I finished.

Color appeared to be actively draining from the top of his head downward. Pools of blood could be spotted through the translucent skin on his neck, above his forearm, on the back of his hand. They looked like wine-colored bruises. If I pushed one, it would bubble to the side like a blood blister. His eyes were hollowed out, as if by an ice-cream scooper. In a span of minutes, he'd gone from awkwardly pale to walking dead. The quiet car ride was more than Adam being the strong, silent type, it was him being the near-dead type.

This wasn't good. This wasn't good at all. I wrung my hands.

"Victor—" he started, lurching forward. I put my palms on his chest to keep him from falling on top of me. "Victor—" He began again before his eyes rolled back into his head and I caught his arm.

"Adam, come over here." I guided him closer to the gurney until I could reach over and drag it the rest of the distance to him. The rusted wheels scratched and stuck. I clasped his arms and helped him onto it. "Lie down," I directed. His elbows crumpled and his head clanged back like a newborn who couldn't support his neck. In a drawer, I found a flashlight and flicked it on, wiping dust from the glass.

I started by aiming it in his ears. The thin skin lit up red with the light. Then I pulled his eyelids apart with my fingers and aimed the flashlight into his pupils. I saw a miniature version of my face reflected in the chocolate-brown irises.

I dropped his lids. "I'm going to try to listen to your heart, okay?" I slid the hem of his football jersey up. The sight of Adam's body sent a tingly sensation under my fingernails that made me want to peel them off and scratch. Pink branches forked across his chest in intricate patterns. Adam stared down and grazed his fingers over the scar tissue ridges.

The hatch marks of intricate scars somehow only seemed to make him more beautiful, like a snowflake that could never be re-created.

I leaned forward and pressed my ear to the spot over his heart. I closed my eyes, listened. At first, what I heard was the sound of nothingness. People might not think this has a sound at all, but it does. It was hollow, a heavy, vaulted absence. I held my breath. My own heart thumped loudly and pumped blood into my eardrums. A dull thud. Then two more. Soft but there.

"It's failing," I whispered. "Do you feel that?"

"Am I . . . dying, Victor . . . ia?" His voice was a rasp. "Again?"

I chewed my lip. There was no word in the English dictionary for someone who died when they were already dead. I wasn't sure I could replicate the experiment. It worked once, but once could mean anything. The success of the experiment could have been a statistical anomaly. No variables had been controlled.

I grabbed a thick research book from a shelf and dusted off the cover before flipping through pages, nose close to the typeface. I dragged my finger line by line. *Experiments in Revival of Organisms*. No. *Soviet Dog Experiment*. *Electrotherapy*. I muttered the chapter titles under my breath, knowing full well that pioneers in a field didn't get to check their work in textbooks.

I slammed the covers shut and paced the room. On the gurney, Adam's eyes started to close.

I snapped my fingers under his nose. "Don't go to sleep," I said. His eyelashes fluttered and he stared at me dazed, but awake.

Okay, his energy was drained. His systems were shutting down. I thought about closed-circuit systems. When the human body grew tired, a person refueled it with food. Even from the fetal stage, a human was only able to grow by receiving calories and nutrients in utero. But Adam wasn't brought into existence through calories and nutrients. So more likely, then, was that Adam's fuel wasn't food at all.

I crossed the length of the storm cellar three more times. If a car engine sputtered, what happened? Someone had to give the battery a jump to restore it to full capacity. I pulled a long breath of air like I was sucking on the end of a cigarette. I eyed Adam, then the claw-foot tub, then Adam again.

"Adam," I said. "I think we're going to have to try to recharge you." I began pulling wires. "Last time, well, you don't remember last time, but you're going to have to trust me." I selected a red wire and a green wire. Both had worn coating so that the copper wires were exposed.

"I trust you."

"I'm going to need to make new incisions. Ones that are less visible. You'll tell me if this hurts?" I dragged the scalpel over the counter into my grip. He didn't respond. "Adam?"

"I'll tell you." His lips were turning blue.

"Good." I pinched the scalpel hard between my fingers. He didn't flinch as I sliced an inch in the soft spot behind his ear and before his skull bone. Blood bubbled into the fresh cuts made on either side of his chest. "I'm going to need your help for this part. You're going to have to focus." He moaned his agreement. "You'll have to undress. And then I'll need you in that tub." I pointed. Adam's head lolled to the side. I used the full force of my weight to roll the gurney as close to the dirt-coated tub as I could. "Okay, Adam. Now, before you're not able to." There was urgency in my voice. I worried he'd lose consciousness at any moment.

I supported him as he struggled to sit up, and then together we swung his feet off the edge and deposited him straight into the empty tub. He peeled off his jersey first, and I caught myself staring not at the tree-branch scars but at the swell of his muscles underneath. When he unfastened the button of his jeans, I whirled around. Heat rushed to my cheeks. "Sorry," I mumbled. This had been so much less awkward when he was dead.

Behind me, I heard squeaks and squawks of skin on porcelain, and once they'd stopped, I announced myself before turning around, feeling more embarrassed than I should have been at the thought of the human anatomy. I was careful where my gaze landed as I reached over to turn the handles on the faucet. The spigot choked, sputtered, and then retched a gush of grimy water. The sound thundered against the sides of the bath.

Adam's eyelids finally closed and didn't reopen. I was reliving the night of the accident. To assure myself that not everything was the same, I put my finger below his nose and felt the soft puff of air against my skin. He was alive, if only barely.

I wheeled the kilowatt meter over and gathered a jar of brine water, working up a sweat as I culled together all the necessary supplies. Since I wouldn't be reanimating a corpse, I reasoned that the power I'd need would be significantly less.

I inserted the wires into the open cuts and applied a short piece of tape to hold each in place. I set the power gauge and, as a final, lucky thought, I pulled ratty old towels and a short stepping stool. I positioned my feet on top of the stool and wrapped the towels around them to stave off the shock. There was no time left to think. Adam was slipping. I had no choice but to flip the dial.

As soon as I did, Adam jerked like a cat dunked in water. The sight paralyzed me. His eyes rolled into his head until all I could see were the whites. He looked possessed. Tremors shot through his body. The water churned. I wanted to hold him but forced my arms to stay pinned to my sides. His jaw clenched and unclenched. Chin stretched up, straining for something. Pain deepened the lines of his face, turning the laugh lines around his mouth into sunken grooves.

I closed my eyes, but I could still hear the enamel clacking together as his teeth chattered uncontrollably in his jaw. This couldn't be right. The hair on his arms stood on end, dimpling the skin underneath with welted goose bumps. Sparks flew. The acrid scent of burning meat.

He let out a strangled grunt and his head whipped back. Throat exposed. His hands twisted into claws. He moaned again. Deep, guttural groaning. I watched as his shoulders convulsed. A grotesque exorcism jolted through muscle and sinewy tissue, racking his body.

"Four!" he screamed.

Startled, I reached for the switch, heart pounding. The soft hum of electricity faded. It left him in waves. Another one shook him every second or so like the aftershock from an earthquake.

Shallow pants came from both of us. Gradually, the last twitch left his fingers. I got down from my perch. "Adam? Adam, are you all right?"

His chest rose and fell. His fists squeezed into balls.

I tilted my head to read him, but shadows disguised all his features, warping them into something frightening and indecipherable. *Four*, I repeated silently. What had he meant by that?

"Adam?" My voice grew softer. Slowly, I reached out my hand, realizing as I did so that it was shaking. With one finger, I prodded him in the ribs beneath the milky water.

His head snapped up. Our eyes met, but in that moment, I wasn't sure he really saw me. His eyes held a glint of hard metal. His top lip quivered over a row of exposed teeth, and a tendon in his jaw pulsated.

I jerked away, finger still outstretched.

"S-s-sorry," I stuttered. "I—"

But before I could finish my thought, his eyelashes fluttered and he tossed his chin quickly. He looked at me as if seeing me there for the first time.

He stretched out his fingers. Examined his hands backward and forward. He rolled his shoulders. He stood up. Bent his knees.

"Why are you staring at me like that, Victoria?"

I closed my mouth. The sound of my own saliva crackled in my ears. "You . . . looked different. For a second." I realized my pulse was still jackhammering the inside of my wrist. I rubbed my neck, trying to shake away the sense of fear that'd overtaken me. Like I'd just escaped a moment that had been teetering on the edge of something very, very dangerous. "How do you feel?" I asked, then cleared my throat. And for some reason the clearest image in my mind at that moment was a faceless missing boy.

"I feel better."

Almost immediately, the pools of blood began to disperse underneath his skin, and the yellow faded out of the whites of his eyes. The more normal he looked, the more normal I felt. I wanted to laugh at myself for being so uptight. I couldn't quite laugh, though. Not when the hairs on my arms still stood on end.

"Really? Because that looked like it hurt," I said with an out-of-place, breathless chuckle that sounded forced even to me. "I don't want to get too graphic, but I thought you were in choking-on-your-own-vomit territory. Not usually a good sign."

He cracked his neck. The bones sounded brittle. "It hurt a little, but not now." I latched onto the word *hurt*. He'd felt something. Something had come back. He had *hurt*. "Thank you, Victoria."

He put his hands on my shoulders. There was a zap of static between us that made me jump. "You saved me. Again," he said, and my throat closed off, trapping any words that I might have had left. *Saved.*

Crickets chirped on my short walk back to the main house. As had become my habit, I scanned the open road that ran alongside our lawn, looking for a car and somebody who knew the truth about me and Adam. But the scattered lampposts that dotted the neighbors' fence lines gave away nothing. The road was empty, and I left it behind to go inside, where Einstein greeted me with her wiggling stub of a tail.

"Come on, girl." I beckoned her into the kitchen. She snorted and sniffed at the linoleum tiles.

This morning's skillet still sat on the cold burner, a layer of eggs caked onto the bottom. I tossed it into the sink with the rest of the dishes and ran the faucet for a few seconds. Two empty wine bottles and a heap of red-stained napkins littered the countertop. With a sigh, I brought the trash can around and scraped the counter off into the garbage.

Dusting my hands off on the back of my pants, I wandered into the living room, Einstein in tow. The blue light of the television flickered on, silent. A mess of crocheted blankets draped from the couch, spilling onto the carpet. Einstein circled and plopped down on the edge of a pilling gray one. I picked the remote off the ring-stained coffee table and sank down into the sofa. I recognized the anchorwoman of the late news and flipped on the volume. The events of the day buzzed in my ears, and it felt good to let her voice drown them out. I was just tilting my head back to rest my eyes when I heard a name that I recognized. Trent. Jackson. Westover.

I jolted upright and clicked the volume louder. Einstein stared up with droopy eyes and shook her collar.

"After the break, we'll give you the tragic latest on Lamar High's missing teenager," the woman said from behind the news desk just before the screen faded into a car-insurance commercial. I laced my fingers together and twiddled my thumbs. The next two minutes lasted an eternity. Car-insurance commercial, cereal commercial, commercial for world's coldest beer. My knee jiggled up and down.

I jammed my finger into the fast-forward button even though I knew I was watching the show live.

Headlights swept through the living room, and my heart constricted. I hurried to the window and peeked through the blinds. I let out a long breath when I saw it was Mom's station wagon pulling into the drive. Behind me, the simple melody of Channel 8's theme song came on and I abandoned the window.

The anchorwoman appeared behind her desk with her helmet of blond hair and bright red lips. "Good evening again. This morning's vote on the water bill passed five to two."

"Who cares, who cares . . . ," I muttered.

Outside, the engine died, and moments later, the screen door clanged shut. "Tor!" Mom called. "I've got pancakes."

"In here," I said, and turned up the volume once again. The woman was now describing how the water bill would affect our county in minute detail. The grooves of my teeth wore into one another.

Mom set a Styrofoam box full of pancakes down on the coffee table in front of me. She wore her blue pinstripe uniform with the cuffed sleeves and white tennis shoes. I craned around her to see the screen.

"And now for the heartbreaking case of the missing high school student, Trent Jackson Westover." My breath froze in my lungs.

"Mom, you're blocking the screen." I shooed her away.

Mom shuffled around to the couch beside me and, before I could react, took the remote and flipped it to her nighttime soap operas.

"Mom!" I shrieked. "Turn it back. I was watching that."

She opened the Styrofoam lid. "My soaps are on," she said. "Tonight we find out if Eliza was really having an affair with Dr. Lee. Oh, I forgot syrup." Mom meandered back to the kitchen, and I clicked the button to return to the news program.

A shot of a lakeshore surrounded by reeds and sinking moss lingered on-screen. A yellow ambulance near the edge flashed red and white lights onto the surface. Below the shot the caption read *Lake*

Crook. A team of uniformed men and women were busying themselves around the water.

"The boy's body was recovered sometime after two this afternoon when a sports fisherman noticed the body being washed against the shore," the anchorwoman continued solemnly. *Body?*

I moved to the edge of the sofa and rested my elbows on my knees.

Mom returned with a glass of wine, a fork, and no syrup. "Tor, I told you I was watching that. It's a very important episode."

"Shhhhh!" I said. "Just a second."

"Tor Frankenstein!" She stood directly in front of the television. I moved a foot to the right to see.

"You forgot the syrup again," I told her.

She looked down at the fork and the brimming glass of wine and cursed. A few seconds later I heard her open the fridge and begin rummaging.

". . . exclusively to Channel 8 to tell us the gruesome details of the body's recovery." The anchorwoman finished just as the screen cut to a man in camouflage overalls and a lure hanging from the brim of his cap.

"I've never see anything like it," the man said. "And I've been fishing here for twenty years and have never seen anything like it," he repeated, rubbing his chin. "It was like an animal had gotten ahold of the boy's ankle. It was that torn up. Like maybe a bear had attacked him. And his other leg, well, it was missing completely."

The camera panned wider and the field reporter turned to face it. "Authorities will be investigating the cause—"

The channel flipped to a man in a surgical mask and scrubs making eyes at a young nurse. I hadn't even noticed Mom come in. I sat pinned to my seat, blood whooshing through my arteries. Trent Westover had been found. It wasn't Adam. I laughed out loud; I was so relieved until Mom slapped at my elbow and hushed me.

"It's not funny," she muttered. "Dr. Lee could lose his teaching job at the hospital. His daughter is sick."

"What? Oh. Yeah." I blinked, still feeling the tickle of laughter building inside. "Sorry."

Then I noticed the heap of pancakes sitting in front of me, and for the first time all day I felt really, truly hungry, so I took a fork and dug in.

SIXTEEN

Hypothesis: A re-administering of the electrical charge will sustain circulatory and organ function.

Process: Same methodology followed with lower voltage.

Conclusion: Experiment was successful, though shockingly (pun intended), Adam seemed to exhibit signs of physical pain post-electrotherapy and elicited incoherent words.

Observations: Personality shift observed right after electro-stimulation. Perhaps stimulus to cranial cortex. Personality shift subsided shortly thereafter and no further anomalies have been observed.

– – –

The discovery of Trent's body buoyed my mood more than it probably should have. For one, it wasn't polite to gloat when a teenage boy was found with one leg mauled and the other completely gone and, for two, it solved only a fraction of one of my problems, which left at least two big, fat, granddaddy-sized predicaments to topple over and crush me at any given moment—there was the shattered phone that, science would suggest, hadn't appeared on my porch by magic and the fact that someone, somewhere, even if it wasn't the Westovers, was probably looking for Adam, my Adam, and if they found him, it wouldn't be either dead or alive.

But instead of feeling the weight of any of those things, I was starting the school day feeling nearly invincible. The experiment was working. The sun was shining. Adam was a student at Hollow Pines High. Today, for the first time, it felt as though it was all beginning to fall into place.

"Um, Tor? Why are people staring at us?" Owen said, smiling through gritted teeth. The sun reflected off the morning dew, bright enough to leave a sunburn. The smell of freshly mowed grass permeated the air. It was summer in September.

Adam trudged through the gravel lot beside us. The pools of crimson that had pocketed beneath his skin had all completely disappeared, and the dark circles beneath his eyes had lightened.

"Huh?" I tore myself from my thoughts and noticed that we did seem to be drawing attention. "I have no idea. Do I have toilet paper stuck to my shoe?"

Owen actually fell back several paces to check. "No, rider, you're clear for takeoff."

"God, you're a geek." I rolled my eyes.

"I think that's been established," Owen said with an uneven strain to his voice. He tugged at his collar and glanced around at the onlookers.

As we neared the Bible Belt, several clean-cut kids in matching T-shirts turned to greet us. "Hey, man," said one. "Heard you had a great practice last night." Adam waved without stopping. The guy turned to watch us pass. "May the power be with you." The Bible Belter put up his fist. "The power of God, that is." At this, a few cheers rose from the group.

"That was nice." I looked back.

"Yeah, but they're always freakishly nice," Owen said. "It's their thing."

"I don't know them," Adam said. "I didn't say hello this time." He smiled. "See? I'm learning." The flecks in Adam's eyes shined golden in the sun. A lock of dark hair slipped over his eyebrow.

"Not exactly what I meant," I said.

As we neared the Billys' trucks, more people began to turn, and it became clear that they weren't looking at us at all. They were looking at Adam. Billy Ray broke from the group, and I had an instinctive, bone-deep desire to run. Science would call this a conditioned reflex. The art of survival. I'd call it high school.

Instead, the three of us slowed as Billy Ray blocked our path. Given that he was the size and shape of a refrigerator, there wasn't really any other choice. He held a football chest level, smashed between his palms. He tossed it to Adam, who caught it easily.

"I heard Coach is thinking of starting you, Smith." Billy Ray's face broke into a wide, fat-lipped grin. He ran his hand over his shaved scalp.

Adam hugged the ball to his chest. "Starting me to do what?" he asked, looking down and hiking his book bag farther up onto his shoulder. A curtain of thick lashes brushed his cheek. If I looked closely I could make out the red slivers behind his ears.

Billy Ray wedged himself between me and Adam, knocking me sideways. He wrapped his arm around Adam's neck. Ruffled the hair on his head. "The game, man. Football!" He released Adam's head and shook his own good-naturedly. "You, Smith! Where the heck did you come from, son?"

"I came from Elgin, Illinois," he replied.

Billy Ray looked over at me as if to say *Can you believe this guy?* As I said, it was a popular look where Adam was concerned. I pressed my lips together and raised my eyebrows. But truthfully, no, I couldn't.

"I would like to start playing more football." Adam bobbed his chin up and down. "That would be good." It occurred to me then that I'd already been thinking of reasons not to let him. It was too dangerous.

We hadn't studied the possible side effects. His state was fragile. It was only when I heard the hopeful lilt in his voice that I had to consider whether I had any right to tell him what to do at all.

I created him, but did that make me the master of his universe, too? I couldn't decide.

"Well, good." Billy Ray thumped Adam on the chest. "Because you keep it up and you're starting the *game*. The big one. Two bye weeks and then you better be ready." He pointed at him with both hands as he backpedaled away. "You, Smith. You're the man. This is the season. I feel it, buddy. This year."

As soon as we were out of earshot, I grabbed Adam's arm. "Group sidebar. Please?" I yanked Owen into the huddle. "I mean now."

Our heads pushed together, except that I was the shortest so mine only reached to their chins. "They're *starting* you?" I said to Adam. "Is this a real thing? Because I'm feeling like this isn't a real thing."

"I'm feeling like you're talking real fast," Owen chimed in.

"I thought people were being uncharacteristically nice or curious or had all suffered some weird, town-wide aneurysm."

"I liked it," Adam said. He was still a man of few words, but even since yesterday I observed that he was just a hair more lively. Less stiff, more natural maybe. "I made friends."

"You made *friends*?" I said. "But you have friends. Why the need for more friends? I've had one friend for the past eight years and you don't see me complaining. You already have two friends. Me and Owen. And what, you're already bored? Don't you think that's being just a wee bit greedy?"

"If you lifted your leg, I think you might be able to pee on him to mark your territory." Owen tilted his head and stared hard at me.

"What's a 'bye week,' anyway? What do you do with 'bye weeks'? They sound like a made-up term."

"It means they don't have games tonight and next Friday to lead up to

Homecoming," Owen said as if he were some authority on the sport now.

I ground my teeth. At least that gave us some time. "Adam, look, these people might be nice to you now, but . . ."

But it was too late. I didn't get to finish. Cassidy Hyde had butted her perky behind straight into our conversation.

"'Scuse me." She spun around. She was holding the ends of a pair of black and orange streamers. "Pep rally decorations." Her smile was blinding. "Go Oilers." She said this with a shrug in her voice like she was partly making fun of herself.

Standing at the steps of the school, I was about to continue with my train of thought when I registered how his eyes were lingering on Cassidy as she pulled the streamers high over her head to wrap them around the top of a column, so that her pierced belly button peeked out the top of her jeans.

"Good morning, Cassidy Hyde," Adam said, formal, flat, but strangely charming because of both those things. "Do you need help with that?" Adam walked over with his stiff gait. He took a pair of streamers from her and stretched up to tape them higher than she could reach.

She put her hands on her hips. "Well, look at that. I didn't think they made real gentlemen anymore."

I felt a scowl overtake my mouth. *They* didn't, I wanted to tell her. I did.

"OUCH-GOSHDARNIT-*DAMN*!" MY FINGER sprung out from under the metal hot plate I was working to pry free from its base. I shook it and stuck the tip in my mouth while it stung.

"How are you *still* single?" The door to the chemistry lab swung closed behind Owen. He cocked his head as I continued sputtering jumbled curse words under my breath. "I mean, really, it's an unsolvable paradox. You have such a sweet demeanor about you. That's what I always say, anyway." I removed my finger from my mouth and examined the broken nail left over. He strolled through the empty classroom to the lab table I was occupying near the back and paused at the sight of my project in progress. "Maybe a little light would help?" He moved for the switch.

"I didn't want anyone to know I was in here," I said sourly. Late afternoon light trickled in through the blinds, casting the classroom in shadowy gray. Trace smudges of dry erase marker covered the whiteboard where Ms. Dot had erased today's notes, and the freshly wiped countertops smelled like antibacterial soap.

"You mean while you're defacing school property?" Owen's white T-shirt read *Wikipedia is accurate.*

"I mean while I'm working." It was nearly five o'clock. Ms. Dot, my AP chemistry teacher, had collected her giant tote bag and stack of manila folders half an hour ago. I had keys to the lab and exactly twenty-five minutes before Adam would be finished with *football* practice. Even in my head, I couldn't say it without a sneer. *Football* practice. Now, scattered around were crucible tongs, a base holder, boss heads, burette clamps, and a hot plate.

"Well, you're doing a good job of that at least. I've been looking for you for thirty minutes," he said, dropping his backpack on a nearby stool. "You might want to consider fixing the whole cell phone situation at some point." I cringed at the thought of my phone splintered on the road and how it'd found its way back to me. Annoyed as I was about football and Adam's sudden rise in popularity, the day had been pleasantly uneventful, and it almost felt as though phones and missing boys could slip into the background and disappear. "We're living in the twenty-first century." I decided not to deal with his cell phone comment.

Since I'd been unsuccessful in wrestling the hot plate away, I gripped the base in both hands and began beating it against the tabletop. Owen jerked and plugged his ears. "What are you doing?" His eyes were wide behind his lenses. I made several more noisy blows before he put his hand over my wrist. "Tor, stop!" I held the hot plate in midair before striking again. "Are you insane?"

"I'm trying to loosen it." I clamped my tongue between my teeth and went to try for another blow, but Owen held me firm.

"Step away from the hot plate." Like a cop disarming his suspect, he slowly extracted the piece of equipment from my grasp. I huffed but folded my hands in my lap. "Now speak in sentences," he said. "What is it that you're trying to do?"

I rolled my eyes. "I'm trying to build this." I reached into my bag for my composition book and flipped through the pages until I landed on the one I wanted. I shoved the notebook in his direction. On the open sheet of lined paper, I'd drawn a circle diagram with four smaller circles inside.

Owen squinted. "Which is . . . ?"

I snatched the composition book back and frowned at the rudimentary drawing inside. "It doesn't have a *name* yet." I glanced sidelong at him. "Adam malfunctioned last night. He completely lost his energy, and his whole body started to shut down." I shuddered. "I . . . had to do it again."

Owen did that thing where he looked over his glasses and made me feel like a little kid in trouble. "Electrocute him?"

"A little," I fibbed, *exactly* like a little kid. "Okay a lot." I nodded. "He was going to die, though."

Owen pushed his fingers into his hair and left it standing straight up. "He already is dead."

"You know what I mean." Footsteps squeaked by in the hallway. A shadow crossed the door before disappearing. "And"—I lowered my voice—"if he's going to insist on playing this caveman sport with all the hitting and running around and throwing of things, his energy's going to keep getting drained."

"Funny. I would have thought you'd have been proud to learn your progeny was turning out to be a perfect physical specimen." He tilted his head. "At least in Hollow Pines terms."

I blinked and felt my forehead wrinkle. "You think?"

"If the cleat fits . . ."

I bit my lip. Adam was becoming every bit the breakthrough that I'd sought out for him to be. Maybe Owen was right. "I'm trying to make a . . . device. . . ." This time I jammed my finger into the page and it tore a centimeter. ". . . To make it easier to, you know, recharge him. But it's not working."

Owen pulled the edge closer and slid his glasses to the bridge of his nose. "Some kind of plate?" He hummed quietly.

"I figured I'd surgically insert it. With portals for the wires and—"

Owen held up a finger and looked away from me. "I am going to try not to be positively offended—no, wait—blasphemed by the fact that you didn't come straight to me before attempting to upend a perfectly innocent laboratory hot plate." My shoulders relaxed. "But I'm here now." He cracked his neck, followed by his knuckles. "We can get to work."

A slow grin stretched across my face. "Really?"

Owen had already turned the hot plate onto its back and was bent over, fiddling with the screws. I glanced at the clock and registered the time. Resting my elbows on the table, I leaned in to watch him work. Owen tinkering, a man in his natural habitat. "Uh, Owen?" His fingers stopped. He turned toward me, our noses an inch apart. "Think you can help a girl out and sort through the rest of this on your own?" I set my chin on my fists and peered up at him. "Pretty please?"

He spared a long-suffering look for the ceiling. "I'm already in this deep, I suppose." He returned his attention to the lab equipment and pinched his tongue between his teeth. "Besides, you're hazardous when it comes to machines, anyway."

"Awesome." I grabbed my bag and slung it over my shoulder. "I'll see you tomorrow. Can you have it ready by then?" I batted my eyelashes.

The right corner of his mouth crept into a smile that dimpled his cheek. "You're not that charming, Frankenstein."

"I am to you." I blew him an air kiss, turned on my toes, and headed out the door.

At least half the school's lights had been turned off, and the hallway was dotted with patches of darkness with only the red glow of exit lights to mark them. Outside the classroom, I fumbled in the bottom of my bag for my keys and looped a finger through the ring. The soft melody from a teacher's radio floated toward me as I made my way to the football field.

A prickle grew along the back of my neck, inching its way up the notches of my spine like a caterpillar. By the time I'd passed the last of the science classrooms, I was able to place the creeping sensation as the feeling of being watched. It slithered and disappeared into the cracks between my ribs, where it forced my heart to beat faster.

I froze in place and spun. My bag banged against my hip. I felt the dead quiet all around me until over my heartbeat I could again hear the small trickle of music coming from the radio hidden behind one of the classroom doors.

Shadows cloaked groups of lockers in even intervals. My eyes focused, and I saw a silhouette. The tingle worked a path down my forearms. The silhouette stepped from the shadow into a shaft of light. The head of a mop landed next to his feet.

I let out a whooshing exhale. "Mr. McCardle," I said. "God, you scared me." My pulse throbbed even as my muscles relaxed. I shook my head, unsure of what had gotten me so spooked.

Blackness filled in the lines on his face. His mouth was curved into a shallow frown. "It's dark," he said.

"Guess so." I lingered awkwardly, remembering when he'd found me rather precariously positioned in the girls' restroom with Adam.

I could only imagine what he must have thought he'd walked in on. I pressed my lips together and rocked back on my heels. Maybe he'd forgotten. Earlier today, I'd seen a few kids playing Pin-the-Tail-on-McCardle, a dumb game where students tried to attach embarrassing signs or stickers to the janitor's back. The game was mean-spirited and cold, but I never removed the stickers for fear that McCardle would think that lots of people had been noticing. "Anyway." I waved. "Just heading out. Have a good night."

He took another step forward when a door behind him opened. "Tor!" Owen popped his head out, brandishing a notebook in his hand. "You forgot this." Owen jogged down the hall, past Old Man McCardle, and deposited my black-and-white composition book into my hands.

The book that contained Adam. I squeezed it to my chest. I never went anywhere without it. Instinctively, I flipped through the pages of data, diagrams, and research, reassuring myself that it was all still there. "Thanks," I said, and meant it. Then I went outside to the emerald field that waited, glittering underneath the glare of the stadium's industrial lights.

SEVENTEEN

I believe an improvement can be made in the administration of the electroshock. Now that we know that the shock will not be a one-time event, it seemed a priority to create something that would negate the need for new incisions, which are not only time-consuming, but the more incisions, the more likely someone is to notice them in the outside world.

— — —

The only kind of pressure I believed in was the ratio of force to the area over which that force was distributed. That's what I told Adam when he practically bounced out of football practice and told me the team wanted him to attend a field party tonight. Peer pressure was for people looking for an excuse to make bad decisions without enough guts to make them on their own.

Of course, I then learned of another kind of pressure. The kind where the boy you killed and reanimated really-really-really wanted to meet up with his new friends, which meant you really-really-really had to tag along to chaperone. Now why wasn't there a name for that?

"Surprised you could make it." Paisley leaned against the taillights of Knox Hoyle's pickup truck. She was only five foot tall, which made her the shortest girl in the junior class.

Not a lot of people attributed this disorder to girls, but I was convinced that everything about Paisley Wheelwright could be explained by the Napoleon complex, a bona fide psychological condition where a person was extra aggressive and domineering just to make up for his or her short stature.

"Surprised you asked," I replied. A group of students had met in the Walmart parking lot to collect ice for coolers and firewood and to consolidate vehicles. I looked around, feeling out of place and without anything useful to do.

This was exactly what I'd been afraid of. First, Adam would join the football team, and before I knew it, we'd be *involved* in things. Hanging out with the Hollow Pines High social elite on a Friday after mandatory school hours definitely counted as involved. It set my teeth on edge.

"I didn't." She turned her back and strode to the passenger side, where she hopped in and slammed the door with a solid clang that shot through the dark parking lot like a gun.

"That's that Southern hospitality I was telling you about," I said to Adam.

"You don't like her." Adam's eyes had a way of boring into me.

"Yeah, well, I don't like rabid animals, either. They bite," I said, climbing onto the back of Knox's truck. My tennis shoe slipped off the ledge, and Cassidy, already perched on the side of the truck bed, caught my elbow.

"Careful," she said, giggling softly.

I stepped over the tailgate, and Adam climbed in behind me.

Even in the dark, Cassidy's legs were tan against her cutoff jean shorts. She wore a white tank top, and her hair fell in loose waves around her face. She smiled and scooted over. I sat down next to her on the side of the truck, wearing an oversized army jacket and shorts with my dirty checkered Vans, while Adam took the seat beside me.

"This y'all's first time?" she asked.

"At least that I can remember," said Adam.

She quirked an eyebrow and I smacked a mosquito sucking on my arm. One minute in and already I could see nothing great about the great outdoors.

"All aboard," yelled Knox. From behind the steering wheel, he reached his hand out the open window and thumped the cabin roof like it was a horse. The other trucks roared to life. Headlights flickered on. Wheels spun and squealed against the asphalt. "Giddyup!"

The truck lurched forward. I fell against Adam and he caught me against his chest. Strong hands wrapped around my waist protectively. "Sorry," I muttered. I put my hand on his thigh and pushed myself up straight as fast as I could.

"You better hang on," said Cassidy. The rushing air off the top of the truck brushed Cassidy's hair back from her shoulders so that she looked like a model standing in front of a wind machine, while somehow the same airflow made my hair stick to my mouth. Knox steered the truck over the curb and onto the neighboring dirt road. I watched as the blazing lights of the parking lot faded. The truck bed rocked back and forth on the gravel road.

After ten minutes of driving, the liquid contents of my stomach had converted into a wave pool. Knox swerved into potholes. He floored the accelerator to pass the truck in front of us. Billy Ray, moonlight gleaming off his white head, gave us a friendly middle finger as we edged in front. I was on the verge of hurling in Cassidy's lap when we reached an open field and Knox decided to perform a doughnut.

I swayed, leaned forward with my head between my knees. Vomit burned the back of my throat and slid into my mouth. I clamped my teeth together while the world spun.

Just when I thought my mouth was about to be converted into a human puke geyser, Knox slammed on the brakes. We went flying forward and all toppled over one another in the bed of the truck. Kids laughed into the open air while watery slime slithered back down my gullet. The bones in my legs had dissolved into mush. Adam offered me a hand and, with a grunt, pulled me off Cassidy, who I'd managed to squash.

"I should at least make you buy me dinner first," she said, propping herself up on her elbows. Her eyes sparkled in the darkness.

I reached down to help her up. "Don't talk about dinner right now," I said, clutching my stomach.

Three more pairs of headlights skirted the field. I was still wobbly and dangerously close to vomiting. Adam held my hips and lowered me to the ground.

I dusted off my knees and looked around at the empty field. Fireflies played hide-and-seek, glowing yellow an inch away before disappearing, then lighting up again another ten yards farther. Crickets chirped out a high-pitched screech that made me watch where I was walking. I didn't know why anyone would want to hang out someplace where there were bugs and no plumbing.

"Smith, catch." Knox tossed Adam a can from a cooler on the back of William's truck. Adam snatched it from the air. "Tor, you drink?"

"Actually, um—" I much preferred being able to think clearly, thank you very much.

"Catch." I caught the glint of aluminum arcing through the air. I shuffled sideways, trying to position my feet. I stretched out my fingers. There was a flash of cold on my hands as the can slipped right through them and landed with a dull *thunk* in the dirt.

"Nice catch." Knox fitted a camouflage baseball cap over his head and pulled the brim low over his eyes before kicking the cooler lid shut with his boot.

"Yeah, well," I muttered as I bent down to pluck the can out of the dirt, "I bet you don't know what forty-eight times thirty-five is either, buddy."

"One thousand six hundred and eighty." Beside me, Cassidy cracked open the tab on her beer.

I brushed caked mud off the side of the can. "Yeah. Um, that's right, actually."

"Don't look so surprised." She slurped the foam off the top. We stood side by side in silence for a few moments, watching kids pile out of the trucks. Adam had been corralled by the Billys and was being introduced to everyone by William and Billy Ray. "So what's a girl like you doing at a thing like this, anyway?" She had one of those sweet-tea accents. I bet she sang out loud to country radio in the car.

"You mean a nerd like me?" I ran my finger around the edge of the can.

She shrugged, not bothering to correct me.

I kicked at the dirt. "I guess we're sort of a package deal." I nodded in Adam's direction.

She nodded. "Man of the hour. You're lucky." Except that luck didn't have a thing to do with it. Unless she was referring to bad luck, in which case there was probably a little of that.

Paisley walked over and bumped hips with her. "Try not to get so sloppy drunk this time, Hyde. Boys at least like a bit of a challenge." Paisley's belly button poked out from a denim vest.

Cassidy shifted her weight and abruptly dropped her beer to her side. I'd heard stories about Cassidy. About things she'd done with boys under the bleachers and in the woods and once in a deer blind. I stared up at the Big Dipper and pretended I hadn't heard.

"Tor, on the other hand." She circled me like a shark. "You could use all the help you can get." She stopped walking and scanned my outfit, from my tennis shoes all the way up to the jacket sleeves that nearly swallowed the tips of my fingers.

Cassidy leaned over. "Seriously, though, if you're going to be bitten by fire ants and mosquitoes for an entire evening, it's best to brave it while buzzed." She slurped beer from the rim of her can.

Paisley's blue eyes were cool and appraising. She brushed away a strand of blond hair. "Knox says there's worse out there than bugs, you know." She put her hand over her eyes, using it as a visor. "Can't even see more than a few yards beyond the headlights and we're a long way from home, *Tor*antula." She stepped closer. "I suppose anything could happen."

"Well, we all know Knox is full of shit." Cassidy raised her beer as if she were making a toast.

Nearby, a ring of onlookers gathered around the beginnings of a fire. William was pushing his leather boot into a Duraflame log to get it crackling. The first orange flames licked the air, and Billy Ray and Knox took turns throwing sticks over the top.

"It's true. This is where Roy McCardle died a couple years back." Paisley ignored Cassidy. "You think if I drew a pentagram right here on the ground, I could raise him back from the dead?" She grabbed a stick from the ground and waved it over her head.

Roy McCardle. The name rang a bell, but I couldn't place it.

"Here?" Cassidy jumped back.

Paisley rolled her eyes. Her bob took on a silver sheen in the moonlight. "Or, I guess it could have been where Tor is standing." Her smile was wicked as she began to trace a five-pointed star on the trampled grass.

I stared off at the fire. "Sorry, Wheelwright. It's going to take a lot more than that to scare me," I said.

She paused from her makeshift drawing. "Challenge accepted," she said. I could tell she was getting annoyed that I wasn't doing a good job of playing with her Ouija board.

"Can you stop that, Paisley?" Cassidy grabbed for the stick, but Paisley snatched it clear.

"Relax, Cassidy. Tor doesn't mind, do you?" She finished another point on her star and drew a circle around the outside.

The name then clicked into place. "Roy McCardle. That's the janitor's son?"

"A-plus, Ms. Frankenstein." She tossed the stick into the shadows.

"Poor Roy McCardle was helping his daddy do some farmwork a couple years back. Riding at the front of the tractor when his pant leg got caught in the wheel. You know what happened then?"

"He died," I said without emotion.

Her lips drew close to my ear. She smelled like Mom's wine. "The thing sucked him straight down." She grabbed me suddenly and shook. My heart jolted awake in my chest, but I kept my face placid. "And the machine ate his legs until they were bone before chewing up his intestines and leaving them as fertilizer."

"You paint a vivid picture, I'll give you that."

"It's more than a picture. I heard his daddy carried him all the way to the road looking for help while his entrails hung out of Roy like a leash dragging in the dirt. Then"—she paused, enjoying her story—"he died. Right there in his daddy's arms."

Cassidy fiddled with the tab, twisting it back and forth until it popped off and she tossed it over her shoulder.

"Not exactly party conversation, Paize." Cassidy gave a nervous laugh.

"I bet his ghost haunts this field." Paisley turned on the spot as though expecting the ghost of Roy McCardle to come gliding in from any direction.

Cassidy shoved Paisley gently. "Shut up and stop trying to scare us. You believe in ghosts, Victoria?"

The night was hot and my shirt was sticky. I was already salivating at the thought of a shower and wondering why I'd been stupid enough to come out here without my own car. "No," I said. "I don't believe in anything that can't be explained through rational thought, and neither should you."

Cassidy bowed her head and peered down at the can of beer she was holding between two hands. "I don't know about that." Her voice was small. "I believe in love."

A short distance away, the fire blossomed to life, sending a tongue of flame up from the ground. I watched Adam, whose figure had been silhouetted against a navy sky, jerk back from the fire and shield his face. Trace flecks of orange and gold floated into the air and disappeared. Adam retreated farther from the blaze into darker shadows. Already, I felt I could mentally trace the lines of Adam with my eyes closed. From the *v* of muscle that winged out from the base of his neck to the pronounced curve of his brow bone. As if sensing me watching, he turned. His eyes scanned the dark surroundings for several seconds, at last landing on me. Adam. My Adam.

"It must be exhausting always thinking that everyone's so much dumber than you, huh?" Paisley's voice penetrated my thoughts.

"What?" I broke my gaze away from Adam. "Oh, yeah," I said absently, although it occurred to me I was supposed to refute what she'd said. "I'm going to go sit in one of the trucks," I said instead. "I think I've reached my outdoor quota for the month."

I started off and had made it no farther than a couple of paces when—"What about *your* daddy, Tor? Ever seen *his* ghost?"

A column of ice wrapped its way around the base of my spine, causing me to stiffen. I didn't turn back to face Paisley. Like a ghost, the image of my father was there the moment she spoke the words. The coroner had told me his death was instantaneous, that he felt nothing. But I could never shake the memory of my father's face when I found him soaked, dead, and lying in the rain. His mouth was open; his eyes were wide and glassy, a look of shock that had been cast onto his face like a mold for me to find. What was left was evidence of an instant, at least one moment where he knew what was about to happen and he understood that the nature he loved so much was going to kill him. Barbed wire punched through my heart, sending fire through the nerves at my fingertips, which I folded into fists at my side.

"Because I heard he was ten times crazier than Old Man Mc-Cardle." Paisley slurred her words. "Is that true?"

"Paisley!" I heard Cassidy hiss. I wrenched my feet from the ground and trudged off in the opposite direction. "Come on, Tor!" Cassidy called after me. "She's only joking! We're sorry!"

Four trucks parked at varying distances formed a semicircle around the growing fire. Their headlights illuminated pockets of the field, casting long shadows that stretched into the darkness. I cut across the beams and walked swiftly around to the passenger side of a red Ford.

I was so eager to disappear into the truck and wait out the rest of the night that I nearly rammed into an open door where someone was rummaging in the backseat. I tried to back away, but Knox's head appeared from within the truck's cabin before I could make it a single step. A silver bottle opener glinted in his right hand. "What are you doing over here?"

Behind the curtain of truck lights, the surrounding field behind us was thick with blackness. The truck's cabin light glowed softly beside him.

"Sorry, just getting some air."

"You're in the country. The air doesn't get much fresher."

"Yeah, that's the problem," I said, feeling more and more irritated with people's inexplicable fascination with being outside. I rocked back on my heel and moved to leave in the direction I'd come from, but Knox caught my wrist.

His mouth cast a ghoulish shadow when he smiled. "Don't have to hurry back so fast, do we?" The cabin light had snapped off, and it was just me and Knox with the scent of beer and cologne hanging between us.

"I think we do," I said evenly.

I tried pulling back again, but he held firm, not enough pressure to hurt, not so much that it might not be mistaken for playful, but enough to send a small tingle down my back. "Come on, the others won't miss you. Besides, I was just joking, you can wait in my truck."

I couldn't see through the tinted windows, but I thought of the locks and the four metal doors and of Knox, and waiting inside no longer seemed like such a great idea. "Like you said, there's plenty of fresh air out here."

He took a step into me so that I could feel warmth radiating off his chest. "Stay, chat . . ." I could sense a definite ellipsis after the word *chat* that turned my stomach sour. "I'm on the *football team*." He stressed the last two words like they were supposed to mean something to me.

"And I won't hold that against you, but still I better get back to the party."

Knox inhaled as though ready to retort when a scream broke through the expanse of black that stretched out into the unseen reaches of the field. I stiffened. Another high-pitched screech. There was a commotion. Someone was screaming and it continued in short panicked bursts. *Adam*. My lungs stopped working.

"What was that?" Knox leaned over to look around me, but I didn't stop to answer. I took off into a headlong sprint. Others from around the campfire were snapping to attention. Some were already hurtling on ahead of me.

My eyes flitted around for any sight of Adam, but I couldn't find him. As fast as my legs would take me, I followed the cries. "Help!" A girl. The urgency was clear. This wasn't a joke. I broke into a run. Why had I left Adam alone? What if something had happened? I followed the forms up ahead, running in the same direction, and closed in on Cassidy, who was surprisingly quick while intoxicated. I stumbled along the uneven ground, pushing aside stalks of grass that grew as high as my stomach.

"Over here." This time it was a boy's voice. Husky. Choked. Not Adam's. I didn't dare feel relieved.

I scanned the area and found two hunkered shapes beside a thin, bone-cragged tree trunk. A ring of people crowded around. I pushed through and there, to my relief, was Adam. He caught sight of me at the same moment, and he took three decisive steps over, grabbed me by the shoulders, and pressed me into his chest. He said "Victoria" into my hair, and I felt a flood of gratitude. "I thought you were hurt."

"I'm fine." I shook my head and let him squeeze me to him for another moment longer, even though his grip was too hard, and when he released me, I rubbed at the spots where his fingers had surely left marks.

When we separated, it was to find Emily O'Malley kneeling and crying in the dirt. Her boyfriend, Mason Worth, stood frozen behind her.

"Is Emily hurt?" Now it was Cassidy. She huffed and put her hands on her knees to breathe. Knox showed up in the small circle of onlookers, too. It was then that we saw it.

Or rather him.

The body leaned against the trunk of a sycamore tree. Someone aimed a flashlight at the lifeless form, and a gasp shot through the gathered crowd. The copper teeth of a bear trap closed around his calf, leaving scores of dried blood and flesh torn from the bone. I swallowed hard. Patches of red stained the grass beneath him. The opposite side of his shorts dangled, shorn just below the hip. Sinewy threads clung to the base of the fabric, hanging on to nothing. The boy's right leg was completely missing.

EIGHTEEN

I call it the "electrification pallet," but I hoped someday it'd get a new moniker based on my name. Like Bunsen burner or Erlenmeyer flask or galvanism. You know, that kind of thing. It's designed to be a built-in conductor plate with ports to negate the need for new incisions. It's brilliant.

--- --- ---

That was how the second body was found. At night. In a field. By teens who'd had too much to drink. It was ugly and real and had left tiny spiderwebs of death clinging to those who'd witnessed it so that I knew, in some small way, each student there would be marked forever, just as I'd been from the moment I found my father.

I couldn't help but be reminded of the eerily positioned cadaver cast in silver light as I stared down at Adam lying on the metal gurney the following day. I glanced away, trying to shake the thought, but my look landed on Adam's legs and my mind instantly formed the image of the porcelain bone sticking out from beneath the snapped trap. The boy's death wasn't a hunting accident. The missing leg had made that clear. Whoever had killed that boy had made good and sure he was dead. I rolled the scalpel handle between my fingers. If there was good news, though, it was that if someone knew about the car accident or about Adam, they seemed to have decided to leave us alone. There had been no more tire marks or evidence from that night left at my doorstep. In fact, the missing boy's death had in some ways offered Adam, Owen, and me a scrap of cover.

"Adam," I said, and I surprised myself at how much I sounded like my mother from when I was a kid. Back before my father had died. "I need you to look straight up at the ceiling, okay? Don't look at me until I say so. Can you do that?"

"But why? You're here, Victoria." He grasped my hand. I set it back down on the gurney, where I gave it a gentle pat.

"Because. I'm—we're—" I gestured to Owen, who was milling in the background, shifting his weight between untied sneakers. "We're going to install this . . . plate. . . ." I pointed to my surgical tray, where Owen's gadget lay next to forceps, clamps, and two more razor-sharp scalpels of different sizes. "So that it's easier for us to keep your energy supply charged. It's an electrification pallet. I invented—" Owen coughed. "*We* invented it. For you."

Adam nodded, looking every inch the child waiting for his measles shot, and directed his eyes up toward the crumbling ceiling.

I pulled a pair of plastic gloves from their box and slid them over my hands, popping the wrists into place, and then slipped into a shabby lab coat. "You'll tell me if this hurts," I said, still wishing we had access to an anesthetic, even though, with Adam, we shouldn't need one. "Owen?"

He stared down at his shoes while he put on a pair of gloves. I could hear him breathing through his nose. He edged around to stand on the other side of the gurney. I zeroed in on the center of Adam's bare chest where his rib cage joined together at the sternum, a flat piece of vertical bone that ran from his collarbone down to the bottom of his lungs. I placed my pointer finger high up on the blade of the scalpel and positioned it in the narrow crease between his pectoral muscles.

Blood seeped out. I drew the incision down twelve inches, slicing through the tree-branch tapestry that decorated his skin. Owen whimpered. At the top and bottom of the line I'd cut, I made two horizontal lines, half the length, so that it looked as though I'd drawn an *I* on Adam's chest. I paused to examine my bloody handiwork.

I then replaced the scalpel on the surgical tray and retrieved a pair of forceps. Using my fingernails and the forceps, I was able to flip up a corner of Adam's skin at the middle seam and peel it back, opening him like the pages of a book. Owen choked. My eyes flitted to him. Milky white had crept up his face and neck. Fog coated his lenses, and his tongue kept protruding out of his mouth before he was able to swallow it back.

"Hold this," I ordered. Owen pinned back the flayed skin.

"Can I look yet?" Adam asked, pointing his eyes obediently to the ceiling.

"No," Owen and I both snapped in unison.

"I can't even look yet," said Owen, voice high with held breath. He stared up at the ceiling, too. "Not much of a view, eh?"

While Owen held Adam's flesh in place, I fetched the plate. Owen had designed it exactly as I'd envisioned, only better. I slid the plate into the gaping wound. The metal grated against bone. The plate was outfitted with four holes, evenly spaced around the perimeter.

"You can let go now." There was no need to tell Owen twice. The flaps of skin fell back into place, and the plate disappeared from sight. Owen cupped his hands over his mouth and breathed hard. "The worst part's over. Now you can stop overreacting."

"Over . . ." His voice shook. "Overreacting. To this?" He waved his hand over Adam's body. "There's a person under there, Tor."

I stared at my nearly completed design. Pride swelled in my breast. "I know."

With a needle and thread, I made quick work of the stitches needed to sew Adam back together. I flipped my composition book open and examined the device measurements, using them to mark his chest where the holes were fitted in the plate. "There . . . there . . . and there," I told Owen. "Now for the finishing touches."

Owen's hand shook as he took the small hand drill from me. He stared for a long moment before positioning the drill over the first hole. A bead of sweat quivered off the tip of his nose as he turned the crank and punctured the skin.

Four times he drilled the holes and four times he filled them with shiny, silver rims through which you could peek through and barely see the plate below.

"It's perfect," I exhaled.

Owen's tongue spilled out of his mouth again. He heaved once and dropped the drill. His shoes pounded up the stairs. He pushed open the hatch door and crawled out into the open air, where I could hear him retching aboveground.

"You're finished," I told Adam.

Dazed, Adam sat up. He pinched his chin to his chest. "Can I see?"

I scanned the room for a mirror. When I couldn't find one, I dumped out the surgical tray and handed it to Adam. I stood over his shoulder while he stared at the distorted reflection without uttering a word.

"See? Instead of new incisions, the wires will go here." I touched the silver rims gleaming on his chest. Owen had even installed the radio transmitter so that the diathermy device no longer needed to be taped to Adam's chest.

It was another breakthrough. Adam ran his finger over and over the length of the incision. Nearly perfect.

Nearly.

NINETEEN

Adam articulates primitive levels of distress at the lack of identity that stems from his memory loss. Teenage identity crisis with a twist. With more experiences, he's showing more promising signs of self-expression.

The recharge process does not seem to be further damaging the nervous system. Rather, the damage to the neocortex and other brain structures appears to have occurred at death and the electricity post-reanimation may be having the effect of jump-starting physical sensation. Physical therapists use a similar process of "waking up" muscles after invasive surgery by using shock therapy.

But I'm not holding my breath.

— — —

The storm cellar door clanged open, and I climbed out of the hole in the ground and onto the surface, stepping into the yellow glow of the flood lamps, where moths were swarming. I took a deep breath of fresh air and wiggled my fingers, which were finally free of the blood-soaked gloves. Owen was sitting on the hood of his Jeep. Einstein lay curled up in the dirt next to his tire. He hopped off and dusted the back of his jeans.

Patches of color had returned to his cheeks, but there were sickly circles underneath his eyes. "Are you reviving him or torturing him for matters of national security?" His chuckle was weak.

I glanced over my shoulder, back down to the cellar laboratory's depths. I'd tested the new device. It had worked, but it hadn't stopped Adam from screaming the entire way through, all the way up until when I shut down the power.

The screen door to the house opened with a loud *thwack*, and Mom ambled unsteadily onto the porch steps. "Tor!" Sometimes when Mom drank, she reminded me of an angry toddler. "Tor!" Reluctantly, I looked back toward the house.

"What, Mom?" My body tensed at the idea that my mom might have heard Adam screaming, too. I looked at Owen, preparing to blame it all on him if necessary.

She craned her neck to look at the roof. "Don't you hear that racket?" My heart thudded. "I thought I told you to fix that weather turner. I know I told you to stop that squawking, Tor." A deep sigh of relief. The first hints of alcohol laced her words, turning them slow and lazy, a telltale sign. It was a Saturday, so she didn't have to work at the law firm, and I knew she'd been nursing her first drinks early.

"It's a weather vane and it's just rusty. Mom, we're busy out here. Owen and I are working." The first sprinkles of stars gathered in the translucent sky.

Her lips pursed, forming deep lines around her mouth. What would my father think of her if he could see her now? She grumbled and glared at the roof again, where the metal rooster spun a quarter turn and let out a hair-raising screech. "Suit yourself." She spat on the ground and disappeared behind the screen door.

"One of these days she's going to figure out what a terrible daughter you are."

I rolled my eyes and rubbed my forehead like a doctor coming out of surgery to deliver the prognosis. "She's not exactly going to be named Mother of the Year," I said, feeling a flush of embarrassment for her. "Anyway, forget her. Adam's in there muttering that he just wants to remember. I can't get him to say anything else," I said. "He's practically catatonic. I don't know. If I could just get him to feel something, maybe it'd help."

"Still nothing?" I shook my head. Owen's mouth twisted. "And emotionally?"

"Still not much improvement there, either."

"Well, what'd you expect? If there was ever an excuse for a man to be emotionally stunted, death has to be it."

"Except he's not really dead."

"Vitally challenged? Is that more politically correct? I'd hate to offend here."

"For your information, he has all of his vital signs." Another unwelcome reminder of the body found in the field. I was only seventeen and already I'd seen three dead bodies in my life. It was beginning to feel excessive. "Anyway, I'm not sure finding a dead body shortly after his own death helped in the emotional-stunting department."

Owen sighed. "Can I see him?"

"Okay, but be nice," I warned, and led him back in. Einstein's collar jangled after us.

Downstairs, Adam straightened upon seeing Owen. His skin was clear and his eyes were sharp with the fresh dose of energy. "Rough day," Owen quipped. Adam didn't flinch. "Right." Owen pulled up a spare stool and took a seat opposite Adam. "A couple questions of my own, if you don't mind," he said. "What's making you, you know, yell like a banshee when Tor recharges you, Adam? Is it pain?"

Adam stared down at his lap. "I don't know. I can't remember."

"So you're not feeling physical pain then? You're screaming about something else."

"I don't feel anything. Except sometimes. Right after. My fingers." He waggled them. "They get . . . tingly."

At this, Owen glanced at me. "That's improvement. And what about happy or sad? Do you feel any of that?"

"I don't know. I can't tell. Mostly, I feel blank."

144

Owen nodded. "That's what I thought. There's a technique I've been studying since . . . since you came along called emotion and memory retrieval. See, the amygdala, along with the hippocampus and pre-frontal cortex"—he pointed to different spots along his own skull—"store emotional memories even if you don't know it. Emotional stimuli are used to retrieve buried feelings along with any associated memory. Since we're working with a blank slate, so to speak, I think we'll have to prompt the resurfacing of those feelings. We've got to create the memories rather than just rely on a mood-dependent mem-ory retrieval system."

"Somebody's been doing extra credit," I said. We'd been taking turns researching Freudian studies of psychosocial development at night, but this was beyond textbook psychology. "So you're saying we're going to unbury what's already in there."

Owen blushed. "It's simple cognitive neuroscience, really."

Adam rose to his feet. His height cleared Owen by nearly an entire head. He peered around the room and then his gaze landed on a small hand shovel. He crossed the room and picked it up. "Here," he said to Owen, eyes wide. "Unbury them."

BRIGHT, COLORED LIGHTS twinkled off the fairground tents. Our shoes kicked through dust. The crowd was thin for a Sunday night. We were arriving on the tail end of park hours. A country song blared through the loudspeakers as we snaked between booths.

Much to Adam's relief, we'd explained that we wouldn't be using an actual shovel to create memories and uncover repressed emotion and physical sensation. Owen suggested that we start by getting Adam out of the laboratory more, and the fairgrounds were his first thought. I stared wide-eyed at the flashing lights of the Milky Way, the main stretch of carnival games, at the entrance of which a man with a handlebar mustache was advertising goldfish as prizes.

"If we're going to make you memories, we better start from the beginning," Owen declared, throwing his arms out wide to welcome us. "Childhood ones." I plugged my ears to block out the sound of a twangy guitar. Owen pushed my hands down. "Stop it. I made some of my best memories here." He reminded me of Willy Wonka, and this was his chocolate factory.

It had been at least ten years since I'd gone to a fair, and even then it was hard to imagine a miniature Tor dying to ride the Tilt-A-Whirl.

Adam sniffed the air. "I'm starving, Victoria."

"Adam, we're here for a reason." I pulled a pen and notebook from my purse. "Now, where to go for maximum impact . . ." I bit the cap of my pen.

"The man needs to eat." Owen rolled his eyes and thumped Adam on the back. "When it comes to caloric intake, my friend, you've come to the right place." Owen led Adam over to a large stall where I could practically taste the grease and burning sugar, and it made my mouth fill up with spit. "They will fry anything here," Owen explained.

"We're wasting time." I tapped my pen on the cover of my notebook. "Our background research tells us that long-term memories are influenced by the emotion experienced when creating the memory as well as the feelings experienced during the memory retrieval," I said, beginning to tick through the steps of the scientific method. "Our unknown variable is whether we're actually causing Adam to re-experience a buried memory from his own childhood or whether this is a new memory altogether. I think for the purposes of the experiment, we have to assume we're combining the learning experience with the emotion of retrieval. I can study the effects under both assumptions when I analyze the data."

Owen looked up at the sign. "Fried Oreos. Fried cheesecake. Fried honey bun. Fried *butter*."

I scanned the fair. "Now, how to test our hypothesis."

"Tor, what do you want?" Owen nudged me.

I glanced at the menu. "Does everything have to be fried?"

"Owen said that you fried me, too, Victoria."

I glared at Owen. He scuffed his shoes in the dirt and whistled, ignoring the fact that I was shooting lasers through his head with my eyeballs. After a few moments of deliberation, he ordered us four fried Oreos and a corn dog to share.

"Now can we please get back to the experiment?" I stomped my foot impatiently.

Owen stooped down to whisper in my ear. "Pro tip: You might not want to refer to the human standing beside you as an experiment. It's tacky. Here, have a corn dog." He shoved the stick between my fingers.

For his part, Adam took in the fairgrounds slack-mouthed and blinking rapidly. A tattooed carny with a giant mallet offered him a chance at a swing to ring the bell. "First one's free," he said, leering. Adam skittered back.

The corn dog burned my mouth, and I handed it off to Adam to devour. "We should do something that combines a strong physical sensation with a strong emotional one," I said.

"Relax." Owen pulled a wad of tickets from his pocket. "I know exactly where to go." Sometimes, I could swear Owen had never met me at all. I didn't do relaxed. Especially when I wasn't in control of all the variables.

Still, we followed Owen past the food stalls and the fair games. He doled four tickets out to Adam and me and tore off two more for himself and, at the front of the line, handed them to the Ferris wheel operator.

We piled into a three-person bench with me crammed into the middle. The operator pulled the bar down over our laps, and the ride lurched to life, jolting us back into our seats. "Hey, I remember this," I said. "My dad took me on this Ferris wheel when I was a kid."

"See?" Owen's eyebrows shot over the rims of his glasses. "It's working already."

The ground swept out from underneath us. The pull of gravity planted me to the bench. We arced clockwise, out and up. Our feet dangled. Adam's hands tightened around the bar and twisted. He pushed as far back into his seat as he could go.

"How far into the sky are we going?" he asked.

Below us, the fairgrounds shrank to a pocket-sized scale. "All the way to the top," I said.

He grunted.

I leaned forward. I liked the view looking straight down where the angle was the sharpest and most thrilling. Adam reached his arm in front of my chest and pushed me back into my seat. The bench swayed in response.

"Be careful, Victoria," he said. His voice was strained.

"I'm with him," Owen said. "Don't rock the proverbial boat, please."

"This was your idea," I reminded him.

The horizon sank lower and lower as we soared over the tree line. Our trajectory began taking us backward as we began to reach the crest. At the top, the ride jerked to a halt.

"Adam?" I glanced over again and found that his eyes were squeezed shut so tightly that wrinkles reached all the way to his temples. "Adam, open your eyes." He shook his head violently and the trolley car swayed. "Adam, this won't work if you don't open your eyes." But I already knew that the experiment *was* working, because the emotion he was feeling was fear. Fear was useful. Fear was good. Fear kept people from running out in front of buses and diving off cliffs. My mind raced with the possibilities of what else I might be able to evoke in Adam. Were the primal responses easier to unearth? If I tried, could I make Adam very angry?

I brought my thoughts back into the bench dangling high above the ground. One thing at a time.

Hands still wrapped in a death grip around the safety bar, Adam peeled open an eyelid, followed by his other. He stared out of the chairlift. Up here, the music couldn't reach. The metal creaked and groaned. Our bench swung gently in the breeze.

"What do you think?" I asked.

"I—I don't know," he said.

I put my hand on his. "You do know. Tell me what you see," I coaxed him. "Describe it to me."

He shifted his weight in the seat. "I see," he paused, "dark." Another pause. "With little lights."

"And how do you think they look?"

He focused on them. "I think . . . they look pretty." I leaned over and gave Owen a meaningful look. "Which reminds me of your hair." He fidgeted again. "At school, even from far away, I can spot your hair and know that you're close and will come to get me. So it reminds me of that. And I like that."

My heart pulled at the arteries that attached it to my chest. I looked down and let my auburn hair fall around my face to hide my grin. Adam was mine. He would always be mine.

"You should write for Hallmark, man." I could feel—though not hear—Owen laughing beside me, and I elbowed him in the gut. "Hey, watch it!" He rubbed at his rib.

Just then, the Ferris wheel motor began to whir, and we were being taken on a slow, controlled fall to the bottom. Adam closed his eyes again, and his knuckles turned whiter than normal.

I had to assure him twice that it was okay to let go of the bar once we'd reached the bottom. He wobbled sideways when he got off the ride, and Owen and I caught his arms.

"Victoria?" he said as we exited the gates of the Ferris wheel. "I learned another thing to add to things I do not like." He craned his neck and stared up at where we'd experienced our bird's-eye view. "Heights."

After the Ferris wheel, I decided we should try to test our hypothesis by evoking a more positive emotional response in the subject. The three of us traipsed over to the petting zoo, which I figured had a good chance of making him happy. This turned out to be a serious miscalculation since the pigs and miniature horses seemed to have a sixth sense about Adam. He spent ten minutes trying to chase them into corners to pet them, and the goats kept trying to nibble his jeans. No sooner than I'd written it, I scratched "interaction with animals" off my list.

It was when leaving the petting zoo that I spotted four people who had the capability of ruining our entire evening. Cassidy, Knox, Paisley, and William were making their way toward the Ferris wheel, which went to show how little there was to do in Hollow Pines on the weekends.

Paisley had a large plush bear straddled over her shoulders. It was pink and was wearing a sombrero and was probably taller than her. Cassidy spotted us first. She squealed when she saw Adam.

"You guys! I didn't know y'all were here." She came running over. Her face turned grave. "It's so nice to get out and do something *normal* after . . ." She lowered her voice. "You know."

"I don't know." Owen shrugged, even though she clearly hadn't been talking to him.

Her eyes were wide as if she were seeing it all over again in her head. "The body. Victoria, surely you told him. My mom is making me be home by ten thirty tonight. Emily's and Mason's parents are going to make them see a shrink. Paisley, look who it is." She turned around to Paisley, who was walking up at a much slower, less enthusiastic pace.

"Well, who would have thought we'd have run into a real, live celebrity," Paisley said. She looked ridiculous parading around with a sombrero-sporting bear. But that was the thing about being popular. It was a self-fulfilling prophecy. Popular kids didn't do cool things. Things were cool because they did them.

Adam looked behind him and to the sides.

"She means you." Cassidy laughed. "Haven't you seen? The papers are already reporting you as Hollow Pines High's resident football savior." She clasped her hands together in a mock prayer. The fact that the papers were reporting anything about high school football practice when there was a killer on the loose was a miracle. Then again, that *was* the Hollow Pines religion.

Adam stopped searching and stared blankly at her.

"Well, it was nice running into you," I said, wanting to extract myself. "We should be getting home early, too. We all like having two legs and our hearts still beating, if you know what I mean." A joke about a murder. That was a classy touch.

Knox narrowed his already squinty eyes. "Hold on a minute," he said. "You're not too good for hanging out with your teammates for a second, are you?"

Adam's eyebrows squished together. "Too good? I'm a good guy. I'm Adam."

Knox's canines caught the light, and I could just make out the shadows of acne scars in the hollows of his cheeks. "Maybe a little friendly competition?"

"We should really be going," I said, remembering how I'd said something similar to Knox two nights earlier.

"One game." Knox held up his finger. "Live a little, Torantula." The guy did not seem to understand the word *no*. I clenched my teeth. Fine then. He could have it his way. This time.

"Great," I said, rolling back my shoulders and cracking my knuckles. "How about that thing?" I pointed to the "Test Your Strength" booth that we'd passed earlier. The tattooed carny was pacing the perimeter, holding his top-heavy mallet.

Knox and William turned to check. William pushed up his sleeves and nodded.

I looked at Owen and then at the twenty-foot-high tower. If the lever at the bottom was struck hard enough, a puck would shoot up the tower and ring the bell.

The group started to cross the distance to the game. "Wait," I called. "How about a wager?"

Knox crossed his arms. "What'd you have in mind?"

I glanced at William. His biceps were bigger than one of my legs. "Twenty bucks if either of you win. Twenty bucks if we win."

William cracked his knuckles. He spit on the ground and grinned.

Knox dug into the back of his jeans and pulled out a wad of bills. "How about a hundred?"

I stared at the crisp green cash. I didn't have twenty bucks let alone a hundred. Adam was big, but William was thicker with a neck like a pit bull. Then again, Adam was Adam.

I stuck out my hand. "Deal." We shook on it.

I tore off two more tickets and handed them to the operator after Knox and William had done the same. An intricate dragon rippled off the carny's forearm as he handed the mallet over to Knox. Fire and smoke breathed down the back of the man's hands and down to his knuckles.

"Batter up," said the carny.

Paisley whistled at Knox, and he made a show of flexing his muscles. "Watch and learn, ladies." He bowed and swung the mallet onto his shoulder. Then, with both hands cupped around the end of the handle, he took a giant lunge forward and brought the mallet head down on the lever with a springboard crash.

The puck traveled just over halfway up the tower, a trail of blue lights following in its wake.

He stuck out his lower lip. "That's harder than it looks."

He tipped the handle over to William. In William's strong grip, the mallet looked much thinner and lighter. When he swung it into position, it appeared to be no heavier than a household hammer. I bit my lip. When it came to brute strength, William must have Adam beat. I shifted my weight, my stomach clenching and unclenching.

He twisted his grip, then, like a warrior bringing down an ax, he wielded the mallet straight over his head and slammed it onto the lever. The puck shot up. It kept going, past the blue lights, past the red, one foot from the top, the lights turned yellow. The momentum petered out, and the puck fell back down to earth.

William ran his tongue along his teeth. "Not too shabby." He strutted. "Not too shabby at all. You're up, Smith."

"Adam." I grabbed him by both arms. "Just swing that hammer thing as hard as you can, okay? You've got this." I held my breath. All I could do now was bet on my horse.

"Will it help me remember things?" he said.

I held out a flat hand and wobbled it from side to side. "Eh. Probably not. But it'd make me awfully happy." My eyes twitched in the direction of Knox and his *I know something you don't know* grin.

He hiked the mallet up. "Okay then," he said flatly. "I'll do it." He walked over and, casually, without stopping, thwacked the lever. He dropped the mallet in the dirt right away and walked over to me.

I slapped my hand over my eyes, and just as I was getting ready to mutter a curse word under my breath, there was a brassy clang up above and then the "Test Your Strength" booth erupted into loud sirens that flashed pink and yellow lights.

"Adam! You did it!" Cassidy squealed. She turned to Paisley and stuck out her tongue and then spanked her backside, teasing. "Told you."

I jumped up and down. Knox and William reluctantly fished for their wallets and handed me fifty dollars each.

I snapped the bills between my fingers. "Thanks, boys."

"Yeah, yeah," Knox said. But he reached out to shake Adam's hand. "Come sit with us tomorrow, Smith," William said as the group began trickling away.

Cassidy grabbed my arm and squeezed it. I could smell the faint hint of alcohol and Slurpee on her breath. "You too, Tor."

I skipped over to Adam and Owen. "A contribution to the Tor needs a new phone fund," I said, stuffing it into my front pocket. "Now let's take a victory lap." I felt lucky, glowing. A sudden rush of energy pulsed through me.

"You guys take your lap of victory," Owen said. "I've got to find a bathroom. I'll meet you back at the car."

I offered my arm to Adam. "Five minutes," I said, and then Adam and I went back into the maze of rides and fairground stalls.

We'd been walking only a short distance when I spotted a familiar ride. "Oh! I loved this one as a kid."

"The Old Mill," Adam read the western-themed sign. "What is it?"

"It's awesome. Or, well, actually maybe it was only one of those things that was awesome because I was a kid, but basically, you get on these little floating boats and you're pulled along a waterway through an old mill and you wind up at a mine shaft." Two of us would barely fit on one boat, but the thought of Adam and me riding the Old Mill together sounded so silly to me that I had to try. "We're making new memories, remember? And if we want to get you to feel the feels, trust me, this is a good one. It'll be fun. You'll see."

I led him up the short flight of steps, forked over my last few tickets, and lowered myself onto the bench of one of the miniature boats. It was shaped like a mill chute, and when Adam followed in after me, the water splashed up around us. He caught himself on the sides for balance and, once settled, peered down into the murky river below.

There was a click, and then the boat dropped down a couple inches, and we began floating into a tunnel.

We were quiet for a moment. The air became dank and musky, and we were immersed in total blackness. I listened to the calming churn of the water.

"What are you feeling right now?" I asked as the boat slid from pitch-black into a well-lit portion of the ride decorated with cheesy animatronic farm animals that greeted us. We passed a bunny waving his carrot. "First thing that pops into your head, go."

"Nothing."

I sighed. "Think, Adam. You have to be feeling something. You just need to learn to express it, okay?"

He dipped his finger over the side of the boat and let it trail through the water. "Like what?"

"I don't know. People can feel all kinds of things. Happy, sad, angry, in love, nervous, scared."

"I was scared earlier."

"And now?"

We floated into a room littered with trees with trunks that had faces and waterwheels that scooped up buckets of water and poured them out the other side.

"Now, I'm not scared anymore." He paused. "Because we're off the big sky wheel."

I pinched my lips together. *Nothing, nothing, nothing*, we kept running up against this great big wall of nothing. We may as well beat our heads against it. After only a couple minutes, we were nearing the end of the ride. I knew because at the entrance of a dark cave was a white and pink sign that read TUNNEL OF LOVE. I scrubbed a hand over my face. I needed something momentous—no—better yet, something *memorable*.

We passed beneath it and the light disappeared. The tunnel was so dark, the hand in front of my face went missing.

I turned in my seat to face him. "Adam, this is purely for academic purposes, okay? And for the furtherance of science."

Before he could ask questions, I reached up and put my hands on either side of his face, and in the name of science, the most noble of pursuits for truth and knowledge known to man, I squished his cheeks together and pushed my lips firmly onto his.

It was then that I made an important discovery. All those stories about couples getting hot and heavy in the Tunnel of Love had been grossly exaggerated. The word *tunnel* itself was generous. Even if I'd wanted to, there would have been no time to get hot or heavy, let alone both. No sooner had I planted my lips, which I realized way too late probably felt like snakeskin, than our tiny vessel had floated clear of the tunnel.

The carnival lights hit my face, and my eyes snapped open. Adam's eyes were round saucers an inch in front of my own. He yelled and jerked away. The boats of the Old Mill were not deep-sea vessels, it turned out, and they weren't made for the pitches and waves of the ocean. The boat tilted with Adam's weight. Dirty water rushed over the side. I shrieked. Adam tumbled overboard, and when the boat tipped back the other way, I was next.

TWENTY

Progress. Real-world memory creation and emotional stimuli appear to have stimulated at least a portion of the neocortex whereby the subject has exhibited signs of nuanced human interaction such as good humor, increased verbal context, and self-expression.

— — —

Last night I had a dream that I came across a dead body while walking in a cotton field. The cadaver stared at me through hollowed-out eyes, its bald scalp glowing in the moonlight. It reached its hands out for me, scratching my jeans with the exposed bones in its fingers. I didn't scream. I didn't even run. Instead, just before I woke, I dropped to my knees and kissed it.

I couldn't avoid Adam forever.

Could I?

I stared down the long hallway where he was shoving textbooks into his locker like I was staring down the barrel of a gun. I took a deep breath and clenched the strap of my bag. Okay, so maybe I'd taken the experiment too far. I could admit that. It was too soon, too weird. Oh god, the look on his face. I might as well have caught him on the toilet. *That* face.

Trust me, if I had any ego about such things, it would be officially obliterated. But there was no rewinding time and no amount of silent car rides and eye contact avoidance was going to fix it. Besides, we weren't twelve.

I came to a deliberate stop at his locker. "Hello, Adam." He jumped and dropped his book bag. Balanced books splattered to the floor. "Let me help." We both bent down at the same time and knocked heads. "*Ooof!*" I nursed the spot on my forehead.

"Did I do that?" Adam reached to touch the mark but poked me in the eye as I was already staging my recovery to collect a book.

"Ow!" I cried.

He snatched his hand back to his chest. "I'm sorry. I'm sorry, Victoria. I didn't mean to."

I cupped my eye like I was a pirate, but when I looked at him through my other eye, the one that wasn't streaming tears down my face, he immediately switched to staring at the floor. I stanched the flow of tears and wiped my cheek. Adam didn't so much blush as go splotchy around the neck.

"Adam," I said. "I have seen you in your boxers." The way that this was related to the kiss was so obvious to me it seemed beyond the need for explanation.

Adam methodically picked up each of his books without glancing at me once before standing. I followed, adding a single notebook to his pile. He stacked them in his locker.

I tilted my face to the ceiling. "I'm sorry I tried to make out with you!" I said, shaking my fists. The space around me fell to a hush. Heads swiveled. Adam's eyes bugged. I stepped in closer. "I thought you would feel something. That's the only reason I did it, and I promise not to do it again."

"It felt funny."

"Right. Off the list. I'm your creator. Strictly your creator. We'll think of something else. Something better."

"Like food?"

I pushed him toward the cafeteria. "Is that all you ever think about?"

The lunchroom stank of French fries and pepperoni pizza. We got both, and Adam got mashed potatoes and gravy, which he'd now at least learned to use a fork to shovel in. We met Owen at the end of the line, where he handed me an extra Diet Coke he'd snagged from the vending machine.

"Thanks," I said, falling in alongside him to walk back to our usual lunch table near the row of overflowing trash cans.

"Wait," Adam called. Owen and I both turned, and I was surprised to find Adam still lingering several feet back. I felt a question mark form on my face. "You said we could eat with them, Victoria?"

"You did?" Owen asked.

"I did." I groaned. "A moment of weakness." I tilted my head and jutted my lower lip. "But wouldn't you rather have a root canal instead?" I asked.

"No." As usual, he didn't get the joke. Spending time with Adam was like bombing a stand-up routine in a comedy club night after night.

I closed my eyes and counted to three. "You coming?" I asked Owen.

He raised one eyebrow. "I think I'd prefer to see about that root canal. You go."

I scowled but followed Adam to the other table, one that was nowhere near the trash cans.

He pulled out my chair for me to sit. Paisley stopped and set her fork down in the Tupperware salad bowl she'd brought from home. She gawked at Adam. "Well, isn't that refreshing." She turned and smacked Knox in the shoulder. "When was the last time you did *that* for me, jackwad?"

Knox stuck his arms up in a cross, shielding himself. "Relax, woman. This isn't the fifties." He tossed his head, and his shaggy hair swooped to the side.

She stabbed her fork into a pile of leafy greens. It was always difficult to tell whether Knox and Paisley loved or hated each other. They'd been dating since the eighth grade and were known for loud fights in the hallway that featured slamming locker doors and a thesaurus full of synonyms for male and female genitalia. Afterward, Paisley would brag about the expensive makeup gifts Knox bought for her. A gold ring. A new phone cover. A steak dinner.

I scooted in my chair. The screeching it made sounded dangerously close to passing gas. I flattened my butt against the seat, looking around to see if anyone had noticed. But Cassidy was busy eyeing my pizza.

I glanced at her and then the pizza. "Uh, do you want some?" I asked, pushing the plate in her direction.

Cassidy jolted to attention. She licked her lips. "No, sorry, I brought lunch." She pushed the plate back in front of me and pulled out hummus and a ziplock baggie full of carrots.

"Really? Because world hunger is an issue very near and dear to my heart." I pressed my palm to my chest.

Catching our conversation, Paisley smirked.

Cassidy snapped off a bite of carrot. "World hunger, huh? You sound like a Miss America contestant. I guess there's a pageant girl in all of us." When I looked blankly at her, she continued. "Former Little Miss Atascosa County at your service." She sat up razor straight and interlocked her hands on the table. "If I had one wish," she recited, "it would be for world peace and to end hunger for little girls and boys everywhere."

"That's two wishes," I said.

She relaxed her posture and waved a hand. "Please, at eight years old, I was better at math than all the judges combined. I wouldn't have done pageants at all, but the winners get scholarships that my mom put into my college fund." She shrugged. "Hard to pass up."

I pinched cheese off the end of my slice and popped it into my mouth. I hadn't realized there were things like scholarships for twirling and wearing bikinis in public.

"Billy was telling us that his dad said we must have just missed the killer," said Paisley. "Because that body was fresh or else we would have smelled it. Can you believe that?" She leaned into Knox's shoulder. "Could have been any one of us."

I stared at my hands, trying to keep my mouth good and zipped, but as usual I couldn't. "That's not true. Well, not necessarily, anyway."

Paisley sat up, eagle-eyed. "And how would you know?"

I scratched behind my ear. "Because bodies don't start stinking until three or four days after they're dead." I looked up at the ceiling, thinking. "Whoever killed that boy could have done it days ago, in which case the killer would have been long gone. It's unlikely that any of us came close to being a murder victim." Everyone was staring at me, and I knew I was about to do that thing where I let my mouth run away just to quit from feeling awkward. "Bodies smell on account of the gas," I said. A few boys snickered. "It's true. A few days after someone dies, these bacteria in the body start to break it down. The pancreas is so full of bacteria that it basically digests itself."

"Sick," said Knox, wiping his forehead with his sleeve, then leaning forward to listen.

"The bacteria creates this really rank-smelling gas that causes the whole body to bloat. The eyeballs pop out of the sockets and the tongue gets all swollen." I puffed my cheeks and stuck my tongue out. "If a woman is pregnant when she dies, the bacteria produces so much gas that the baby will blow right out of her. It's called a coffin birth."

Cassidy covered her nose and her mouth.

"Jesus Christ." William thumped the table with his fist excitedly. "How do you know all this stuff, Victoria?"

Victoria? I blinked, remembering who I was with and what I was doing. I registered the strangeness of being called "Victoria" and felt the stillness of Adam behind me. The realization that I'd been going on and on about death and dying and corpses decomposing while one was sitting right beside me. "It's just science," I said, then fell silent.

Adam wasn't going to bloat and expel eyeballs out of his sockets, was he? His organs wouldn't liquefy. His skin wouldn't blister when I touched it in a week, a month, a year, would it? I thought of Adam's discoloration just before another shock set his organs back in motion. The green and blue-black bruising that surfaced under frosty skin. Sure signs of death.

"Sorry," I said to Adam when the conversation had picked up again. "That's . . . that's not you. I didn't mean—"

He moved his hand and placed it on my shoulder, his expression as still as a grave. "Just do me one favor," he said.

A rush of maternal instinct hit me squarely in the chest. "Anything," I said.

"Let me know if I start to smell."

"Adam!" I wanted to clap but kept my voice at a whisper. "Was that your first joke?"

He dropped his hand from my shoulder. The line of his brow curved down. "No," he said, and I realized that he hadn't been kidding at all. His takeaway from my conversation was that he actually did want me to tell him when he started to stink. So much for progress.

The table's conversation had turned to spray-on tans and shampoo brands. I pushed my chair back. Cassidy looked up. "Where are you going?"

"To the bathroom." I drew out my words and hiked my thumb over my shoulder. "Is that okay?" I said when she stared at me as though I should have requested a hall pass.

"Oh." She shoved the hummus and carrots aside. "I'll go with you."

"That's okay. Really." I moved to leave without her. Call me crazy, but I'd been peeing alone since I was five. Cassidy, however, had the quickness of a wild antelope. It must have been all those hours on the elliptical. They'd left her backside both perky and deceptively functional, and I had no problem hating her for it.

She was on my tail before I could take a single step. She trotted along beside me. "This is good, I needed to stretch." She put her arms up in the air and arced sideways. The bottom of her shirt lifted, leaving a space of skin above her jeans that didn't lump over the waistband like it did for everyone else. "Coach made us do squats for a half an hour straight on Friday because Ashley was late for practice."

"She does know torture is an international crime, right?" I swung open the door for the ladies' room and made a beeline for the nearest stall.

Cassidy didn't enter a stall of her own. In fact, when I sat down, I could see the toes of her shoes pointed in my direction just, I didn't know, standing there, I guessed. Was she seriously going to wait and listen to my urine stream? Was this normal?

"So," Cassidy began the moment I'd committed to start peeing. "It's . . . well, I guess we've never really gotten to hang out before."

"No time like the present, apparently." My eyes flitted up to the tiled ceiling, where there was a smattering of chewed-up gum. I twisted my head. How on earth did people get it up there?

"It's weird. Our paths just, like, never crossed until now."

I squeezed my eyes shut and tried to tune her out. "Ninth grade," I said through gritted teeth. *Idiot.* I regretted saying anything the instant it came out of my mouth.

"Huh?"

I sighed, unfurling sheets of toilet paper. "You put fliers up at the football games. A superunflattering picture with my number and the caption: *Call for a good time.* Effective, but zero points for originality." One of the Oilerettes had caught me picking a wedgie in my PE uniform and snapped a photograph. Three days of prank calls and I was convinced I'd have to get a new phone number. Finally, I just stopped checking voice mail altogether, a habit that had stuck.

"Oh." Her toes disappeared from my line of vision. "Right. It wasn't just you, though."

I wanted to say something to this, but I wanted to pee even more, so I did and then kicked the handle to flush.

"I'm really sorry about that." Cassidy followed me to the sink. In the mirror's reflection, I saw her bite her lip. "It wasn't me. I swear. Paisley has a tendency to take things a little too far." I stared at her through the mirror. "Okay, a lot too far."

I wiped my hands on the back of my jeans. Something in the way Cassidy said this felt sincere. "It's no big deal."

She lit up with the kind of smile you'd see on the "after" pics of an acne commercial. "So, how long have you and Adam been hooking up, anyway?" she asked all nonchalant. She even turned her nails over to examine them up close.

I wanted to leave, but Cassidy was standing directly and strategically between me and the door. "What does hooking up mean, anyway? People always say that—hooking up—what *is* that? Does it mean dating? Making out? Boning? These seem like pretty important distinctions except that no one ever knows what anyone else is talking about. I move for the uniformity of the phrase 'hooking up.' Who's with me?" I put my hand out, team-huddle-style.

Cassidy had a Tinker Bell laugh. "You're funny." She crossed her arms over her chest. "But seriously, how long have you and Adam been hooking up?"

I rolled my eyes. "We're not." I determined that at least in the Victoria Frankenstein dictionary, planting a surprise kiss during a carnival ride didn't meet the hookup threshold.

Her eyelashes fluttered over her cheeks. "Not?"

"No way." My neck felt sweaty and gross. "We're, I don't know, like brother and sister or something."

"Not hooking up," she repeated under her breath, now turning to fluff her hair in the mirror.

"That's what I said." I rocked back on my heels.

She pulled a canister of lip gloss out of her pocket and glided the wand over her mouth from corner to corner. "So you wouldn't mind, then, if I did." I could tell by the drop in her intonation that Cassidy wasn't asking a question. She smacked her lips together and stepped back to admire her reflection.

In that moment, I'd suddenly forgotten what to do with my hands, and my throat felt like someone had poured a bottle of Elmer's glue down it and the only thing that I could gurgle out was a weird strangled version of, "Of course not."

Of course not. I really was getting used to this lying thing.

TWENTY-ONE

The experiment results are unprecedented. The subject displays keen athletic ability, a pleasant demeanor in social settings, and the ability to interact with peers. A once-dead body has been absorbed by a high school. Adam is a near-perfect specimen. I'm reminded of the great scientist Ian Wilmut, who could find not one fault in his cloned sheep Dolly. I must be vigilant, though, if the story of Dolly is to be recalled, since that sheep had only half the life span of other sheep of her breed, so Wilmut must have been missing something.

— — —

In ten thousand years, creatures like you and me will be completely phased out, and the world will be overrun by Cassidy Hydes." I'd made the mistake of telling Owen about my lunchtime adventures, and this was his response. "And then someday a kindly old scientist will come extract our DNA from a preserved sample of fossilized amber and they'll create a whole park filled with misfits and rejects, and people will come from far and wide to gawk at the hideous creatures that once roamed the earth." Owen performed a dramatic sweep of his arm. "And that's when we'll go all crazy-eyed and try to rip their hearts out, and they'll try to Tase us or something but will ultimately decide that they should have never re-created us in the first place and leave us to be weirdo misfits all alone together on an island where there will hopefully be mai tais with those little umbrella straws."

"You have issues." I fitted my lab goggles over the bridge of my nose. "You know that, don't you? Real problems. You should see a psychiatrist."

Owen slid the lab sheet off the table and skimmed through the instructions. "Not this one again. Didn't we do this foam experiment in class last year?"

Students were busy carting buckets of supplies over to the four-top lab tables.

"No, year before that." I grabbed a Bunsen burner from the back counter. "Cassidy's not *that* good-looking."

Owen crumpled up the instructions and tossed them toward the trash can. He missed. Of course. "You can't ignore the facts, Tor. Process of natural selection. Girls like Cassidy Hyde are genetically superior to the rest of us."

"Gee, thanks," I said, lighting the burner. "I'm not exactly a troll, Owen."

He did a once-over. "It's hard to tell," he said matter-of-factly. "Because you dress like a boy half the time."

"I do not!" I looked down, pouting. "I dress, I don't know, boho . . . chic. That's a thing, right?" I tugged at the frayed edge of my over-sized tee, trying to recall the last time I went shopping.

Owen measured out a half cup of 6 percent hydrogen peroxide. Our teacher insisted that we do the experiments with the rest of the class, but we were allowed to work on our own projects afterward. "Why are you getting your granny panties all in a wad? Who cares? I would take you over a Cassidy any day." He smirked. "They're a dime a dozen, which"—he scratched his chin—"observationally really serves to further my hypothesis on the increased prevalence of physically gifted human specimens, but that's beside the point."

I filled the beaker with water and turned the valve to start the flow of propane gas. My chin hovered an inch over the tabletop. "You know, maybe you're *right*." I frowned, straightening. "Take black panthers for instance. They're more plentiful than the spotted leopards but they actually *are* leopards. They're just melanistic."

"Meaning?" He poured a tablespoon of yeast into the beaker once the water had started to bubble.

"Black panthers are hot leopards. The color is a recessive trait but since it's more advantageous for ambushing . . ." I bit my lip, thinking. "They win."

"See, and all this time I thought we were talking about Cassidy."

I added green food coloring to the mixture and turned up the flame while Owen drained the hydrogen peroxide. "I'm saying that physical characteristics are the greater indicator of genetic evolution."

"At least two significant parts of her are *highly* evolved." A dollop of dish soap. An ingredient Owen and I had thought to add on our own without consulting the teacher.

"That's it." I walked around the lab table. I could never think while stationary. "Doesn't the greatest scientific breakthrough of the century deserve the best model on the market?"

The flame reflected two orange flecks in the lenses of Owen's glasses. "I think what you're referring to is the eugenics movement. Probably not ground you want to tread." I ignored him. What I was proposing was not the select breeding of the human race for the most desirable characteristics. I was thinking about Adam. And he at least was one of a kind.

The beaker's mint-green liquid had begun to transform and expand into a swirling foam that overflowed the glass and spurted out onto the table.

"Need I remind you that you're contemplating letting Adam date people that once left a dead fish in your gym locker to convince people you'd stopped showering again."

"It was your idea," I snapped. "Plus, the weird part is that everyone was *nice* to me today. It was like they all had amnesia and made a collective decision to forget who I was. Even Paisley was tolerable."

"People in town would give up both kidneys if they thought it'd make our football team win. Hanging out with you is mildly more comfortable than death by organ donation. If Adam likes you, then so do they. Stir." He pointed. I grabbed the pipette and swished it around our mixture. I had promised Adam we'd find some other way to make him feel, and while I watched froth tendrils crawl along the black surface of the countertop, I realized that I might know what that something was. What he needed was a chemical reaction.

"Can I borrow forty bucks?" I picked my bag off the floor. The lab partners next to us had somehow succeeded only in boiling water, or at least that was what it looked like.

"Were you even listening to me?" Owen scratched behind his ear. "Because sometimes I get this weird sense that voices in your head are way louder than the voices out here." He drew a circle in the air with his pencil eraser.

"Please, you make me sound crazy."

"I think you accomplish that all on your own."

I held my hand out, palm up. Owen stared at it.

"You literally just won a hundred dollars last night at the carnival. What do you need a loan from the Bloch Bank for?"

I tapped my foot on the floor. "Because I need *that* money for a cell phone, remember? Again . . ." I shrugged. "Your idea."

He rolled his eyes but fished his wallet out of the back pocket of his jeans and reluctantly forked over two twenties. I snatched the crisp bills and folded them in half. "Thanks. You know, sometimes I think I'm the only sane one here." I headed to the front of the classroom, and just as my hand found the doorknob, a shrill voice came from behind me.

"Ms. Frankenstein?" it said. "Where do you think you're going? Class isn't over for five more minutes."

I knew the "time is relative" joke wouldn't fly on Ms. Dot, who taught chemistry, not physics, but that didn't stop me from considering it. Instead, I turned slowly on the spot, composing my mouth into something I hoped resembled a smile. To put this in perspective, for the past seven years, every single photograph in a yearbook that appeared over the words, *Frankenstein, Victoria* depicted a girl with a haircut that no matter the grade always seemed to be recovering from some sort of salon calamity and absolutely no smile. So I wasn't what one would call a traditional "charmer."

"Owen and I finished our experiment, Ms. Dot." Smile stayed pinned in place. "I'm sorry, did you have something else planned for today?" *Keep smiling, keep smiling.*

Ms. Dot was a woman of cheesy holiday sweaters and, just by looking at her, you could tell she knew how to knit. The corners of her glasses swooped into purple wings that mimicked the patches of frizz on either side of her head. "No, I suppose not. But there's still—"

"Thanks, Ms. Dot." I cut over her like *but there's still* were a perfectly natural end to whatever it was she was trying to say, and I didn't feel bad because, really, if teachers expected me to sit through an entire period, wasn't it their job to keep me interested enough to stay there?

The later lunch slot was still in session, and the hallway smelled like cafeteria burritos. I heard the door open behind me, and I picked up my pace, expecting to hear Ms. Dot.

"What are you doing?" This was a Ms. Dot thing to say, but unless Ms. Dot had swallowed a teenage boy whose voice just cracked, it wasn't her.

I turned to see Owen following after me in what had to be the least athletic run of all time. His skinny legs bowed inward, and his ankles seemed to be made of melted cheese.

"Setting up an experiment," I said. "Keep up, Bloch." I led him to a card table draped in orange and black streamers and a puff-painted sign. A girl glanced up from her phone screen. "Four Homecoming tickets." That was a sentence I never thought I'd say.

Owen's money disappeared into the girl's lockbox, and Owen groaned. "Has anyone ever told you, you don't have a lot of patience?"

I counted the four tickets and handed one to Owen. "No, I try not to talk to anyone besides you and Adam."

The bell rang to mark the end of the period. I grabbed Owen's hand and pulled him toward the school's west wing, where Adam had History. Students began pouring out of classrooms, and it was like trying to walk up a waterfall.

I spotted Adam's head over the crowd, the expression on his face as vacant as if he'd truly been dead. I waved my hand. His eyes brightened, and he returned an excited wave, knocking a passerby in the skull with his elbow. He didn't notice, and the kid slunk away, rubbing his scalp.

I had to admit, it was a good feeling being someone else's Christmas morning. Adam hugged me, and my feet lifted off the ground. "Adam." I held him by the elbows so that he would focus. "Remember what we talked about this morning?"

His eyebrows squished together. "No more kissing?"

"Wait, *what*?" Owen butted into our brain trust.

"No more kissing *me*," I corrected.

"Wait, huh?" Owen looked from me to Adam then back to me. "When did *this* happen?"

"I need you to do something, okay?" I asked Adam. "You like Cassidy, right? Well, I want you to take these two tickets and ask her if she wants to go to Homecoming with you. Say it nicely, though."

"Ask her to come with us?"

"No, ask her to go with you. Only you." I put my finger on his chest.

"Can we go back to this kissing thing?" Owen was asking. Another bell rang. "Because I feel like I missed something here." He raised his hand. "Follow-up question: Was there tongue?"

I spotted Cassidy applying fresh lip gloss in her locker mirror. How many times a day did a girl need to apply goo to her mouth, I wondered, and for a second, I questioned my plan to send Adam gallivanting off into the arms of someone who probably spent upward of ten minutes a day maintaining the appropriate level of goo to a part of the body that was intended for eating. And kissing, I quickly added in my mind. At least for girls like Cassidy Hyde.

It didn't matter. She was, as Owen said, a perfect specimen, and it helped that she also wasn't completely brain-dead. I pointed to where she was now shaking her long hair over her shoulders and pulling it into a ponytail. "She's right over there. She'll like it, Adam. I promise. You like Cassidy, right?"

Adam looked between us. "Yes, she's nice to me and smiles."

"Great, then go. Shoo!" I waved him across the hall toward her and shrank back to observe.

Like a kid being sent to his first day of preschool, Adam ventured to the other end of the hall with his tickets in hand, only a single glance back at us. I tugged Owen along for a closer view. We stayed half hidden behind a trophy case. I leaned forward so that I could see better.

"You have officially become a creepy helicopter mom. Does this concern you? I mean, you're only seventeen, and conventional wisdom would say that you should probably be getting drunk and making out with dudes of the non-dead variety."

"Shhh!" I slapped Owen's arm. Adam was talking to Cassidy. Adam looked happy about talking to Cassidy. True, Adam liked just about everyone, but he watched Cassidy Hyde as all guys watched Cassidy Hyde. This was good. This was what was supposed to happen. *Positive feelings*, Adam. My teeth dug into my lip like I could will him to feel something for her. Who knew? Hopefully, I could.

"What?" Owen whispered. "I'm just saying, I'm available, too."

Maybe Owen was right about me turning into a helicopter mom, because I had this weird, expanding sensation in my chest like someone were tying a balloon animal in there. Adam shoved the tickets in Cassidy's face. I cringed. It wasn't exactly a smooth presentation. What did helicopter moms wear? I had a flash of myself wearing pearls and a cable-knit sweater while I led my man-child Adam around by the hand. *Right, scratch that.*

I steepled my fingers in front of my chin. *Come on. Come on.* Cassidy Hyde was the good-time girl, the biggest flirt in school, and all I could do was pray that she didn't fail me now.

Cassidy stared at the tickets. Daintily, she picked one. With her hand on Adam's shoulder, she stood on her tippy-toes and whispered something in his ear, and then her overly glossed lips drifted to within a centimeter of Adam's, hovering close so that I knew she must feel the puff of his breath on her nose. My stomach clenched, and I held my breath for what felt like an excruciatingly long moment before she closed the gap and fit her mouth into his. Adam closed his eyes and wrapped his arm around the small of her waist, and he kissed her.

TWENTY-TWO

Adam's scars have turned from pink to silver-white. They are smooth, stretched skin that branch across his chest and torso. His other cuts continue to heal, too. Many of the scabs on his legs have peeled off. The cut on his side is a dark red and looks like it will take longer to heal, but it's not fresh and there's no gangrene, so I'll continue to watch it and hope for the best.

— — —

Three days until the Homecoming game and a foreign visitor—if our town ever *had* any foreign visitors—would have thought the Olympics were coming to Hollow Pines. In reality, it was a football game. A *high school* football game, no less.

The closer the game got, the less the town thought about the dead boys whose legs had gone mysteriously missing. Hopes for the Oilers' season dominated the headlines, and the recent memory of the gruesome murders floated into the background.

"Gray or black?" Cassidy held up two suits for Adam, Owen, and me to judge. After what had started as two Homecoming tickets, an ingenious plan by me, and a kiss, Adam and Cassidy had been dating for an entire week. The presence of googly eyes were at an all-time high, but I was already busy counting this phase of the experiment as a rousing success. The two clearly liked each other. Thank you, raging teenage hormones.

Both of the suits that Cassidy showed us looked linty under the fluorescent lights of HP Gold Formalwear, a store located conveniently between the food court and Foot Locker. I'd only agreed to come so I could pick up a cheap prepaid cell phone and rejoin the land of the living.

Almost overnight, Adam and Cassidy had become the front-runners for Homecoming king and queen, the winners of which would be announced the Saturday following the game at the Homecoming dance. It had all the makings of a fairy-tale ending if your small-town fairy tale involved a sticky gymnasium floor and a balloon arch. I could tell Cassidy's did.

Adam scratched his head and glanced over. "Don't look at me," I said. "I fully intend to wear these." I tapped my Converse sneakers.

"You two are hopeless." She dropped both hangers to her side and returned her attention to the racks.

Stage 3 of the experiment: take Adam's emotional development from animal instincts to actual feelings. Here I observed as Cassidy turned Adam into what is known in layman's terms as a "boyfriend."

"Check this out." Owen held out his arms to model a powder-blue blazer thrown over a Smokey the Bear T-shirt. "Looks pretty snazzy, don't you think?" He thrust out his hip and struck a pose.

"Focus!" Cassidy clapped her hands. "Now, Adam, which do you think would look better with a red dress. Gray, black, or this pinstripe suit?" She leveled her chin and stared up at him like he was supposed to be making a choice between his children or something.

Adam rocked back on his heels and put his hands on the sides of his face. "I don't know," he groaned. "Can Victoria please choose?"

One look at me and Cassidy sighed. None of us exactly screamed "fashion critic."

"Let's try them all on," she said, and added another suit in a different shade of gray to the pile. I started to sit down in one of the chairs reserved for people-who-hated-to-shop-so-much-they-could-no-longer-physically-stand, but just as my rear end grazed the cheap, red velour fabric, Cassidy snatched me by the elbow. "Not so fast. We need you in there."

Owen was performing a slow pirouette in the mirror. "I think I'm going to get this," he said, tugging on the lapels. "I look very dapper, if I do say so myself."

"You're missing the pants." I pointed at his jeans, cuffed over a pair of untied sneakers.

"Ew, Tor. These are rentals. Someone else's balls have been in those."

Cassidy glared. Owen blushed and he tugged on the neck of his shirt.

Cassidy pulled Adam and me toward the back of the store to a row of dressing rooms. I cast Owen a *help me* look. He responded by waving, then returning to browse.

The dressing rooms of HP Gold Formalwear hadn't been updated since back before that powder-blue blazer was in style. Four narrow stalls with full-length mirrors lined the back wall. The carpets were a sea of shaggy red. The store seemed really into the red motif. I guessed it was supposed to be fancy or romantic or something. It all looked as if it could use a good cleaning.

I thought about Owen's "balls" comment. Something told me patrons would be even less pleased to learn that a dead guy had worn these clothes, not to mention while he was actually dead.

People were weird about getting too close to death. It was like it was contagious. There was a house down the road that took five whole years to sell because the former owner had killed himself in the kitchen. Even then, the buyers mowed it down and used the land for farming. Pretty soon, the field where we found the body would have its own urban legends, I imagined.

Cassidy stuffed a heap of suits onto a set of hooks inside one of the fitting rooms on the right and ushered Adam in. "You have to come out and model," she said, closing the door behind her. We both plopped down on a bench—more red velour—outside of the fitting room.

Underneath the door, we could see Adam's jeans drop to his ankles. I wondered if Cassidy would be horrified to learn how many times I'd seen Adam in his underwear.

Cassidy bumped shoulders with me and looked at me out of the corner of her eye with a small smile playing on her lips. "Paisley says I should worry about you." At this, she rolled her eyes. "But you know her. She can be such an alpha bitch sometimes. It's been such a freaking relief having you around. Seriously, Victoria."

Seriously what?

Fabric rustled from behind the closed door, and I watched as a pair of socked feet stepped in and out of slacks. Cassidy kept her voice low. "If I didn't know you two were practically siblings, maybe I'd feel threatened, I guess. I mean, I'd have to if y'all's connection was more full frontal than familial."

A strangled sound came from the dressing room. "Are you okay in there?" I called.

There was a grunt and then a pause before the door flew open and banged into the wall behind it. Adam stood in the frame. His eyes were dark pools, hooded in shadow. I recognized the clench in his jaw as the same look as after a recharge. Something was wrong.

The gray suit was too tight around the chest and not long enough in the leg. The hem hovered an inch above his tennis shoes. Cassidy crossed the space between them and led Adam to a larger mirror with three reflective sides so he could see the panoramic view. She hovered behind him and tugged one of the sleeves down over the cuff of his white dress shirt. "A little snug, but what do you think of the color?"

Adam mumbled something unintelligible. I didn't think Cassidy was even listening, because without another word, she pushed him back into the dressing room. "Next! Don't forget, the black suit goes with the black shirt." Turning to me—"Did that color say Wall Street or James Bond to you? I don't want to go too middle-aged corporate, if you know what I mean."

"It's strange. Menswear has always been very quiet around me."

"Ha. Ha." She sat down again and crossed her legs. "You know, no girl is too good for a dress. Not even you, Victoria Frankenstein. I could help you look for one."

It wasn't that I was too good for a dress, it was that I had better things to do than care about dresses, but it wasn't worth explaining the difference.

Owen strolled up with his chin lifted and a plaid ascot tied around his neck. "Ladies." He adjusted the puffy neck scarf.

His expression drooped when Cassidy totally ignored him. When it came to my scrawny, towheaded best friend, she seemed to have a wide blind spot. "Seems like he's taking a long time, doesn't it?" She went to the door and knocked. "How's it coming, Adam?"

Moments later the latch clicked and the door slowly drifted open. Adam was breathing heavy. His fists constricted into tight balls at his sides. His lower teeth jutted out in front of his upper ones. The all-black getup only served to make him look more dangerous.

Cassidy buttoned his collar. "If you don't like this one, maybe you'll like the pinstripe better." The black suit was long enough for each of his limbs and the pant legs reached all the way to the floor as they were supposed to.

"No." Adam's eyes cut away from her.

She cocked her head. "Navy then? You really do look handsome in the black, though. With a silver tie, I think." She frowned.

He trained his gaze on his tennis shoes, which looked out of place when paired with the dress pants. "I look like a monster."

My eyes snapped up. A monster. The word roared in my ears like the sound of an 18-wheeler on a highway. I peered around him into the fitting room and the long mirror inside, and it all clicked into place. Adam didn't have a mirror in the cellar. Adam had been given strict instructions not to change or shower with the other boys on the team.

Adam was different. But he'd never seen the full extent of just how much so.

I felt as if I were trying to swallow a wad of steel wool. Cassidy's laugh was shaky and high-pitched. "You're a tough one to figure out, Smith." Then she balanced on her tippy-toes and kissed his cheek. Adam couldn't feel it, I knew, and seemed only vaguely aware that Cassidy's mouth was grazing his own cold, dead skin.

A monster.

I wouldn't have thought of it like that, and I was a little angry at him for using that particular noun. *A monster.* His features grew darker and more sunken in, as if Adam was actually retreating into himself. Before now, he'd looked down and seen the scars left on his body. Why didn't I realize the full extent of the damage, once finally appreciated, would bother him?

"One more." Cassidy held up a finger. "Pretty please? For me?" What was it about attractive girls that made pouting an acceptable means to an end after the age of four and a half? "White shirt with this one," she said.

"I thought the black shirt looked nice," I added hastily. "Maybe keep it on."

"With pinstripes?" Cassidy gave a small shake of her head. Adam clomped back into the dressing room, where a pinstripe suit awaited. I drummed my finger on my knee. I would have ripped the mirror off the wall if I could have, but it would have been hard to come up with an excuse for Cassidy. Only vampires and ghosts were afraid of mirrors. Maybe I could claim he was one of those.

Cassidy, Owen, and I fell quiet. I imagined that we all felt like intruders listening to the struggles of man versus fabric taking place within the tiny confines of that fitting room. I heard the rip of a seam and a frustrated growl. Owen's eyes went wide. A heavy crash. Then the din of cracking glass like a fault line traveling through an iced-over pond.

When Adam bellowed, it sounded like a trapped animal. Fibers split and scraps of black fell to the floor. The door flew open and banged against the wall. That was the moment the shards of mirror lost their hold and clattered to the ground around Adam's bare feet.

"Adam," Cassidy gasped.

A river of blood flowed from his knuckles. Red spotted the white tails of his untucked shirt, which had been ripped at the shoulders and collar. Adam's eyes were hard, as if they'd died two weeks ago along with the rest of him. But this time for good.

Unseeing, he shoved past the three of us, just in time for the store manager to see him break into a run out of the store. "Sir!" the manager called. "Sir, you haven't paid for those."

Cassidy hadn't seen this side of him. Neither had Owen, not really. Only I had. "Get his things," I ordered Owen. "I'm going after him."

The bell attached to the door jangled on my way out. I knew they'd expect us to pay for the damage. I also knew I didn't have the money and my list of repairs—phone, car, Adam—was already long enough as it was.

I found the nearest exit to my left and sprinted toward it. Orange light seeped out of the horizon, turning the sky's clouds into an inverted map of the world. Below, the dimming parking lot was empty. I ran both ways, searching. "Adam!" I called. "Adam! Wait!" I wheezed the last few words before I had to hunch over and put my hands over my knees.

"What the hell was that?" Cassidy demanded. She marched to the edge of the curb and looked at the same thing I was looking at, which was a bunch of cars and nothing.

Owen had Adam's shoes in one hand and his jeans and shirt in the other. "Yeah, what was that, *Tor*?" he asked flatly.

The only option was the truth. Or at least some version of the truth.

I scanned the parking lot one last time for Adam. Cars whizzed by on the adjacent road.

"Adam doesn't like his scars," I said. "He . . . he was in an accident. He never likes to look at them. You have to promise me, you won't ever try to look," I told Cassidy.

Her lower lip trembled. "I'm sorry. I didn't know. He didn't tell me. What kind of accident?"

My eyes flitted over to Owen. "A car accident." The more truth I told, the fewer lies I had to keep up with. "He doesn't like to talk about that either, though. You can't ask him."

"I won't," she answered quickly, then traced a cross over her heart with her fingernail. "Cross my heart. Can we go find him?"

No, I wanted to scream. *We* can't go find him. Not while my creation was in a self-examinatory tailspin of epic proportions, but instead I just said, "I think it'd be better if it was just us."

A thin line of water sprung from her lower eyelid and balanced there. She nodded. "I'll go deal with the manager in there, I guess." She placed her hands on my shoulders and said, "Just take care of our boy, okay?"

After that, I couldn't get away fast enough. It sure wasn't Cassidy slicing open his chest and stitching it back together, so I couldn't grasp what her claim to him might be. She made out with him? From what I gathered, she'd done that with plenty of boys and never claimed any sort of ownership over them.

Owen drove, so we found his car in a sea of SUV crossovers. He dumped Adam's belongings in my lap.

"That's it. We're screwed." He thumped the steering wheel and then rested his forehead on it. "I knew this would happen. Elvis has left the building, people." Owen was still wearing the powder-blue blazer and ascot.

I slid the seat belt across and clicked it into place. "We're not screwed," I said. "Just drive, okay?"

Shaking his head, Owen obeyed, removing his forehead from the steering wheel, which had left a red indent on his skin. He reversed his Jeep out of the spot and guided it out of the lot and onto the road. "Which way?" He sounded resigned.

I scanned the roads. "That way." I pointed down a long stretch of road lined with half-full rain ditches on either side. "Toward my house."

Owen pressed the accelerator, and the car lurched onto the road. "We're three miles from your house."

"Just do it." We followed a minivan with one taillight out. The driver of the minivan must have been ninety years old because she—or maybe he—was driving slower than a sloth with cement bricks for feet. "Go around them."

"I can't go around them. It's a double yellow line."

I slammed back against the headrest, then thought better of it and reached over to honk the horn. "Get out of the way!"

Owen swatted my hand. I leaned closer to the windshield and tried to make out what was farther down the road. I thought I saw something bobbing along the side.

"I told you we would get caught." Owen shook his head. "Didn't I tell you?" Owen looked deranged in his evening clothes. "My face is way too innocent for prison, Tor. Look at it. It's the face of a child. Someone will shank me with a knife made from toilet paper rolls and bedsheets before I can even learn how to make moonshine out of rotten fruit."

I grabbed Owen's arm too hard and he swerved. "That's him." I scooted to the edge of my seat. "That's him!"

Owen nudged the brakes so that we could drive at the same speed as Adam was running. I rolled down the window. "What are you doing?" I asked. Blood covered his hand and the torn shirt. What he looked like he was doing was running from the scene of an ax murder. He grunted but kept running. His bare feet slapped the pavement. "Adam, will you please get in?"

"I'm hideous." Sweat soaked the tattered white dress shirt. "Why did you not tell me I'm hideous, Victoria?"

"You're not hideous. You're special." His breaths came in powerful huffs. "This is crazy, Adam. You knew what—I mean, you knew *who* you were. Why are you running?" I asked.

He didn't answer, but he didn't stop, either. Nothing we said or did persuaded him to get into the car. And so it was blood-splattered and sticky that he finally finished the three-mile run to my house. He didn't speak. Instead, he retreated into the depths of his lair and was gone.

When I moved to climb out after him, Owen caught my wrist and held me in place. "Tor, hold on." His eyes darted between mine. "There's . . . something I haven't told you. I didn't think it mattered. Just stupid high school stuff." With my seat belt off, the door began to chime. "Until today, that is."

A prickle worked its way up the back of my neck. "What?" And I could hear the distrust creeping into my own voice.

Red crept into Owen's pale cheeks and splotched his neck. "It's about Adam. See, I've been keeping tabs on any mention of his name in Hollow Pines. I know it's not his real name, but I figured if anyone, I don't know, said anything about him, we should know."

"Why didn't you tell me?" I snapped.

Owen let go of my wrist and ran his fingers through this hair. "Well, first of all, you've been pretty busy trying to turn him into a 'real boy.'" He curled his fingers into air quotes. "But, I—look, I didn't think it'd matter, but something came up. People—only a couple people, really—are saying that he might have had something to do with those two boys." I sucked in a mouthful of air and let it sit in my lungs. "Look it up for yourself. The Lie Detector. They're these web-sleuthing forums where people discuss their theories on all these crimes. It's kind of sick, but . . ." He looked down at his lap. "Check it out."

"You think it's true," I said. "I can tell." The hatch through which Adam had disappeared was still.

Owen lifted his chin. "All I'm saying is, how much do we really know about him?"

TWENTY-THREE

Possible neurobiological sources of violence include chronic traumatic stress, testosterone, or dysregulated serotonin. The most common sources of violence, though, are developmental neglect or traumatic stress during childhood. I will plan to test hormone levels to measure possible concerns surrounding impulse control.

— — —

Darkness had descended over my house. I knew this sounded melodramatic topped with a generous helping of teen angst, but it was true. Adam wouldn't speak. Not in words, anyway. He hugged his arms around his knees and rocked and tuned me out like I was a staticky channel on an old television set. So the only sentence that I bothered him with was to tell him that I'd be in later tonight after Mom had gone to bed to administer his *electrotherapy*, the euphemism I'd adopted for the shock. I wished I were better with words, but I was hardly any better than Adam.

Now, with my toes tucked into the comforter of my bed with the squishy, sinking, quicksand middle, my mind turned to the broken mirror, and I ran the search for the Lie Detector. A dated blue-and-white message board appeared on the screen, loading in slow motion, one piece at a time. I read through the long list of topics. The Black Dahlia. Lizzie Borden. Amanda Knox and the murder of Meredith Kercher. The list went on. It was an inventory of the grisliest crimes.

Outside my window, I heard the shrill screech of the weather vane twisting on its pole. I checked my watch. Mom must have fallen asleep in front of the TV. If it woke her, she'd be furious I hadn't gotten around to fixing it yet. I plugged my ears against the spine-scratching sound, hoping for the wind to die.

Halfway down the screen I noticed a title topic: the Hunter of Hollow Pines. Ominous, I thought darkly, as I selected the new thread. I was surprised to find that there was already more than a page of responses to the original entry.

Hollow Pines wasn't famous for much of anything. Our two sources of industry were feminine pads and canned soup and hardly anyone cared where those things came from.

But here it was causing strangers to sit up and pay attention—or at the very least, take a break from playing their Xbox. I was part of it, I realized. I was there when they found the second body. And I felt this messed-up flutter of achievement. I squashed the wings on it when I remembered why I was digging around the bowels of the Internet in the first place.

The static post at the top cataloged the two known deaths. The moderator emphasized the "known," and I felt a shiver run down my back to think about what exactly that meant. Right away, I could tell that the overwhelming majority thought there'd be more.

Escalation. That appeared to be the word *du jour.* The unsub's— after a quick search I determined this meant the unknown subject or killer—pattern was escalating. A poster with the username Dead-Bunny pointed out that he was growing more confident. He'd refined his method. A bear trap to capture his victim and a souvenir limb.

All but one of the users were certain that the unsub was male. Apparently almost all unsubs were men. Women were rarely serial killers. But the fact that this unsub targeted teenage boys made it different from most cases, more likely that a woman could have been the attacker. *But how would a woman overpower a teenage boy?* Dead-Bunny wanted to know. The user, DiadeMuertos, spit back that

DeadBunny was just being sexist. Call me crazy, but a stronger disposition to become a murderer was something I was okay letting the XY chromosomes take.

When I'd combed through the responses, I flipped to the next page. This one was shorter. Not as many responses. I skimmed. There was one poster who believed that it was a vagrant oil-rig worker and that the concentration of crimes was a usual part of his modus operandi, only he wasn't at one place for long, so the cops never pieced it together. This added to the fact that as a rig hand, he would prey on small towns, ones with incompetent police forces, which by the other comments, incompetence seemed to be the prevailing opinion with regard to all police forces, anyway.

I was buying into this theory hook, line, and sinker until Dead-Bunny swooped in with another of his fatal counterpoints. The unsub had stashed the bodies in two completely independent areas, signaling a comfort level with the area. It couldn't have been a nomad. It had to be a local job. I chewed through a flake of dead skin on the side of my thumb and swished it off my comforter.

Hollow Pines, Texan here, an anonymous post began. *I've been following these events with interest and I've carefully drawn out the timeline and I've noticed one thing. A new student started at Hollow Pines High the very day before the first body was found and he was even present when the second body was found. Coincidence? Could be. His name is Adam Smith.*

I snapped my laptop closed as though it might bite me. Or worse. My chest rose and fell. Shallow breaths. Nothing felt real. I clumped my blankets into my fists and squeezed just to feel grounded. Buzzing filled my ears. I looked around, unable to process what I'd read. Everything seemed normal. Posters, books, college paraphernalia. I slid my legs out from under Einstein. She looked up at me through wrinkled lids and sneezed into the soft cotton.

"Come on." I scooped her up in my arms and set her down on the carpet. She shook her hide, jangling her collar. I held my finger to my lips. "Shhhh." I didn't know if she understood, but she waddled after in silence, completely content to have been allowed to come along.

I tippy-toed across the living room's shag carpet and through the kitchen all the way to the back door. I jiggled the doorknob until it opened without a creak. Einstein rolled off the ledge, onto the driveway, and I closed the door behind her. She shuffled ahead and scratched at the cellar door.

I paused. It was one user. One person's harebrained theory about what could have happened to those boys. None of it was true. Adam was mine. I knew him. I created him. And I could trust him.

But if that were true, what was I doing? I'd recognized the cold, metal glint in his eyes as something dangerous. I'd wondered. I'd felt my own blood run cold when he screamed beneath the shock. I'd heard him call himself a monster.

With my heart pounding, I pushed Einstein away with the side of my leg. Tonight held the first real hints of fall. There was a coolness that had been hidden all summer by the ferocious blaze of the Texas sun. That warmth had disappeared like a shower with all its hot water used up, and I slipped my hands into my sleeves before descending into the dark cellar.

TWENTY-FOUR

The brain stem includes the medulla, the pons, and the midbrain. These three parts control autonomic processes like breathing and digestion. The cerebellum sits at the back, underbelly of the brain anatomy. It controls motor skills, balance, and other cognitive functions like language and procedural memories. The medial temporal lobe near the divide of the left and right hemispheres holds the brain's declarative and episodic memory. Finally, the hippocampus possesses the ability to store long-term memory and the adjoining amygdala processes emotional and sexual behavior.

— — —

Adam?" I flicked on the lights. The glass jars magnified the specimens bobbing inside them. I quickly scoured the room. The open-jawed skeleton standing in the corner mocked me. "Adam? Come out." I sounded angry. I imagined him cowering, scared. But he wasn't there. The room was empty and, for the first time since Adam had taken up residence in it, it felt abandoned.

I made a promise to myself not to be mad. I'd ask questions, give him a chance to explain. I grabbed a flashlight from the workbench and left. I ventured back up to the surface and around the back of the house, casting the beam of my flashlight over the open field. The thing about small-town darkness was that it had the consistency of molasses. Thick and sticky, it sucked up everything below until what was left felt like outer space. Not far away, the light was eaten up entirely. I couldn't see past the initial wall of high grass and wire fences.

I moved to the edge and tried holding my flashlight up high. "Adam?" I said as loudly as I dared without waking Mom. It was silly being scared of the dark. Childish. But that didn't stop my heart from taking up residence at the top of my throat. I looked back at the house and then, with a show of being ten times braver than I actually was, I took my first step into the field. "You coming?" I patted my leg for Einstein to follow. For once, the clumsy, thick-jowled mutt would have been a welcome companion.

She whined and scooted her back end, but she didn't cross into the field. I slapped my thigh again. "Come." Once more, she whimpered and pawed at the dirt, but she didn't come any farther. "Fine, stay there," I grumbled. "Some guard dog you are."

She flattened her belly to the ground and rested her head between her paws, looking guilty. Her jagged underbite made it look like she was actually pouting. I rolled my eyes and tried to convince myself that it didn't matter, but the flashlight handle was slippery in my hand, and I had to keep telling my legs to go forward.

The crumbly clay soil under my feet grew softer. The breeze blew the scent of young sweetgrass. Soon, it was soaking the shins of my plaid pajama pants. I waded in farther, thinking that I should have changed. Moisture seeped through my slippers. I swept the beam over the field. Everywhere it touched, it turned the green grass a golden yellow.

I struggled to keep my nerves in check. I was alone in the middle of the night. There was a killer loose in Hollow Pines. How could I be so sure that he would only do what he'd done to boys? An image flashed of my body lying faceup, staring at the stars.

Then an even colder thought: I could be out here searching for the killer right now.

I swallowed. I couldn't think like that. And even if I was, I thought I felt something in my gut click like a lock being latched down, and I knew that even if Adam was responsible, I might still protect him.

My resolve teetered on the edge of a cliff. The *swoosh-swoosh* of my pants drove me mad. It sounded like someone following me. Each time I stopped so did the swishing. *Chill out*, I ordered.

Turning back, I realized I could no longer see the house or hear Einstein's snorting breaths. Goose bumps spread over the back of my neck. I swallowed. "Adam?" This time my voice cracked. "This isn't funny, Adam." I tried to sound loud, brave, but my pulse fluttered as fast and light as a hummingbird's.

Keeping my feet planted in one spot, I revolved around and around, until I lost track of which direction I'd been facing to begin with. Everywhere I looked was darkness and field. Panic bubbled. My ears strained to differentiate sounds—was that the brush of the wind or someone else in the field along with me? Sweat pooled in my armpits.

I made another feeble call of his name. Terror burned through my veins, and I dropped the flashlight to my side. Before I could talk myself out of it, I ran.

A minute later I arrived panting back at Einstein. She heaved her girth off the ground and came to lick the dew that coated my pants.

I gritted my teeth. I had to find Adam. He was my responsibility. I ducked inside the house to grab my keys off the nail but found that they were gone.

I covered up a sharp intake of breath. Then I eased around the corner of the big house to where two cars should have been parked in the drive.

There was only one.

This situation had just gotten worse. Way worse. He could have gone anywhere. He didn't have a license. He didn't even know how to drive. Or did he?

I stole my mom's keys. Tire marks snaked wildly through the dirt road, and there was a deep rut like one of the wheels had spun out. *Not good*, I mouthed, wanting to kick mud.

I loaded Einstein into the passenger-side seat of Mom's station wagon and kept the headlights off until I'd pulled out of the drive.

Where would he have gone? My first thought was the obvious one. The football field. It was where he felt most comfortable and competent. I headed back to school, realizing only when I was pulling into the parking lot how crazy this was. It was the middle of the night and no one but Einstein knew where I was.

The hulking green figure of Bert loomed in the parking lot. I experienced a slight loosening in the pinch of worry at finding myself on the right track.

I parked in one of the teachers' reserved spots alongside the empty car. The deserted stadium loomed up ahead.

A few weeks ago I might have considered this the most rebellious moment of my teenage years, but that was out the window. Now, it'd be lucky to break the top ten.

Elongated shadows spread across the empty parking lot. I leaned into the steering wheel, peering up through the bug-splattered windshield. The lights had been cut like an after-hours merry-go-round. Nearly as creepy, too. Reluctantly, I turned the key in the ignition and the engine died. After another second, the headlights faded as well. Einstein's breath left little cloud puffs on the window.

"Let me guess? You're staying here again?" On cue, she lowered her rump to the seat and reclined in a lazy heap against the door panel. "Okay, but next time you can't find your bacon treats, don't go looking at me." I clanged the door shut and pressed the lock button. At least one of us should be safe.

I hugged myself, less because I was cold and more because I didn't know what to do with my hands. The school building looked on with hooded windows as I cut across the grass. Alone and out in the open, I felt as though anyone could be watching. The familiar prickle crawled over my arms. I tried to rub it away, and a pit solidified in my stomach.

I was still in my pajamas and slippers. Not exactly the outfit I'd prefer to be wearing if caught by the cops . . . or worse. The creak of metal bleachers and the crisscrossed network of support beams groaned in the wind like an abandoned swing set. I scaled the short stack of aluminum steps to the stands and mounted one of the bleachers.

I kept my footsteps quiet across the beam, spiriting along the length of the football field. Every twenty yards or so, I stopped and listened, too scared to call his name and afraid of what might be lurking out of sight.

When it came to fear, I was a faithful follower of logic. How likely was it that someone would try to break into my house the one time I forgot to lock the door? I was twice as likely to be killed in a car accident as I was to be murdered, though this statistic somehow still felt high, and lately I'd seemed to be gunning for both. But, still, there was no reason to be inherently scared of being in a place alone at night. The odds that something bad would happen were slim. That was the logical answer, anyway.

I tried hard to focus on mathematical probability while I looked under bleachers and up in the announcer's box. I ventured onto the field, taking hesitant steps onto the turf. Adam was nowhere to be found, and I was beginning to feel that the ghostlike car parked in the lot was a cold lead.

I was picking my way down from the highest bleacher when I saw a rectangular sliver of light. It was faint, nearly hidden, and it was just to the left side of the stadium. I narrowed my eyes and stared hard. There was definitely something there. I rushed the final few rows and used the railing to skip steps onto the track.

I looked around, still fighting off the sensation that someone else was here with me. When I could finally convince myself that I was alone, I cut straight across the fifty-yard line and past the concession stands on the other side, where the signs had turned a dull gray in the faint light of the moon and dried-out mustard stains coated the sidewalk.

As I approached, the light grew brighter, and I could see it was the outline of a door on the side of the main building. My heart raced. I suddenly had sympathy for the horror movie heroine at whom the entire theater audience was screaming, "Don't go in there!" because I was totally going in. Logic be damned, this would add at least five points to the statistical probability that I would be murdered in the next hour.

I jammed my fingers between the door and its frame and pried it open using the full weight of my body. I then found myself peering into the boys' locker room. I poked my head inside.

A dying fluorescent light flickered overhead. I inched my way over the threshold. The acrid scent of caked-in sweat and the inside of a jockstrap overwhelmed me to the point I could taste it, sour, on the tip of my tongue. I took each step gingerly, rocking my weight from heel to toe, scared to so much as breathe.

I glanced between each row of lockers. They were eerily empty. The strobe-light effect didn't help. I felt the distance growing between me and the door. I swiped clammy palms across my pajama bottoms and swallowed.

A little farther, I promised. Someone had been in here. Someone had turned on this light. "Adam?" My voice came out hoarse.

Just then I heard a shuffle beyond the lockers. Past the rows, the room darkened where a row of sinks led to a short line of bathroom stalls.

Another scrape across the floor sent a chill up my arms. I could hardly wrench my legs forward. My footsteps grew shorter. I reached the last bench, where I caught my own spectral reflection in the mirror and rounded a tiled wall, and then I saw it. *Him.*

His body writhed in the group shower on its side, centered between two drains. The lights hadn't been turned on here, and it obscured the form. Its—*his*—back was facing me. His legs twitched, and the shuffling sound they made was louder from here. Barely human.

Adam, my Adam, rocked back and forth. His breathing sounded tortured and husky against shower walls. I stepped closer. He was hunched into a ball and hidden from view. There was a metal taste in my mouth. Reality shattered over me like broken glass, the pieces of what was happening.

Water hummed through the walls. The building creaked. My hairs stood on end. I switched on the light, then kneeled and placed a hand on his shoulder.

Quieting, he turned his chin to face me.

"Victoria," he croaked.

"Adam."

His eyes were colorless. Yellow seeped out into a piss-colored shadow between his cheekbones and lower lashes. The thin layer of skin stretched across his forehead was a vampiric shade of white coated in pearly slime. His cracked lips parted.

"What are you doing here?" I whispered. My voice quaked. I tucked my feet underneath me and scooped his head into my lap. I ran my fingers through dark, sweat-matted hair. My eyes searched his. "What happened?"

His pupils—the only shade in the runny egg whites of his eyeballs—followed my movements. His teeth chattered. The rest of his body fell still, as if he'd been paralyzed.

"Adam." I patted his cheek. "Adam, stay with me." The charge. He'd needed the charge after running home and he'd been too stubborn and I'd been too consumed to give it to him. I cradled his head. I was stupid. So stupid. What if a full resurrection could only work once? What if I couldn't replicate the past results? His jugular swelled with the effort of gulping down his saliva.

"4-0-8." The numbers were feather-soft when they crossed his lips. I bent my ear down to him. "4-0-8," he repeated, and this time I was sure I'd heard correctly.

"408?" I shook my head. "I don't know what that means." It felt important that I grasped the significance, but every time I tried to reach into my mind and close a fist around them, the numbers slipped through and I came up empty.

"The house." His head lulled toward me. I put my palm to his forehead, cool from being against the shower tiles. "I saw the house."

I nodded in that whatever-you-say way I used to have with my grandma right before she died, too. I felt him slipping. It was as if his body actually became lighter in my arms, and I knew that he'd be gone from me and that I'd have nothing to show for that night except for skin and bones and a rotting pile of organs.

I traced the outline of his jaw and the ridge of his brow.

He coughed and it sounded like his lungs were tearing out drywall. "We have . . ." He sucked air as though a hole had been torn in his rib cage, making the entire effort useless. ". . . to find . . ." His tongue pushed against his teeth, leaving behind tiny spit bubbles. ". . . the house."

And with that, the darks of his eyes rolled into the sockets, and he was gone.

TWENTY-FIVE

Physical deterioration between recharges seems to compound. Adam's motor functions visibly slow once the electric half-life in his body has reduced to critical levels.

Purpose of later experiments will be to develop a way to maintain functionality for longer periods of time.

— — —

Wax dripped in fat rivulets down the sides of melting candles. The wicks had sunk into caverns. Each stick was half the size it was when I lit it. I kneeled beside him, listening to every whisper of breath, straining to hear his heartbeat.

"You should get some sleep." I jumped when Owen's fingers brushed my arm. "I can keep watch."

I shook my head. When I called, he'd arrived faster than an ambulance. I now watched as wisps of color returned to Adam's face and the yellow stains dissipated from underneath his eyes. Dark pools of blood spread out and vanished as his circulation returned. The wires used for the shock lay about like dead snakes.

Eventually an eyelid quivered, and first one, then the other, peeled open. Adam stared up at the ceiling. The deep, chocolate brown had returned to his eyes.

"Oh, thank God," I said. Without thinking, I threw myself over his chest.

Gentle fingers petted my hair. I wiped my nose on the back of my hand before prying myself away. I hadn't even realized that tears had slipped from the corners of my eyes. That's how I was when I was focused on something.

He sat up and cracked his neck, looking somehow more human than before.

"I should have come sooner," I said.

He frowned. "Thank you."

"I think it's safe to say that I have carried your body far more than any other man's body in my life," Owen said.

I wanted to tell Adam right then and there that this was all my fault. The second I thought I might lose him, I'd remembered Meg. I didn't know who she was and I hadn't tried to find out, but I knew I must have been taking something away from her and, worse, from him. A screw tightened in my chest. Except, I couldn't help but believe that Adam belonged to me, not her, and that as long as no one knew Adam, there was no one to ask questions. My kneecaps dug into the floor.

"I've been seeing something." His voice was deeper and more sure. He stared straight ahead like Owen and I weren't even in the room. "When the shocks come, I can make out images."

My hands slid from my face. "Images?"

He pulled his knees closer to his chest and rested his arms across them. "Only one image, actually. But it's real. Like something I'm remembering, Victoria." He squeezed his eyes shut and pinched the knotted skin. "The electricity. It's tearing memories free. I can feel it in here." He pointed to the breastbone beneath his red tree-branch scars. "And here." He touched his temple.

I scooted closer. "Tell me about them. What are they like?"

"I saw a house. There was an address painted on the curb in white. 4-0-8." He recited it carefully like he'd been trying very hard to memorize this exact sequence. "It's only for a second and then—" I inched forward. "It sucks."

"What does?"

He held his hands out and shook them. "Bbbzzzzzzzzzzzz," he said, mimicking being electrocuted. "Everything. It burns and my head feels like it's being stabbed."

"Why didn't you say something?" I should have seen past his stoic routine. Adam wasn't going to win any awards for self-expression. In fact, he was a locked box when it came to his feelings. All the signs had been there. Clenched jaw. Furrowed brow. I'd ignored them.

"It's not your fault."

For a moment, I couldn't speak. Because the truth was that it really was all my fault. Every single moment of this story was my fault. "I'll help you find it," I blurted out. I felt my eyes tighten at the corners. I wasn't sure I'd wanted to volunteer that. But my heart softened when he sat up straighter. *My* Adam. I could do this for him. I should do this for him. "The house. I'm sure we can locate it, just give me some time."

"Really?"

I felt a worm of guilt niggling its way into my stomach. If there was a piece of him that I could help click into place, I knew I'd rather it be shaped like a house than a girl named Meg. Houses, at least, didn't ask questions.

I RUBBED MY temples, wishing another mug of coffee would materialize in my hand. Instead, a girl in a band uniform slammed into me with her tuba case. My shoulder throbbed. The stress of Adam's disappearance, his near re-death, and the knowledge that he was remembering hit me like a bag of bricks to the face.

I looked after the band girl. "Excuse you," I called, my words drowned out in the hustle and bustle of the hallway. I was an island in a sea of blissful ignorance, and that sea was called Spirit Week.

Everywhere I looked students were tacking up posters. Student council members were selling tickets to the Homecoming dance.

Hollow Pines High pride was at its all-time peak. It was such a stark contrast to my night that I felt as if I'd entered a very peppy alternate dimension.

Historically, I dreaded Spirit Week with the fervor of my annual teeth cleaning. It'd be way more interesting if it had to do with spirits of the paranormal variety, but instead, it looked like a monster had vomited pom-poms and streamers over the entire school.

I ducked under a pennant smeared in puff paint. The energy this year, though, was electric, and that was Adam's doing. Adam, the most talked-about boy in school and ostensibly *my* best friend. People I hardly knew waved at me as they went by. They smiled. They called me Victoria instead of Tor. The only thing missing was a soundtrack.

I spun the dial to my locker and pulled out my physics textbook and stuffed it into an already overstuffed book bag when out of the corner of my eye I saw Cassidy dressed head to toe in orange and black. She squealed as soon as she saw me lurking and dragged Paisley over.

"Happy Junior Class Spirit Day!" she said as though this were as natural a thing to say as *Merry Christmas!*

Bah humbug, I thought while struggling to zip my bag. I was losing track of the days, but if it was the junior class's day, that must have meant it was Wednesday. Freshmen on Monday, sophomores for Tuesday, seniors on Thursday. Yes, Wednesday. I made a mental note. Each class was in charge of making one of the days of Spirit Week "special." I didn't take my duties seriously.

Cassidy spun her bag around and unfastened a giant round pin that read *Get Loud* in school colors. "Thank God I thought to bring you one, Victoria. We're selling them for student council. You look the opposite of spirited. You look . . ." She curled her lip, taking in my fitted black shirt and sneakers. "Apathetic."

"I'm not apathetic," I insisted, feeling defensive. "Apathy is for kids pretending to be smart and stoners. I'm neither of those things. I'm an independent thinker. Like, I don't know, Galileo." The zipper finally closed, pinching the tip of my finger and causing me to jerk it back. "Or something."

Paisley sputtered out laughing. "I told you not to waste your time, Cass."

A heart-shaped pucker formed between Cassidy's eyebrows. A slight frown creased either side of her mouth.

"That's not true," I said quickly. It turned out I would do just about anything to prove Paisley Wheelwright wrong.

Cassidy grinned. "See?" She stuck her tongue out at Paisley, who dismissed her with a wave. "I knew she'd like it." Cassidy threaded the pin through the fabric of my previously plain-Jane tee.

"Go Oilers?" I said lamely. My outward show of school spirit was no doubt a surefire sign of the coming apocalypse.

As though in response to this cosmic shift in the balance of the universe, there was a ripple through the hallway. One of those invisible movements you felt like a magnetic force field. It started somewhere at the far end from which the commotion was beginning to carry. There, the crowd of people was beginning to churn like sharks spotting chum in the water.

Cassidy and Paisley turned.

"What the hell's going on?" Paisley asked.

The current of bodies was reaching us now. Girls leaned in with cupped hands and sidelong whispers. Paisley marched up to one and tapped her on the shoulder, demanding to be let in on whatever had the attention of the entire student body. I could tell she wasn't used to not being the first to know. I wasn't used to caring.

Paisley's eyebrows shot up. Her blond bob swept her shoulders as she shook her head. Cassidy and I shared a look.

The first bell rang, but instead of hurrying off to class, students were leaving the building. "Come on." Paisley grabbed Cassidy by the arm.

"That freshman told me there's something on the building and the administration hasn't been able to cover it up yet." While not exactly an invitation, it was enough of one for me. "I hope it's about Principal Wiggins."

I ignored the first bell sounding through the intercom and followed them past the administration office and out onto the front lawn. Students snaked like a trail of ants toward the stadium, stopping short and curling around the side of the building.

A clump formed at the end of the line where they all stood staring in the same direction. There seemed to be an invisible line across which no one would step.

Finally, we joined them. Across the exit to the boys' locker room red dripped in stringy rivulets down the side of the school building. Jagged letters scrawled across the tin door, spilling onto the brick on either side. The writing had the metallic taste of violence, as if the brush had been wielded like a weapon, and positioned below it, like an abandoned puppet, was a third body.

Someone shrieked. "Is that *real*?"

An arrow stuck out from the boy's throat. Silvery netting wound around his legs and up his torso like a fly stuck in a spider's web. The boy was small. He couldn't have been more than a freshman, with skinny arms that poked out of baggy sleeves. His chin drooped onto a frail chest. A ring of burned flesh was carved into the scalp. His feet splayed out from the school, shoes that were too big for his body like he might have shot up next summer if he'd been given the chance. There were more screams now. Girls shielded their eyes. I couldn't take mine away. At his sides, the boy's wrists pointed up like a sacrifice. And he might have been sleeping or passed out.

If he hadn't been dead.

If it hadn't been for the missing eyes.

I stared into the hollows where the whites had been carved from the sockets and blood left tearstained streaks down his cheeks. The vacant expression leftover haunted the daylight and drained the warmth from my skin. Bloodied eyelids hung limply, half covering the empty holes.

Kids covered their mouths, and I flinched at every muffled gag that sounded from nearby. I gulped down my last memory from that locker room last night. Adam lying on the floor. Damp, water dripping. Crickets and nighttime and no one around. The thought sent a shudder through me. The spaces between my fingers grew slippery.

"Back inside!" Coach Carlson had arrived on the scene and was yelling into a megaphone. "One week's detention for anyone that's not in their seats in five minutes."

The wail of sirens grew closer. A teacher shuffled in front of the students, herding them away, shooing them. She kept glancing over her shoulder at the dead body, too, and the empty sockets. Glancing and shooing, glancing and shooing, as if we were all passing by one giant car accident.

I didn't know if it was the threat of detention or the approaching sirens or if everyone wanted to get away from a spot that felt all of a sudden unconsecrated, but the herd began to slowly turn back in the direction of the front entrance.

I took a final glance back at the glistening words, penned in dripping blood.

The Father Said Drink In The Blood & Share Ye The Resurrection.

I then flitted my eyes away, worried that the act of reading itself marked me as one of the damned.

TWENTY-SIX

The subject has lost five pounds in the last two days. His eyes are dilated. It's becoming increasingly clear that a new energy source, with a longer half-life, is needed to sustain him or we'll risk losing the progress shown to date in the data.

— — —

Instead of class, the school staff corralled the entire student body into the gymnasium and told us to sit on the bleachers and when those were full to sit on the floor. We caught sight of Owen and Adam, and while I knew she'd never admit it, I got the feeling Cassidy found the emergence of a crisis on school grounds to be *très romantique*. An excuse to leech onto Adam, who, to her credit, was tailor-made to play the strong, silent type.

We climbed up a set of bleachers after the other upperclassmen, with Adam and Cassidy trailing. Owen rolled his eyes. "Someone get the fair lady her smelling salts before she faints," he said.

I looked back. "Don't be a jerk. We're making progress. I think he actually likes her. Look at how he watches her."

"I think it seems as if he likes everyone."

We scooted past a row of students to a few empty spots near the top of the bleachers. "What do you mean by 'it *seems*'?"

"Nothing." He sat down and slid over to make room. I didn't peel my eyes away from him. His shoulders scrunched up to his ears. "*Nothing*," he repeated. "God, you don't need to go all mama bear on me."

The roar of a thousand voices filled the gymnasium.

Adam tapped me on the shoulder, his face calm and serene and innocent as ever. "Victoria, what are we doing here?"

The corner of my eye caught the red scabs on his knuckles, and I quickly glanced back up. "Damage control."

On cue, Mrs. Van Lullen waddled out in a tight black pencil skirt and orange cardigan. She dragged a screeching podium to center court. She tottered away on clunky heels, and Principal Wiggins, who was built like a bullfrog, appeared, tugging at the tie around the spot where his head and shoulders met. The man had no neck. He tapped the podium microphone, and the thumping reverberated around the room. He leaned over. "Hello?" Mrs. Van Lullen reemerged and whispered something in his ear. "Oh." He cleared his throat. "Okay then." A hushed silence blanketed the room save for the choked heaving of a single person's sobs. "Most of you know why we're here," Principal Wiggins began. He spoke close to the microphone with his head bowed, probably trying to strike the right balance between authoritative and grim. "We're not releasing the name of the victim at this time, but a student's body was found this morning outside of the boys' locker room." This sparked a round of tittering, and Principal Wiggins had to hold up one hand to make it stop. "This marks the third murder in Hollow Pines in the span of weeks. Precautions must be taken to protect our students. If you spot anything or anyone that looks suspicious, report it to an adult immediately. Students are to go home directly after all extracurriculars, and the Hollow Pines police have asked me to convey that all persons under the age of eighteen will be subject to a ten o'clock curfew as an added safety measure."

This time the crowd elicited a collective groan. "But it's Homecoming," called a voice in the crowd.

"Which will now be over at nine," said Principal Wiggins. "In order to ensure that everyone has time to get home for curfew."

"This blows," yelled another voice to shouts of agreement.

"His body's not even cold yet," I said to Owen. "And already his death is an inconvenience."

"Surprised you're not going to try to bring him back, too," he whispered. "You could have an entire army of—" I elbowed him. He croaked and shut up.

Principal Wiggins raised his voice over the crowd. "The police will be pulling certain students to question them."

Cassidy bent forward to talk to us. "I wonder if they'll question us since we were there. You think?" She said this like it was a good thing.

"Why? We don't know anything," I said too quickly.

My heartbeat picked up. Adam plus police plus alibis. Under scrutiny, it all seemed to add up to a mudslide of worst-case scenarios, and I was standing at the bottom waiting to get buried.

When Cassidy returned her attention to the gym floor, I tilted toward Adam. "You didn't see anybody here last night?" I asked, voice low, half wanting him to say that he had, that he hadn't been the only one on campus. "No other cars in the parking lot?"

Principal Wiggins continued to drone on about the closure of the boys' locker room and where counseling would be available for students that needed somewhere to cope with this most recent tragedy. Adam shook his head. "Is this my fault?"

"No." I closed my eyes and willed myself to be patient with him. "And don't say that, either. To anyone. Don't mention that you were there."

"I should lie." He said it as a statement, one that I wished he'd have said more quietly.

"Think of it as leaving out part of the truth. It's more of a secret. A secret between us. You like when we have our secrets, right?"

"Just us?"

I squeezed his hand, then felt Cassidy watching us, monitoring. I pulled it away. "Just us," I said.

"Um, Tor?" Owen nudged me. "You might want to take a look at this." He tilted the screen of his phone toward me. I recognized the basic blue-and-white background of the Lie Detector message boards.

I snatched the phone and scrolled the page. I couldn't reach the bottom. It was as if the comments on the Hunter of Hollow Pines thread went on forever.

"The number of posts has more than quadrupled in the last hour," he said.

"Are they about . . . ?" I clicked the screen off and shoved it back into Owen's lap like it was contaminated. *Adam*, I thought, but didn't say it.

"Some of them." His mouth formed a hard line. "But if the rate continues, more than five hundred people will have viewed the comments by tomorrow. It's out there, Tor, and I'm not sure you can stop it."

I refused to let myself contemplate how much time Adam had had unsupervised this morning once we'd arrived at school. Had it been fifteen minutes? Thirty? Would that have been enough? And if so, enough for what?

My throat was parched. I folded my hands in my lap and stared at the podium and Principal Wiggins behind it. "Then no more mistakes," I said. "We have to make sure there's nothing else to get out there, okay? It's simple. We just have to be perfect."

We can be perfect.

TWENTY-SEVEN

Stage 3 of the experiment will revolve around a new energy source for the subject.

— — —

The administration locked the doors. Off-campus lunch privileges were revoked. All PE classes were held indoors until further notice. For the rest of the day, we'd been trapped inside a cinder block cage with what felt like a shrinking oxygen supply. At the final bell, students rushed for open air. I was one of them. I grabbed my things and headed straight for the stadium to wait out football practice. At this point, there was no way I was leaving Adam alone. Not in Hollow Pines. Not with the Hunter on the loose. And . . . for other reasons, too, reasons that lodged painfully in my throat like a pill that refused to go down. Reasons that couldn't be true. They just couldn't be.

I scaled the stadium steps to a spot a few rows from the top bleachers. It looked like every sport except for the football team had canceled practice today. But this was Hollow Pines and this was Homecoming we were talking about. *The show must go on*, I thought drily. I popped off the orange-and-black pin fastened to my shirt and tossed it into my bag. My books made a loud clang when I plopped them down on the metal bleacher beside me. The seat was hard and cool. Up high, a strong wind swelled, peeling back the covers of one of my textbooks. I pinned it in place, then wrapped my arms around my knees, shuddering in the unexpectedly brisk air. The weather was changing. Above me, stray leaves fluttered before falling onto the sidewalk below.

I searched the field for Adam's face as Coach Carlson took the team through warm-up drills. A familiar rush of panic crowded my lungs when I couldn't immediately find him underneath the matching helmets and hulking football pads. The panic settled without fully disappearing once I spotted his uniform, number 88, and could just make out the swatches of dark hair and deep-set eyes hidden behind the bars that covered his mouth, chin, and nose.

In the background, a wide border of yellow crime scene tape marked off the outside of the boys' locker room. A lone news van lingered a few feet off, and the occasional black-coated official ducked under the tape and jotted things down in a notebook.

The body was gone. But the image of the missing eyes still haunted me, so much so that I startled at the sound of another pair of feet clomping down the bleacher aisle toward me.

"Boo," Owen said with a smirk, catching my jolt to attention.

"You shouldn't sneak up on people like that." I let go of my knees and crossed my legs underneath me.

"That would hardly qualify as sneaking. I literally walked right in front of you." He swung his backpack onto his hip and unzipped it. "Anyway, I wanted to show you something."

I glanced back to where Adam had just flattened a teammate on the field. I felt the curve of a small smile on my lips. He was really *good*. "What?" I asked.

Owen flipped open a spiral notebook and took a seat beside me. "This," he said, pointing.

I held back strands of my hair and leaned over to see. "It looks like a map."

"Exactly. This"—he turned the notebook horizontally and moved his finger to the upper left-hand corner of the page, where he'd drawn a squiggly blob—"is Lake Crook. And these two lines over here . . ." He traced what looked like a river with a winding turn that crossed the page. "This is State Highway Twenty-Four. I figured right around here is where you . . . well, where you found Adam." My back tensed. "It's about a fifteen-minute drive. A longer walk but doable."

I looked up from the page, stared hard at Owen, who I knew better than anyone else on the whole planet, who understood me better than anyone else except for maybe my dad, and he was gone. "Stop, Owen," I said.

But Owen didn't stop. The twitch was already in his fingers, the way it was when he was working on a tricky bit of machinery. He was fiddling, testing, probing, the cogs were turning. "Here's the field. I've marked the time the body was found approximately based on what you've told me. Adam was there, too."

"Owen . . ." The wind picked up again, fluttering the page. He ignored that, too, and I felt my throat get all tight and narrow like I'd been stung by a thousand bees. Suddenly I felt too exposed out here in the stadium, in the open air where any bird could simply fly over.

"Finally, we know we found Adam at the locker room," he continued, "the night before a boy winds up dead at our school, outside of that *same* locker room." To Owen's credit, his tone was grim. There wasn't an *I told you so* in sight. Just the bare-bones facts, exactly how I liked them.

My joints were stiff. "Let me see that." I leaned over, then, as Owen was handing it to me, I snatched the notebook, tore out the page, and crumpled it into a ball.

"Hey, that took effort!" I hated it when he whined.

On the field, Coach Carlson blew the whistle, and the team huddled together. I kept switching my attention back to Adam after short intervals.

"Yeah? Well, then it was a waste," I said, tossing the crumpled paper out of Owen's reach and shoving the rest of the notebook back into his hands. "These are coincidences, Owen. I thought you'd know the difference. I was on Highway Twenty-Four that night, too, remember? I was at the field where the body was found, and I was also with Adam and *you* at the boys' locker room last night. Does that make me a killer?"

Owen looked down at his untied laces propped up on the bleacher below. "No."

"And who are you looking out for, anyway? We're supposed to be looking out for Adam, not piecing together his prosecution." I was on my feet without realizing it. "I suppose he's just storing his spare eyeballs and legs in, what, his locker?"

"I don't know, Tor. He's dead. I think we should at least think through the possibility. Before somebody else does. And FYI, the person I'm looking out for is you. You don't know what you've gotten yourself into."

"See, that's where you're wrong." I pulled the strap of my bag over my shoulder and collected my things. "I'll see you later, Owen," I said, despising the niggling worm of doubt that squirmed inside me. "Find me when you remember who your friends are." After that, I didn't look back.

The bleachers shook underneath my clomping feet as I stormed down the stadium rows and out into the parking lot. The cool breeze wrapped itself around my neck and throat again, making me walk faster. Adam was mine. Owen would never have had the guts to create him. He would have never even tried. Owen's fear of Adam was that he was different. He had questioned Adam's existence since before he'd taken his first breath. Now he was looking for an excuse to be right.

I fished my keys from a front pocket of my bag, unlocked Bert, and slumped onto the fake leather seat. The cabin smelled moldy from where the moisture had seeped in through the crack in the windshield.

What I needed was to find a way to make sure last night didn't repeat itself, to make sure that I didn't find Adam on the brink of dying again—or worse—beyond saving.

I bit the nail on my pinkie finger down to the quick. The only way to do that was to find energy that would last.

On the opposite side of the parking lot, I watched Owen lope across the gravel, chin down and shoulders hunched. For a brief moment, he lifted his head and stared right at Bert. I wasn't sure whether he could see me or if he could only see the fractured mess of my car that would remind him of that night. Whatever the case, he must have decided something, because he walked the rest of the distance to his Jeep. Soon his taillights were glowing red, and he was backing out of his spot.

The band of skin where I'd chewed away the nail was pink with blood, and I squeezed it in my fist. Maybe I was too hard on Owen. Maybe—

A shadow crossed behind my car, and the light was blocked momentarily through the back windshield. I jolted upright, gripping my hands tightly around the base of the steering wheel. What was that? My brain conjured the first words that came to mind: *the Hunter.* Only a few cars were left in the lot. I glanced around. I was being stupid. The place had been swarming with cops only hours earlier. This was probably the safest place in town now. Footsteps crunched in the gravel directly next to Bert's passenger side, and, despite my internal monologue, the hairs on the backs of my arms stood on end.

But it was only Old Man McCardle. I tilted my chin up to the ceiling and shook my head. He appeared carrying a stick with a sharp point. He'd speared an aluminum Coke can and was now depositing it into his trash bag, which was exactly the sort of thing a school janitor should do. Not the Hunter of Hollow Pines. I exhaled. Apparently, the murders were getting to me, too. I slouched into my seat as the janitor crossed in front of the hood of my car, bending down to pick up a piece of garbage. Still, I had to admit, McCardle gave me his own brand of the creeps ever since he'd driven to school with a dead deer in the back of his truck last year and Principal Wiggins had insisted he return home.

I turned the key in the ignition and the headlights flared. He stood up, shielding his eyes. He stared at me with his watery blue eyes through the glass. *Sorry*, I mouthed without feeling all that sorry. I was eager to get away without having to talk to him. Even though I hated seeing the other students play stupid tricks on the old man, I couldn't help having the same instinctual response to want to distance myself from him. The truth was, Old Man McCardle wasn't even such an old man. Sun had been hard on his skin, thinning and wrinkling it like animal hide left to dry, and his hair was a silvery white with patches of a sun-spotted scalp peeking through. But he couldn't have been much older than Mom.

The gear still in park, I gently pressed my foot on the accelerator, and the engine revved. His lips worked without making any noise that I could hear, and at last, he dropped his hand and shuffled out of the way, trash bag in tow.

Relieved, I eased Bert out of the back row and left McCardle behind without sparing another thought, just as the players began to trickle out of practice and climb into the remaining cars.

I made a wide arc with the wheels and pulled up next to the sidewalk.

"Nice ride, Torantula." Knox shook his sweaty hair and flashed me a grin. Right as he was crossing in front of the hood, I laid my heel into the horn and let it blare in his ears. He jumped in surprise.

I smiled sweetly and folded my hands into my lap. Adam's face showed up at the window. He knocked and I unlocked the door for him to come inside.

"You're loud, Victoria," he said, folding his legs like a lawn chair to fit in the seat. "Why are you making the car yell?"

I let the foot off the brake. "Sorry. Thought I saw a rodent." I shrugged. "My bad. So how was practice?"

"You never ask how practice is," he said, no hint of accusation in his voice. He buckled his seat belt.

"You're awfully observant today, aren't you?"

"Yes." Adam smelled like mud and grass stains. I wrinkled my nose. I liked him better when he smelled clean, like rainwater.

I sighed and turned at the stop sign. The stadium faded from view. I hadn't realized how good it'd feel to get away from the school and to distance myself from the lingering image of the boy with the missing eyes. When I asked Owen whether Adam was storing a set of legs and eyeballs in his locker, I'd meant it to be rhetorical, but what had he meant when he'd responded that he didn't know? That Adam was dead.

I glanced sidelong at Adam. His face was serene. He seemed utterly incapable of harming anyone. But then there had been the mirror in the dressing room and the times just after his recharges that I could hardly recognize him. This, I realized, was further evidence of the need for a more permanent solution, something that didn't change Adam into . . . something else. Something darker.

"So no one asked you anything today? No police officers, I mean. They didn't come to talk to you?" I ventured while at a red light.

"No, no police officers. Was I supposed to talk to the policemen?"

"No," I answered too fast. "I was just curious." I slid my hands down to the bottom of the steering wheel and let my foot off the brake. If the Lie Detector's forum kept finding an audience, it was only a matter of time until the authorities would want to speak to him. The question was, how much time?

We drove through the small town center of Hollow Pines, past the two-theater cinema and Walton's Drugstore. The red cobblestone made the wheel axles rattle, and we bounced down Main Street until we got to Grimwood Drive and took a right where the cobblestone changed into dusty road and the buildings faded into miles of land-scape that was no more hilly than a sheet of cardboard.

"Home, sweet home," I said when, after ten minutes, we pulled up to my house. The weather vane screeched and howled in the breeze. I glanced up to see it pirouetting on the spot. Nails on a chalkboard. The wind blew an empty pail across the yard.

Adam put his hand to his stomach. "Can we have the tater tots?"

I laughed. *This* was the guy I was scared might be a monster? "I'll see if we have some in the freezer." I had already learned that Adam could consume an entire bag all by himself.

I was stepping out of the car when I noticed something different about the hatch. "No." My eyes got big. I left the car door hanging wide open. "No, no, no, no, no." I jogged over to the door of my laboratory. It was boarded shut. Plywood lay across the length of it, with bent nails sticking halfway out. "What?" I tugged on my hair. "No!" Everything was in there. All that I needed for a recharge. All my data. All my texts. What was it doing boarded up?

I spun back to Adam and held out my palm. "Stay inside," I said. "Stay down." He dropped back into his seat, and then when I motioned to him again, he lay down, disappearing from view but for the barely visible curve of his back. I looked back one more time at the spot where Adam was hiding and then at my laboratory. Einstein let out high-pitched barks from behind the screen door.

"Mom!" I yelled, stomping into the main house. "Mom!" I repeated. "Did you see someone boarding up my lab—the cellar? It's all blocked. I can't get in. Mom!" I tore through the kitchen, passing the piles of dishes and pushing a wicker chair out of my way.

I didn't have to look far, because I found her waiting for me in the living room, twirling a glass of red Merlot like she was at a fancy din-ner party instead of in the middle of our crummy living room.

"Mom!" I shouted again. "Somebody nailed boards to the cellar." I pointed outside.

"I know," she said, and took a long slurp from her wineglass. "Because it was me." She grinned. The wine made her mouth look toothy.

"You?" The rest of the words lost their sound the moment they tried to leave my mouth. I stood dumbstruck. The fact that my mother conceived of this scheme and then succeeded in actually carrying it out was almost too much to comprehend. "What are you talking about? You can't do that," I shouted, panic climbing up my throat. "That was Dad's cellar. He wanted *me* to have it. What were you thinking? All my equipment is down there. I'm doing my best work. Why would you do that?"

She pointed her finger at the ceiling, where, through the roof shingles, we could hear the metallic squeal of the weather vane. "I've been telling you to fix that racket, Victoria Frankenstein. I've been telling you more times than I have fingers or toes. But all you care about is your *laboratory*. And your *cellar*. And your *science*." She said these words like a playground taunt, and I felt the skin around my neck flame. "You're just like your father."

"Good!" I screamed. As long as I was nothing like her. Fury clawed at me. I wanted to break something. A chair. A vase. Anything. I stuffed my hands in my pockets and seethed.

Her shoulders shook with laughter. "I told you, you think you're smarter than everybody, but I'm still your mom."

Tears burned the back of my eyes. Tears that never came for my father but were now there in a white-hot rage. "You are the opposite of helpful! You are worse than Einstein!" I yelled, and stalked out of the room. I sounded like a teenage girl, which I absolutely, positively hated, but my mother was standing in the way of progress. What I was doing was important. It was maybe the most important work on the planet right now. Didn't she realize that Dad had been killed by a single shock, but I'd manage to create life from the same source?

Of course she didn't. She knew nothing. I knew when I'd been beat. Breathing hard, I retrieved the ladder from our garage, which acted more as a storage shed than a place for cars. I dragged the ends of the ladder across the dirt until I could prop the top of it against the roof. I put my foot on the bottom rung and shook it to make sure I wouldn't fall to my death. Mom would probably think that was my fault, too.

When it seemed secure enough, I scaled the rest of the rungs and pulled myself onto the roof, still wishing I had any mother but the one I had. The shingles were warm and gritty. Bits stuck in my hands and dimpled the heels. I couldn't believe she had the nerve to take a hammer and nails to my laboratory. It made me want to stomp through the roof and break the ceiling.

Instead, I pushed my way up from my knees, knowing that my mom had won this round. Her weather vane was going to get fixed or there'd be no peace for any of us. Up here the air conditioner hummed, and a mysterious substance was leaking from a spot near our chimney. Adam was afraid of heights, but they didn't bother me. My dad used to come up here and take notes on the cloud patterns. Sometimes I came with him and lay bellydown, reading my textbooks. That was why I didn't want Mom to take down his weather vane.

But as I crossed the ridges of our roof, I realized that his presence had disappeared. My dad was gone from this place. Barely his memory even lingered. It'd been years since I'd seen the weather vane up close. From here, I could see that the rooster ornament used to be painted red. By now, though, most of the paint had flaked off. The directions were each marked with elegant letters: *N, S, E, W.* It must have been an antique even when my dad got it.

I kneeled beside it, put my hands on the crossbars, and wriggled it off its post. The weather vane fell to the roof with a clatter, and I dropped backward on my rear end.

I wiped my hands together and stared out at the horizon. From here, I could see the whole of the town clearly. The lights cropped up from the town center, the factory, and the rest of the city limits, which faded into the Hollows, an evergreen forest that bordered our town. For a moment, I just sat there and stared out at the fuzzy green treetops that carpeted the horizon. They were beautiful. A peaceful stretch of countryside. It was strange seeing them this way again. The last time I'd been into the woods, my dad had been killed. Now, when I thought of the Hollows—if I ever thought of the Hollows—it was about how they hid the flashbacks from me, or, if I thought too hard, about how their branches reminded me of the scars left behind on my dad's chest, the angry rivers of red that charted the course of his death. I leaned forward, cupping my hand and staring harder out into the forest. Because I remembered now that they hid something else, too.

In a second, I was pushing myself to my feet. Why hadn't I thought of this before? In the Hollows was hidden my father's great masterpiece. His prized experiment. The thing that killed him. Three dormant behemoths rested in the woods, waiting. They had killed my dad, but electricity had killed my dad when it had saved Adam, and this just might be the same thing. My heart pounded in my chest. This was it. This was the answer. The solution I'd been looking for.

The generators would need to be reawakened.

TWENTY-EIGHT

The lightning generators work off a series of silk pulleys, a belt, wire combs, a metal dome, an electric motor, and a column. The design is similar to that of a Van de Graaff generator, though on a much larger scale. A similar endeavor was first attempted without the generators by German scientists in the Alps. The scientists used a two-thousand-foot iron cable and an adjustable spark gap across a valley, but the space between the mountains was too vast for harnessing and the experiment ultimately failed.

— — —

Back up and tell me where we're going again. Am I being kidnapped? Because if I'm being kidnapped, I'd like to make some demands up front." Owen scooted to the middle of the backseat, wedging his head between Adam and me. Outside, evening fell in stages. The darkest blue began at the top, where it stacked itself onto brighter hues that ended in a golden ribbon of light on the horizon. "First of all, I'll need a bathroom break every hour. Second, I have a sensitive stomach, so I'd like to suggest a bland diet of Pop-Tarts and Nutri-Grain bars. No sodas, or we'll need to up the bathroom-break quotient."

My broken windshield fractured the sky, turning it into a giant puzzle as I edged my car up to the fringe of the Hollows. The forest bordered the western edge of Hollow Pines like a prickly petticoat made from pine trees and oak. Beside me, my dad's old map was sprawled over the center console.

I glanced in the rearview mirror, still annoyed with Owen. Only as annoyed as I was, I happened to need him more at the moment, so I'd have to play nice.

"We're going in there." I nodded to the tree trunks now framed in the windshield like a photograph. Once off the rutted side road, I pushed the gear in park. We'd been driving for ten minutes. The headlight beams penetrated only a short distance into the woods' heart, where gnarled branches crossed arms as if in warning to keep out.

Owen ducked his head to peer through the glass. "Oh, great, that quells all of my worst fears. The creepy woods at night. Perfect, *just* perfect, Tor."

"Victoria has a plan. She told me," Adam said without turning in his seat. He stared after the high beams into the forest. Maybe it was stupid, maybe it should have been the complete opposite, but I somehow felt safer going out there with Adam nearby.

Owen patted Adam on the shoulder. "That, my friend, is exactly what I'm afraid of. Is part of that plan getting murdered by the Hunter?"

I lifted my eyebrows. "Oh, are you worried he's out there now?" I said. "Because I was under the impression . . ."

He pushed back into his seat. "I'm worried period, okay. It's easy for you. The Hunter seems to prefer boy legs, but Adam and I, we happen to like our appendages where they are—attached." I tilted my head but tried to mask a smile. Owen was at least trying. He was trying to believe Adam wasn't the Hunter. He was trying to be on my side. "Okay, fine." He tossed his hands up. "What's this plan?"

I unbuckled my seat belt and twisted to look back at him. "I've told you about my dad's death, right?"

"Oh sure, that was after we made friendship bracelets but before we held hands and sang 'Kumbaya.' I can hardly get you to shut up about it."

"Point taken." I turned back and, across the steering wheel, unfurled the map. A red triangle with a circle around it marked the three matching points. I peered over the map's curling edges into the forest. "My dad left something in there. He was brilliant, you know. My grandparents, they were just regular people who worked at the plant, but not my dad. He could have never been happy doing just that. He wanted to know things. Bigger than Hollow Pines."

I felt Owen inching closer behind me. I could feel the hot tickle of his breath on my arm. "What did he leave?" Owen asked.

"Was it treasure?" Adam said, and I remembered he'd been reading Robert Louis Stevenson's *Treasure Island* in English class.

"Not exactly." I closed my eyes. I was trying to picture the generators, but time had worn away the edges of the memory, and now they only loomed like a legend in my mind. "My dad had figured out a way to harness atmospheric voltage."

"What is that?" Adam asked.

"Electricity that's in the sky," Owen said.

"Lightning," I nearly whispered. "The theory goes that if someone could control the atmospheric voltage, then there would be enough energy to disintegrate the atom."

Owen's intake of breath was sharp.

Adam's eyes widened. "You're going to disintegrate Adam?" He touched his finger to his chest and frowned.

I put my fist over my mouth to keep from laughing. "No! The *at-om*. Tiny little microscopic particles. Don't worry. No one is disintegrating you."

"But if you could disintegrate the atom, you would have not just energy, but a supersource of energy. Enough to charge a whole city. Enough to charge—"

We both stopped and stared at Adam. On the outside, my creation appeared so normal, beyond recognition for what he really was. But hidden underneath was the tapestry of scars and organs sustained by a steady hum of current destined to fade like the passing tide.

"Yep," I said. "That's pretty much the idea."

The ink scratches of my dad's handwriting on the satellite picture were like whispers from the dead. Coiling the map, I retrieved the clunky GPS device from the glove compartment, then opened the door with a tinny pop.

From the trunk I pulled Owen's bag of tools, which I'd ordered him to bring. Metal clanked around in the canvas bag. I plopped it in the grass behind the trails of the car's exhaust.

"So I guess that means you're done being mad at me," he said as he bent down for the handle. "Now that you need me."

I slammed the trunk. The sound rang through the open air like a gunshot. I dusted my hands. "Yep. That's pretty much the idea."

I doled out three flashlights, and we each snapped them on. The yellow beams trickled through the dying sunlight. We crossed the tree line just as the day took its final breath.

The ground was a soft bed of pine needles. A few steps into the forest and we found a world emptied of sound. No birds chirped or squirrels chattered. I hadn't set foot in the Hollows since my dad's death, and I felt like I might see him pass through the spaces between the trees at any moment.

Adam held up a low-hanging limb for me, and I ducked underneath and shuffled through the leaves scattered half decomposed over the mud. Soil clumped onto the soles of my shoes, making them heavier. I passed a snapped trunk. Shards of charred wood poked out from either side like a broken arm, and I smelled the remnants of smoke.

We trudged in silence. I noticed Owen snapping his head left and right, searching. It was easy to create the story in our heads of the Hunter lurking and for it to begin to feel true. But there was no reason the Hunter would be here in this spot with us right now, so I ignored the distant snaps of branches and rustling of leaves.

With the tip of my finger, I brushed the bark. My skin came away with a black smudge from where lightning must have split the tree some time ago. After a short distance, I handed my flashlight off to Owen and cradled the GPS in both hands. The numbers on the screen glowed green, changing as we tracked east and north in the direction of the Arkansas state line.

I studied the shifting digits harder now and tried to match them with a few recognizable landmarks from my memory. A fallen log with a gaping hole in the center like a howling mouth. A red rock, flat on the top with three points.

The numbers told me I was getting closer. "This way." I adjusted our course to veer left. The digits scrolled up. Closer, closer.

My pulse quickened and, with it, my pace. We picked through strands of spiderwebs that formed invisible nets between the trees and broke twigs from their boughs. Then, as the numbers bled one into the next, the thicket cleared, and we stumbled into an open space ringed by the warped trunks of trees. *Here*, I thought.

"Jesus . . . ," Owen mumbled.

This was it. The three columns of my dad's lightning generators rose nearly twenty feet into the sky. Dormant gray orbs made a triangle in the secret circle. They stood like lost relics from a different era. A temple to the gods of science.

I separated from Adam and Owen and walked to the center of the triangle. Instinctively, I held my breath, feeling as though I was stepping onto hallowed ground. The carpet of pine needles was thick and undisturbed. I stared straight into the sky, where stars were beginning to prick holes into the navy blanket above. Thick white cables connected each of the generators. I traced their paths. *The lightning cage*, my dad had called it, and I missed the low-frequency buzz of electricity running through them.

I turned to see both Adam and Owen watching me. "You say you can fix anything," I told Owen.

His eyes traveled up the length of the gargantuan generators. "You bet your ass." He followed me and motioned for Adam. "Buddy, come here and hold the light," he said.

Owen circled the first generator. Around and around he went, running his hands over the smooth cylinder from the base to as far up as he could reach. Then his canvas bag was on the ground, unzipped and puking out tools. Owen's front teeth dug into his tongue. Adam held the flashlight over Owen's shoulder while Owen kneeled in the dirt.

I could hardly see the tiny grooves, but Owen nestled the screwdriver tip into the screws and twisted two free until he was able to flip the lid. Inside, there were three switches, each pointed down and coated in thick rust. A beetle crawled up the side, and Owen flicked it off. For two years the monoliths had been in a coma. The outer build was cool to the touch.

I bit down on the inside of my cheek. Owen flicked the first switch, the second, and, finally, the third. Nothing happened.

"I suppose that would have been too easy," I said.

Owen grunted and flipped the switches back down. He used the flashlight to discover four more screws and removed a plate that opened into a tangle of wires, like the generator had intestines. They were every color, and beside them were a series of cogs frozen in place with age, a thin ribbon wrapped around each cog and attached to the next, disappearing into the underbelly of the generator where I couldn't see.

"Bingo." Owen licked his lips.

I left Owen to tinker and Adam to help. Though I felt Adam's stare stretch after me, he didn't follow. I found myself drawn away not by an electromagnetic source, but by something deeper. I crossed over the invisible line created by the three generators to a spot just before the end of the glade where the tree line resumed.

My fingers tingled. I bent down and touched the nest of leaves. I could feel the place in the marrow of my bones. This was where it happened. This was where my life had changed. I closed my eyes and remembered. The smell of the rain. The splatter of droplets on glass. The static playing through the speakers . . . and him.

"Wait in the car," my dad had said. I'd kicked my boots together over the floorboards of his dusty old truck and played with the lightning-bolt bracelet around my wrist, spinning it around and around in an endless loop.

My dad crawled out into the rain that was busy sliding over the windshield in great torrents, turning the world into an Impressionist painting. His yellow galoshes splashed in the puddles. He looked up at the sky, shielding his eyes. I wasn't sure what he was looking for, but it made me mad that I couldn't see it through the roof of the car.

He pulled the hood of his equally yellow rain jacket up and disappeared into the forest. Even though I knew it was strictly forbidden, I waited only thirty seconds or so before I followed him. The moment I stepped out of the car, the downpour beat against my cheeks, softening only once I'd crossed into the forest.

I'd been into the Hollows with my dad dozens of times before, but this time Dad seemed different. The printouts of his Doppler readings screamed with orange and red. The storm was coming. And now he wanted me to stay in the truck and miss the whole thing. I didn't think so.

I stayed close to the trunks of trees to avoid being spotted but soon realized that my dad was farther in front of me than I thought. I became more brazen, hopping over fallen logs and undergrowth, hurrying so as not to miss the big event.

I was so consumed in reaching the clearing that I nearly ran straight into the middle of it without realizing. I came to a screeching halt at the edge when I saw my dad's bright yellow gear and was brought back to reality. The rain masked any noise I made, and because I wasn't supposed to be out here in the first place, I had no bright raincoat to give me away. On the other hand, my skin was soaked, and I was shivering down to my underwear.

Above us the generators were alive with the electricity in the atmosphere. A blue-white glimmer zipped across the cables. I stared at them, quivering, as if they were living beings. It was better than anything I'd ever seen at Disney World. Because these were real. These were science.

A roll of thunder shook the pine trees around me. I squatted behind a trunk. Dad pulled out a plastic-coated paper of some sort and eyed the sky, rotating in place, always looking up. The first fork of lightning split the clouds, making the raindrops appear like falling shards of light. It was close enough to smell the burn in the air.

My dad was smiling now, laughing. He thrust his fist over his head. He was yelling something I couldn't hear. It made me want to laugh, too. But then the next streak of lightning burst through the clearing, and at first, I waited to celebrate, thinking that my dad's experiment had worked. That was, until I saw his yellow galoshes on the ground, the toes pointed up. The rest of my dad lay sprawled on the ground. His hands and arms fanned out from his body like an angel.

I broke my cover. I no longer cared. I sprinted over to him and wrapped my small hands around his face and shook. He didn't wake up. Frantic, I found the zipper of his raincoat and tore it open, bursting apart the buttons on his shirt, ready to try to perform CPR as I'd seen on TV. But I choked. There on his chest was a web of red scars, and they snaked all the way up to his throat.

I was frightened at once. I wanted for the night to disappear. I remembered skittering back on all fours, heaving, while inside the lightning cage bolts of lightning twisted and writhed, casting a luminous glow across my father's dead body.

Something hard on the ground brought me back to the present. I'd been touching the leaves idly when, from the damp earth, I felt something cross my palm. I curled my fingers around it and turned my hand over. I sucked in a quick breath. There was a gold lightning-bolt charm threaded through a string of frayed twine. I pinched the ends and held the shiny trinket eye level. It was a gift from my father for my thirteenth birthday, and back then I never took it off, even to shower. The rope had unraveled and become threadbare until I realized that it was just gone. Sometimes it was my naked wrist and the missing charm, more so than my dead father, that woke me up in the middle of the night in a cold sweat, feeling like I'd lost something.

I used my teeth to tie the twine into a tight knot around my wrist. The lightning bolt bounced softly against the bulb of veins that gathered at the crease before my hand.

Behind me a motor clicked before shifting into a high-pitched whir like the sound of a plane engine taking off. I spun. A white spark spat from the first sphere's surface, followed by a strand of light that started at the ball and looped in on itself.

"You did it!" I exclaimed, running back to join them. "You did it!" I threw my arms around Owen's neck, and he toppled over.

"One down . . ." He stared up, smiling. The first generator was alive.

It took Owen an hour to jump-start the two remaining. Adam and I helped. Beneath the buzz of the generators' electromagnetic pulse, I replaced the lid on each cylinder and screwed it tightly to the base.

I felt a swell of hope. My dad's experiments were being resurrected.

Just as the last generator was issuing its first rusty roar and I was screwing the lid over the switches and wires, we heard a string of rapid breaks in the branches.

"Did you hear that?" Adam asked.

Owen swept his flashlight beam over the trees, but we couldn't see past the border. "Yes."

More cracks came from the other side. "It's just the forest," I said, keeping my voice low. "Probably a deer."

Every few seconds another branch snapped. Owen rested a hand on my shoulder. It made me jump. "We should go."

Slowly, I rose to my feet. I felt the cords on my neck grow taut. Owen shouldered his bag. Adam's hand was on the small of my back. He drew close. I imagined a faceless Hunter watching us, casing us as his next victims in Hollow Pines, and my blood ran cold.

A rustle of leaves. It sounded close. A hush had fallen over our group. I thought I saw movement between the trees. "Come on." I motioned to the others.

We tried to keep our pace calm and steady, but as we left the clearing, it continued to escalate. Twigs split within earshot. The three of us broke into a jog, twisting our chins over our shoulders to check to see if somebody was following. Then we were running. Our flashlights bobbed in and out of tree trunks. We sprinted back the way we came. Although I knew Adam could outrun me by a mile, he stayed a few inches behind, and I could feel his protective presence envelop me.

"It's farther to the right," I huffed.

"Are you sure?" Owen asked, but he followed me.

As we ran, I began to think of how the boys died. My mind jumped to the body in the field with the bear trap snapped around the anklebone, and I aimed my flashlight at the ground, scared at any moment one of us would feel the iron jaws clamp down on our foot. My heart turned into a wrecking ball hell-bent on destroying the inside of my chest.

We clambered through the woods until we couldn't hear the snapping of branches. The trees thinned. I could see the road. One by one, we arrived at my car. I rested my hands on Bert's hood and tried to catch my breath. Owen dropped the canvas bag and collapsed with his back to one tire.

"Are you okay, Victoria?" Adam put his hand between my shoulder blades as they rose and fell.

I nodded and looked back into the woods, wondering whether I should feel silly, if we'd let shadows chase us from the forest, or, instead, whether what we'd feared was real.

TWENTY-NINE

Stage 3 of the experiment has been initiated, but we will have to wait for the right set of conditions to apply it to the subject. For now, I've continued to monitor the subject through regular tests of his pH levels, blood pressure, platelets, and weight. Adam's emotional range continues to progress as evidenced by careful observation of romantic behavior with the female variable.

- - -

The moon punched a hole in a clear sky of navy so dark and fathomless it seemed to go on forever behind the haloed glow of Hollow Pines High's Friday night lights. I'd spent the last two days keeping an eye on the colorful blobs of green and red and yellow as they expanded and shifted along the Doppler radar images while the fifteen-mile radius around our town remained hopelessly blank. I stared up from my spot on the bleachers. Nothing.

Somewhere across the city line, three lightning generators buzzed with life. I now tracked the weather, charting storm systems in my notebook with the obsessive fervor of a Vegas bookie. Hollow Pines, Texas, could look forward to a weekend of clear skies and crisp fall weather. Lucky it.

Back on earth, the stadium benches wreaked havoc on my tailbone. I couldn't imagine why anyone did this whole rah-rah school spirit thing for fun. The whole place smelled like artificial cheese and corn dogs, and, only five minutes in, I'd already stepped on an open mustard packet. I kept my knees pinched together and my hands folded in my lap. This seemed to be the safest position to avoid either touching the guy beside me whose face was painted orange or getting caught in one of those crowd waves I'd seen on television.

"Watch out. Coming through. Beep, beep." I scooted left when I spotted Owen picking his way down the row toward me and balancing an overflowing bag of popcorn and a monster cup of soda. "I come bearing gifts," he said, spilling a few kernels on my lap when he plopped down beside me.

"Excuse me," I said, stuffing some of the fallen popcorn into my mouth. "But hell hath frozen over." I leaned forward to get a view of the orange lettering on his hoodie. "Is that an Oilers sweatshirt?"

"When in Rome, right?"

"Sounds a lot better than here at the moment." I took a long sip of Coke from the straw and squinted at the scoreboard. "How long do these things take, anyway?"

"Longer than a prostate exam, shorter than open-heart surgery." He reached into the pouch of his sweatshirt and pulled out a Twix and a bag of Skittles. "Drugs to numb the pain."

I snatched the Twix bar and unwrapped it, sinking my teeth into the crunchy chocolate and caramel. "I'm going to need, like, five more of these." I stood up on my tippy-toes and leaned over the bleacher railing to see if I could spot Adam, but the players all looked nearly identical dressed up in tight pants and football pads. I worked to search out his jersey number. The freshly watered grass sparkled emerald green. Just because my Hollow Pines pride happened to be running on empty didn't mean I couldn't feel a tiny surge of satisfaction at the thought of my own brainchild on the starting line. To think, it'd taken Adam only some minor persuading to get me to come.

Suddenly, the band began trumpeting a version of "When the Saints Go Marching In," and the fans rose to their feet, clapping. I looked around, searching for the invisible clue I missed. "It's starting? How do people know it's starting?"

I jumped and plugged my ears at the sound of cannon fire.

"Get 'em, boys!" Owen whooped.

"What are you doing?" I pushed Owen's arms down to his sides. "You're one whoop away from starring in a beer commercial."

A few minutes later, to the tune of "Deep in the Heart of Texas," Knox kicked the football. It arced, end over end, landing a disappointing ten yards past the center to unified groans from the crowd.

The limp kick was an omen of things to come. It'd been a point of pride that I'd managed to live my entire life in football country without learning a single fact about the game, but by the end of the first quarter, I'd learned that a touchdown was worth six points plus a chance to kick a field goal for an additional one. And it didn't take a girl genius to ascertain that we didn't have any.

Adam barreled through the other team like they were dominoes. He was a force to be reckoned with, much like gale force winds and garlic breath, but halfway through the second quarter, we were still down by fourteen. Owen held his fingers to his lips and whistled.

When he caught me staring at him like his body had been taken over by aliens, he shrugged. "Must be the sweatshirt."

Just after halftime, we earned a touchdown back. Adam bulldozed the defensive line, and Billy Ray was able to throw for a touchdown. Cassidy, Paisley, and the rest of the pom-pom brigade leaped into the air and twisted their legs into unnatural positions as though they were cheering for something other than our team's ribs getting cracked by total strangers. It was barbaric. And okay, maybe a teensy bit thrilling.

Adam himself, though, was his own phenomenon. When we broke even, Owen yelled like a banshee. "Do you think it's muscle memory?" I said, screaming over the crowd. "To explain, I don't know." I pointed down at the field. "All of that."

"Who cares," Owen called back and shoved the bag of Skittles into my hand. I stress-ate a handful.

The two teams held even for a whole quarter and a half, nobody budging. The trouble was that while Adam was the best man on the field by a long shot, the other team had at least five guys half as good as Adam, which made them twice as good as all the other Oilers players. He was outnumbered. I couldn't watch. I had to watch. I was witnessing a losing battle. Custer's last stand.

Two minutes left on the clock. I found myself literally biting my fingernails. Owen quirked an eyebrow. "What?" I glanced away. "It's your darn sweatshirt. I think it might be contagious." I made a show of shuffling away.

Oilers' ball. The seconds ticked by with excruciating regularity. The ball was hiked. I bobbed on the balls of my feet. The whole stadium held its breath.

Until Billy Ray's face ate Astroturf. Adam shook his helmet and punched his fists together. Second down.

This time, despite being outmanned four to one, Adam managed to block the onslaught long enough for Billy Ray to progress several feet. But it wasn't enough. The clock no longer had a number in the minutes' column. The seconds counted down lower and lower.

I dug my teeth into my fist. Third down.

The ball was hiked. Rather than block, Adam backpedaled toward Billy Ray. When he emerged around the other side, the ball was tucked underneath his arm. I could *see* Billy Ray screaming at him, face turning maroon as he waved at Adam to run. *Run, Adam, run*, I saw him shout.

I would deny this with my dying breath, but I screeched. Like girl-at-a-boy-band-concert screeched. Because Adam—*my* Adam—Adam, who had been dead and brought back to life by yours truly, was sprinting down the field. I was a science goddess. A genius. Fifty-yard line. Forty-yard line. Thirty.

A skinny kid with ninja-quick legs chased him from the side. When he got close, he leaped onto Adam, but Adam caught him in the neck with the side of his arm. His head whipped backward and he flipped onto the ground, where the red jersey rolled before lying in the grass, his knees curling up.

Twenty yards. The roar of the crowd was deafening. A thicker player, built like Einstein, had cut across the field and was now closing the gap between him and Adam. As Adam reached the ten-yard line, the player hooked his arms around Adam's waist and twisted. Adam stumbled. Now the rest of the crowd had joined the chant, "Run, Adam, run!" He dug his cleats into the ground. But he didn't fall.

The other player's legs splayed out from under him, and he was dragged across the field, clinging to Adam's waist. Slow, but still standing, Adam inched toward the one-yard line with two entire teams in pursuit.

My eyes stayed glued to the field. *Come on, Adam, come on.* They were going to catch him. But as the numbers on the game clock slipped down to two seconds left, Adam lunged across the line, landing with a thud on his shoulder.

"He did it!" I screamed. "He did it!" A shotgun blast marked the end of the game. The drum line erupted into rolls of percussion. "Oh my God, he won!" I said. I flattened my palms together and put them up to my mouth, and I just stood there, staring down at the field like a proud parent.

Pretty soon, the stadium had turned to pandemonium. This was the first Homecoming game Hollow Pines had won in ten years. Fans stormed the field, and I rode the rush until the soles of my shoes hit plush green and I was searching for Adam in the crowd, reading the numbers on grass-stained jerseys, peering past the grates of face masks. My insides bubbled. It was so uncomplicated, this sports thing. And it was all Adam. *My* Adam, I repeated this. A mantra. I did this.

So flushed with the glow from Adam's win, I didn't mind the sweaty arms brushing by me or the stink of hard-worked boys. I pushed through to the center of the crowd. Never had I felt a pride so pure as the one throbbing through my heart for Adam. My Adam. When I spotted him only a few yards away, I thought it may burst through my chest. This contrivance of my own device, of my own sweat, of my own tedious work, late night, and bloodshot eyes.

I squeezed through a pair of local reporters interviewing a pair of Billys, and I was about to shout for Adam when there was a blur of orange sequins and skin. Cassidy straddled Adam, wrapping her arms around his neck. He twirled her, and when he did, I could clearly make out the smile plastered across his face, and I knew then that I'd succeeded. Adam felt something. But it was all Cassidy's.

She returned gracefully to the ground, her hand clutching his shoulder.

"There you are!" She caught me looking on. "Did you see our man?"

Something sour brewed in my stomach. Who did Cassidy Hyde think she was? *Our?* I swallowed down the piping hot mixture of jealousy and righteous indignation that had risen to the top of my throat.

Adam peeled off his helmet, and my intestines untangled themselves. I couldn't help but smile. Hair stuck to his temples, masking the incisions I knew were there. Beads of perspiration dripped from the tip of his nose. He shook his head like a puppy, and sweat flew in all directions.

When Adam's eyes landed on me, the effect was undeniable. His grin lit up the whole of his face. From there, it reached into my chest and gave my heart a gentle tug. Okay, so it wasn't the same way that he looked at Cassidy. Instead, it was as if I were the sun and he were one of my planets. He looked at me with such awe that I both simultaneously shrank and expanded beneath it.

"Victoria, I did it," he said.

"You did it. Congratulations," I said, keeping a healthy distance.

"I saw you clapping."

"I'll deny it with my last breath."

Billy Ray barged into the conversation. He lifted up Adam by his thighs and hoisted him up into the air three times before dropping him. "Thatta boy!" He slapped Adam's back. "Party at Knox's house. One hour."

I looked down at my watch. "What about curfew?" The ten o'clock quarantine was still in effect, and the third body lingered like an invisible presence at the same time every night. *Better get home or you'll wind up dead*, it whispered to us silently. Only tonight, nobody was listening.

"Best not to get caught, then." Billy Ray pointed at Cassidy and then Adam and then turned to me. "Don't flake out now. Winners don't flake."

"Oh, well then, I feel personally entitled to continue to flake," I said.

Cassidy did that thing where she tucked her hands under her chin and shot out her lower lip. "Come on, Tor. You guys have to be there. Knox's parents own part of the Texans."

"The who?"

She laughed. "The pro football team. They're on the road this weekend. Nobody will ever know."

I sighed. "I don't know." The truth was I had already been dreaming of plaid pajama bottoms and bunny slippers and, oh yeah, the idea of not being murdered. "I mean, I got up real early and I wear, like, a retainer at night." I frowned. I didn't think it looked nearly as convincing as Cassidy's princess pout. "Really just, like, a whole headgear situation. It's not pretty. And, I mean, it's probably best just to skip altogether." I looked at Adam for help. After all, he needed to be recharged by morning, but he was searching me with pleading eyes.

"Shut *up*, Victoria." Cassidy grabbed both of my hands and held them in hers. "You two have to come. Promise me you'll come."

The merriment surged around us, and the pesky memory of the

third body seemed to float farther and farther away. I looked up to the cloudless sky and decided what the hell. "Okay, okay, I promise. For one hour. That's it."

Cassidy narrowed her eyes and held out her pinkie to me. "Cross your heart and hope to die?"

I rolled my eyes but locked my finger into the crook of hers. "And hope to die," I said.

THIRTY

Subject's Stats:
  Height: 6'3"
  Weight: 196 lbs
  Blood pressure: 142/96
  Eyesight-good; hearing-normal

— — —

An hour later my teeth were rattling from the bass pumping through Knox Hoyle's home, a massive ranch-style house that reeked of oil money from the stone facade to the shrubs that were manicured into evenly spaced orbs and planted along the circle drive. I peered up at the vaulted ceilings, feeling instantly underdressed. I wondered how anyone could live in a place where they felt awkward wearing sweatpants.

Cassidy, on the other hand, surveyed the place like this was her natural domain. "Hang on. I'll get us all a round of drinks," she said, then took off toward a back door.

Adam and I stood a couple of feet inside the entryway, staring at our shoes and looking conspicuous. "So, uh, this is what it's like to have money." I stared up at the dangling chandelier. Crystals quivered from the beat of the music.

"I don't like dead things hanging from walls," Adam said matter-of-factly.

A deer head stared out at the party from its place over the mantel.

Near a set of towering bookcases, Mr. Hoyle had hung the shaggy head of a buffalo, and across the room, another antlered animal—maybe an antelope—had reached its final destination nailed to a mahogany plaque. Each had hard marble eyes that reflected the flashing blades of the ceiling fans.

"I don't like white furniture," I said, noting an entire living room upholstered in cream. "I get the urge to throw drinks on it. Seriously, don't let me near that stuff."

Adam dipped a hand into a bowl in the foyer and pulled out a red chip. He took a bite and then spat it back out into the bowl. "I don't like that stuff."

"I think that's potpourri. You're not supposed to like it. You're supposed to smell it."

Adam picked up the glass bowl and held it up to his face, where he scrunched his nose. "Oh, nice."

I lifted my eyebrows. "Look at us. A couple of party animals. Watch out, next we'll be sampling the room spray."

Knox swaggered down a white marble corridor toward us, clutching a bottle of vodka by the neck. "You know, at a party, you're supposed to actually venture *into* the party. That place where the other people congregate?" Knox had changed into a pair of rumpled khakis and a collared shirt that poked out from underneath a gray sweater. His freshly showered hair was darker than its standard wheat hue.

I stuffed my hands in my pockets and rocked back onto my heels. "Beautiful home. Adam and I were just saying."

Adam still clutched the glass bowl like he was about to take a long drink of dried flowers. "I thought you hated the furniture."

Knox narrowed his eyes, took a swig from the bottle, and then shook off the burn. "Guess there's no accounting for taste," he said, casting a look from me to Adam and then back to me. "Obviously."

"Right. Anyway, great party. Really top-notch." I gave him an awkward thumbs-up. Not even a minute in and I was already wishing that

Owen had decided to party-crash. Screw the no-invite rule. Besides, Knox gave me the creepy crawlies.

His eyes flashed, snakelike. "Better with a little of this." He shook the bottle of vodka. "Strong enough to ward off serial killers, I hear."

"That doesn't sound scientific at all. And thanks, but Cassidy's on drink duty, anyway. There she is." I pointed at no one in particular and grabbed Adam by the arm.

"I'll come find you later, Tor," Knox called after me, and for some reason, it sounded like a threat.

Deeper into the Hoyles' house, the music grew more earsplitting. I found a spot where I could move in a two-foot radius without bumping elbows with someone spilling beer on me. I pressed my fingers into my temples, trying to drown out the music that was pounding around in my skull. I pulled Adam down to my eye level, speaking close to make sure he could hear me. "Listen, I don't think alcohol's a good idea tonight. We don't know how it'll affect you, and I don't think the time to experiment is now." I dropped my voice low. "Right after a game. If you know what I mean. We're going to be here for one hour. Tops."

I glanced back toward the door where more people were pouring in. Red cups had been set up on the dining room table, and guys were tossing Ping-Pongs into them before downing the contents of each cup. I felt the worried pull of my forehead. "Can you promise me you won't drink?"

He put his hand on my shoulder. Half his mouth swooped into a smile. Leftover black paint smudged his cheeks. Adam Smith, whoever he was, really was kind of adorable. "Cross my heart and hope to die."

"You're learning," I said, and felt the gleam in my eye.

"Ahem." Cassidy appeared, balancing three drinks. She looked to Adam, then to me, and then back to Adam. I stood up straight and took a step back from Adam. "Am I interrupting something?" She had to yell over the music, and I wasn't sure if she'd meant for the question to come out quite so angry.

"Nope." I stood up straighter and backed farther away from Adam. She handed me a drink, which looked like Coke. "Yours is just soda," she said when I bent down to sniff it. "I made an educated guess. Hope that's all right. We can switch if you want." She swirled a straw in her drink of clear liquid.

I took a sip. Just Coke. "No, this is perfect, actually," I said. At least I knew the random party attendance hadn't ruined my nerd cred.

Cassidy's cheeks pursed when she sipped from her drink. She hadn't changed since the game. A fringed leather vest hung open over an orange sports bra, which showcased her toned torso, and her silky brown hair cascaded in loose barrel curls over her shoulders.

"Adam, I want to show you the pool," she said like she was the Hoyles' Realtor. "It has one of those infinity edges and a waterfall Jacuzzi. You can come, too, Victoria, if you want." I understood from her tone that I wasn't supposed to want to come. I didn't, anyway. I'd seen pools before, and I'd seen Adam and Cassidy make out, so I assumed there was nothing much more for me that I hadn't already experienced a time too many.

I raised my glass in salute. "No, thanks. I'm going to forage for food, I think." That was what lame people did at parties, right?

Cassidy gave a tight smile in thanks, and I wandered off in the opposite direction. I pushed my way through the middle of an Oilerette talking to the president of the junior class.

"Uh, how about excuse me?" said the Oilerette with the blond ponytail, jumping back.

"You're excused," I mumbled, and knocked back a gulp of soda. The ice clinked together in my glass.

The house was filled with faces that were familiar but that I couldn't quite place. I wandered through the living room, filled with its dead animal heads, where exposed bra straps seemed to be the fashion.

241

That, and drunken staggering that I gathered through my finely tuned powers of observation was supposed to double as dancing. Booze seeped from people's pores, and I caught sour whiffs like bad breath whenever I passed too close.

By now I'd gotten used to the bass and the way it punched at my organs. My whole body buzzed with the music amid curls of smoke that reflected in the dim lights. The air was fresher in the kitchen, where I was pleased to find a bowl filled with tortilla chips and an open jar of salsa that had vomited tomato chunks onto the marble countertop. I cracked a chip in two and popped one half into my mouth.

New stainless steel appliances gleamed from every corner of the room. I ran my hand over the stovetop to a block of wood that displayed a dozen shiny butcher's knives. I wrapped my fingers around one and pulled out the blade, examining the sharp edge. Probably one of those infomercial ones that could cut through a penny.

I fished around in my pocket to see if I had one to try.

"Are you allergic to parties or something?" I whipped around to see Knox open the freezer, realizing too late that I was wielding the point of a knife in his direction. He held up his hands in surrender. "No need for violence, Frankenstein. I'll go willingly wherever you want to take me." He winked.

"You're going to make me gag." I replaced the knife in its slot.

"I bet you're into that kinky stuff, aren't you?" The fluorescent light of the freezer lit his face as he stooped to dig for another bottle of vodka to replace the empty one he'd deposited on the island. From the looks of it, he had an endless supply to choose from.

"Hate to ruin your fantasy, but not all geeky girls are closeted sex freaks waiting to be unleashed."

He chose a bottle and kicked the door closed. "Well, now you're just being mean." He glanced at my watered-down glass of Coke. "Looks like you could use a refill."

"It's just Coke," I said when he took the cup.

He waggled his eyebrows. "How very responsible of you. Okay, just Coke then."

I waited while he opened the refrigerator and poured me another glass.

"There you are." Paisley stomped into the kitchen dressed in an identical uniform to Cassidy's. "What's taking so long? The natives are getting restless without their refreshments. And nobody knows where Ashley went. Caroline is freaking the hell out. Thinks she wandered off and—" Her eyes fell on me and then narrowed. "Oh. You've got company."

Knox reappeared from behind the refrigerator door and handed me a refilled cup. I sniffed it and couldn't detect any alcohol. "I'm being a host, Paize. Chill out."

"Can you please hurry? Ashley's been gone for, like, twenty minutes, and Caroline is convinced she's been abducted by the serial killer or whatever." Paisley looped her arm through Knox's, but shot me a hard stare as she dragged him off.

Bored, I wandered out, drink in hand, of my safe hiding spot in the kitchen. A team of guys was holding Billy Ray upside down. He held the keg spigot between his lips and the audience was chanting. "Three . . . four . . . five . . ."

I twisted my head for a better view of a red-faced Billy Ray. Did it taste better from that angle? I watched as the counting grew more and more energetic. Was he able to swallow or was it just sitting there in his mouth about to explode. It was as if we were all spending New Year's Eve in Times Square waiting for the ball to drop instead of watching a sweat-stained white tee creep ever closer to the nipples of an even whiter hairy chest.

The front door opened, and there was a shriek. A lanky girl with curly brown hair ran across the room and hugged a freckled redhead. The redhead turned an unflattering shade of pink. "What's going on?"

The brunette pressed her hands to her friend's cheek. "Where have you been? I thought you were . . . that maybe someone had taken . . ." She was slurring her words, but her tears made her seem genuinely distraught.

Knox stood up and raised his hands over the crowd. "New rule," he shouted. "Nobody leaves. Everyone stays right here in this house. There's a killer on the loose, people."

There were cheers and hoots. Only in Hollow Pines, Texas, could a murderer turn a party into a *better* version of itself. The beat picked back up, and Billy Ray stepped up onto a coffee table and thumped his fist against his chest. "Who's doing the next keg stand?"

I scanned faces for Cassidy and Adam. Maybe the celebratory mood was contagious, but as I weaved in and out of dancing bodies, I felt my lips working their way into a smile and had the faintest hint of champagne bubbles floating around in my head.

I held my near-empty glass of Coke to the light and then sniffed it again. I shrugged.

When I emerged from the throng, I spotted Adam near the fireplace. I was giddy at the sight of him. Giddy and a little bit groggy. I hadn't known those two feelings went together. *Weird.* The thought was fleeting, and I pushed through the cluster of kids from my school. How did all these people go to my school? That was another weird thing. Why was I hanging out with them somewhere other than on campus? I squeezed my eyes shut. My head was beginning to feel like it'd been stuffed with cotton balls. I hoped I wasn't getting sick.

As I came closer to Adam, I had to squint. He wasn't looking right. His skin had that splotchy texture that made him look like he was coming down with a rare tropical virus. He stumbled and caught himself, using the mantel.

"Smith's wasted!" a boy nearby crowed.

Wasted? I registered this in the back of my mind as my tongue would a leftover bit of chicken stuck to my teeth. Adam wasn't supposed to drink tonight. Hold on. Neither of us was supposed to drink tonight. I flattened my hand to my forehead. The world seemed to have just performed a quarter rotation, and I had to steady myself to keep from spinning with it.

Where was Cassidy? I had to concentrate hard on each face in the room. They lurched in and out of focus. I didn't see her. Adam's knees buckled. A few more hollers of encouragement from the peanut gallery. Adam did indeed look drunk. Obliterated. And maybe he was, but I didn't think so.

I cut across the room—or maybe not cut—since I swerved once or twice. This wasn't good. I squinted at the ice cubes floating around in my drink. What was *in* this? My feet felt three times their normal size, and it seemed as though no matter how fixated I stayed on my target, which was, in this instance, Adam, he continued to jump to my left or right and I'd have to align my path all over again.

"Adam." I caught his elbow. His name turned my mouth into marshmallow fluff. This wasn't good. I wasn't feeling right. I forced myself to concentrate. Through damp hair, he peered up at me. His arm, hanging from the mantelpiece, supported his weight. He tilted his chin as if to study me. "We have to get you out of here."

"You're different," he said.

"I'm fine." I glanced to either side. Then I put his arm around my neck and began leading Adam, my Adam, down a dark hallway. I chose the first door that was unlocked. I guided him inside, then made sure to turn the latch behind me.

We were standing in the Hoyles' master bedroom. I lowered Adam to the floor on top of a plush oriental rug. The king-sized bed was a four-poster fit for royalty.

Inside the bedroom, the bass was a muted echo, muffled further by the cotton-ball stuffing that had taken over the space between my ears. I stretched my jaw, trying to make my ears pop. Something was definitely wrong. Adam lay on his back. His chin tilted up. His back arched slightly. His breaths were shallow.

"Victoria." His fingers gripped the air and tightened into fists. I hated the cat-vomit-colored circles that spread out from his eyelids. "You're drunk."

"I didn't have anything to drink except—" A moment of clarity wormed its way through my foggy brain. *Knox.* I closed my eyes for a moment too long, and the earth took off spinning. My eyelids snapped open, and I used the bed to steady myself. "I'm fine," I insisted. My arms felt as though someone had filled their veins with cement. How much of that drink did I have? I tried to remember backward. All of it. I was pretty sure I drank all of it.

Adam closed his eyes and for a second lay very still.

I dropped to my knees and shook him. "Adam? I'm sorry." I clutched his hand. "But I think the game drained you faster than normal."

He stared up at the ceiling. My thoughts felt as if they were swimming through molasses. I could figure this out. I would figure this out.

I stood up and nearly fell back down. My surroundings spiraled, and I struggled to reorient myself to begin taking stock of the master suite.

There was a large walk-in closet with fancy, sliding racks for shoes and little else. I opened up drawers and found sachets, dried fruits and herbs tied up in bows to make rich people's socks smell floral. I shoved each drawer shut with my hip. There was nothing in here I could use.

I stumbled and grabbed for the nearest thing to keep me from falling. It was a fur coat, and it drooped onto the carpet. I left it there.

When I returned to the main room, Adam's eyes had rolled back into the sockets. "Adam?" I slapped his cheek. He didn't wake up. I considered dousing him with a cup of water but kept looking instead. Where was a generator when you needed one?

Under the bed, in the nightstands, nothing. Finally, I turned my attention to the bathroom. I'd never seen a tub that wasn't also part of the shower before. Again, there was the siren call of a place to nap. I resisted. Instead, staggering, I rummaged through the vanity and other drawers until I found the first thing with a cord: a hair dryer.

I turned it over, feeling the weight in my hands like a gun. I looked at the dryer, then at the bathtub, then again at the dryer. The plan was simple, which in this case was a nice way of saying dumb. But it was science.

I plugged the drain and twisted the knob. Water began pouring into the bath. Next, I went to the clock radio on top of one of the nightstands. The numbers blinked from red to nothing when I tore the wires out of the back. I carried my bouquet of red, yellow, and green wires back to the bathroom.

I pushed my thumbs into my eye sockets. The back of my throat turned slimy with mucus. My hands shook and my insides turned seasick. I couldn't think about what would happen if I was too late. So I focused on getting him undressed, pulling off his jeans and jersey until he was stripped to his boxers. Stitches framed the cavity in his chest that masked his metal plate, and the electrocution scars formed white tree branches across his chest.

"Adam, we have to get you up. We have to get you into the . . ." My eyelashes fluttered and I swayed. "The tub." I hooked his arm over my shoulders and together we crawled and dragged him to the bathtub. He collapsed inside, and his pupils stared up at the ceiling. Crossing myself, I poured four shakes of expensive bath salts into the water in an attempt to replicate brine.

I attached each of the wires, per my usual routine, to the rings left open in the conductor plate. Steam billowed into the air and caked the mirrors with fog. I saw Adam, sliced and cabled, for the first time aboveground, and he looked even more grotesque in this position than usual. Almost inhuman. Like a creature stolen from the lab. I wanted to look away. But instead, I switched on the hair dryer, held it over the bath, and dropped it.

THIRTY-ONE

It was only on Owen's suggestion that I thought to look into the power of suggestion as a possible source for the subject's "memories." The power of suggestion is a process by which one person's thoughts or feelings are guided by the allusions made by another person. This psychological process can be so strong as to create false memories. Think of people who confess to murders after a grueling interrogation only to be proved innocent later. However, I've been able to pinpoint no potential sources of allusion that could be creating these memories in Adam's head.

\- - -

T he lights blinked off, swallowing the room in black ink. Orange and yellow sparks burst from the socket and died midstream. There was a thrashing in the tub, like a shark churning up water. Skin flapped on porcelain, thick *thwacks* of suction-cupped flesh. The music stopped cold. Muffled shrieks and squeals trickled through the walls. In the bathroom, where I stood motionless, the noises stopped. I held the air in my lungs and could still hear the shallow pulls of someone else drawing in oxygen.

I fumbled for the light switch and flicked it on. Nothing happened. I must have shot the circuit breaker.

"Adam?" I whispered.

A grunt. I dropped to my knees and slid in his direction, feeling with my hands out in front of me until my palm landed on his arm.

I slid my fingers down until I could grasp his hand. He squeezed and, in the darkness, where no one could see, I smiled.

"You're alive," I said.

"I was never really alive."

My fingers wriggled around to his wrist, where I could feel the throbbing of the veins underneath. "You have a pulse. You have a heartbeat. You have blood coursing through you," I said softly.

"Are those the things that make a person alive?" My eyes adjusted. "Look at me." A shadowy outline of Adam reached up and snatched the wires attached to his chest.

I recognized the dark shift of mood that came over Adam after each recharge, but I still hated it and wished it away with a selfishness that was childish.

Our hands didn't leave each other. The darkness distorted my perception of the distance between us, but I sensed his closeness like a charge in the air. The short space between our two faces. The hairs on the backs of my arms raised.

"I saw fire," he said. "The house." His voice was strangled. "The one that I always see, it was burning." He pulled his knees to his chest. "I heard people screaming."

"And you're sure it's not, I don't know, a nightmare or a hallucination or something. It could be anything. It could—"

"I was there, Victoria. I can smell the smoke. I can feel the ashes falling in my hair. The fire's hot. It pushed me back. I couldn't go any closer or else I'd burn . . ." He trailed off. "They're screaming in there."

I gulped. If Adam's memory was, indeed, returning, how long until he remembered how he'd died? I wanted to tell him. In the dark, here, when he couldn't see my face, but I was too chicken. And then the lights flickered on. Adam and I squinted against the sudden brightness. I felt woozy. The floor seemed to rock.

Someone pounded on the door.

"Let me in." My head snapped up. Cassidy. "They saw you go in there." The doorknob jiggled. I stood up and helped Adam to his feet. We looked at each other, then I searched for a window.

Too late. The doorknob stopped jiggling. A metallic click and the door swung open. Cassidy stood wielding a bobby pin, which she quickly returned to her hair.

Adam and I were now shoulder to shoulder in the bedroom opposite Paisley, Knox, and a very pissed-off Cassidy. Her fists made tiny balls by her sides. Her bangs fell askew across her forehead. "I knew it," she said. Her accent came out thick and mad.

Paisley gasped. An accusing finger flew up and pointed at Adam, who, I realized at that moment, was standing dressed only in his boxers, dripping water onto the carpet. Tracks of silvery scar tissue left twisted rivers of raised skin across his stomach and ribs. Angry sutures pinned muscle and fat over bone. "*Freak*," Paisley said.

Cassidy's eyes widened as she took Adam in. My shoulders slumped. "It's not what you think." A hiccup punctuated the end of my sentence.

A boy. A girl. A party. A locked bedroom. Cassidy was good at math and she'd already run the calculations.

She tore her gaze from Adam's chest and focused on my face. "Everyone said I shouldn't trust you." Tears pooled in her eyelids. Her pink-stained lower lip trembled. "And they were right." She spun on her heel and pushed through the onlookers.

Adam snatched his clothes from the floor and tugged on the pair of jeans and jersey. Black paint ran down his cheeks. His raven hair stood on end. He was wild. He shoved through Paisley and Knox. "Cassidy!" he called. "Wait!"

"Nice scars, you mutant freak." Paisley scoffed and then trained her cold blue eyes in my direction. "Now I see what he saw in you. The circus sideshow and the Whore of Babylon. You deserve each other."

When Paisley turned to leave, her form split in two. I pushed the heels of my hands into the side of my head and groaned. The carpet seemed to be tilting at a sharp incline. The outline of everything multiplied like a TV with a bad signal.

"Turn the music back on," someone yelled from the other room just before a rap song blasted through the surround sound speakers. The pounding bass nearly buckled my knees.

"You don't look so good." I couldn't make out any of the features on Knox's face.

"I'm fine." I staggered toward where he stood near the open hall. My shoulder banged into the doorjamb. *Deep breaths, Tor.* If only this house would stay in one place.

I followed Adam's path more slowly, leaning against the wall for support.

"Slut," someone said to me as I passed. This garnered hearty chuckles all around that took on a fun house echo.

I made it down the hallway in time to see Adam punch his fist through drywall. The crunching sound reverberated in my head, and I had to shut my eyes against it. *Too loud, Adam,* I wanted to say. But my lips felt as if they belonged to someone else.

"Christ, dude! That's my wall!" Knox hollered over the music, which had revived into the soundtrack of my own personal nightmare.

I stretched out my arm, reaching for Adam and misjudging the distance, because now it seemed as though he was much farther away. So much space stretched between us. He tore out chunks of plaster when he jerked his hand, unfeeling, out of the hole he'd left, and went after Cassidy.

My chest tightened. My brain wouldn't function. All I could see was the crumbling of Cassidy's face. The tears splashing her cheeks. Adam's fist charging through a wall.

A sea of unfriendly faces glared at me. I swatted the air. My cheeks drooped along with the corners of my mouth. My tongue, suddenly too big for my mouth, was working up words. I wobbled sideways. The house zoomed in and out of focus. The judging faces surrounded me.

Everywhere I turned. Mean. Nasty. "You don't know me," I slurred. "I'm a genius." I poked my finger into my chest. "A real live genius!"

Someone whistled. "All aboard for the train wreck."

They laughed. They were all laughing. It roared inside me. I pressed my fists into my eye sockets. *Make it stop, make it stop.*

"Maybe you should lie down." There were gentle fingers on my shoulder. I thought vaguely that they belonged to Knox, but I wasn't sure. I tried to remember why this mattered. "You can use my room," the voice said. "It has a big, comfortable bed with your name on it."

I whimpered at the mention of bed. *Yes, please. Bed.* Even the word sounded enchanting. *Yes, yes, let me crawl under the covers.* I thought I managed a nod. Wet sand filled every inch of my body. I leaned on the arm that was offered to me. It was too much effort to keep my eyes open, so I didn't. Instead, I caught flashes of carpet through my lashes. Muted footsteps. A lock clicked. A door creaked. Inside there was a dark room that smelled like cologne. I needed to lie down. There was that word, only now it was in object form and it was even more enchanting than when I'd heard it suggested. *Bed.*

"You'll feel better in the morning," said the Knox-voice. He led me to the great, big, fluffy bed. I dragged myself onto the mattress and fell into a heap on top of the comforter.

I felt like I was floating. I stretched my hand out in front of my face. It seemed as if it belonged to somebody else. There was something I was supposed to remember. Something important.

"Just for a second," I mumbled. "Just need to lie down."

He ran his hands through my hair. Only, it didn't feel like my hair. It felt like someone else's, too. How funny. I watched a shadow lean down, and then there was a warm mouth on mine. I didn't know what I did with my lips. I hated the taste, but I couldn't move. I was consumed by the bed, which seemed to have taken hold of me like a Venus flytrap. If Venus flytraps could be fluffy clouds of comfort.

"Knox!" A girl's voice drifted in to meet us. "Where are you?" I was drifting, too.

A finger replaced the lips. "Shhhh," he said. I shut my eyes. I heard footsteps. "I'll be right back." The door clicked again.

I wanted him to take his time. Finally, I could sleep. *Finally, finally, finally . . .*

The weight of a deep, dark slumber wrapped itself around my torso and pulled me under. Conscious thought lapped at the edges of my mind. I was supposed to remember something. It was bothering me. Like an itch on the bottom of my foot that I was too lazy to scratch.

Sometimes I could lay awake for hours at night while my mind spun off into a dozen universes of thought. But this was the opposite. This felt like someone had poured Pepto-Bismol between my ears. My mind was quiet. Too quiet. Except for this one stubborn thought that wasn't a thought at all.

Why did I feel so funny? The answer rose slowly to the surface like bubbles. *Knox.*

My drink. Knox and my drink. I tried to connect the two ends, forcing myself to roll onto my side. I let out a pathetic moan and peeled open my eyelids. I was still in the dark room. On the big, fluffy bed. Knox's bed. The door was closed. I needed to get out of there.

I hoisted one leg over the edge, followed by the other, and slid to the floor. Somehow, in the last two hours, I had gained about a thousand pounds. Pushing myself to my feet, I stumbled for the door. It took me three times to grip the door handle and then to twist it. The light from the hallway nearly blinded me.

I started to close myself back into the room just to avoid the light but then remembered what it was that I was doing. Knox would be back any moment. My sense of time was gone, along with all my other faculties, so I had no idea how much time had passed since he'd left me sprawled on the bed with his leftover spit on my mouth.

I put one foot in front of the other, and when, after a couple steps, I grew tired, I slumped against the wall. The sound of voices and music amplified. I wanted to cry when I heard laughing. I didn't care if they were laughing at me. Blurry figures moved at the end of the corridor. I stretched out a hand. One of these figures was coming toward me.

"Help," my voice rasped.

He was only inches from my face when I realized it was Knox and he was towering over me. "I thought I put you to bed, Victoria."

I shook my head. Strands of hair got tossed over my eyes. "No." I was working in slow motion, but I gathered all my strength and I pushed his chest. He didn't budge.

Knox, with his sharp teeth and wax-slicked hair, actually laughed. I didn't enjoy his laughing at all. "You know Adam's not your only ticket in," he said. His fingers closed around the bones of my wrist, crushing them. His words tickled the peach fuzz on my ear. "I thought you had a thing for other girls' boyfriends." His eyes danced. "It's the thrill, isn't it?"

Knox was towing me back toward the dark corner of his room. I dug my heels in and did the only thing I could muster. I sat down.

"You're drunk, Victoria," he said loudly, like he was acting on a stage.

I shook my head. I shook it over and over. My head spun even more. I felt tears slide down my cheeks. Then I looked up, and Adam was on him. I thought I was dreaming. Knox's mouth morphed into a snarl, and it happened before I could blink.

"Don't hurt . . ." Adam grunted as his pawlike hands wrapped around Knox's shoulders. "Victoria."

Knox's eyes bulged. His feet left the ground. Adam shook him.

I reached for Adam's leg. "Adam, stop!"

I was too late. There was a flash of recognition that appeared on his face before the feral pitch of anger broke and Adam released him.

Knox stumbled. He was too far back on his heels and his footing too off-kilter to catch.

Almost in slow motion, he toppled backward. His right arm hit the floor at a sharp angle. There was a pop like the seal on a fresh canister of potato chips. He crumpled, and the arm disappeared under the full weight of his body.

Paisley rushed past me and kneeled by Knox, who shoved her away. "You broke his arm, you freak."

Adam let out a strangled yelp.

"It was an accident," I said. Then more loudly, "It was an accident. He didn't mean to." There was no way to be sure I was saying these things out loud. The floor rocked beneath me. Then Adam was gone. As if into thin air.

Knox groaned. "You will pay for this!" he shrieked. "Don't think I won't find you, Smith. Don't think you can get away with this. I don't care who you are."

I pressed my palms into the carpet. In the battle between me and gravity, gravity finally won. I sank onto the floor and forgot everything.

THIRTY-TWO

The subject has exhibited the telltale signs of retrogression in his impulse control that raise concerns that perhaps he is sliding into more primitive and instinct-based behaviors. A propensity for violence and aggression shows a marked change in the subject's behavioral evolution.

— — —

I woke up tangled in a heap of flannel sheets and a plaid comforter that smelled nothing like cologne. A puddle of drool soaked the blue pillow next to me, and I scratched crusted saliva off my chin.

"Good morning, sunshine."

I propped myself up on my elbows. "Where am I?" My eyes darted around, still trying to focus. The hood of my sweatshirt drooped over the side of my face. A roaring pain erupted in my eye sockets, and I immediately lay back down.

Owen appeared over me, sipping a steaming cup of coffee. My stomach turned. "Casa Bloch. Welcome."

The blurry room in which I found myself sharpened, and I recognized the poster of *A Brief History of Time* and the shelves lined with the complete series of Harry Potter.

My insides rocked like a deep-sea fishing boat. Maybe if I stayed very still, I wouldn't puke. "This is it, Owen. I'm dying. I need you to put me down like Old Yeller."

He rolled his eyes. His hair stuck up at odd angles. He took another swig of coffee and shook his head. "Here, have some of this." He handed me his mug. I wrinkled my nose and pushed it away. He insisted. "It'll help."

Thunder rolled through my brain, making it impossible to think. I raised the hot cup to my lips and swallowed a mouthful of coffee. I wanted to hurl again but managed to keep it down and took another sip.

I looked around at the slender twin bed and narrowed my eyes suspiciously. "Where'd *you* sleep?"

He took the mug from me. "You know, you make it awfully hard to want to be hospitable." He gestured to a pile of sofa pillows stacked near his desk. "I slept on the floor. Like a gentleman."

I lowered my eyes, feeling a healthy surge of insta-guilt. "Sorry."

"I broke curfew for you, you know," he said.

"Bastard." I bit my lip and wrinkled my nose.

Owen dropped onto his desk chair, leaving the cup of coffee with me. "Not quite the thank-you I was expecting," he said, interlocking his fingers behind his head.

"Not you." I breathed in the steam. I felt as though I'd been punched in the nose. "*Knox*. Knox Hoyle is a bastard of the highest order."

"Is this just your standard Saturday fare or did He-Who-Must-Not-Be-Named do something particularly heinous in the last twenty-four hours."

The hot liquid scalded my tongue. "He slipped something in my drink." Owen's hands separated and he leaned forward, resting his elbows on his knees. "I had sworn myself to carbonated beverages only. Knox got me a refill. Next thing I know, I can't see straight."

"That explains the 'Queen of the Sloppy Drunks' comment."

"*Whose* comment?"

"Don't get mad." Owen slid a Wolverine comic book from his desk and flipped through the pages without stopping to study any of the illustrations. "Cassidy called me. She . . . had some choice words to share about you." He idly returned the comic book to its stack. "But, uh, she thought someone should come get you, so she tried me."

Something snagged in my stomach. She *did* that? For me. My chest felt warm and melty right before the deep, sickening regret sank in.

"They saw his scars," I said. "And . . . they think we hooked up."

"What does 'hooked up' mean, anyway?" Owen asked.

"I don't know, but whatever it is, it's not good." I sighed and launched into the whole story. Or at least I tried to make it the whole story. I wasn't sure whether parts of it made sense. Bits of my memory were holes, like a rat had come and chewed through parts of the night. Now I knew how Adam felt. "I'm pretty sure Knox's arm is broken," I finished. "His parents will destroy Adam."

But then again, there wasn't really any Adam to destroy. Adam Smith was a thing we'd made up—invented—and once they punched through that facade, I worried that the person they'd find hiding behind it would be me.

ADAM WAS MISSING. Again. Only this time he wasn't at school and he wasn't in the cellar and he wasn't in my car. He'd vanished. Owen and I had been searching for him for hours, ever since I woke up cursing Knox Hoyle's name in Owen's bed. I hadn't even brushed my hair, let alone my teeth, and this solitary stick of gum in my mouth was starting to have the consistency of wet cement.

"This is useless." Owen drove slowly down the side roads while I hung my elbows out the open passenger-side window and scanned the blocks for a sign. "We should go home. You should take a shower."

"We're not giving up. Either we find him first or Knox's parents do. Which of those sounds better to you?" Owen propped his elbow on the window and kept driving. "That's what I thought."

I probably should have been more panicked than I was. I probably should have been freaking out. And I was, but it was a dull kind of freaking out. Like a blade that had been used too often. I was thinking about the shell-boy that I'd created and what would happen if that shell stopped being such a good hiding place. What would happen to me then?

But this could all be fixed. One tweak in the formula. One change in the variables and—presto—all would be well. The contents of my stomach felt swampy, and the drugs in my system wouldn't let go. I felt hot and listless. Beads of sweat gathered on my upper lip. I wiped them away.

"Does it look overcast to you?" I asked. A dingy blanket of clouds hovered over the cotton fields, absorbing the puffs of smoke from the city's factories.

"Yeah, why?" Owen kept licking his lips and leaning over the steering wheel to see better, I guessed.

I rested my chin on my arm and stared out. "The weather report said a storm was coming in five days," I said. "Doesn't look like it'll hold that long to me."

Owen drove us into town, and the landscape stretched into a curved pyramid in the side view mirror, where I knew the three lightning generators waited, hidden from view, coursing with a power so strong it could stand your hair on end.

Once in town, the wooden train tracks we'd been running beside disappeared between brick buildings. Owen drove around the deserted parking lot of the old red Movies 8 Theater with the black-and-white checkered ticket booth, then into a strip mall.

"Try the square," I said. "Town's not that big." Last I checked, there weren't even twenty-five thousand people in Hollow Pines. Sure, Adam was a needle, but the haystack wasn't all that large.

At a stoplight, Owen turned left onto Grand Avenue. Flat, front buildings with block-letter signs lined the street. A large clock on an iron lamppost marked the time as a quarter past six. It was already getting late.

My stomach growled. As we drove slowly past the streaked windows beneath a flat green awning, a sheet of paper taped to a stop sign caught my eye. I hung further out the car, noticing the face on the poster as it drew closer. "Stop!" I yelled.

The wheels screeched against concrete. I popped the lock and slammed the door behind me. The flyer fluttered against the metal pole. I tore it down and held it in trembling hands. A black-and-white picture of a dark-haired boy with deep-set eyes and a straight nose stared out at me with the word *Missing* branded over his head and the words *John Wheeler* printed underneath it. Unlike when I'd first seen the picture of Trent Jackson Westover, I knew immediately that this boy was Adam.

Only less dead.

I scoured the surrounding area. Not ten feet away, there was another, identical flyer pinned to the display window of a jewelry store. I marched over to it and stripped the paper from the window.

John Wheeler. That name was a punch to the face, waking me up to what was real. And that was a boy named John.

I saw another one a short distance farther. A corner tore off when I ripped it down, crumpling the page in my fist. Owen's horn blared behind me.

I worried that I was being watched, that someone would see me. I crushed John Wheeler's photograph over and over as I followed the trail of flyers. An engine revved beside me and a door slammed. Lock beeped twice. Footsteps ran toward me as I reached up for another flyer. I was two blocks away from where I'd begun.

"What are you doing?" Owen said, spinning me. "I'm double-parked."

I crammed the freshly picked flyer into his chest, and he shuffled back. Peeling the paper away from his body, he stared down at the picture. There weren't very many words on the page, but Owen looked for a long time. His lips pressed into a white slash. "It's him," he said at last.

I took a deep breath. "It's him."

Owen and I collected flyers like bread crumbs, destroying the evidence and the search for John Wheeler. The fact that anybody might have seen these was enough to make me break out in hives. I handed my collection to Owen, and he stuffed it in a garbage bin.

He straightened and froze. "Look." He nodded up the road where a stoplight blinked from yellow to red. Near a sign that marked the way toward State Highway 24 was a girl taping a poster to a storefront with boarded-up windows. She stood on her tippy-toes and fastened the paper to the wood.

I took off toward her.

"Tor," Owen hissed. "Where are you going?"

I didn't pay attention to him, and he didn't follow. When she heard me approach, the girl snapped her chin up to meet me. At first, I thought that I'd misjudged and maybe she was just a kid, but when I got closer, I saw that she was only small. She clutched a stack of papers in her hand and a roll of duct tape.

"Just posting, if that's all right with you," she said in a thick country accent. This girl was all pointy elbows and sharp eyes. She wasn't unpretty exactly. I could appreciate her in the same way I might the appearance of a starving raccoon. Cute, but scrappy. Tattered jean shorts hung off her hips, exposing a heart-shaped freckle on the bony ridge of her pelvis. "Been putting these all over town," she said, tearing off a strip of tape with her teeth.

I hadn't prepared anything to say. She stared at me expectantly, like she wasn't sure whether to call a doctor or the police. At this point, both were probably worthy choices. "Who—uh—" I pointed. "Who is that? Do you know him?" In my mind I repeated the words she had said: *all over town*. My palms began to sweat.

She looked at me sideways. "Why? You seen him?"

I folded my arms, squirmed, and then scratched my temple. "Me? No. I—there's just been a lot of boys going missing around here, you know?" I rubbed my arms to fight off imaginary goose bumps. On a hazy day like today, it was always tough to tell when the sun was beginning to set, but I noticed her shadow stretching along the length of sidewalk and knew that the day's light was fading. "Hard to feel safe anywhere."

She nodded. "I heard about that. The Hunter of Hollow Pines. Gives you the creeps, doesn't it?" She made a little visible shiver. "If it eases your mind, though, I don't think he's one of them."

"Oh." I forced a smile. "That's good to hear."

I couldn't pull my eyes away from the poster. Heat crawled up my neck. I tugged at the fabric around my collar. I wanted to snatch the poster away and add it to my trash collection.

"How do you know that he—" I kicked the ground, hiding my face in case I was a worse liar than I thought. "Isn't, you know, one of the other boys that went missing?"

She started to open her mouth when another round of honking came from the road. I looked over to find Owen had pulled even, and he was waving me in, mouthing, *Are you crazy?*

"Looks like your ride's here." She offered a small shrug and handed me a flyer. "If you do hear or see anything, call me, okay?"

"Sure," I glanced back over my shoulder at her. She was already taping up another flyer. We'd have to circle back to tear down the rest of them later. I folded Adam's face in half, then in quarters, until he was hidden from view, but not from memory. The boy smiling in the picture was genuine. He was more than decaying energy racing through his blood and forcing his neurons to fire. He had history. And he had Meg.

THIRTY-THREE

I wish I had access to a CT scan. Then I could really see how Adam's brain is functioning. By my best estimate, the brain stem and cerebellum would be lit up, firing on all cylinders. The frontal lobe would exhibit moderate coloring, and the hippocampus would be waking up to the first blooms of light on the scan.

— — —

Victoria Frankenstein." Owen put the Jeep into park and extended his hand, palm up. Moonlight gleamed off the windshields of dozens of empty cars in the school lot. "Will you go to the dance with me?" A sly smile dimpled his cheek. His eyes danced under his lenses.

I rolled my eyes. "Don't make this worse than it already is." I climbed out of the car and stared up at the school gymnasium. "Let's just go."

Owen's door banged shut. "Is it because I'm underdressed? Because I must say, you look positively stunning if I do say so myself. Who are you wearing? Is that Levi's?"

Okay, I probably did look like hell caked over and then left to ferment in the sun. I was still wearing my clothes from last night, which now looked like they'd been left for three days in the dirty laundry bin. Instead of heels, I followed the sidewalk in a pair of threadbare high-tops. I had meant to stop home before heading to the dance, but then we'd found all those flyers and we spent every spare moment ripping them down, a difficult task when they seemed to multiply faster than fruit flies. At least my face had stopped throbbing like one giant zit waiting to be popped.

"Save your corsage," I said. "We're just here to find Adam."

In front of us, the gym was busy barfing up orange and black balloons and techno beats. A white banner welcomed us to "A Night in Paris," the theme of this year's Homecoming dance. We walked through a cardboard cutout of the Arc de Triomphe, where a chaperone offered us a glass of "French champagne." I sniffed the cup. My stomach rumbled. The last thing I'd eaten was a handful of tortilla chips in Knox's kitchen. I drank the swigs of sparkling grapefruit juice in two quick gulps and wiped my mouth.

"Just so you know, if I see Knox, I'm going to kill him."

"One illegal act at a time," Owen said. Together, we surveyed the crowd. Adam had now been missing for nearly twenty-four hours. We'd looked everywhere we could think of, and this now seemed like the best possible bet for an Adam sighting. Unfortunately, there was no scientific term for "last-ditch effort."

The dance was in full swing. A flock of girls passed by, hair twisted up into unnatural knots, rhinestones sparkling off chiffon dresses. "I think we should split up," I said. "Cover twice the ground."

"Cell phone signal?" Owen asked.

I pulled out the clunky prepaid phone I'd purchased at the mall. "Check."

"Meet back here at the Arc de Triomphe if we haven't found him in thirty minutes."

I nodded, and then, without a backward glance, I disappeared into the mass of people. Even though I was a slight person, slipping through a horde of dancing bodies wasn't easy. It was tougher still since the definition of dancing seemed to be grinding one's rear end against the front end of someone else. I searched faces for anyone who had been at the party. "Have you seen Cassidy Hyde?" I yelled into a girl's ear. She shook her head and kept dancing. At the center of the throng,

I knew I'd reached the fifth circle of hell, where all the people who were coupled up came to make out beyond the reach of the chaperones' watchful eyes.

I wedged my way through to the other side, where I was, at last, able to take a breath of fresh air.

"You've got to be kidding me."

I looked up to find that I had stumbled into Cassidy and Paisley, who were halfheartedly dancing in a clear space close to the stage that had been set up at the far end of the gym.

Cassidy peered down her nose at me. "I didn't think this night could get any worse," she said, turning her cheek. She wore a shimmery green dress and teardrop earrings that made her look like a fancy mermaid.

I guess in her eyes I deserved that. In any event, I wasn't there to clear the air. "Have you seen Adam?"

She pulled her shoulders back and tossed her hair over them. Behind her, there was a backdrop of velvety black curtains borrowed from the auditorium. They were pulled shut across half of the stage. Silver, decorative balls hung from the hidden rafters along with a gold cutout of a crescent moon that, put together, were supposed to represent the Paris sky. "Not since I caught him naked in a room with you."

My guts made a fist. The key was to stick to the script. The rest wasn't important. "Not after that, though?" I asked evenly.

Tears sparkled in her eyes, and for a second I actually felt sorry for Cassidy Hyde. All she had wanted was her small-town, balloon-arch fairy tale, and it had been shattered by a boy who was shattered before she ever met him. "Oh, you mean when he attacked my best friend's boyfriend?"

"He wouldn't have had to if your best friend's boyfriend wasn't such a creep," I muttered.

Paisley, who was half listening while crossing her arms and tapping her foot to the beat, snapped to attention. "What did you say? You know all of this is your fault. Knox probably won't be able to play for the rest of the season, and now he's got this hideous orange cast. It's a disaster." Her lips, which were painted a bright scarlet, tightened into the shape of a cherry.

"Tragic. I'm just looking for Adam, okay? I don't even want to be here. Trust me," I said, craning my neck to search the room. At the edges, round tables covered in white cloths speckled the floor and glowed with soft candlelight. Blue, red, and purple spotlights spanned the ceiling.

Cassidy trained her stare on me, and I could tell by the way the tendons on her neck kept constricting into guitar strings that she was fighting back tears. "You know, you really are no better than us, Tor."

And I didn't know what to believe when the first thought that popped into my mind was, *That's not true.*

But just then the music shifted. The volume lowered, and two white spotlights circled the crowd. "What's happening?" I asked.

Cassidy and Paisley both turned to each other, lips drawn into solemn lines. "I hope you win," Cassidy said, taking Paisley's hand.

"Thanks," Paisley replied, nodding and turning back to face the stage without letting go of Cassidy's hand.

"It's that hour." The DJ's voice boomed through the microphone. "Time to crown this year's Homecoming king and queen." He hit a button and a drumroll track played.

The ring of light looped over the heads of the crowd.

Knox appeared next to Paisley, holding a plastic cup in his good hand. "My lady." He gave a slight bow of the head. With his bad hand he fumbled with the cap on a flask and tipped a splash of a mysterious substance into the drink. He caught me watching. "Want some, doll face?" He winked.

The contents of my stomach roiled. I turned my chin away. "I'd rather take cyanide, thanks."

"Suit yourself." He stashed the flask back into the inside pocket of his suit coat. Paisley grabbed him by the elbow and forced him to face the stage.

Everyone's heads bobbed up and down as they leaned and stood on tippy-toes to see where the rings of light would land. I squinted and stepped back when the circle stopped moving and fell over not Paisley, but Cassidy. Her jaw dropped. "Please welcome to the stage, Hollow Pines's finest, Miss Cassidy Hyde." The DJ, who was wearing sunglasses, hit another button, and the sound of applause came from the speakers. Cassidy flashed a quick smile and played with the hem of her dress. Her fingers unlaced from Paisley's, and I immediately noticed Paisley's hand curl into a claw at her side.

A tune began to play, and Coach Carlson beckoned Cassidy. Slowly, she scaled the steps to the stage, where she stood in the center, shifting her weight between her feet like she wasn't sure she was really supposed to be up there. The edges of my teeth dug into my lower lip. After last night, I could see that the balloons on Cassidy's balloon-arch fairy tale had already been popped, and no amount of canned applause was going to fix it.

I didn't know why I felt bad for Cassidy standing up there, only that I did. I wished I could tell her that there were things going on here that were bigger than her, that there were matters of life and death bubbling under the surface of this stupid Homecoming facade, and that she had just been one part of the experiment. But, of course, I could never tell her any of that. I could only do what I came here to do, which was to find Adam.

The second spotlight traced a figure eight until it stopped, dead middle, on Knox. I felt my face screw up like I'd just mixed orange juice and toothpaste.

"Please welcome our new Homecoming king, Knox Hoyle." The DJ hit the cheesy prerecorded applause again. Knox stepped easily away from Paisley without a second look. He smiled broadly and waved to the crowd with his good hand. *That weasel*, I thought.

But I couldn't linger, because the crowd behind me had begun to murmur as Knox made his way onto the stage to stand beside Cassidy. When Cassidy smiled, she looked like she was baring her teeth. A freshman boy and girl came out from either side of the stage, holding the winners' crowns. Cassidy was taller than the girl, and she bent down, knees pinned together, and let her fasten a shiny, plastic tiara to the top of her silky, loose curls. Owen was right. Cassidy Hyde was beautiful. She was a perfect specimen.

Once crowned, Knox thrust his fist in the air and crossed over to the microphone propped up at center stage. "Anybody have a drink?" He glanced around the stage. The two terrified-looking freshmen shrugged and retreated into the backdrop. "I'd like to propose a toast."

The stage lights glared so brightly it turned the strands of Cassidy's hair into a glowing halo, but the newly announced royalty couldn't hold the crowd's attention. A ripple continued through the student body, moving closer and closer to the front. The throng of people parted down the center until it broke open entirely and spit out Adam.

My Adam.

"Last night," Knox was saying. "We defeated Lockwood for the first time in ten years. And it wasn't one man . . ."

My heart practically leaped into my throat and out of my mouth I was so relieved to see him.

"Adam!" I waved. I felt a sharp pain in my foot and buckled over. "Ouch!"

I looked down to see the needle-thin spike of Paisley's stiletto. Her nails were at my scalp, and she yanked my hair back. "Stay out of this one, Frankenstein."

She released my head, and I rubbed the spot where she'd pulled.

Adam's fist was clutching a bouquet of handpicked flowers. They drooped and sagged over his grimy hands. He was still wearing his jersey and crusty jeans, and traces of black paint smudged his face, so faint now that it only looked like dirt. His forehead smoothed when he looked up to see Cassidy standing on the stage, sparkling in her sea-green dress.

Adam looked around. I separated from Paisley and tried to make my way to Adam, but it was too late. He was already tromping up the steps to the stage, carrying those wilting handpicked flowers. Just as he had for me once. Exactly as he had for me. My glands began to sweat. Cassidy gritted her teeth and angled herself away from Adam.

The crowd was rapt. *No, no, no, no, what are you doing, Adam?* I thought.

Knox stopped mid-sentence. He cocked his head, watching Adam approach. "What do you think you're doing, man?" he said into the mic. "This isn't about you. The game is over. It's over for you, Adam."

Adam kept coming. He pushed the flowers out in front, ignoring Knox. "For you." I could barely hear him say this. Cassidy looked sideways without turning her head. It felt like I was watching two cars barreling toward each other and we could all already sense the explosion in the air.

"She doesn't want to see you, dude." Knox stepped off the microphone stand and held up both hands to stop Adam's progress. "Did you hear me?"

Adam was like a machine. He tried stepping around Knox, but Knox headed him off.

"For you." I saw Adam's mouth form the words again. And there were those pathetic flowers.

"You wanna go?" Knox shoved Adam. "We can do this right here, right now."

This rattled Adam. He looked Knox in the eyes for the first time. I scrambled to get closer, to reach Adam in time, for what, I didn't know.

"You're a freak, Smith." Knox pushed again. Someone threw an empty soda can at Adam. It bounced harmlessly off his arm, but he jumped at the sound it made clattering onto the stage.

The DJ cut the music.

"Cassidy." Adam stretched out his hand with the flowers. Another can, this one at least a little bit full, hit Adam in the ear. His head jerked sideways.

I froze in place. This was happening. They were turning against him. They were calling him a freak.

"Stay away from me." The venom of Cassidy's words stopped Adam. He turned as if noticing the onlookers for the first time. He turned and they booed.

Knox ripped the flowers from Adam's hand and tore them at the stem before dropping them. "She said, get lost." He pushed Adam again.

This time Adam pushed back. My heart stopped beating. *No.* Time stood still. Every clock in town stopped ticking if only for that one crystallized moment. Knox's arms windmilled wildly. I caught a glimpse of his eyes as he fell from the stage. They weren't foxlike at all, but wide and keenly aware of the feeling of nothingness into which he was careening.

His head hit the dance floor first. A pop fired off. Screams came from everywhere. Knox Hoyle lay still, his hair tossed over his eyes, his neck bent at an unnatural angle and a sickening bulge sticking out just above his collarbone.

Bile burned my mouth. My eyes watered. I had to get Adam out.

"You did this." Cassidy was backing away. Her throat was tight. She barely opened her mouth to speak. The words oozed out. "You did this."

Knox Hoyle was dead.

And Cassidy was right. Adam did this.

I scrambled to the stage and crawled up. "We have to leave," I told him. "We have to go right now." I reached for Adam's hand. He grasped my fingers. I was blind with panic. Our shoes squashed petals as we rushed off stage left.

I spotted a red exit sign glowing in a corner behind the stage. "This way," I said. I didn't look back. I pulled Adam as fast as I could out the door and slammed it behind us. We cut back to the front of the building. I spotted headlights swooping sharply around a turn, and then Owen's Jeep was parked in front of us. He rolled down the window. "Get in."

I didn't ask questions. We piled into the backseat, and Owen slammed on the accelerator. I heaved for air, sticking my head between my knees and trying to breathe. "What . . . the hell . . . was that?" I said.

"That, Tor, was a very dead Knox Hoyle."

I pushed myself into a sitting position. Owen drove faster than I'd ever seen him drive before. It was good. We needed to be as far away from there as possible. I wrung my hands. Adam's eyes were bottomless in the dark backseat with the evening landscape whipping past. My Adam. My perfect Adam. What had I done?

"I'm sorry, Victoria," he said, and I wished that his voice held more emotion. Just this once.

But it didn't matter. Sometimes, the results of the very best experiments were different from what you'd expected. Sometimes you failed. I'd been wrong all along. I couldn't fix Adam. His time was up. I reached into my pocket and pulled out the last flyer, the one that the girl had handed to me.

I spread the page out on my lap and punched the number into my keypad. The tone rang three times before an answer.

"This is Meg."

THIRTY-FOUR

The subject will not be progressing to Stage 3 of the experiment. The regression of Stage 2 has been complete. Subject has failed to integrate into society and is no longer a productive member. Impulse control has devolved considerably. Subject is a menace to himself and to others. I can't help but think that this inability to control is caused by his lack of memory, which would serve as an anchor to his behavior. In any event, the experiment has failed.

— — —

What started off as a car crash on a rain-slicked road had splintered. We had collateral damage. First the mirror, then the wall, followed by Knox's arm, and now someone was dead. I paced the short distance from wall to wall of the cellar. My laboratory, since yanked free of my mother's wood boards, felt more like a storm bunker than ever, only it wasn't a tornado we were trying to keep out. Adam raked his fingernails down the sides of his face and neck. Owen's head bent low as he tinkered with the back of a broken pocket watch.

"Adam, where were you today?" I asked, trying to keep the rage from my voice. It was there, it had been quietly boiling for some time, I realized. I checked my phone again. Precious minutes were melting away. They would be looking for him. Where was she?

Adam rocked back and forth in place. "I was searching for the house. 4-0-8. You told me that you would help me find it," he said.

My teeth clenched. I squeezed my eyes shut. "And I would have,

Adam. If you gave me the chance." I idly closed an anatomy book with pencil scribbles in the margins. "Now everything is ruined."

"Tor . . ." Owen looked up from the pocket watch. "Come on . . ."

I couldn't believe that Owen was the one standing up for Adam. Especially after tonight. None of us spoke for a long moment until we heard the sound of three knocks on the hatch door.

"Who is that?" Adam hardened. The muscles in his forearm twitched.

Owen's screwdriver went still. He looked to me, then the stairs, then to me again. He seemed to make a decision. It took him three steps to reach me. He positioned his back to Adam. His fingertips were stronger than I expected as they applied pressure around my arm. His mouth was close to my ear. "You have to tell him, Tor. Tell him how it happened. He deserves to know at least that much about why he is the way he is. This isn't all his fault and you know it."

Our cheeks touched when I shook my head.

"He might . . . remember." His voice was low. "When . . ."

I swallowed. Before any of this, there was me. I killed John Wheeler. But I was too afraid to say it. Three more knocks came from above. Held breath burst in my lungs. I pulled away from Owen. My heart slammed against my chest.

"It's a surprise, Adam," I said, trying to keep my voice light, a noticeable shift from moments earlier. This was the end, though. There was no point in acting mad. There was no point in acting anything. "You'll like it, I think."

"A surprise?"

"Tor . . . ," Owen insisted.

"Did I hire you as my conscience? No? Then maybe you should stop trying to be one." There was no turning back now, anyway, and I failed to see what telling Adam the truth would solve. I hurried up the steps, the smell of the cedarwood stairs thick in my nostrils, and turned the hatch lock. At first, all I could see was the moon half hidden by a cloud, like it was wearing a dirty sock. Then the silhouette of a girl cut a dark notch into the already dark sky. "I came as fast as I could," she said.

"Did you park on the side road?" I asked, and eyed my mom's station wagon out in the drive. Through the curtains I could see the soft blue glow of the television set.

She nodded. "Can I come in?" It felt too late to say no.

All the words I possessed were colliding in my head, so when I moved aside, it was without saying one of them. I felt the end of something drawing near, and I wasn't sure that I was ready to let go or that I would be ready for what it meant to hold on. She stepped gingerly onto the first creaking step. I wondered what kind of girl went willingly into the basement of strangers.

The kind of girl, I supposed, who was a boy's last word.

She cupped her elbows, holding her arms tightly to her body. She wore the same white tank top that she'd been wearing earlier this afternoon. With her back to me, I noticed a raised scar like a cigarette burn on the back of her arm.

She stopped at the bottom of the stairs. For a second Adam appeared invisible to her. Her hand found the railing, and she leaned on it for support. "What *is* this place?" She took in the bowing shelves, shriveled specimens, mason jars full of viscous pea-green liquid, tubes that attached to crusted Florence flasks, life-sized skeleton, preserved rats, and rusty claw-foot tub.

"This is my laboratory," I said, squeezing past her. "This . . . well . . . this is where I saved him."

"Saved?" Her pitch shot up.

"Do you know her, Victoria?" Adam's shoulders were as hunched and tense as those of a guard dog.

Meg let out a soft cry. *"John?"* Her hands flew to her mouth. "It's you. Oh my God, it's really you."

I waited, expecting him to remember something. And wanting to take it as some kind of sign if he didn't.

"Who is John?" Adam rose to his feet. He retreated back a few steps.

"What are you doing—I mean, how?" She pressed her lips together and pushed back her hair. Meg wasn't beautiful. She was a girl who looked as if she were still trying to grow out of her tomboy years. She had thin lips, a straight waist, and mosquito-bitten ankles. The whole of her looked like it'd been scraped together with not enough material. She wasn't a Cassidy. She wasn't the type who automatically went with an Adam. But based on the way she was looking at him, I knew that somehow she did.

Owen cleared his throat. "Perhaps you should introduce them."

Meg's mouth fell open. "What do you mean *introduce* us? This is John. My John."

I blinked, coming back to attention. Swallowed what felt like a thorn stuck in my throat. "Adam." I cut her off. "This is Meg, she's, well, I think she knew you before."

He extended his hand to meet her. "Hi, I'm Adam. I'm from Elgin, Illinois."

She left his hand hanging in midair. *"Adam?"* She glanced between us like we were playing a trick on her. "This isn't Adam. His name's John. John Wheeler. John, tell her she's mistaken."

"Victoria, why is she calling me the wrong name?"

I sighed. "Adam *is* his name . . . here," I said. "He doesn't remember anything. Including any recollection of John." Her eyes widened. "It's a long story. Way, way too long for what we have time for now. Trust me. But I found Adam late one night." I avoided Owen's look. "He'd gotten into a car accident," I said slowly, remembering the story I'd told Cassidy. "He was in bad shape. Dying. I didn't have time to take him to the hospital, but I was able to jump-start his heart. So to speak, anyway. I'd been working with animal anatomy previously and was able to transfer the findings over to him. Only, since then, he's had no memory of before."

Meg took slow steps over to where Adam stood. The dark, cold look still lingered in his eyes. Her hand trembled as she raised it haltingly and touched his forehead, his cheekbones, the ridge of his nose, his chin. Adam's face relaxed under her touch. His eyes warmed. "You saved him?" Meg's voice was breathless. "But . . . he doesn't remember me." I heard the heartbreak in her voice. I saw her knees quivering like she might collapse.

"How do you two know each other?" Owen asked. He had a problem with prolonged silences. They made him uncomfortable. Besides, I sensed his eagerness to move on from Adam, to do what we should have done all along—return him to his people.

A smile flickered. She didn't look away from Adam. "John's been in love with me since we were eight years old," she said, and I thought I could detect the same hint of pride that I got when I talked about him. It was aimed at something completely different, but I still recognized it as there. "It took me a little longer to come around, I guess," she said. She lifted her fingertip from his brow and quietly clasped her hands together. A pale pink rose to her cheeks. "I think I need to sit down," she said. I gestured to a nearby stool that Owen dragged over for her. She perched on top and shifted her weight. "I always had a problem trusting men. It's easy to get that way where I come from. It was almost too late by the time I came around on trusting John, but the two of us"—she twisted her mouth sideways and gave a small shrug—"we were always—I don't know what to call it—meant to be. Like something out of the movies."

"I—" My voice was hoarse. "Well—that's very romantic." I coughed into the crook of my elbow, hoping to clear the cobwebs that had suddenly taken up residence on my vocal cords. My mind was spinning. None of this felt real.

"John . . ." Adam sounded out the name, trying it on for size. "Victoria? But—"

So much had happened today. I had to look away from him. I studied the skull of the skeleton dangling near the far wall. "It's true, Adam. I found a flyer just before the dance, and I knew the photograph was of you. Meg was searching for you."

It's for the best, I told myself. *This is what has to happen. The experiment has failed. Adam killed.* But it didn't feel right.

She shook her head and stared at her knees. "I . . . just can't imagine that he wouldn't remember me. Don't get me wrong. I'm grateful, but to have it all just be gone." The last word was choked in the beginnings of a sob. She took a deep breath and recovered.

"He's in trouble," I said, making sure to stare past Adam and directly at Meg.

She nodded. "I guess he seems to find trouble wherever he goes then."

Adam looked between the two of us. Here we were, the most important women in his life. "I don't want to be in trouble. I'm good. I want to be good." He knitted his hands together. "Victoria, I didn't mean to break the wall or the mirror or Knox. I'm sorry. I can fix them. Right? Can't I fix them? Victoria, you can bring him back. Put him in the tub. I know you know how." The veins writhed in Adam's forearms, twisting like snakes.

"It's gotten a little bigger than you, buddy." Owen put a hand on his shoulder. Owen gave me a small frown, meant to be reassuring.

"What kind of trouble?" I asked Meg. I probably should have offered her something. An iced tea. A Diet Coke. But I had nothing to give, and besides, the situation seemed beyond niceties.

For the first time, Meg looked grim. She took a deep breath and looked between Owen and me. "Like you said, it's a long story, but John took off after a . . . fire. He's wanted from here to the Mississippi, I imagine. I wasn't sure I'd ever see him again."

"Fire?" Adam and I both said at once.

She studied us. "Yes . . . But I thought you said . . ."

"I've seen fire," Adam explained, and I thought of him searching for the house, searching for numbers painted on a curb, searching for answers. "Bits of my memory. They come back. Mainly that one bit. The fire. I can see it sometimes. Victoria said she would help me find it, but she never did."

Meg's shoulders fell. "Oh." And I could see she was disappointed that his first memory wasn't of her.

"There hasn't exactly been a lot of downtime since Adam's arrival," I said.

"Better that you didn't. I thought maybe you were dead." I could tell she wanted to touch him again, but she held back. "There are some bad people after you. Some things you—we—got mixed up in. I would have come sooner, but I thought you were gone." She looked down at her shoes, and when she looked up, the sparkle of tears danced in her eyes. "I guess you were, almost. When they found your car near Lake Crook, that's when I started looking."

I felt Owen's eyes snap onto me. A fugitive on Lake Crook. I knew what he was thinking, but just because of Knox didn't make Adam the Hunter. The methodology was all off.

We waited several heartbeats when it began. It was soft at first, so soft we could have been imagining it. But then, from above, came the sound of sirens.

"They're coming," Owen whispered. Light flashed over his glasses. We both cast fleeting looks around the room. The cellar felt like an animal trap. There was nowhere to go.

"What's happening?" Meg tilted her chin to the ceiling. "Are they coming for him?"

"You guys have to leave," I said. Adrenaline took over. "Owen, grab the wires," I commanded.

Adam looked at me, and it was as if an entire chasm had opened up between us. "But I want to stay with you," he said, pushing past Meg. I turned my shoulder to dodge his touch. The specimens, the lab equipment, the maps, and notes, they all belonged here. Adam didn't. Not anymore.

"Wires?" Meg spun in place. Owen tugged at the ends of his hair and muttered to himself, but he retrieved the wires. We should have been more prepared for this.

I picked alligator clips from a surgical tray, then crossed the room and cupped them into Meg's hand. "Meg, the method to keep his heart beating, it's not permanent." I zigzagged through the laboratory, every step familiar. I tore the kilowatt meter from the wall. The small generator. "Brine, Owen." He retrieved jars from the shelves and pushed them into Adam's arms. "Salt will work in a pinch," I said. "It's a conductor. You need water and then attach the wires to the notches in his chest. Adam, you remember how it works."

"No, Victoria," he said, but I knew it wasn't in response to my question. "No, don't leave me. I'm Adam. *Adam*," he repeated.

My Adam.

I steeled myself. "Your name is John," I said. "John, you have to do the charge exactly as I've done it. You remember." I stared intently at him. Adam wrapped himself in a hug, his fingers tucked into his armpits as he rocked back and forth, clearly perturbed. The sirens were a high-pitched drone now. I stared up at the ceiling. Time had run out. "Where are you staying?"

"Victoria," he said. "Please. Don't make me go. Victoria."

"It's Tor," I said. "It's always been Tor." And I felt my arteries snap and my heart drop to my bowels.

"At the Queen's Inn," Meg replied, clutching the heap of supplies close to her chest. "A few miles down the road." Everyone knew only truckers and lot lizards stayed at the Queen's Inn. The two-story motel bred cockroaches and venereal disease in equal quantities. I tried not to think about it.

I hovered at the bottom of the stairs. "Wait five minutes. Owen and I will buy you enough time to leave." I tore my attention away from Adam's pained stare. The skin bunched around his eyes, and the image seared into my sockets like a brand. Adam. My Adam.

For once, Owen made no smart remark. Maybe there wasn't room for it. Maybe he was that scared or maybe the whole thing just wasn't funny anymore. Like at all. He did come to stand loyally at my side, though, my lead foot already starting up the staircase. "Good luck," I said. "I'll . . . I'll come find you." And it was a strange thing that I didn't know whether I meant that.

Adam was John. Adam—my Adam—had failed in some fundamental capacity, and I felt my heart closing up, like somebody sliding shut the seal on a ziplock bag. He wasn't my Adam anymore.

I didn't turn back. I pounded up toward the hatch and shoved it open. I climbed out and dusted off my jeans. I pulled Owen out after me. We slammed the hatch door closed with an aluminum clang that rocketed through the night.

I looked around, suddenly grateful for the country dark. Red, blue, and white flashed on our front lawn. "Come on." I held fast to Owen's hand, and we ran around the back of the house in a loop so that we were spit out on the other side. I had little to no plan when I saw the two cop cars parked in the dirt in front of my house.

From inside I could hear Einstein already hoarse with barking. Her nails scratched the door. "Quiet, Einstein," I muttered too quietly for her to hear.

I arrived to greet them, panting. A middle-aged officer with a blond mustache and a holster strapped around his pregnant-looking belly got out. He rested his hand on his gun.

"Is that dog dangerous, miss?" He nodded toward the front door. She whined and scratched some more.

"Who, Einstein? Only if you're afraid of excessive amounts of drool." Owen nudged me in the ribs. "Right, I mean, no, she's harmless."

"We're looking for an Adam Smith. Heard he might know something about the murder up at the school. People told us to try here. That you two were close friends, and that he might have left the gymnasium with you." He nodded at me.

The question knocked me off balance. Adam had left with me. What could I answer?

"What do you need Adam for, sir?" Owen stood up straight, stalling. He was good with adults. He had that nerdy charm that convinced them he was no trouble at all. I, on the other hand, seemed to lack that quality entirely.

"Just a few questions," replied Officer McMustache. "That's all." By now his partner had climbed out of the car and was looking out at the property. I felt the seconds ticking by.

"I . . ." I swallowed down what felt like a wasp stinging my throat on its way down the pipe. "He left me. After the gym, he took off," I said, sticking with some version of the truth. I forced myself to quit talking, not to ramble, not to offer any details that could be used against me. People were always too quick to volunteer the details with which to hang themselves.

"Shoo, shoo," I heard from behind me. On the porch, a door thwacked against the wood frame. Einstein resumed barking. "What's going on?" My mom's bare feet stepped onto the grass. She had managed to wrap a robe around her shoulders. "What are you people doing on my lawn?" Without makeup and with her red hair all askew from a few hours' sleep, it was easy to see how much she'd aged in the past few years. I could hear the empty wine bottle in her words.

Go back inside, Mom. Go back inside. I made a silent wish.

"We're looking for Adam Smith, ma'am. Is he here?"

My mom's face screwed up in the headlights. She noticed me standing a short distance to the right, and then she noticed Owen. "That's Owen. Owen Bloch," she said, and seemed so pleased with herself for remembering. In other circumstances, I would have been quite impressed myself.

"Has an Adam Smith been residing at your house the last few weeks, ma'am?" Officer McMustache widened his stance.

"Don't you think I'd know if a boy was living here in my house?" She said her consonants extraloud, like somebody was adjusting the volume on her remote control without her looking.

McMustache looked to his partner and then back at Mom. "Yes, ma'am, I suppose you would. But, all the same, would you mind if we had a look around?"

"Yes!" I pressed my lips together. Just once could she not—"Yes, I mind!" she shrieked. And that was when my mother's robe flew wide open, revealing only an oversized Lynyrd Skynyrd T-shirt with nothing on underneath but her bony, white-sheet legs.

McMustache's partner took off his hat and crossed it over his chest. Both of them averted their eyes to the ground. Owen scratched his temple and squinted one eye like he didn't know *what* to do.

With the sound of the sirens cut, I heard a distinct creak from the back of the house that made my armpits sticky.

"What was that?" The younger partner raised his hand to his holster.

"Probably just the dog," I said quickly. "She's always knocking things over." I looked over my shoulder. Every so often, I could hear Einstein's frantic puffs of breath underneath the threshold.

"Ma'am, maybe—" continued the officer while definitely, most certainly not looking up at Mom.

"Did you not hear me right? *I* didn't give you permission to be on my lawn," Mom shouted. "I didn't give any of you permission. Get off!" The sleeve of her robe fluttered. "Get off! All of you! Scram!" She pointed back at the robe and took several more barefooted steps toward the police. "This is my property. Don't go telling me who is on my property like I don't know."

I wanted to laugh and cry and hug my mother, open robe and all.

The officers exchanged looks again. McMustache cleared his throat and said, "We apologize, ma'am. You'll let us know if you hear anything, I'm sure."

To that, she spat on the ground. Then she pulled the robe around her chest and marched back into the house. The younger partner raised his eyebrows. Then to Owen and me he nodded. "Y'all take care. We may be back around if we hear anything else."

As the sirens faded and the lights disappeared, I felt the emptiness spread out over my house like the first day of winter, cold, bleak, and alone. The realization seeped into the pores of my skin. Owen wrapped his arm around me and tugged me into his side. I leaned into his chest and listened to his heart thud steadily against my cheek. The experiment was over. Adam was gone.

THIRTY-FIVE

I return to my father's favorite quote:
"Many of life's failures are people who did not realize
how close they were to success when they gave up."
—Thomas A. Edison

— — —

I slid my textbook off my desk at the end of Dr. Lamb's class and stuffed it into my book bag. I wasn't sure if I'd dozed off those last few minutes or if I'd just turned off my brain. That seemed to be happening more and more these days. I had these long stretches of time where the outside world was filled with white noise and afterward I couldn't remember anything.

"Tor." Dr. Lamb was peering at me over her glasses. Her chunky half-inch heels clacked over to her desk, where she took a seat in the rolling chair in front of a poster of a rocket launch. "Can you come here for a minute?" she asked.

I glanced around the room at the other students packing their bags and heading for the door and thought about pretending I hadn't heard her. But since I knew it'd only create twice the hassle tomorrow, I dragged my feet over to her workstation. "Did I do something wrong?" I asked. I had done so many things wrong in the last few weeks I wouldn't know where to begin.

She rested her pointy elbows on top of a pristine desk calendar. "Is everything okay, Tor? It's been a week since you last raised your hand in class, and I don't think you even bothered turning the pages of your text today. You're usually one of my brightest students"—I chafed at the phrase "one of"—"so I hesitate to say anything, but so much has been going on, and I want you to know we have resources here to help you process anything that might be upsetting you."

"You mean about Knox?" I asked, relaxing my posture. "We weren't exactly friends."

"Knox . . . and the other boys."

"Right, them," I said absently, kicking my shoe on the classroom floor. "I'm fine, but thanks. Was there anything else?"

She frowned. The corners of her eyes crinkled. "No, that was it, Victoria."

SOMEHOW IT HAD wound up Thursday. Or maybe it was Wednesday. I couldn't remember anymore.

"Watch it." Billy Ray's arm caught me in the shoulder, and my books sprayed onto the floor. I kneeled down to collect them. A sneaker stepped right across the spine of my physics workbook. I pinched the cover and wriggled it back to safety.

For a moment I stayed near the ground, watching the pairs of legs pass by. Worn jeans, tights, boots, tennis shoes, wedges. Part of me wanted to give up, to stay there. What difference did it make, anyway? Knox was dead, and I was in some ways worse off than dead. I was invisible.

I crawled to my feet. No one offered to help. I passed by Cassidy's locker. She wasn't there, but I'd seen her yesterday collecting her assignments after math. No sign of Paisley yet.

I met Owen at the cafeteria entrance. "Want to go see that Stan Lee documentary at the cineplex after school? It'll be over before curfew."

I yawned. "No, Owen, not really." Only, I couldn't remember if I'd bothered to say that out loud.

— — —

WAS IT FRIDAY already? God, how did that happen?

I stared out the window of the chemistry lab. Dark clouds were beginning to congregate over the school's campus and beyond the forested blanket of the Hollows. Below the windowsill, zebra grass bowed in the wind. The American flag beat wildly. It had been almost a week since I'd set foot in the cellar, but I imagined the mercury in my father's glass barometer plunging with the pressure. The Doppler radar, which I'd been studying so intently up to this point, would be electric now with orange and red beginning to spread toward Hollow Pines.

"Tor." The voice felt far away. "Tor. Hello? Tor."

I jumped when I felt a hand on my shoulder. "What?" I snapped.

Owen jerked back. His face looked longer, leaner. It was impossible to miss the purple bruises under his eyes that gave away that he hadn't been getting much sleep. They reminded me of Adam. The amused smile always brimming just at the surface of Owen's eyes was gone. And that reminded me of Adam, too. "Are you going to help?"

There was nothing clever in Owen's delivery. He didn't try to make me laugh. He just pointed to the small lab prep of our would-be science fair project. Set up in the empty classroom was a test tube fitted with a rubber stopper, a piece of glass tubing, and a two-liter soda bottle.

I sighed and turned from the window, where the first droplet had splashed the pane. Owen and I had agreed to abandon Mr. Bubbles. The experiment had already failed. I'd played God and created a monster. Besides, the lower mass and muscle density with that level of voltage would probably never work, anyway.

My lip curled at the sight of our new project, an archaic production of sulfuric acid from sulfur and saltpeter. I dropped my elbows onto the table and looked over Owen's equations for balancing the reaction:

$$KNO_3(s) + S(s) \dashrightarrow K_2S + N_2(g) + SO_3(g)$$

It was all painfully unoriginal. "Have you done the stoichiometry calculation yet?" I asked, my cheek pressed into my palm.

"Not yet," he said, rinsing the walls of the soda bottle using the small sink in the center of the lab table and leaving them wet.

I sighed again. I was becoming a professional sigher. It was pathetic. Or maybe it was apathetic. God, weren't those basically the same thing? I picked up a pen. It felt like a lot of effort. And I quickly ran through the calculations to determine the number of grams of salt-peter needed to react with a gram of sulfur. When it came time for the fair, we'd translate the process in neat print onto a colorful poster board, hell, maybe we'd just tear out the page of my notebook and slap it onto the poster board. Honestly, who cared? This was nothing compared with what I'd accomplished. This was pointless. Kid stuff.

When I'd circled the answer, I returned to staring out the window. Adam was out there with Meg. I had to keep reminding myself that he had killed Knox, that maybe he'd killed other people, too, except I could never get my mind around the idea that Adam was the Hunter. Something didn't add up. He had a violent streak, but he wasn't sadistic. It was more that he was being driven mad by how different he was. The truth was, I didn't want him to be different. I wanted him to be perfect, and when he wasn't, I had to send him away. I had no other choice.

Did I?

Outside, I watched the sky darken. Even though the sun hadn't set, the looming storm made the use of lights inside mandatory. I glanced at the clock. It was after three in the afternoon. I chewed on the end of my pen and wondered for the millionth time this week what he was doing.

The first flickers of lightning lit the bellies of the clouds like camera flashes sparking behind a gray veil. I lifted my cheek from my palm. I thumbed the lightning charm dangling from my wrist and rubbed it between my fingers, making the gold metal warm to the touch. The little zigzags in the bolt dug into my skin when I pressed. The bulbs went off again. And suddenly, it was like the lightning had struck me. Maybe the experiment with Adam *wasn't* over. Maybe he still could be a perfect specimen. Before, I hadn't had the answer. The generators. But now . . .

The pen clattered to the table. Owen glanced up from fiddling with the fit of the glass tube. "What?" he asked.

"The storm's only going to be here overnight." I grabbed my rain shell off a stool. "After that it might be too late."

Owen gently set the glass tube down on the counter. "What do you mean 'too late'? What are you talking about? Too late for what?"

"The experiment."

"*This* is our experiment, Tor."

I punched my arms through the sleeves of my coat and pulled the hood over my ears. "This is college sophomore science, Owen, and you know it. I'm talking about the generators." I pointed out the window where the fog rolled over the tops of the woods. "I'm going to get Adam. This isn't over yet. I think I can fix this."

"Tor." Owen stepped toward me. I was already making my way for the door, skipping backward. "You can't fix a body count. It didn't work. We tried."

"I know, but maybe I should still fix him. I have to go," I said. "I'll call you later."

I backed out of the room, still watching the storm brewing outside.

"Tor!" Owen called, but I just pivoted and ran, ran for my car, ran for Adam, ran to chase the storm breaking overhead, and just hoped that I'd get there in time.

THIRTY-SIX

Lightning is caused by an imbalance between positive and negative charges. A single cloud-to-ground lightning bolt can contain up to one billion volts of electricity.

— — —

A nswer, answer, answer." I shook the phone. This was my third call in a row. I dashed down the abandoned school hallway, dodging a yellow sign marking a puddle on the floor.

"No cell phones in school," barked Old Man McCardle. He pushed the mop back and forth across the white tiles. The silver wisps of his hair covered only pieces of his bowed head, sun-pocked and wrinkled with age. A yellowing bandage, stained with dirt and sweat, wrapped around one of his hands.

I cupped the receiver. "I know, but it's an emergency."

I hurried past while he grumbled something after me.

Just as I made it outside, the line clicked over to voice mail. "You've reached Meg. If you'd like to leave a message, do so after the . . ."

"Meg, it's Tor—Victoria—Frankenstein. I've been trying to get ahold of you. This is urgent. I have something that will help Adam, but I need you to meet me at the lightning generators in the Hollows as soon as possible. Even if it's raining. Tell Adam. He'll know the spot."

I could have sworn I'd told her to answer her phone if I called. Then again, maybe it shouldn't have taken me a week to call. I crossed the parking lot and dropped into my car. I crumpled the flyer that I'd pulled from my backpack and threw it on the dash. *Think.*

I stared at my cell phone. But it remained quiet. Maybe this was some kind of sign. Maybe Owen was right. I'd been down this road. As unpleasant as it was to admit, Adam had malfunctioned. That was my doing.

The sky was a wash of gray, and I leaned into the steering wheel to watch it darken, like spilled ink coming toward us. I twisted the key and felt the motor rumble underneath me. I'd almost forgotten. I didn't believe in signs.

I was going to the Queen's Inn to find Adam for myself. A few minutes later I crossed Main Street on my way to the southeast corner of Hollow Pines. As I drove, the houses got rattier. Weeds scaled the fences of overrun lawns. The windows of a gas station had been boarded up with plywood. Meanwhile, the clouds above me engaged in a valiant standoff with the threatening downpour. The sky held steadfast, with only a few spare drops slipping through the defenses and plummeting to earth like warning missives that splashed onto my windshield.

There'd be more. A lot more. The radio's weather report beeped with severe thunderstorm warnings and a tornado watch in the area until midnight. I pulled into the seedy lot of the Queen's Inn. The motel was a squatty two-story building with bars on the windows of the bottom-floor rooms and craggy asphalt with painted yellow lines fading in the parking lot. The place reeked of imagined cigarette smoke and crushed dreams.

Most of the spots in the lot were empty. I parked mine in a back row, nearest the road and the vintage sign with slide-in letters that read VACANCY. Or that was what it would have read if the *y* wasn't missing from the end. My hands twisted over the steering wheel. What if he had left town? What if she told someone our secret? My stomach chewed over these possibilities. I still had time to turn back while the experiment was still in the loss column. But, instead, I unfastened my seat belt and climbed out of the car into the part of town that nice girls never went. I looked both ways and crossed the parking lot to the front entrance of the inn, where I pulled open a door with ten years' worth of fingerprints smudged on the glass.

A sleepy-eyed man with a comb-over slid his elbows off the counter upon seeing me. "Can I help you?" His tone urged me to say no, but that wasn't going to happen. A roll of thunder so faint it could have been mistaken for my stomach growling seeped through the door.

"I'm looking for a girl's room. Her name's Meg." When he blinked, his hoodlike eyelids had only a short distance to travel. "She's about this high." I held up my hand an inch over my own head. "Dark hair. Pointy features. Scrappy. She's with a boy named"—I hesitated—"John Wheeler." I thought I saw a flash of recognition, a moment where his wiry eyebrows twitched.

"Sorry. We don't give out occupants' room numbers." This was the type of place that called their customers occupants instead of guests, and I found this to be the most honest thing about the Queen's Inn.

The clerk returned to picking bits of lint from the front of his shirt.

I cleared my throat. I'd been expecting this answer. After all, it was no surprise that occupants at the Queen's Inn wouldn't want to be found. I leaned on the counter. "Then could you call them to let them know someone's here?" I used my girliest *please help me* voice, a skill, although not mastered, that was maybe the one plus I'd picked up from the Oilerettes. "I'm sure they'd like to know."

He looked as if he didn't want to commit to moving, but, finally, he picked up the receiver. "Meg, you said? Meg what?"

"I don't really know," I said honestly. "I—Well, truth is, I'm better friends with John and, this girl Meg and I, we're on more of a first-name basis only. Know what I mean?"

He grunted but didn't seem perturbed. In a place like this, there were probably plenty of people who had reasons for obscuring their name for some reason or other.

Behind the counter, he ran his finger down a list.

"She's skinny," I said. "Pretty. I guess, anyway."

He didn't glance up. "I know the one." His voice was gruff. "Not a lot of young kids like you staying here." He perched a pair of glasses on his nose and peered down through the lenses. With a dirty fingernail, he punched the numbers into the phone's keypad and I watched, holding my breath.

First a nine. That was to be able to dial, I figured. Then a two, followed by a one, then another two: 2-1-2.

Room 212, I recited silently. I waited for the phone to ring in his ear. I worried the guy would go narcoleptic on the phone, but he hung up and stated, "They're not answering."

I shrugged. "No problem. Thanks for trying."

At least I knew that they were still staying here. I left the dingy clerk's office armed with Meg's room number and stuffed my hands into my pockets to keep them out of the wind. Without stopping, I climbed up the two flights of steps that ran alongside the fire escape.

I found Room 212 four doors down. The second "2" hung cockeyed from its nail. Inside, the window blinds were drawn.

I used the tarnished brass knocker to rap on the door. "Come on, come on." I bobbed up and down on my toes. I knocked again. The bottom had dropped out on the atmospheric pressure, and the temperature was falling along with it. The storm was strengthening. But where was Adam?

Again, there was no answer. I glanced over my shoulder. No one was around. I dug my teeth into my lower lip and wiggled the door handle. Locked. My heart thumped. I wondered if I'd officially lost my marbles. But that was the thing about losing it: You were usually too far gone to care. From my back pocket, I pulled my wallet and slid out my driver's license. Bending down, I inserted the license between the doorframe and door and slid it down toward the latch. It took several attempts until I heard the *click* that meant I'd successfully maneuvered the license in between the lock and frame.

With a whiny creak, the door popped open an inch. The room inside was a dark, tea-stained brown. The soles of my shoes sank into a spongy, carpeted floor as I slipped in and pulled the door shut behind me. I chained the lock and pressed my back to the door, letting my eyes adjust. A musty odor emanated from the comforters on two separate beds.

"Hello?" I called. The room was quiet except for the buzz of the window air-conditioning unit. All I needed was a hint of where they might have gone or when the last time was that they were here. I forced myself to move away from the wall and made a beeline for a duffel bag squished tightly between the television and minifridge.

I dug into a pile of clothes. If I had any doubt as to whether I had the right room, it went out the window when I found the treasure trove of cutoff denim. The girl loved to take scissors to jeans—shorts, skirts, it didn't matter. Soon, I was squatting amid a denim massacre.

But it was underneath a pair of underwear that I saw the glint of a screen. I pinched a red thong, the kind I'd never personally own, between two fingers and dropped it on the pile of clothes.

I picked up the shiny black tablet. The silhouette of my face reflected off the screen. I swiped my thumb across the bottom, and the tablet came to life. Bingo.

The background lit up blue, displaying a dozen icons. I tapped the one for "mail," but it wasn't set up. I cursed under my breath and closed out of the application. I selected the Internet app instead and the browser expanded.

I navigated to Meg's search history. A long list appeared, showing the last two weeks of activity. I scrolled. I didn't even know what I was looking for. A clue. Anything. Shopping websites filled the bulk of her history, and I grew impatient as I paged my way through.

From the hallway, I heard the sound of approaching voices. I stiffened, glancing around for somewhere to hide if I had to. Under the beds? The bathroom? They got closer. Shadows crossed the blinds. Footsteps. They were at the door, and then, in the space in which I was sure a key would slip into the lock, the footsteps began fading. They passed by the room. I let out a long whoosh of air and returned to the contents of the tablet.

Partway down, though, the word *fire* caught my attention. The link was to a news article. I clicked it, and the screen went white before flashing to the local news site for Hugo, a town north of Hollow Pines, across the Oklahoma border.

The headline, at once, stopped me cold: *Fatal house fire was intentionally set, officials say.* I read without wanting to. I read knowing what I might see. But the important thing was, I read anyway.

Unified Fire Authority investigators ruled out natural gas as the cause of a fire that destroyed 408 East Trice Street in Tuesday's late-evening hours. Unified Fire Battalion Chief Aaron Blanton issued a statement confirming, ". . . some other form of accelerant was spread in several places throughout the house."

James Flacco, 21, perished in the fire. An autopsy will confirm whether Flacco died as a result of the fire or whether his death occurred at some time earlier in the night.

My skin went from hot to cold to clammy and sweat-ridden like I was consumed by fever. I had finally found the house. My hands quivered. I set the tablet down and heard it knock against something hard in the bag.

I pushed a rolled-up shirt to the side, and my finger grazed something smooth and hard. Carefully, I lifted a gun out of Meg's bag.

My veins whooshed against my eardrums. Despite living my entire life in Texas, I'd never held one before. The short, angular handgun was light in my grip. I balanced it between handle and barrel.

My thoughts tumbled one on top of the other, roaring like a waterfall. Adam. The flashback. The screams. The fire. Meg. Gun.

That was what Meg meant by trouble. Someone died. I stared at the words on the screen. I hadn't created the monster. I'd just uncovered the person there waiting. It was John lurking underneath the surface. Not my methods. *John.*

But my loyalty was to Adam.

Still shaking, I stuffed clothes back into the bag, then tucked the gun unnaturally underneath my arm. When I stood up, my head filled with hot air, and I had to wait three *Mississippi*s for the feeling to pass.

The world around me was sharp and dreamlike all at once. I unchained the lock and slipped back out onto the balcony. Still no sign of Adam. In the parking lot, a blue truck was parked next to my car. It looked empty, but the motor was running. I caught a silhouette of my own reflection in the truck's window as I passed by.

I threaded my way through the space in between and popped open the door to my car. From the center cup holder, the screen of my phone flashed blue. I leaned over, maneuvering my knee onto the seat so I could pull out the phone. I recognized Meg's area code on the missed-call notification. My heart jumped. *Finally.*

I was entering the phone's password when I felt a shadow cross me. A whiff of tobacco. Then a brush of hair on my cheek. I didn't have time to scream before a coarse rag was shoved over my mouth and nose. The grip of strong arms hugged me to a stranger's chest. Something sweet filled my nostrils, and a wave of nausea rushed up my throat just before the world disappeared.

THIRTY-SEVEN

A half-life will grow shorter the more energy that is released. Therefore, a vast quantity of energy is needed as a starting point to sustain Adam for a greater length of time. It would need to be a supersource.

— — —

Pressure filled the space between my temples in waves. I lay still as a possum and counted to five, then to ten, then to five again to see if the last surge had left me. When the pressure faded, I dragged my forehead from a hard wooden surface to a world where everything was blurry. Tilted. Unrecognizable. I tried to sit up. Somewhere outside dogs barked, and I briefly thought of Einstein. My arms scraped the wood. Splinters flaked off and stuck in my skin. I groaned. The back of my throat burned like it'd been seared with acid. My hands, I realized, wouldn't budge. They were paralyzed. Stuck together. My feet felt as if needles were attacking them. They tingled, dead asleep. How long had I been lying here? I squinted through my eyelashes. An intricate knot looped around my wrists and ankles.

I jerked. My cheek scraped what I now understood was the floor, and I felt the fresh sting of raw skin. Panic seized hold of my lungs. I spent several long seconds writhing on the floor, trying to break my hands free. It was no use. The rope wore into my wrists, and the prickle of welts spread underneath it. Trying a new tactic, I dug my elbows into the ground and pushed myself into a sitting position. I was breathing heavy. Strands of hair fell over my eyes.

I made myself tick through the things I knew for certain. At some time before now, I'd been at the Queen's Inn. Someone had drugged me. That someone must have brought me here. I swallowed back tears. It wasn't much to go on. I glanced down at my clothes. My jeans were buttoned. My shirt appeared untouched. I didn't feel like anything . . . indecent had happened. At least not yet, anyway. I thought of lost girls on national news programs and tried to imagine myself as one of them. My pulse pounded in my ears. I sucked in uneven breaths. Shallow. What was going to happen to me? The answer formed instantly.

The Hunter.

The words shot through me, igniting a fresh rush of horror. I yanked against my ties, using every muscle in my body to slide my hands out of the trap. My wrists screamed with pain, and I curled in on myself. "No," I whimpered. "No, no, no."

Slowly, I sat back up. Tears streaked my cheeks, and my hair stuck to them. *Breathe*, I commanded. *Focus*. It wasn't doing anyone any good to dive into hysterics. I steadied my lower lip and forced myself to take in the surroundings. I was in a dim room, one that looked like it hadn't been used for years. Dust covered the floor. A twin bed had been shoved against the wall. Moths had eaten through spots on the thin green quilt that dripped off the brass bed frame. A yellowing crocheted blanket covered the nightstand beside it.

The room smelled like the inner pages of an old, forgotten book laced with something else, something I couldn't place but that felt unmistakably out of context.

At the foot of the bed, I noticed a curious trunk that appeared to be made of glass and filled with a pus-colored liquid that might account for the smell. I couldn't imagine what could be inside, but whatever it was it seemed foreign to the haunting nostalgia of the rest of the room's untouched decor.

"You see him now," said a voice coming from a far corner.

I gasped and cast my gaze around, searching through the dust-speckled air between us. "Who's there?" I said. I scrambled, driving my heels into the floor, until my back met the wall behind me.

It was then that I noticed the sliver of shadow beneath a small window that was part of an alcove cut into the wall. The shadow moved. No, the shadow was rocking. I heard the creak of wood. A shiver raced up my spine. As the chair rocked forward, the pale light from the window revealed a hand curled over the chair's arm. Behind him, the sky was bleak.

"Look." My voice quaked. "I—I don't know what you're talking about or who you are even, but we don't have to do anything rash here. It's not too late to let me go, and we can forget about this whole thing."

I felt vulnerable on the floor so, with great effort, I wedged my feet underneath me and worked my way into a standing position by using the wall to support me.

"Look at him." The man sounded familiar, but I wasn't sure why. I narrowed my eyes, trying to cut through the room's murky depths, but it was like trying to open my eyes in the ocean.

"At who?" I asked. Then my eyes landed on the glass trunk at the foot of the bed. "But I can't move," I whispered. "You've tied my feet together."

"Are you going to run?"

"No. I won't run." My knees knocked together. "I promise."

He stood up. Meg's gun glinted from his belt loop. He noticed me staring at it. "That's right. You're not going to run." The shadow slid from his face, and standing before me was Old Man McCardle. He wore a camouflage vest with a utility belt tied around his army green pants.

I stammered. "It's you. It's—" But I couldn't finish. Evil had roamed our school's halls unnoticed and untouched. Fear left a gaping hole in my insides.

He didn't answer. McCardle crossed the room. He bent down beside my feet. I saw that his left hand was wrapped in bandages. The smell of tobacco choked me. A blade flashed. I shrieked and shut my eyes, but then the ropes fell loose from my legs. I rolled my ankles, stretching them. At least one part of me was free. I wondered if his other victims had been so lucky and tried to tell myself that there was still time to win.

McCardle's eyes were sharp and cunning. He pointed to the glass trunk. "And the Lord said, 'Look upon my son.'"

I hesitated, then caught another glimpse of the gun. My feet still numb, I advanced slowly until I could see over the lip of the open glass casket. I brought both hands to my mouth. My knees buckled. Inside the syrupy liquid was the floating body of a teenage boy. Much of him had been decomposed. Bits of his teeth showed through the pruned skin of his cheeks. The nose had begun to recede into the skull's abscess. Tufts of hair were missing from his scalp. But none of that was the most grotesque part.

The eyes bulged from the sockets. Crusted blood formed a ring around them. I thought of the boy with the missing eyes and knew at once that I'd found them stuck haphazardly to fit into the naked corpse. *The first to decompose*, I thought. The eyes were the first thing to decompose. My head grew woozy.

Each of the boy's legs was a different shade of flesh. One was pale and the other olive-skinned. Jagged stitches attached the thighs to the hip joint. Between stitches, skin flaked from the wounds, and it was clear that the old and the new body had never healed together.

"The hand," I said, and I wasn't sure whether I'd meant to say it. Only that my eyes were glued to the floating cadaver festering in pustule liquid. "None of the bodies were found missing two fingers." I stared at the boy's left hand, where a new pointer and middle finger had been attached using the same barbed stitching. "There's a body that hasn't been found yet?"

I peeled my eyes away from the monstrosity to look back at Mc-Cardle. He held his left hand up, and I noticed now that the bandages ended in nubs on his left hand. He'd used two of his own.

I closed my eyes and breathed through my nose. "This is what you're going to do to me? You're going to use me for parts. You're sick." Then a piece of my memory clicked into place. Paisley at the field party. Old Man McCardle, his son, and the tractor. I turned back to the corpse. The legs, which had been caught in the machinery. Perhaps his fingers had been, too. "This is your son. The one that died. You're trying to re-build him. You can't fix him. He's gone. You've gone mad," I screamed. "You don't need to hurt me to make him whole."

"Of course not," he said. His tongue slid over his lips. I didn't know if he was playing some kind of joke on me. Toying with me as he would prey. The Hunter of Hollow Pines was standing right in front of me, and I felt the clock of my life winding down.

Thunder crashed overhead, shaking the walls and causing me to jump. I struggled with the ties on my hands again. "You can't do this. You can't."

McCardle came closer, taking even steps toward me. I retreated until my calves were against the cool glass of what I realized wasn't a trunk at all, but a coffin. "He was buried into death in order that he be raised from the dead by the glory of the Father to walk in the new-ness of life. So sayeth the Lord."

"I don't understand," I said.

"Then the Lord formed him of dust from the ground," McCardle boomed. "And the man became a living creature."

I shook my head. Mucus dripped from my nostrils. Tears flooded my eyes.

"Come ye the resurrection where the hunted are born again."

I sniffled. My body froze. "What are you saying?"

He was so close now that I could make out a long scar that ran from his ear to his chin. "I am saying that I know."

Static buzzed in my ears. I remembered the tire tracks, the shattered phone. And now my stomach threatened to betray me. I'd ignored all of it, and I was here.

"How?" I rasped. I squeezed my eyes closed and reopened them free of tears. "Where . . . are . . . we?" I asked cautiously. But as soon as I asked, I knew the answer. I knew it because it was the only possible answer. I peered out the window, and sure enough a short distance away was the highway. He had seen me. Then he had seen Adam. That night came rushing back. The farmhouse with its lights on. The barking dogs. A scream lodged in my throat. This felt like a nightmare. One that lived and breathed and bled into the day to torment me.

"Bring him back," McCardle said.

My spine went rigid. Already pressed to the coffin, I tilted my head and stared down at the amalgamation. "I can't. He's . . . he's a monster. He's gone. I can't do it."

I cringed away from the body, but McCardle caught me by the wrist. He ran his bandaged hand over my forehead and down the bridge of my nose. "I suppose then that my boy could use a new nose. Maybe ears." He crossed my face to the lobes. "Patches of skin. What do you think?" he hissed. His breath was sour like curdled milk.

"No." I breathed. My mind began reeling. I needed time to figure this out. I needed to buy time.

He yanked me into him.

I bit my lip by accident. A small shriek escaped. The room was spinning. "What—what I mean is, I can't do it here. I have to have . . . my equipment."

"If you think I'm taking you back to your house, where you can call the cops . . ."

"No," I added quickly. "Nothing like that. The lightning generators. They are . . . my father's invention." The spit was so thick in my mouth

I could hardly speak. "Without those, the resurrection, as you called it, it won't work. We have to go to them." A part of me begged to collapse on the moth-eaten bed, but I remained standing. Time. That was what I needed. As much of it as I could get. "I can show you."

Some of the gauze around his hand loosened, and I could see the spots of blood that had seeped throughout the layers. "I already know where they are," he said. And a cold fever swept through me.

THIRTY-EIGHT

Coordinates: 33.6627589 degrees north, 95.7891265 degrees west
  Take left at the lone oak
  Forty paces to due west
  Look for the clearing in the woods

— — —

How long had McCardle been following mc? I wondered. My teeth rattled against one another as we forked off onto the country road that bordered the beginning of the Hollows. The rope still knotted around my wrists rubbed deep grooves there, and I winced every time we went over another bump.

McCardle knew where the generators were. The thought sent icy tentacles around my throat. We hadn't been alone that night. We'd been right. The Hunter had been watching us, tracking us. Who knew what he might have done, especially if I'd gone alone.

I rode silently on the front bench of the blue truck that left no divider between us. A white rabbit's foot dangled from the rear-view mirror. Something told me he didn't buy it at a gas station for a souvenir.

The sky was breaking. Drops of rain spattered the grimy windshield. The darkest clouds now hung directly above us, grumbling like monsters. The occasional ripple of lightning flashed through the clouds' bellies, but I had yet to see one break free.

I stared silently out the window. Through the side mirror I could see the blue tarp that covered the glass coffin loaded into the truck bed. During the drive, I'd been waiting for a plan to come to me, but I was no closer to one than I had been when I'd first woken up, drugged and groggy, in McCardle's creepy farmhouse. My only thought was to get to the generators and wait for an opportunity.

"We're almost there." He ran his hand over the steering wheel. Thumped the bottom with the base of his hand. He was anxious. Anxious could be good, I figured. I might catch him off guard. But anxious could also be unpredictable, in which case all bets were off.

I cleared my throat. "You know, it wasn't your fault what happened to your son. It was an accident. Everybody knows that."

He watched the storm swirl above. "It's really starting to come down out there."

I shifted in my seat. "Yeah," I muttered. "I guess it is."

We rounded a bend in the road where there was a small inlet large enough for two or three cars to park. I didn't think I could ever go near that spot without thinking of my dad leaving me behind in his truck to go chase the lightning.

I inhaled sharply. Another car was already parked there.

"Who's here?" McCardle's voice was a bark.

I tensed. "I don't know. I swear. I don't know." This was mostly true. I didn't recognize the silver sedan, but the Oklahoma license plate gave me a good idea to whom it might belong. My spirit lightened. Hope fizzed in me. They'd gotten my message. Adam and Meg were here. I tried to keep my face neutral.

I glanced sidelong at the black hilt of Meg's gun still tucked in McCardle's waistband. Maybe it was selfish of me, wishing they were there, but I couldn't help it. I wanted to survive.

McCardle pushed the gear into park. The rabbit's foot swung and then stopped. "Doesn't matter," he said, climbing out.

I craned around to watch him pull the tarp off the glass coffin and roll it carefully, lowering it to the dirt. The mutant corpse now stared up at the sky with his stolen eyes. Next he loaded the box of tools I'd told him I'd need. For what, I didn't know yet. I didn't have a plan. "Not much longer," I heard McCardle murmur to the body. "So close."

I turned back on the bench. What did he mean it didn't matter? He'd sounded so sure of himself. A vague uneasiness spread through my limbs.

He opened the door, and misty rain sprayed my cheeks. "Get out," he said.

"You're going to have to untie me." I stared straight ahead, unmoving. "I'm not going to be much help if I have my hands tied together."

Another spike of fear punctured my lungs when the buck knife slipped between my hands. There was a pop, and the ropes fell to the floorboard. I rubbed my wrists and moaned.

McCardle spat on the ground then took the gun from his waistband and flipped off the safety. "Well?"

I climbed out. The storm breeze flattened the shirt against my stomach. Even though the generators belonged to my dad, the woods felt like McCardle's territory.

"You move him." McCardle wiped his nose on his sleeve and trained the gun's barrel at my heart.

"Me?"

He nodded with the barrel, a language that translated universally. I went round to the back of the truck. McCardle had rigged a crude wagon, where the casket lay on a plank of wood with four wheels and rope tied to it. I shuddered to think where else he'd taken his son.

He grabbed a lantern from the truck bed. The yellow glow cast a short path in front of us. I strained my weight against the rope, and together we entered the forest.

My back tightened against the weight of the coffin as I pulled it over uneven ground, stumbling every few steps. My eyes kept scanning the trees for signs of Adam. The soles of my shoes dug into the soft ground. Only spare raindrops fell through the canopy. Icy cold, they stung at my skin. The rustling of brittle leaves from above drowned out all sound.

Nearby, McCardle stalked through the woods, walking heel to toe like a predator. He swept the surrounding area with his gun. I was breathing hard now under the burden of the casket. A monstrous curiosity caused me to keep looking back, to study the body with the bulging eyes, which was only a shadow now sloshing over the forest floor.

Thunder cracked overhead, shaking the trees to their roots. I chewed on my cheek and continued our crawl forward. With every step, I expected to see Adam. Where was Adam? He'd saved me from Knox. He'd stayed close when he thought I was in danger. I needed him now more than ever.

We were getting closer now. McCardle stretched out his arm, the one with the lantern. "*Shhhh*, do you hear that?"

I strained my ears to listen. My pulse thudded. "No."

We walked a few more yards, then I heard it. It sounded like crying. I felt the beat of my heart like a ticking time bomb in my chest.

"Someone's come to join us." I didn't like how he said that. "Watch your step now," he said. "Follow right after me."

My ears rang. Or else what?

I heeded McCardle's advice. We snaked our way through the trees. He watched the ground closely. The crying grew louder.

I jumped at the sound of a metal clap behind the wheeled coffin. McCardle paused. He held his lantern high over his head. "Looks like you found one." On the ground, the jaws of a bear trap had clamped shut after one of the wheels had passed over it.

McCardle lowered the light and continued on. I hurried to stay near.

"Hello?" I heard the quiet call of Meg's voice over the rustling branches. "Hello, is someone there? We need help."

The rain poured harder over the foliage. More of it trickled onto the bare spots of my skin. My hands were freezing around the rope. We entered the empty clearing. The sobbing felt nearby now. I looked frantically around before I saw Meg's face, a few paces away on the outskirts of the clearing. It was twisted in agony. She sat on the ground next to a figure that was lying prostrate.

"Adam." My voice was hoarse. "What's wrong with him? Adam?" I called.

"I don't know." She wept. "I don't know. I don't know. I don't know. He just gave up."

McCardle's boots trampled the wet grass. Rain now soaked through our pants, our hair, our everything. Lightning streaked through darkness like a network of blood vessels. He held the lantern over the pair. Meg's hands were wrapped around her ankle. A trap bit through her foot. She rocked back and forth. Close by, another trap had caught Adam around the anklebone. He groaned but didn't move.

I stopped myself short of blurting out the obvious. Meg hadn't recharged him. Who knew how long it had been. Days? A week? My eyes darted to McCardle. I didn't want to volunteer any extra insight.

No. That was all that was going through my head. No, and this couldn't be happening. There was no one here to save me. I was as good as alone.

"I need to help him," I yelled over the storm.

He shook his head and looked up into the heavens. "Come on. They're not going anywhere."

"Tor!" Meg screamed.

McCardle pointed the gun at me. I weighed my options. I wanted to run to Adam, but the gun was a convincing reason to stay.

"We need to go in there." I pointed to the center of the generators. "Is my leg going to be snapped in two if I walk any farther?"

McCardle grunted no. We passed beneath the shadows of the three great columns. I stared up at the giant orbs. Their motors hummed with life. A low charge hung in the air. *Think, Tor.*

My steps were heavy. I marched to the center of the ring of generators. McCardle's mouth hung open as he took them each in. In the middle, I stopped and stared up, turning in a slow circle. The lightning was gathering closer and stronger.

"Stop stalling," he said.

I dropped my chin. "Right, sorry." But stalling was my only plan. "I, uh, have to prepare the body. It's . . . complicated." I let go of the rope and went around to the back wheels where my borrowed tools were. "I . . . may need your help. We'll see."

I felt his eyes on me as I carefully sifted through the equipment he'd brought. Instead of a scalpel, there was a small Swiss Army knife blade and a rusty razor. I pressed my thumb to the knife's point, testing it. I wasn't sure what good it would be against a gun. Besides, McCardle seemed to know his way around a blade just fine.

I glanced over my shoulder. McCardle had yet to so much as look away as far as I could tell. I found a screwdriver, a hammer, a few copper wires. I stared at the tools. I had no plan of actually resurrecting the corpse, but I still felt shorthanded.

"Victoria . . ." I stopped at the moan coming from Adam. "Victoria . . ."

McCardle waved the gun at me again, and I lowered my head.

My hand trembled. I balanced the Swiss Army knife between two fingers and stared down at the body. Its shriveled lips hardly looked human. Rain dripped from the tip of my nose. I bent over and gingerly pressed the blade at the point between the boy's collarbones. He sank a few centimeters in the viscous liquid before finding the bottom. I pressed harder. The skin opened up. The insides were yellow like a dissected frog. Not a hint of blood on the knife's blade.

I lifted the back of my hand to my mouth and stifled a gag. I cut along the ridge of his sternum, all the way to the bone underneath. Foam squelched from the open wound. Another flash of lightning lit up the clearing. When it did, I nearly screamed. I had seen Owen unmistakably making his way through the woods toward Adam and Meg. The lightning abated, and his figure was blotted out. I looked to McCardle. He was still watching me closely. He hadn't seemed to notice anything amiss.

Owen. Owen was here. I had almost forgotten that I told him my plan was to go to the generators. I wanted to cry with joy and with fear. My mind raced. Somehow my entire life seemed to have converged on this moment. The loose threads of a plan began to dangle in front of me, waiting to be knitted together. *Keep the old man distracted.* I could do that.

"Is this what your son would have wanted?" I asked the first question that fell on my tongue. Over my top lip, beads of sweat mixed with the rain.

McCardle's features were twisted, and, in the rearranged pieces, I could see underneath where the guilt and the years had worn at him like termites on damp wood. "He shall see his offspring, he shall prolong his days, the will of the Lord shall prosper in his hand. So sayeth the Lord." He was eaten alive by the death of his son, and what was left over was a haunted shell of a man whose blood had been transformed to poison.

Instinctively, I looked away, like I was witnessing something that no one should ever have to, the unbuttoning of a man before my very eyes. So I sliced downward on the corpse's body until I reached the bottom of his breastbone. I hardly noticed the chill of the stolen eyes staring up at me anymore, and long moments passed when all I could see from the forest was darkness.

I kept my eyes on the corpse, scared that I'd give something away, that maybe the hope would show in my eyes. "And the boys that you murdered." My voice shook. "What would the Lord have to say about that?"

Thunder vibrated the air around us, and the bowels of the clouds above let loose. Cold rain poured over us with renewed intensity.

"For just as Jonah was in the belly of this fish," McCardle called, "so will the Son be in the heart of the earth, for his subsequent rescue from death is what vindicated his mission to go forward." He turned his face up and let the rain fall on his forehead, run into his eyes, and wet the thin strips of hair on his scalp.

I flattened the kinks of four copper wires in my hand. I was running out of time. The orbs above us had begun to glow a dull bluish tint. Sparks zipped between the cables that connected the generators.

At the next burst of lightning, I saw Owen fiddling with the traps. My breath lodged in my throat. *Careful*, I wanted to tell him. *Don't get too bold.* I wondered if he had seen the gun or if Meg had told him. I was thankful for the blustering storm that offered a cloak.

At the center of the ring, I peeled back the layers of skin, exposing the mealy rib cage underneath. There, I inserted two of the wires in the crevice I'd created. The chest cavity matched Adam's almost exactly but for the fact that I had no metal plate to give this dead boy.

Another groan came from the distance. The sobbing had continued nonstop. *Quiet, Adam.*

"He'll look like an abomination of your son," I said. "He'll be an idol. A fake. Look at him." And there was no mistaking that I was right. This person, this thing, was nothing like Adam. He might have started as someone's child. He might have been good and kind in life, but there was nothing left of him that was sacred. Dwarfed by the giant monoliths of the lightning generators, I felt like McCardle and I were in the midst of a sacrificial ritual. I wiped water from my eyelashes.

"And thou shalt believe," McCardle murmured. He turned his face up to the sky and let the rain pour over him. "And thou shalt believe in thine heart that God hath raised him from the dead."

The sky above was being torn apart by light. The generators were doing their job. "It's not safe here," I said, beginning to shake. "We could be killed."

The next burst of lightning came from directly overhead. When I looked over, I saw that Owen was gone. And so was Adam. A jab of dread filled me. What if they had left? Was that less than I'd deserve for killing Adam and for lying? I wedged the Swiss Army knife in my fist, ready to fight.

The next lightning strike looked as though it landed somewhere in the forest. The brightness flickered. And then I saw Adam's face inches away from mine. This time I did cry out.

"Victoria." He staggered, looking less human than he had ever looked before. His joints were stiff. He teetered unevenly on stilt legs.

Now I smelled the first hint of smoke.

McCardle wheeled around. He dropped the lantern. It rolled on the ground. Another burst of lightning. But this one lingered, caught between the generators' crosshairs. I had a split second to react.

"Now!" I shouted as if this had been my plan all along. With all my might, I grabbed Adam by the arm with both hands. I wrenched him over, pushing him on top of what was left of McCardle's son. He splashed into the liquid.

Above, lightning tangled, mixing and blurring. I shielded my eyes. The orbs lit up bright blue, electric with energy. I scuttled back. One great, combined streak of lightning shot down. The glass coffin was a wash of white-hot color.

There was the sound of glass cracking like a footstep on a frozen lake. I held my breath for a heartbeat. The coffin shattered. Liquid poured from broken shards.

"No!" McCardle howled, and it sounded like a dying animal. He lunged for the heap of flesh where his son's body lay at the same moment that the silhouette of one body emerged. The outline that was Adam arched his spine. He rolled back his shoulders. McCardle realized his mistake too late. He should have known by now what Adam was capable of.

Adam stretched out his arm, grabbed McCardle by the neck, and flung him sideways. The old man crumpled to the ground. The wind burst from his lungs, and he wheezed, clutching his chest. The gun skittered an arm's length away.

Adam's eyes shined in the flickering light of the lantern. They were cold. He lowered his chin, and his brow hid his eyes in shadow. I recognized the look from just after his recharges or in the moment that he hurled Knox off the stage. He moved methodically toward Mc-Cardle with a slight limp to his gait.

McCardle cowered on the ground as Adam closed on him. He lifted an arm to shield his face. "You . . . would save her?" The old man's voice was ragged, and he puffed for air. "The girl that killed you?"

I went limp. The truth, the one I'd been holding on to with a death grip, the one that every day I'd had an opportunity to share and that every day I'd chosen not to, was out. What could I say now that hadn't already been said in one bone-crushing sentence?

Adam stopped. When he turned, his expression was a raw wound. His eyes held pools of sorrow. "Victoria?" There was still awe there and hope, and I felt it begin to crumble through my fingers.

"I killed you," I said softly. "It was me that night." A strangled groan, nearly inhuman. "It was an accident." Since the night of the wreck, we'd come miles, but when I stared across an endless chasm at my creation, I felt that I'd returned to our start. I stood dripping wet in front of him, begging for his forgiveness, pleading with him to understand. I didn't know whether I deserved it, only that I was what I was and he was what he was and that neither of us could hide from it. Neither of us were perfect, only special.

He wrapped his hands around his head and pulled his elbows over his face like a cage. The air between us crackled, and I mentally readied myself for an attack. I could feel the violence raging within him. My own creation may kill me with his bare hands, I realized.

Find the thing you love and let it kill you. That was what my father had done.

He lowered his hands. His entire body was shaking now. "I remember," he said. "It's . . ."

Out of the corner of my eye, there was movement. I tensed.

McCardle stretched his fingers for something. The gun on the ground. "Adam!"

There was less than an instant. Adam's decision balanced on the edge of a razor before it tipped over and fell. Forever. Irrevocably. And then he was mine.

He lurched on a damaged leg and pinned McCardle's arm. "Not . . . Victoria." I watched horror-struck as Adam's hands wrapped around the neck of the man who used to be our school's janitor. Tearing myself from the spot, I reached for the gun, pulling it to safety and out of reach. The weight of it in my hands again felt deadly and even scarier now that it had been pointed at my brain. Milliseconds went by that felt excruciatingly long. McCardle began to gurgle. His frail lips worked for words.

I could have stopped Adam, but I didn't. I was ready to watch McCardle die, when suddenly, Adam released his grip. He slid away from the old man and sank his head into his hands. "Not yet, Adam," I said, too quietly for anyone to hear.

"My son," McCardle wept. "My son." The contorted evil that had engulfed his features had vanished, and what was left was just a man stricken with grief.

I sensed the defeat in McCardle as he dragged himself to his feet. The retreat in his step. I watched as he tried to shift into the shadows, to disappear into the woods he knew so well. The Hunter of Hollow Pines. Only, it was too late. I couldn't let that happen. He knew our secret. He knew what Adam was. He knew what I had done.

My hands were slick with sweat. I held the barrel of the gun straight out from my body. I had to do something. I always knew when something hard had to be done and when someone special had to do it. So I did. I fired. The first bullet missed, whizzing by to lodge in a tree trunk somewhere. Lost. I fired a second shot.

This time Old Man McCardle doubled over. He clutched his stomach. The word *son* made it halfway out before he collapsed. The muscles in my arms dissolved, and the gun plummeted from my hands.

THIRTY-NINE

A description of the event: The storm approached Hollow Pines from the northeast corridor. As it neared, it became clear that the lightning was both attracted to and reinforced by the presence of the generators. A few stray lightning bolts hit close to home, but when, at last, a series of bolts found their mark, the electricity was harnessed and strengthened through the use of the adjustable spark gap. The tangle of lightning was too bright for the bare human eye to view without discomfort. A single, combined bolt made it to the ground, amplified in brightness and intensity more than any observed in nature of which I am aware.

- - -

The adrenaline drained from my body with the waning storm and we were left with the damage. The final shot rang in my ears. My eyes were too wide. I stumbled to the overturned lantern, barely seeing. I stared at the wreckage, which seemed to fan out from me like I was a bomb that had already detonated.

McCardle's son stared into the vast nothingness with eyes that would never close. A puddle surrounded him. In the debris, the stitching on his legs had loosened to expose the ends of whitewashed bone that glistened in the moon now beginning to peek through the passing clouds. I hugged my torso. My sopping clothes chilled me to the core. A single trickle of blood dribbled from the corner of Old

Man McCardle's mouth. Red blossomed through the front of his flannel shirt. I stepped over his legs when I heard Owen's voice calling.

I'd been so lost in the small blown-up world between the generators that I had forgotten all about Owen and Meg. It felt like I'd spent hours in a cage match, and yet it couldn't have been more than minutes. I glanced back at Adam, who was still hunched over, catatonic. Reluctantly, I left the circle. I followed the sound of Owen's voice and followed the light of the lantern. The sobbing had stopped, and I now heard faint whispers through the noise of the rustling branches.

I found Meg with her arm wrapped over Owen's shoulder. She'd taken off her shoe and held her foot a few inches above the ground.

"Easy does it," Owen said as he guided her closer. The lantern glinted off his glasses. His forehead wrinkled when he looked up. His face broke into a broad smile at the sight of me. "Tor," he said. "You're okay. What happened?" He caught my wrist and pulled me into a tight hug, which ended up being crowded with the three of us, and it was like we were long-lost friends reuniting. "Janitor McCardle was the Hunter?" he said.

I nodded. "I guess he really was as crazy as people said he was. How bad is it?" I gestured to Meg's foot.

She winced. "He says it will heal and that I was lucky it only got my foot."

"The puncture wounds are deep," Owen said grimly. "And there are probably a few small fractures. She should keep it still and elevated as much as possible. See a doctor . . . if she can."

As though drawn by a magnet, we gathered back at Adam. Meg whimpered at the two remaining bodies.

"I was going to kill him." Adam was still hunched over. He let his hands fall from his face. "I already killed two people, and I was going to kill him, too. With my bare hands." He turned his hands over, examining them front and back. "I remember now."

A cold sweat spread to the backs of my knees. The three of us standing shared glances between us. "What did you see, Adam? What do you remember?" I asked.

"Everything."

I bent down. A tuft of his dark hair fell over the bridge of his nose. I brushed it away.

"I'm John Wheeler," he said, staring at his boots. Blood seeped through his pant leg where the trap had caught him, but he didn't seem to feel the same pain that Meg did. "But I'm Adam, too." He looked at me imploringly. The naive boy I'd created was fading and being replaced by something wiser and less familiar. "I saw it," Adam said. "I know why the house was burning. I—I killed someone. I punched him. I didn't mean to kill him, but, I punched him again and . . . I don't think I was sad. I was standing over his body." He squeezed his eyes shut and pinched his chin to his chest before continuing. "Then there was gasoline. I . . . poured it in the house and then I lit the match." He sucked in a deep breath like coming up for water. "And you were there." He cocked his head and narrowed his eyes at Meg like this was the part he couldn't quite place. "You were screaming for me. You told me to go. So I went."

Owen and I both looked to Meg. Her eyes watered, and I didn't know if it was from pain or the memory. Who knew, maybe the memory was pain. "Here's what you have to understand," she began, taking a deep breath. "Hugo is a piss-poor excuse for a town." I started to open my mouth. "Wait. I know you think because you're not exactly from New York City that you've got the whole small-town bull nailed down, but this place deserves its dot on the map. Where we come from, people sit around waiting to die. And when they're bored, they sit around thinking of ways to speed that process up. John was going somewhere. He was an athlete. He was dynamite on the football field. Probably would have gotten a scholarship." Her smile was soft in the trickles of moonlight. "But John's biggest problem was me. Like I said, he's been in love with me since we were kids. He'd have walked through fire for me if I asked him."

I set my jaw. "And did you?"

"I didn't have to. I got involved with this guy, see."

"I thought you said you two were madly in love," I said.

She looked down at her knotted hands. "This guy and his friends were bad, and being with him meant being involved with both. I did some things I shouldn't have. I'm young. I experimented. We all did. Better than sitting and waiting to die." She rubbed her arms like she'd caught a sudden chill. "But by the end, I owed them money and I wanted out. When I tried to stop, Jimmy wouldn't let me." I recognized the name. Jimmy, short for "James." James Flacco, the man who died at 408 East Trice Street. "I told John that Jimmy had been hitting me. It wasn't true. But I did believe he might have killed me. Sooner or later, anyway. I knew John had . . . a temper. There'd been a few other incidents. Lots of guys in Hugo were angry, though. I knew when I told John about Jimmy that he'd lose it. So I let him and that was when it happened. . . ." She trailed off.

My eyes flashed with anger that she'd done this to Adam. But then again, there would be no Adam without her. "Then how come *you* had a gun?" I demanded of Meg.

She let out a short, mirthless laugh. "I knew that looked familiar. For protection. From Jimmy's friends," she said. "I'm not exactly the most popular girl in town right now. John even less so. The question is why'd you go searching through my things."

"I needed to find you."

Adam studied his knuckles. "I killed Knox. I killed Jimmy. I would've killed him, too." He looked over his shoulder at McCardle's crumpled body. "I'm a monster."

I grasped his chin between my finger and thumb and looked into his eyes. "The generators worked, Adam. You're not a monster. If I'm right, the energy source should hold. At least a lot longer. You can be Adam."

"I can only be both," he said. I cut my glance to Meg. She looked away, shifted her weight. "And I'll always be this," he continued. "Dead."

"No. Don't say that. I made you."

"I know, Victoria. Thank you. But you *made* me."

My intestines writhed like slime-laden earthworms. "Adam, you can't stay here," I said. "Not after Knox. Not after Jimmy. You'll never get a fair shot." I had destroyed the keeper of the secret, the one who knew *what* Adam was, but *who* he was could still catch up to him.

"Victoria, no."

I shut my eyes to block out his pained expression. I'd abandoned him once, and now I was doing it for a second time. "You have to. It's the only way that makes sense. At least for now."

All around us, the clearing was cast in an eerie light.

"My aunt has a house in Laredo," Meg said. "We'll head there for now."

"What about your injuries?" Owen asked.

Carefully pinching the fabric, I peeled up Adam's pant leg. Deep lacerations churned up loose skin. Blood coagulated in the sunken wounds. I was pretty sure the cuts went down to the bone. "His platelet count has been double what it needs to be. It may be enough to heal him more quickly."

Beads of rain dripped from his hair. I thought of the tree-branch scars that braided his chest, and I wanted to memorize him, all of him.

"Adam," I said softly.

"Victoria."

I breathed in from my nose, out through my mouth, and tore my eyes away. "The charge should hold, but if it doesn't, don't let it get too far. Always stay alert." I glared at Meg when I said this. "You let him get too far gone. You see what happens now. Promise me."

"I promise," she said, and I knew I had no choice but to trust her, even though I still didn't.

The rain had nearly dissipated. The sky had turned milky. The night clouds swirled in uneven patterns, blotting out the stars.

"Go," I said before I could change my mind. "We'll take care of all this."

My throat became sore and achy. With Adam's last look, he didn't hug me. We didn't shake hands. He only held my gaze for what felt like a small eternity, and then he was gone. Owen wrapped his arm around my shoulders and squeezed as the pair of them disappeared into the Hollows.

FORTY

With a heavy heart, I'm closing the Adam file today. Adam has been my greatest achievement. I'm looking into the possibility of getting recently euthanized cats and dogs from the local animal shelter. Will report with availability. Otherwise, I may have to look into less palatable means of getting large mammals.

— — —

People would believe anything that fit within their version of reality. Some days I was convinced that the people of our town chose not to see Adam for what he really was. Now he was nothing more than a memory in Hollow Pines—a ghost—which was funny seeing as how he'd been dead all along.

I stood with Owen next to our flimsy piece of poster board, waiting for the judges to evaluate our project. By now the burns around my wrists from McCardle's rope were a ring of ragged orange scabs, half peeled from the skin. I used my sleeves to cover them up and the nubs of my fingernails to scratch them now that they itched constantly. The judges consisted of two senior science teachers, a junior college professor, Principal Wiggins, and an oil-rig engineer. All around the cafeteria, students sat with their creations—oozing volcanoes, models of the solar system, and seeds sprouting weeds.

"That kid blew up balloons using Pop Rocks," I said, crossing my arms and eyeing a set of three soda bottles whose necks were covered with blown-up latex. "And I thought our project was bad." Science fair projects were mandatory in most science classes, but effort tended to be lackluster. The school fair was only a stepping-stone, anyway, for the team that got to move on to county and then state. Owen and I had won every year, and this one was supposed to be our best. Our brightest.

Instead, in front of our poster board, Owen had displayed the Florence flask and the sulfuric acid that had resulted from our chemical process. The whole thing lacked pizzazz. It was boring, and I was sulking as a result.

"We're lucky we even have a project given that our other one is currently on the run and, oh yeah, a federal crime," he muttered out of the side of his mouth.

I touched the lightning-bolt charm dangling from my damaged wrist. I still hadn't tried to contact Meg's phone. It seemed smartest to lay low and submit stupid, subpar science fair projects like nothing much had changed.

One of the judges passed with a badge pinned to his lapel. I stared down at my shoes. When he passed, I turned to Owen. "How long do you think until they stop searching for the body?"

Owen's mouth formed a line. "I don't know. Another week? I—" He took a deep breath and shook his head. "It's hard letting all those people go to all that trouble searching for something they'll never find." He pushed his glasses up to the bridge of his nose.

A couple days ago, the city had started dredging the lake for Adam's body. Twenty-four hours after the Homecoming dance, he was declared missing. Shortly after that, he was presumed to be one of the boys killed by Roy McCardle Sr., the Hunter of Hollow Pines.

It hadn't taken long for Owen and me to mastermind the crime scene. We'd used a screwdriver to whittle away the serial number from Meg's gun and placed it in McCardle's lifeless hand. We'd wiped clean the tools and the traps. Owen insisted on searching the grounds for the rest of them. We found seven more bear traps and made sure that they snapped closed by using a thick stick to press the triggers. I had wanted to burn McCardle's old house down, but Owen was right, I had never been in the criminal system and any hairs they found there would be a match for no one. One anonymous tip from a pay phone and it was all shockingly simple. They had found the mutant body with the pieces of the missing boys. There were suspected to be more out there. Especially since there were two unidentified blood samples left in the bear traps. But no one had found anything yet.

"Stop worrying about them, Owen. This town has never paid attention to us. Why should we feel bad about it now?"

I read the Lie Detector religiously, devouring any mention of Adam. Commenters thought it'd be a matter of days before they found Adam Smith's body strung up somewhere in the countryside. Adam had received some "posthumous" sympathy for Knox's death, which many now viewed as an accident. Of course, there were fringe commenters who created a conspiracy theory where Adam had been working with McCardle and was now in hiding. I appreciated their creativity if nothing else. Or others that thought he'd just gotten spooked and ran after Knox's death. But few were convinced that a high school boy could get very far on his own without getting caught.

Owen and I fell silent. We'd been doing that a lot the last few days. Another judge—the junior college professor—passed. I watched the judge linger over the Pop Rocks experiment. When I turned back, Cassidy was standing in front of me. I jumped and knocked over our poster board.

"Sorry," she said softly. "I didn't mean to startle you."

Behind me, Owen righted the project. I could feel him listening.

Her fingers worked, twisting themselves around and around. Her hair was pulled up into a bun, and she looked sickly thin, like she hadn't eaten or slept in days. She parted her lips and, at first, no sound came out. I just stood there staring at her. She blew a long breath out and began. "I just wanted to say, I'm sorry, for . . . not giving Adam a fair shake." She glanced away. A tear slipped onto her cheek, and she quickly brushed it away and took another deep breath. "We all saw what Knox did. What he was doing and . . . I know you're not Adam, but I can't say it to him and this doesn't change the fact that what you did to me was terrible. But, you know, I just want to find him." She sucked in her lower lip. Her nose was turning red, but she was holding it all together. "I feel responsible in some way."

I noticed Paisley on the outskirts dressed in all black. She was shaking hands with people and holding a hot-pink handkerchief. She'd been scheduling her breakdowns for smack in the middle of class for days. Paisley's "grief" was on full display.

"Anyway," Cassidy continued when I didn't say anything. She had appeared on the five o'clock news to talk about her boyfriend, Adam Smith. To her credit, she didn't pull a Paisley. There was no choreographing the wardrobe or doing her makeup. Cassidy appeared bare-skinned, wearing a fourth-grade Mathletes tee and looking the worst I'd ever seen her. "I just wanted to tell you that I'm sorry for your loss." Her throat contracted.

"Thanks," I said. "He actually really liked you. I wish you hadn't turned against him."

At that she made a little hiccupping sound and spun on her heel. She grabbed Paisley by the elbow and whispered something in her ear, and then Cassidy Hyde was gone. I wondered if I would ever talk to her again in my life. Somehow I doubted it.

"They're handing out ribbons," Owen said.

I craned to see Principal Wiggins shaking the hand of the third-place winner. I tapped my foot, wishing he would get on with it already. The next place should have been second, but I saw Principal Wiggins walking our way.

I looked around, seeing what other candidates there were for second place. Before I knew it, though, Principal Wiggins was standing in front of us.

I swallowed hard. "Congratulations on a fantastic science fair project," he said, extending his hand to Owen. He then said something else, but I wasn't listening. He reached his hand out to me, but all I could do was stare at the color of the ribbon he held in his hand. It was red. And after he was finished shaking my hand, he fastened the red ribbon to our board. I bit into the side of my cheek until I tasted blood. I didn't stop until Principal Wiggins had moved on to find the first-place winner.

"What is wrong with you?" Owen leaned over.

Suddenly it felt like I didn't know Owen at all anymore. I had thought he was the one person who got me, but here he was wondering what was wrong with me, and he had never seemed more alien.

"What's *wrong* with me?" I ripped the red ribbon, tearing the poster board in the process. I stared at the second-place prize and then crumpled it in my fist. I felt tears burning my eyes, and my nose starting to run. I lowered my head. "Really, Owen?"

He came to stand beside me. "I'm sorry. I didn't mean that. I know you lost him. I'm sorry. I shouldn't be so harsh."

I sniffled, and with tears blurring my vision, I looked up at him, wiping spit from my lower lip. "It's just such a shame that the experiment had to end. I worked so hard to tie up everything with McCardle, but—"

Owen's eyes narrowed. His body separated from me. I felt the cold spot where his torso had been. "What do you mean, 'tie up everything with McCardle,'" he said slowly.

"Just that he's dead, that's all."

"Adam was a person, Tor." It was like Owen's brain was spinning. He turned on the spot and tugged at his hair. "Oh my God, you actually did it. I knew it. I knew that moment. You killed him on purpose." His head shake was slow and disbelieving now. He pressed a fist to his lips. "What did you do, Tor?"

My tears dried. I wished that they wouldn't have. The delivery would have been so much better if only I reacted like other people. Even with Owen. That was what he wanted. I knew that now. But I couldn't cry. Like I'd said before, I wasn't that good of an actress.

"He killed people, Owen. He killed people and he knew the truth. It's not a big loss for the universe."

Color drained from his face. "McCardle did what he did out of grief." He stared at me for a long moment. He bit down on his lower lip. "You made this whole mess, Tor. It was you. None of this would have happened otherwise. None of it. Adam may have been unnatural, but you Tor . . ." His nostrils flared, he pointed his finger at me, and I knew what he was thinking. That I was the monster.

In the end, I watched Owen go, and I felt mostly as I felt with all people—detached. Like I was watching an argument happen to someone else. I wiped the leftover tears from under my eyes and squeezed the wrinkled ribbon that was growing sweaty in my palm.

I found the first-place winner not far away on a fancy corkboard designed to look like a space background. On it, the winner had pinned personal photographs she had taken days earlier. All were of a giant lightning storm that had been witnessed just this past week in Hollow Pines. She explained in great detail through paragraphs she had clearly pulled from articles on the Internet what might create such an intense "lightning event."

When the girl wandered away, I tore the pictures down and put them in my pocket. These belonged to my father, and they would come in handy as part of my research.

After all, I figured, I could always use them. For next time.

ACKNOWLEDGMENTS

THIS BOOK WOULD literally not exist without Liz Gateley and Tony DiSanto, who both nurtured and guided the story of Tor and Adam since its inception. Liz, you have acted as a mentor, always striking the perfect balance between encouragement, critique, and business savvy, while, Tony, you have invariably understood what I'm trying to achieve in no small part because of your limitless creative references, which, of course, are always on point. Thank you to the team at DiGa Vision for not only creating some of my favorite TV shows, but also for being behind this book.

While this story may exist, it would be a far lesser novel without the direction of Jean Feiwel and Holly West. Endless thanks for fruitful brainstorming sessions and your willingness to push me (and Tor) in new directions. I'm so glad we get to do this again.

I would have been lost without the eagle eye of my copy editor, Veronica Ambrose. For the rest of the team at Feiwel and Friends and Macmillan—Christine Ma, Nicole Moulaison, Johanna Kirby, Kallam McKay, Molly Brouillete, and Rich Deas—I have tremendous gratitude for your work in taking this manuscript and turning it into a real, live book.

I have to thank Andy McNicol at William Morris for making sure this book found a home and my own agent, Dan Lazar, and his assistant, Torrie Monro–Dougherty, for wrangling my schedule and being there for me each step of the way.

Love to Kelly Loy Gilbert and Shana Silver, who suffered last-minute phone calls when I was stuck and doubting myself. It has to be said that I might have never finished this book without Charlotte Huang and our daily e-mails. It's also true that everyone should be so lucky as to have amazing friends like mine, who include Lee Kelly, Lori Goldstein, Virginia Boecker, Jen Hayley, Jen Brooks, Kim Liggett, Emily O'Brien, and Kelley Flores—thank you, thank you, thank you.

To my sweet girlfriends, Erica Amadori, Stacy Koski, and Emma Kate Scovill, I'll always look back fondly on our times riding around in Bert, and I appreciate your letting me borrow him for a cameo in this novel.

Not enough can be said about my parents, to whom this book is dedicated. Your unflagging support means the world.

Finally, to my husband, Rob—it's no secret that I can have a little "Tor" in me when it comes to my writing. Thank you for encouraging me to pursue it sometimes to the detriment of our social lives and housekeeping, but thank you even more for reining me in and showing me when I've already done my best work. You're the best.

THANK YOU FOR READING THIS
FEIWEL AND FRIENDS BOOK.

THE FRIENDS WHO MADE

TEEN FRANKENSTEIN

POSSIBLE ARE:

JEAN FEIWEL, Publisher

LIZ SZABLA, Editor in Chief

RICH DEAS, Senior Creative Director

HOLLY WEST, Associate Editor

DAVE BARRETT, Executive Managing Editor

ANNA ROBERTO, Associate Editor

CHRISTINE BARCELLONA, Associate Editor

EMILY SETTLE, Administrative Assistant

ANNA POON, Editorial Assistant

Follow us on Facebook or visit us online at mackids.com.

OUR BOOKS ARE FRIENDS FOR LIFE.